SORCERY & SACRIFICE

SORCERY AND STRIFE

TWO

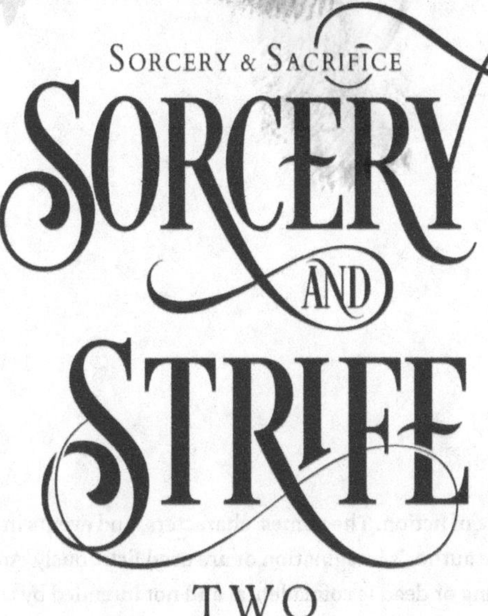

KRISTIN L. HAMBLIN

This book is a work of fiction. The names, characters, and events in this book are the products of the author's imagination or are used fictitiously. Any similarity to real persons living or dead is coincidental and not intended by the author.

SORCERY AND STRIFE

Kristin L. Hamblin – kristinlhamblin.com

Copyright © 2025 by Crown of Laurel Press, Owasso, OK

Cover Design by saintjupi3rgr4phic

Editing by Lisa Lee Editing

Map by Cartographybird Maps

Library of Congress Control Number: 2025901412

Paperback ISBN: 978-1-959230-09-0

To Aunt Sharon and Uncle Skip, the kindest souls you'll ever meet.

THE FAE REALM
EMBIDIAN SEA
TROLL HIGHLANDS
EASTERN BANKS
AMELYN RIVER
OLDINGER FORTRESS
ALBERRY
WESTWATER LANDS
THE FAE KINGDOM OF ASENTIA
GOBLIN KINGDOM
WESTLAND GNOMES
DIATEM
LIRIAN FOREST
UNICORN SANCTUM
SOLICE
SPRITE FOREST

THE HUMAN WORLD
CORDELIAN OCEAN
MARSO RIVER
PULTON
NORTHLAND FOREST
TIMBERCROSS
FALLHOLD
KINGDOM OF TAUNFALAN
HUNTERTON
RICCI PLAINS
ALBERON
DEVSHIRE
PARNUVIAN DESERT

CHAPTER I

Fenity Stormbrook held her breath, every muscle quivering with excitement just begging to burst from its stillness as the sprite approached her outstretched finger. His rainbow-hued wings glinted in the soft morning light filtering through the forest canopy. Sprites *never* approached fae, so this one must be young and overly curious. He tilted his head, shoes made of bark barely touching her skin as he hovered, studying her.

There had never been a more beautiful summer day, which was perhaps why this little one had been keen to come to her. The creek babbled peacefully nearby, water rolling over stones smoothed by the passage of time. Rays of sunshine touched upon Fenity's face and unbound red hair in random fits and spurts as the breeze waved the leaves about. The seedlings were in full swing, carried on the wind to grow into new and beautiful things.

The sprite, naked from the waist up with bottoms made of blue leaves, landed fully on her finger. Fenity held in her squeal

1

of excitement and instead offered an encouraging smile. She didn't dare speak for fear of spooking him away.

"My lady," a male voice called behind her, beyond the tree line.

The sprite's eyes went wide, and he zipped away between the towering oaks, gone as if it were a dream.

Fenity's shoulders sagged. She turned, aiming her ire at whoever had interrupted such a beautiful moment.

"My lady," her pata's steward said, stopping beside a thick tree to huff and puff when he saw her expression. "Your mata needs you back at the keep. There's been word. From the king."

The king? She looked forlornly at her newfound sanctuary, the only bright spot about moving to this so-called keep and having strangers address her as 'my lady'.

"Thank you. I will return at once." He'd come a long way to summon her, so it had to be important.

Fenity left the steward behind as she crossed out of the forest's edge and entered the meadow at the back of her pata's new holdings. The king recently named him High Lord of the southern edge of the Kingdom of Asentia, an extremely high honor, and one he'd served for decades to achieve. With the title came the lands, servants, and the house—or, keep. It'd been a month, and Fenity still didn't know what every room was for.

But she'd worn a trail in the grass to the woods.

She followed it now, leather boots stepping light and sure over the waving stalks. Her parents' keep rose before her, blotting out the pink sky and the lake beyond. The land was beautiful, but *stars above*, she ached for her old life. Their simple hut in the heart of the Lirian Forest with days spent hunting and nights spent studying the sky. Though she tried to be happy for her parents, the forest would always be the home King Sidian had taken away when he'd given her pata his title.

She couldn't help the foreboding in her heart at this summons. Was Pata going back to battle so soon?

Fenity entered the kitchens—one of the first rooms she'd identified upon their arrival—and snagged a nectar muffin off the cooling rack, ignoring their new cook's scowl. She nibbled it on her way to the family room where they all still spent most of their time. Mata, Pata, and her—they weren't used to all this space.

Mata rose from her chair, fidgeting with her dress—they were almost royalty now, and the High Lord's wife must dress properly.

They tried to get Fenity to wear a dress. It did not go well. Her heart belonged to the forest.

"Daughter," Pata said from beside the fireplace. A fire roared in the hearth despite the warm summer day—what a waste. He held a letter in his hands, wax seal broken. "This has arrived via wind transfer."

Wind transfer... only the king and the extremely wealthy could afford to send messages on the wind to the receiving stations. And only for urgent news. Bad news.

Mata went to stand beside Pata at the mantel. They stared at her in a way that sent Fenity's heart to skittering.

"What does the king want?" Her voice rose in pitch, replacing the pin-drop quiet of anticipatory silence and filling the space from fine carpet to tall, beamed ceiling.

Had the king changed his mind about pata's new title? Had the goblins finally invaded like they always claimed they would?

Her parents grinned wide, pleased grins. What in the world?

"You've been selected for the Strife!" Mata burst out, though her eyes crinkled with worry.

Fenity's mouth went slack. "Why would you joke about

that?" The Strife was already set. All the eligible ladies of the court were chosen at birth, and she was definitely not on that shortlist.

"This is no joke, Fen," Pata said, looking to Mata for support. "We move in two days."

"What do you mean 'move'?" Fenity's breaths became shallow. "We just got here."

The ceiling swirled above her. Was her reality being upended again?

"We have so little time to prepare," Mata said, tugging at the neck of her dress. She flitted around the room, straightening pillows and sweeping non-existent dust off the furniture, her restless energy needing release. She, too, hadn't adjusted to having servants to do all the work.

"We have no time. The Strife is... What? A month away? Please," Fenity said, grounding herself with a hand against the cool stone wall. "Tell me what's going on."

Pata crossed to her and passed her the letter. "It's true. Though my status as High Lord is new, King Sidian has deemed you eligible. You're to join the other ladies of the court for a chance to win Prince Renic's hand in marriage."

Fenity's heart pounded in her ears. This was the stuff of dreams, the kind every female wished to the stars would happen for them. A chance to compete for the prince's hand? She could be queen.

Well, that wasn't her dream. And she didn't want it.

All her plans, her carefully crafted design to leave her parents' lofty keep and return to the forest and carve her own path were evaporating before her eyes. The school she planned to open to teach other families how to survive the cold, the people she could help. She hadn't even gotten to the part where she told them that was her dream. The timing had never been right, with all the changes happening so fast. But they had to know she was unhappy here, right?

Fenity finally found her voice. "Please send my regrets to King Sidian. I'm sure Prince Renic has enough ladies fawning over him without me."

Mata gasped. "Fenity!"

"This is not a request," Pata said, deep frown unmarring his youthful face. His family had always had influence. His grandpata was a noble alderfae in Alberry—the oldest elder—respected for his wisdom and often sought by the king for his long memory. Pata even had an older daughter, Fenity's half-sister, who was decades older than her. But that was before Pata found Mata—his mate. Now he'd fallen back into the role of rich noble with ease, commanding servants and proudly wearing his tailored shirts and trousers. "We will accompany you to the castle where we will live as guests of the king until the Strife trials are complete and either you are chosen as Prince Renic's bride, or sent home."

"I don't want to participate in the Strife." The last Strife had been a hundred years ago when King Sidian chose Queen Lara. Since then, they'd produced one heir—Prince Renic. The Strife was all she'd heard about since forever, how they'd hold one once the prince came of age, and the gossip about who was most likely to win. She'd looked forward to the festivals and celebrations with all the other townspeople, but it was never supposed to be her. She was never supposed to be in it.

"This is a great honor," Pata said, anger now in his tone. "The highest honor. You will not refuse the king, and you will not shame our family with your legendary stubbornness. I am High Lord now, and you will accept this is your life."

"I don't want this life." She swept her arms around the room at all the finery. "I want my old life, where I worked hard and set my schedule, and I actually made a difference in people's lives." She'd just started teaching the youth in the nearby town of Solice about gardening when Pata had been lorded. She'd seen too many starve not to pass on what she knew.

"I worked hard to give you *this* life, daughter. And I won't have you ruining it with your stubbornness. I've let you be because it was a big change coming here from the forest, but now you must learn to be a lady of the court." He turned to Mata. "Make her see reason." He shook his head and stormed out of the room, frustration getting the best of him.

Fenity's lips parted. She'd messed up. Pata was over ninety years old, with plenty of time to master his emotions, yet she still found ways to upset him. They didn't share the same bond she did with her mata—he hadn't been around.

"See reason, Fenity," Mata said, having long given up on tidying. She sat carefully on the edge of the couch. "I know this is not the life you thought you'd have, and it's far different from how it used to be, but there's no choice here. You can't say no." Her mouth creased in a look Fenity knew so well—when she was about to make the best of a situation, even knowing there was no good side. Like when Pata was supposed to come home on leave, but the king canceled it. Or when they nearly starved one winter after an early freeze destroyed their garden. "It will be fun. I hear the prince is handsome. And think about all the dresses and festivals." Mata turned her face away and scrunched up her nose.

She missed the forest, too.

Fun wasn't dresses and stuffy competitions. Fun was freedom, not being told what to wear or having her time dictated to her at all hours. Fun was making crowns of laurels while kicking her toes in the chilly brook and listening to the dicaidas chirp about way more important things than who the prince might marry.

Was this really happening?

She sat beside her mata and took her hands. "I didn't mean to upset Pata. But why even bother at this point? I'll never be ready in time." The Strife was an impossible competition for the prince's hand for females borne of privilege and wealth. Just the thought of it made the room spin again.

Mata squeezed her callused hands. "You'll work hard, as you know how. You'll be ready, my daughter, and you'll make us so proud."

Fenity thought of her forest sanctuary, wishing she'd never left.

CHAPTER 2

Mata let out an exasperated sigh from the carriage that made Fenity smile to herself as she walked beside them. They were an entire entourage, a parade of sickening excess—Mata and Pata in the horse-drawn carriage like the fancy rulers they now were, plus teams of guards and warriors in front and behind, servants, and wagons holding the clothing and items they'd need for the next several months.

Or, at least the items her parents would need. The palace had instructed they would provide all of Fenity's provisions—dresses, shoes, and even jewels.

Fenity just wanted the dirt. To feel the trail beneath her feet, the way the rocks tested her balance and the wind whipped her unbound hair. None of these fae accompanying them understood her—what female would choose a life of ruggedness over one of finery? But she had little time left to be herself, and she would take every bit of it she could.

So she mostly walked or rode beside her parents' carriage,

rather than relax on its soft cushions, earning plenty of stares and whispered rumors.

After two weeks of travel, they would finally arrive at the king's castle in Alberry tomorrow.

She had agreed to go only to appease her parents and to avoid the consequences of disobeying the king. Despite her mata's fretting as they readied for this journey, it was impossible to prepare for what was to come, impossible to combat the immeasurable ways Fenity was unqualified for this competition. She knew nothing of court, her competitors, the contest, and even lacked basic skills, like how to dance. Because those things hadn't mattered in the game of survival in the forest.

But they mattered now.

She didn't stand a chance at being picked, for all those reasons and more, but she wouldn't disgrace her family by not trying. She'd give it her all, learn the silly customs and perform the ridiculous rituals, so in the end, when she still lost, no one could say she didn't try.

After one last night at an inn in a little town south of Alberry, Fenity rode in the carriage with her parents as their party crossed the bridge over the Amelyn River and approached the castle gates.

She clamped her teeth together to keep her jaw from coming unhinged as the enormity of the palace reoriented entire thought processes in her brain. She never knew anything existed in the world this size—at least not fae-made. If she thought her pata's new keep was grand, the palace dwarfed it one hundred times over. There were too many sights and sounds to take in as they barreled on—tons of fae on foot or driving wagons loaded with goods, guards and warriors in glinting armor beside every gate and on every wall. Turrets and wings and spires of stone rising high into the sky.

Pata had been here several times, and his light-hearted

chuckle warmed the carriage in regular intervals as he watched Mata and Fenity's reactions. Fenity may have kept her mouth shut, but that hadn't stopped her from craning her neck far out of the carriage window.

An alarm bell sat high in a tower, poised to sound if ever danger invaded their world. It was the first to greet them as they slipped through the open gates and seemed to follow her as they passed underneath it. She stared wide-eyed as the battlement walls swallowed her party up. Echoing stone and flapping flags replaced sounds of chirping birds and whispering wind, the sun blotted by the towering turrets. The air turned instantly colder.

Servants and townsfolk stepped aside as they proceeded through the brick-paved streets and into the courtyard outside the castle. They spoke to each other as they pointed and stared, but Fenity couldn't hear them over the clatter of the carriage and the horses' clopping hooves. Fenity narrowed her eyes on them until Mata pinched her side.

"First impressions, young one." Mata smiled overly large—pretending to belong—until they stopped before the castle doors. She lowered her voice to a whisper. "Court opinion is important, but remember who you are and where you come from. Don't let this place take it from you."

A host of servants appeared to escort them into the castle, helping the females down from the carriage. Fenity ignored their proffered hands and weighty looks. She'd chosen not to wear a dress. Not just yet. This was her last chance to be herself, so she'd stolen it.

The carriage creaked as she stepped down in the courtyard. Fenity gave a quick intake of breath. The castle was going to be impossible to navigate. Steep stone walls decorated with stained glass windows and banners of green and blue rose impossibly high and wide. Manicured trees and gardens lined everything, from the staircases to the walls and out to the pristine, sprawling lawn.

"Welcome to Alberry," a servant said, bowing to Pata and then to Mata. "I will show you to your wing." He turned and ascended the steps to the castle doors where servants were already hauling their possessions.

Wing? They got their own castle wing? Fenity scanned the courtyard but saw no signs of anyone royal—the prince or the king or queen. Fenity's arrival wasn't important enough for that kind of reception.

The inside was as impressive as the outside—their entire keep could probably fit into the entry hall. As tall as it was wide, with smooth, marble columns lining the perimeter and towering three floors high with balconies on all sides. Her boots skidded over smooth floors that gleamed, reflecting the light from the many sconces lit by magelight—a luxury they didn't even have at Pata's keep. A hearth graced the far end of the long room, so far away she practically had to squint to see it. The servant led them up a staircase—more marble—and then down one of the many branching hallways.

If the goal was to get her so impossibly lost that fleeing would never be an option, then job well done. Several courtiers dressed in regal finery stopped to eye them as she passed. One female in particular, wearing an elegant red dress, sneered at Fenity's clothing before turning her nose up in the air. Another, with soft blonde waves wearing a bright yellow gown, gave her a tentative smile before moving on. Several young males around her age nudged each other, grinning, which sent heat to Fenity's cheeks.

Some of these females would be her competition, and they'd already passed judgment.

Fenity pulled at her tunic. Maybe it would have been wise to wear a dress.

Eventually, they reached a set of double wooden doors that looked important with carved reliefs and gold trim.

The servant pushed them both open at once. "The Starsend Wing," he said with a proud smile as Fenity's parents oohed and aahed. "This may be the smaller of the wings, but this floor is all yours for the duration of the Strife. I'll show you to your rooms."

The wing was a hall that ended in tall windows, the outside world obscured by colorful glass—but was that an actual tree blowing in the wind? A carpet runner decorated dark wood floors, and the same sconces graced the walls alongside paintings of landscapes. They each had their own individual suites off the hallway. Fenity gawked unabashedly at hers. She'd barely gotten used to the large bedroom and bathing room at the keep, but this was nothing like that. There was a receiving room that led to a bedroom, a separate bathing room, a sitting room, and another room she couldn't guess the use of and was too embarrassed to ask.

The servant left to show her parents to their rooms, but someone took his place, a female this time, who led her around the suite. Every surface was either graced with fresh flowers or trimmed in gleaming gold, and the wood shined with polish. The cream walls had a bumpy texture when Fenity traced her fingers over them, and the carpets were soft and intricate.

"The comfort of the ladies of the Strife is of the utmost importance to our generous prince," the new servant said after Fenity had toured her rooms. "The Strife will provide everything you need, including dresses for everyday wear and dancing." She eyed Fenity's leggings meaningfully, though there was a hidden kindness in her stern eyes.

"What about dance lessons?" Fenity shrugged at the servant's wide eyes. It wasn't her fault she didn't know about all this madness.

"Your attendants and I have our work ahead of us, I see." The servant frowned, and Fenity took real notice of her for the first time. She didn't wear servant's clothing at all but a dress like a lady, though not as nice of quality as Mata wore. Her dark hair was swept up in a perfect twist with colorful feathers tucked into it. She carried herself with confidence, someone important to be taken seriously.

"You do?"

"I'm to guide you through the Strife." She extended her hand. "My name is Arinia Thornreach, my lady."

Fenity took it hesitantly. "Do all the females get a guide?" Or just her, because she was woefully behind. "And you don't have to address me as my lady. Fenity is fine."

"Protocol must be observed at all times, and you are a lady of the court." Arinia eyed her like she'd already failed a test. "And yes, all ladies of the Strife have a guide." She guided her to the sitting room, and then ordered tea and cakes from a waiting servant. She sat prim and proper on a cushioned chair with elegantly carved armrests. Fenity considered copying her, but what was the point? She was what she was.

"Unfortunately," Arinia said, "you are at a disadvantage."

"Oh, I'm well aware I've been thrust into this completely unprepared." Fenity sighed.

"It's more than that. Most of the other participants have guides that were here during the last Strife."

"And you weren't?" Last to arrive got last pick. Of course.

"My duties were elsewhere." Arinia smoothed her dress of deep green satin. "But don't let that discourage you. I've trained for this since Prince Renic was born."

As if that small piece of news would be what discouraged her. "So what do we do first?"

Arinia paused while a servant rolled in a tray covered in

dainty glasses and steaming tea, with mouthwatering treats and sandwiches.

"Today, you rest. Tomorrow we prepare." With that extremely vague answer, Arinia left without touching her mini cakes.

Fenity couldn't shake the sense that Arinia felt disappointed in her somehow. Surely she had known what kind of contestant she was getting. Had the king not warned her?

Fenity ate Arinia's cakes and left her suite. She needed dirt.

Mata's voice sounded down the hall, directing servants where to unpack their possessions, so Fenity went the other way, toward the trees she spied through the windows. Down a different marble staircase, she kept as close to the outside wall as she could, turning to where the pull of the sun directed her.

There were so many more rules here already than at the keep. So much more formality and structure. Even less freedom than she had before, and none of this was part of her plan to return to her old life.

She needed air. Needed to breathe. She was suffocating under the weight of these walls and everything she didn't know was coming for her in the Strife.

She had attendants? And a guide? How had things come to this, a great lady at the capital of their great kingdom, competing to marry the prince and become the next queen in a competition she had no clue what it entailed?

Fenity burst through the first door she found to the outside. The sun poured over her skin, and she took deep, gulping breaths. She'd entered a garden of some kind, with tall, manicured hedges and beautiful roses circling the perimeter. But instead of the rainbow hue of the trees around the world, these had leaves of green—all of them. A dull green with no varying hues or colors. And she loved it. The walls could almost be forgotten among the green. She shrank against a tree trunk and put a hand to her chest as the sounds of wind-rustled leaves and insects calmed her once more.

"Are you alright?" a male voice said.

Fenity squeaked and jumped. The male stood a stone's throw away, hands raised and green eyes wide. His long black hair hung loose and wavy to his shoulders, pointed chin, and fine, tailored clothes clinging to muscled arms.

"I'm fine," Fenity said, straightening and dusting tree bark from her butt. "You startled me is all."

He lowered his hands, shoving them in his pockets. His mouth twisted into blatant skepticism. "I thought I should intervene. You looked ready to scream."

Fenity blinked at him. He wasn't far from the mark.

"I know the feeling," he added quietly.

His admission gave her courage, and she smiled gratefully. "I might have screamed, but someone interrupted me."

"Why did you feel the need to scream?" His genuine curiosity was etched in his open expression. The honest innocence had her wanting to bare her soul to this male she'd never met. Why not tell him the truth? Maybe he could be a friend in all this.

"I only just arrived here. It's a big change for me. I'm not used to being closed in so." She tucked her hair behind her pointed ear. "In more ways than one," she added under her breath.

"Oh? What ways?" At her tilted head, he shrugged. "Just trying to help."

She studied him, but there was no judgment there. "Okay, fine. I feel closed in by these walls." Fenity waved her hand to the tall stone wall beside them with more heat than propriety probably dictated in front of a lord at the castle. Even if covered in ivy, it was still a wall. "And I feel like I'm not in control of my life or my destiny." She hadn't meant to add that, didn't even know that was how she felt until voicing it. But it was true.

"I know all about those things. The trick here is not to let them see it get to you." He smiled, and it was like a gift she'd earned without trying. "My apologies for interrupting your scream, Miss..." He raised an eyebrow, eyes trailing her clothes.

"Oh, no one." She chuckled awkwardly. "Just the gardener." She plucked a dead leaf from the closest tree.

He studied her actions. "These are the last of the trees imported from the human realm, or so they say. King Sidian is very proud of his collection."

Fenity snatched back her hand and stepped away from the scratchy bark. Why would anyone want to keep something from the human realm? She shouldn't be here. "Yes. Good day, m'lord." She hurried back inside, even as he called for her to wait.

Was she even allowed to talk to other males while she was here? She'd probably just broken enough rules to get her disqualified from the competition. But how was she supposed to know?

Fenity returned to her rooms with the goal of staying out of sight and out of trouble until Arinia's instructions tomorrow.

CHAPTER 3

Fenity was already awake when Arinia came for her the next morning. She'd always been an early riser, working when the sun was up, but apparently that was not how royals functioned. Arinia flowed into her bedroom, eyes lighting up when she spotted Fenity perched on the windowsill, staring at the sky instead of sleeping the morning away. Today Arinia wore another dress, this one green with long sleeves and a high neck, hair swept up as before. A host of servants—both male and female—entered with her, and Fenity swallowed the urge to flee.

"These are your attendants," Arinia said, lifting her arms to them like it was a grand reveal. They all wore simple green tunics and trousers embroidered with silver thread. Six in total, they stood behind Arinia studying Fenity as much as she was studying them, though they looked friendly enough, with smiles and polite nods.

"They will serve you—and only you—for the duration of the Strife." Arinia snapped her fingers, and the group broke apart into different sections of the suite, some into the dressing closet, some to the bathing room, others to the sitting room.

Fenity shuddered. More servants?

"Don't worry." Arinia placed a hand on Fenity's shoulder. "I picked them myself and can vouch for their characters, so you don't need to worry about spies."

Spies? Fenity watched her attendants scurry about carrying combs and clothing as her mind tried to grasp what Arinia implied. She hadn't thought much about being part of the Strife, other than ways she might get out of it. After all, she'd grown up hearing about it her whole life, knowing one day the prince—who was eighteen, like her—would come of age. Her mind still clung to the safe thoughts that she was outside of all this, that she could learn to love dresses and dancing, and it could be fun as her mata had said.

Was the competition so fierce that the ladies would actually spy on one another to gain an advantage?

Of course it was. This wasn't just a temporary chapter to endure and move on. Her life would be forever changed, even when she lost. The Strife was the biggest competition of the century. It determined the next queen, for valley's sake. How could she have been so naïve? Showing up in her regular clothes—the other females must think her a fool, not worthy of the title. Thank the moons no royals had been there when they'd arrived. She prided herself on not caring what others thought, but she couldn't embarrass her parents by not playing the part.

Then, after it was all over, her life would be hers again. Changed or not, she would go back to fulfill her dream of helping people.

"Arinia," Fenity said, looking her guide in the eyes, "can you make me look like a lady of the court?"

Arinia smiled wide. "That's what I'm here for." She clapped her hands, and the attendants got to work.

After being thoroughly scrubbed in the luxurious, sweet-smelling bath—which had turned the water an embarrassing gray—she led Fenity to a dressing room as big as her entire hut in the forest. Clothes—mostly dresses—lined every wall, interrupted by shelves covered in gleaming jewels and rows and rows of shoes.

And every bit of it was green. Not just any green, a light forest green. Like the moss that grew on their true home in the forest.

"Is green the only color I'm allowed to wear?" Fenity sat as directed, in front of a large vanity table already scattered with combs, brushes, makeup, and hairpins. Green just happened to be her favorite color, but no one here would know that, so why green?

"His Majesty says it's easier to identify the contestants this way." Arinia selected a comfortable-looking dress. "Each of the forty contestants has their own color."

Forty? She gaped at Arinia through the mirror. She hadn't realized there were so many eligible females in all the king-dom. To be eligible, they had to be of age but no older than fifty, unmarried and unmated, without any offspring, and connected to the royal court.

And if someone was eligible, they had no choice but to compete, apparently.

An attendant picked up a brush and combed through Feni-ty's damp hair.

"I can do that." She reached for the brush.

The attendant didn't speak but turned a questioning eye to Arinia.

Arinia gave a tight, knowing smile. "I'm sure you grew up perfectly capable of doing everything yourself, but here, you're a contestant, and we do everything for you. These are the rules. You'll learn to enjoy it."

The feeling of being useless and helpless was barely subdued by the relaxing indulgence of having someone else brush through the knots.

While the attendants quietly styled Fenity's hair, Arinia paced the dressing room, which was more than large enough for pacing. "The point of the Strife is not to win Prince Renic's heart, it's to win the pillars. But it definitely helps to have his favor, and there are no rules against seeking him out. Precedence establishes that it's an acceptable practice."

"What about relations with other males?" Fenity grimaced as an attendant jabbed a hairpin in place.

"Absolutely not." Arinia stepped back, aghast. "You're not mated, are you?"

Everyone in the room seemed to pause.

"No! Of course not." She wasn't too young to have found her mate, but no male had ever even come close to turning her head.

"Good, good." Arinia handed another hairpin to the attendant. "There will be several events—all part of the pillars—to rank all forty eligible ladies."

The Five Pillars of Faedom. The basis upon which fae morals were founded. Strength, poise, leadership, compassion, and integrity. Everyone knew what they represented, but how that translated into the Strife was at the king and queen's discretion.

"I know about the pillars. I also know the competition is never the same twice." Fenity watched the transformation happening in the mirror before her.

They coaxed her into a green silk dress, and it wrapped delicately around her slim figure in a crisscross pattern over her chest, leaving her arms sleeveless. It fit straight at the top, not squeezing too tight like the dresses at the keep, and flowed down from her waist. The color set off her fiery hair, and they'd pulled half of it up into intricate braids while the rest tumbled over her shoulders. They'd used too much makeup, covering up her freckles, but her eyelashes were accentuated, and green eyeshadow matched her dress and complemented her pink cheeks.

She looked like a true lady. Though not a queen.

"Yes, the Five Pillars of Faedom. We already know about poise—you must stand in full queen regalia wearing a crown the longest without fail. And you're correct. The other challenges differ with every Strife. Some pillars may even have multiple, separate tasks. And the challenges rarely happen in order."

"Well, that sounds horrible." And impossible. What in the stars above had she gotten into?

Arinia frowned. "Last time for leadership, the contestants had to host a ball, start to finish. For compassion, they had to develop a program to help needy children." She paused. "Oh, the competition for the First Pillar always comes first and never changes, of course. Strength. You must display your energy. Easy."

Fenity stopped breathing.

"Oh, no." Arinia and the attendants exchanged nervous glances. "You *can* control the energies, right?"

"I, um…" Fenity hid her shaking hands. "No, I can't."

"This is not good. This is horrible news." Arinia's face crumpled. "If you can't control the energies, you've already failed one of the five pillars."

Failed? "What happens if a contestant fails? Do they get to go home early?" Fenity went still.

Arinia put a hand to her chest. "Not every contestant will succeed in every pillar. Some can even have more than one winner and loser. What kind of test would that be if we sent someone worthy home early, before she'd had a chance at the other pillars?"

"Is there no hope, then?" Fenity willed her heart to calm. Her secret was safe. She was safe.

"A lot of factors contribute to winning the Strife. How well you do at each pillar combined with Prince Renic's preference —which will reflect the court's preference—all come together to determine a winner by the end." Arinia paused. "And you're sure you possess no energy? Your great grandpata is the alder-fae. Has a seer ever tested you?" She fanned herself, her cheeks flushed, making her look downright panicked.

The attendants cast her looks of pity and even sympathy. While they stayed silent, Fenity saw the wordless conversations they exchanged across the dressing room.

"I'm eighteen. I'm too old for energy to come to me now." Fenity tried to shrug as if it was no big deal. The truth was, it was the biggest deal. But Arinia must believe the lie.

If the court knew Fenity possessed prophecy-unleashing, world-ending energy, her life and her entire family's lives would be forfeit.

"This is dire." Arinia waved for the attendants to continue, then took a deep breath. "Of course there is still hope. Like I said, no one gets sent home. We'll simply work harder at excelling in the other four pillars. Come on, we're late." She took Fenity's hand and pulled her from the bedroom.

Fenity barely had time to adjust her strides to the dress and shoes before being dragged out of her suite and down the hall. "What are we late for?"

"Part of having an advantage is getting to know the competition. The ladies like to dine together at breakfast."

"So they can use each other's personalities and secrets for their own gain?" Fenity asked, disgusted. What kind of friendship was it to get to know someone just for what they can do for you?

"Yes, exactly. The trick is to open yourself up enough to let them in without revealing anything about yourself. In turn, you learn about them. Their families, their likes and interests, their faults and failures. What can you use against them?" She paused. "Don't make that face. Trust me, they will do the same to you."

"But I have nothing to hide." Almost nothing.

Arinia stopped her with a hand on her arm, stepping off into an alcove in the hall with a pair of cushioned chairs surrounded by tall windows of colorful glass. "You have everything to hide. The fact you grew up poor, that you don't know what you're doing, or how to find your way around here, the fact you don't have energy. Some of them will use everything to bring you down. Because despite the rules and rumors, the ultimate decision for Prince Renic's hand is up to the prince. And his decision will be influenced by the king and court. You can pass all five pillars and still fail if your reputation was dragged through the mud the whole time. Win with honesty and integrity, which means using their weaknesses covertly."

"It's so underhanded." Fenity shook her head. "Make friends just to find their weak points for the knife?" That wasn't who she was, and it certainly wasn't someone she wanted to be.

"And stab where no one can see, and no one can trace it back to you." Arinia kept going at a breakneck pace, so Fenity followed, though she wanted to even less now.

She couldn't win that way. She wouldn't tear the other ladies down to boost herself up.

Down several flights of stairs and more unending corridors, the dining hall was alive with chatter when Arinia led her through the archway. "You are the last to arrive—to court and to the palace—the others already know each other. You have a lot of catching up to do. So be careful." She gave her a little nudge and then left the way they'd come.

Very vague advice. What about who to avoid or who to watch out for? Or how to eat like a lady?

Long rectangular tables stretched along the room with white cloths and silver vases of fresh flowers. Chandeliers with crystals and energy orbs cast twinkling light around the room. Wood beams lined the ceiling, and servants lined the walls. No windows, but a mural on the far wall surrounded a low-burning hearth. Fenity watched mesmerized as the mural shifted and moved, as if the colorful flowers and depictions of unicorns and woodland creatures had come alive. Fae were raised not to use nature's precious energy for unnecessary feats, so the display of power and wealth was overwhelming.

There were only females dining, and they sat already eating at the tables. They were dressed like Fenity, trussed up in regal finery in all the colors of the rainbow, except they looked like they belonged here, with fancy food harvested and cooked by someone else, in expensive gowns they didn't have to make.

They all looked up as she crossed to an empty seat between two others, conversations pausing. One immediately set down her napkin and moved to another table, a plain-looking female in a light pink dress. Fenity smiled at the one who stayed, noticing it was the blonde female in the pale yellow who had smiled at her the day before.

"Ignore her," the female said. "We all do. I'm Nisha."

A servant sat a plate in front of her covered in aromatic dishes—eggs with mushrooms, crispy meat, and fruit with some kind of sweet-cream dip. "Nisha. I'm Fenity. Thanks for the warm welcome yesterday."

"Of course." Nisha took a bite of bread with berry jam. "It can be lonely here."

Arinia's little speech had Fenity wondering if Nisha's kindness was genuine, or a way to get Fenity to trust her and show her secrets and failures. Fenity hated that little worm that was now working its way into her mind, trying to ruin what could be a genuine friendship. She mentally smothered it. Distrust and constant second-guessing were no way to live. She would trust her gut and her heart.

"I'm starting to figure that out. How long have you been here?" Fenity bit into bread with fresh herbs baked into the crust and slathered with butter.

"Only a few months, like the others. Contestants are not allowed here until four months before the Strife begins. Unless they live here, of course. My pata is High Lord of the Eastern Banks. He couldn't be here because of a skirmish between the goblins he's overseeing, but my mata came with me. Have you met the prince yet?"

Fenity swallowed hard. There were contestants who lived here? Had grown up here? "Besides my guide, you're the first person I've met."

"You might see him around, but you're sure to see him at the opening ball. Every lady gets a turn to dance with him." Nisha lowered her voice. "Since you're new here, I'll tell you who to stay away from." She tilted her chin to the table beside them. "See the female in red with her back to us?"

Fenity nodded. It was the same female who'd turned her nose up the day before, the same hazelnut hair and hostile energy.

"That's Lady Sarafine. Her pata is High Lord of Alberry. She grew up here. Though, I think they should have made her live elsewhere. They knew one day she'd be part of the Strife. Her parents have been planting the seed since before her birth. Rumor is she's dating Prince Renic in secret. In her mind, she's already queen."

"A queen with an attitude," Fenity whispered back, then regretted how petty it made her sound. Maybe Sarafine was really nice but having a bad day yesterday?

Nisha snorted. "Exactly. Hey, I heard you got Arinia as your guide." Her face contorted into something like pity.

"I did. She's really nice." What was wrong with Arinia?

"Oh, that's too bad. She wasn't a guide at the last Strife, you know." Nisha speared a small bite of eggs. "Did you know they get an award if the prince chooses you? The attendants too."

A servant carrying a tray of goblets brushed past them. Her foot caught on the leg of the bench, and she went down. Hard. Metal goblets crashed to the ground, dark berry juice splashing on the floor and the hem of Fenity's dress.

"Oh!" Fenity hopped from the bench and helped the servant to her feet while the other contestants sniggered or gasped. "Are you alright?"

The servant's face turned deep red, and she stammered an apology. "Your dress."

"It's just a dress." Fenity took the tray and piled on the empty goblets.

With her actions, the room went silent.

The contestants stared at her with varying expressions. Fenity had messed up somehow. Nisha gaped, Sarafine rolled her eyes, and others began whispering. About her.

Had she broken some other rule?

The servant reached for the tray. "I'm alright, don't trouble yourself, my lady."

Since when did simple kindness become an unworthy action? Fenity gritted her teeth and finished picking up the goblets. Nisha finally sprung up and offered her napkin, while servants mopped up the mess.

"It's no trouble." Fenity smiled and handed the tray to the servant, who smiled with nervous gratitude.

Nisha quickly excused herself, promising to tell her more about the other contestants and share more of what she knew later. Fenity ate the remainder of her meal alone, but she left the dining hall glad to have made a friend.

She didn't have to wander too long before Arinia found her, scolded her for ruining such an expensive gown, and told her she was going the wrong way for lessons.

"What kind of lesson?" Fenity asked.

"Every kind."

CHAPTER 4

Every part of Fenity's body was sore by the end of the first week. Most of all, her mind. She awoke early each day to be drilled in names and etiquette, only to be ushered off to dance lessons, and other unnecessary-for-real-life things, like how to throw a proper tea party. As Arinia pointed out, there was no way of predicting what skills would be relevant for the Strife.

All the lessons were private, of course, as she was the only contestant here who needed them. That didn't stop the attendants of the other contestants from constantly poking their heads into her lessons until Arinia shooed them out, mumbling about gossip hoarding.

Everything she learned only further convinced her she did not want to marry the prince and live this life. Nor stay at her pata's keep and live that life. How was knowing the right way to curtsy going to fill her belly come next winter? Or anyone else's, for that matter.

But Fenity absorbed it all, staying up late to study, determined to make up for lost time and not further embarrass her parents. She'd hardly seen them since they'd arrived, both busy with the rest of court.

The opening ball was in a few days, and Fenity was already tired of being here. She hadn't set foot outside the castle since the first day, and the lack of sun and green was depleting her—at the next break in this endless routine, she was going to make a run for it to the first patch of grass she found. But she had learned how to get to the dining room and back without getting lost. And when Arinia had found Fenity half-stuck in one of her dresses, she finally convinced her it was okay to pull the servant's bell to ask for help.

This might be the day that broke her, though. Today she joined the rest of the ladies for painting in the ballroom. She'd never painted a day in her life.

"Just don't embarrass me," Arinia said, cringing as she not-so-gently nudged Fenity out of her suite.

"The only way that's going to happen is if I feign illness and stay here." Fenity held her breath. It wasn't a bad idea.

Arinia's lips turned up, but then she frowned. "The opening ball is tomorrow and you'll finally meet the prince. This could be your last opportunity to make some allies. You can do this." She closed the door in Fenity's face, leaving her to find the way. None of the other contestants needed an escort to keep from getting lost in the palace, so Fenity was glad Arinia didn't accompany her.

Besides, she knew her way to the ballroom after all the dance lessons there, and the solarium was supposed to be near there, so she made her way, watching the passing trees through the windows. She wasn't the last to arrive, but Nisha had saved her a seat at the table beside hers. Despite Fenity being the odd one out, Nisha had always been kind, even as the others had snubbed her.

It was as if they were waiting to see if she'd fall or fly before deciding to approach her.

Fenity quickly decided the solarium was her favorite room in the castle so far. It was vast and cold—like every room—but the back half was comprised of windows. Windows for the walls and windows slanting to make a ceiling of clear glass. The most gorgeous garden in colors varying more widely than the contestants' dresses graced their view. With the fresh sun pouring through, it was the closest feeling to home she'd had.

Every contestant had their own table, spaced far enough they wouldn't be on top of each other, with an easel, blank canvas, paints, and different sized brushes. Each chair had an apron draped over the back, so Fenity put hers on, copying the others.

A female Fenity had never seen walked through the room toward the front, scrutinizing them. She wore a dress like a royal, but not so fine—plainer in detail with less expensive fabric. Not uncommon among servants of rank.

"That's Uda," Nisha leaned over and whispered. "None of the contestants like her. She runs the pre-Strife events, but she doesn't have a kind bone in her body. Best not to cross her."

Fenity flashed her a grateful smile. Spare time with her new friend was nonexistent, but Arinia told her Nisha's holdings were small, not enough to be significant, but enough to earn her place in the Strife.

"Today," Uda began when she reached the front, "you will paint whatever you see fit, and I will inspect your progress."

"Are we being judged for this?" a lady across the room squeaked. "Is this a pillar?"

Forty elegantly dressed silhouettes sat up taller.

Uda frowned. "You are always being judged, and you should know that by now."

"But the contest doesn't begin until the ball," Fenity whispered to Nisha, who gave her a sympathetic wince.

"But, no," Uda continued. "This is not part of the pillars."

"Why is the ability to paint so important?" Fenity asked quietly.

Uda jerked her head. "Who said that?" Some of the ladies gasped.

Oh, moons. Fenity cleared her throat. "What I mean to say is, I'm curious why we are here if it's not part of the contest?" That sounded more polite in her mind. She should have held her tongue.

Uda stomped over to her, ire rolling off in waves that Nisha visibly shrank from. "So, you want to change centuries of tradition, do you? This wild female of the woods who barely even qualified to be here." She scoffed. "Our future queen will be well-rounded, with several talents and skills with which to grace our kingdom and future heirs."

Fenity curled her anger into her fists. "Thank you for explaining." Uda's lip lifted as she turned toward the front, but Fenity wasn't done. "In the future, a little kindness with your explanations would be appreciated. One of us will be the future queen, after all, so you'd only be serving yourself."

Uda spun around so fast, part of her hair fell from its bun. "I have nothing to fear from you. You'll never be fit to be queen." She lifted her chin. "Pick up your brushes and paint!"

The ladies quickly complied, but Fenity held Uda's stare until she was called away to assist someone else. Fenity already knew she wasn't fit to be queen. She didn't want it anyway, so she had nothing to lose putting bullies in their place.

"You shouldn't get on her bad side," Nisha whispered while hastily mixing paint colors on her wooden palette. "She reports directly to the king on our progress."

Stars. Fenity paused, reaching for a brush. Of course she did. Which meant Pata would probably hear about this, too. Maybe if she kept on her best behavior from now on, Uda would forget about today?

Yeah right.

But she didn't regret standing up for herself.

"You don't want to end up in the bottom ten." Nisha swept her paint over the canvas with expert efficiency.

"The bottom ten of the contestants? Why not?"

Nisha's mouth parted. "You don't know?"

"Quiet!" Uda commanded.

Nisha snapped back to her work.

Fenity gripped her paintbrush. She couldn't worry about it now. First, she had to figure out how to paint.

The room was silent with only the swish of brushes delicately sliding over canvas and the occasional clink of glass when someone dipped a brush in water. Some ladies still gave her the side-eye, but all were well into their paintings. Flowers, Alberry Castle, the outline of a portrait of the king and queen, the royal crest. One painted a rough picture of a male who was probably the prince. Even with different subjects and techniques, everyone in the room had clearly received extensive lessons.

"I don't know what to paint," she whispered to Nisha, who was outlining a gorgeous mountain range.

"Paint something you love. This is my home." Nisha smiled at her work, the peace radiating off her something to envy.

The last time Fenity had felt that peace was... She knew what to paint.

Starting with brown, she painted tall tree trunks on either side of the canvas, using gradient blues to give them full, billowing canopies. The forest floor and babbling brook were trickier, but she lost herself in the painting, finally capturing a bit of the peace Nisha displayed. She'd almost forgotten where she was by the time Uda told them to put their brushes down.

Hers was a splotchy mess compared to the other females, and she had to squint to see the vision, but it was beautiful in its imperfection. Like the woods themselves, it was wild and free. She loved it.

Uda started at the front and worked her way back, complimenting some contestants—even if their work wasn't that great—and critiquing the others. She clearly had her favorites. Fenity knew at least some of the contestants' names after Arinia's instruction, but Sarafine was the alpha here. Fenity couldn't see her painting from where she stood across the room, but then she lifted it and turned, as if eager to show the room. Copying others—or more likely they'd copied her—she'd painted the king and queen, doing a masterful job given the timeframe, of course. Uda gushed over it for quite a while.

Fenity considered taking her painting and leaving before it was too late. Before she had to endure the harsh remarks sure to come her way, tempting her confidence into believing one person's opinions mattered.

But she stayed put as Uda approached.

"Needs more shadowing," she mumbled to Nisha, who visibly deflated before her flawless landscape painting.

Nisha was on Uda's bad list, and it was probably Fenity's fault. What happened if they ended up in the bottom ten?

Actual laughter burst from Uda's lips when she beheld Fenity's painting. "Oh, child. They really ought to amend the rule that says you can't refuse an invitation to the Strife." She shook her head and scribbled something onto parchment.

Fenity's cheeks burned with anger.

Sarafine led the eager pack that came for a closer look at the spectacle. Some of them tittered behind gloved hands.

Some looked bored and sauntered out of the solarium. Sarafine just shook her head and walked away.

"Well, I like it." Fenity removed her apron and reached for the painting.

Uda stopped her. "All paintings, regardless of skill, now belong to His Highness. They will be hung for all to see in the grand hallway." A satisfied gleam entered her eyes. "Properly labeled, of course."

"Excellent." Fenity rose. "I appreciate the opportunity to display my skills for His Highness." She gave a nod and left the room, hurrying to catch up to Nisha who'd left without her.

She wasn't embarrassed about her painting. She'd done the best she could given she'd never had a lesson a day in her life. And the painting turned out better than she could have imagined. So why let the others' opinions affect her?

"What happens if you end up in the bottom ten?" she asked as she caught up with Nisha. "I've never heard that rule."

Nisha slowed her pace and lowered her voice. "Look, I didn't want to do this. It's not who I am, but I can't associate with you anymore."

Fenity's legs stopped moving and her chest constricted. She'd been trying, hadn't she? Did succeeding really mean compromising who she was?

"They obviously have you marked as unfit, and by association, I'm unfit too." Nisha took her hand. "I hope you can understand, though I know I don't deserve your understanding. Even so, I have to protect my family."

"We're all here for ourselves, right?" Her pain couldn't help but seep through as sarcasm. "I wouldn't want to ruin your family's reputation."

"I'm sorry." She pulled away.

"Just tell me one thing. What happens if you're in the bottom ten?"

Nisha glanced from side to side, but the hallway had mostly cleared. "The unspoken knowledge is that the bottom ten mysteriously fall out of favor with the king. My parents think it's because our bloodlines are found wanting. He shuns them until they are practically obsolete from society, only calling them for the bare minimum, like wars and the like." She lowered her voice even more. "The lowest among us will quietly have their lands and titles stripped from them." Nisha looked at her meaningfully. A door opened down the hall, and she rushed away, leaving Fenity alone and stricken.

The lowest had their lands and titles stripped. Fenity couldn't get any lower if she tried.

CHAPTER 5

There was only one place to take solace after hearing her parents' entire future depended upon how well she did in the Strife. Only one place that would clear her mind and let her think.

Fenity held up her exorbitantly fine gown as she tread barefoot in the cool grass outside the castle walls, though still within the battlements—the guards made it clear contestants weren't allowed any further unescorted. Fae weren't meant to wear such fancy clothes and live in the confines of a stone castle. They belonged to nature.

But here she was, wrapped tightly in a forest-green silk dress her mata and Arinia chose to complement her red hair, warning her 'she'd better not ruin it.' She'd never worn a dress before coming here. It represented every change thrust upon her with her pata's new title, and so she'd held out as long as she could.

Fenity sighed, relishing the brief connection to the earth, the energy that swirled within her she could never release. It wasn't the dress's fault she'd come so far from where she wanted to be. It was the king's.

She'd lived within the king's walls for over a week and had yet to catch the eye of Prince Renic. That might have been fine before, but now her parents were at risk of losing their dream if she didn't find a way to give up on hers.

It was no choice at all. What kind of daughter would she be if she wasn't willing to do this small thing for them? What kind of person?

The Strife officially began tomorrow—the end of her chances to slip away for time to herself. All her efforts would go to keeping out of the bottom competitors. That meant doing her best at each pillar and every moment in between. Fate had given her a rare opportunity. Now it was up to her to work hard enough to earn it, for her parents, if not for herself.

"Lose your shoes?" a snide female voice said from behind her.

Fenity jumped and dropped her skirts in the dirt. Lady Sarafine leaned against a low stone wall, nudging Fenity's silken slippers. She wore her signature red, this time as a looser-fitting dress that somehow still showcased her busty chest and bony hips. The look was complete with a red hair clip to hold her golden-brown hair off her slender neck. The precious stones glinted in the sun.

"Hello to you too, Sarafine." Fenity rolled her eyes and dusted off her skirts. Maybe Mata didn't have to find out. Some of her red hair slipped from her bun, and she blew it out of her face.

"As wild as a sprite." Sarafine laughed. "Prince Renic will just love that." She shook her head and made her way back from the gardens.

"Why the hostility?" Fenity called after her. "I've given you no reason to treat me as you do. Why not be civil?"

Sarafine paused. "Your pitiful wailing won't keep the king from stripping your lands when you end up in very last place. Oh, and you have paint on your face." Her upturned nose led the way back to the castle.

Fenity scowled and scrubbed at the crusty smear on her chin until it was gone. There might have been a better way to confront Sarafine about her actions, but remorse didn't stir in Fenity's gut at all. She wouldn't be mean, but she also wouldn't bow down to any superiority Sarafine felt entitled to simply because she'd had more time and money to prepare.

Fenity gave up dusting her hem, letting the dress hang back in the dirt. She was a mess. She knew it. Mata and Pata knew it. Probably all the Strife contestants knew it, too. It'd been easier to ignore Sarafine and the other judgmental females when Fenity first arrived at the castle.

"You don't look like a gardener," a male voice said, startling her. He walked toward her from the distant tree line carrying a hunting bow. It was the lord from the garden, the handsome one. Dirt smeared his hunting leathers and mud caked his boots. But the dinge couldn't hide his beauty. If anything, the grime only brought out the green in his eyes, making them all the more striking when framed by dark hair.

Another male with bright white hair—nearly as handsome with serious eyes—trailed behind.

Heat brushed Fenity's cheeks, and she crouched a little to hide her bare feet beneath her dress. He was clearly someone important here, though not too important if he carried his own bow and didn't mind getting dirty. While the white-haired male hung back, the handsome one studied her dress, a clear giveaway she wasn't who she'd claimed to be.

"I'm sorry I lied. I don't know why I did." She smoothed her dress, ensuring the hem covered her toes. "I'm here for the Strife." She waited for some kind of reaction from him—disappointment that she was unavailable, perhaps, but his eyes gleamed.

"You look happier today." He said it softly, as if it pleased him to see her happy. Or maybe it was her imagination.

Fenity sheepishly lifted her dress, exposing her bare feet covered in dirt. "Outdoors makes me happy."

The male lord tilted his head back and laughed, a sound that started deep in his belly and radiated over his whole body. His glee was contagious.

Fenity found herself smiling.

"I'll join you." He tossed aside his bow, then kneeled down to unlace his boots. One by one, he tugged them off, followed by his stockings, then pushed up his trousers and stood back up with a grin.

His companion backed to a discreet distance, leaning against the stone wall and playing with a knife, as the lord trudged through the grass. High Lords' sons, perhaps? He stopped close enough for her to feel his warmth. Instead of making her want to back away, she had to resist the instinct to step closer.

He dug his feet into the cool dirt, and the sigh that escaped him matched her own contentment. "I won't tell your mata if you don't tell mine."

Fenity watched him, searching for signs he was mocking her, but he truly appeared to appreciate the connection to the earth almost as much as she did.

"I'd have to know your name to tell your mata." Now that it was clear he wasn't about to mock her, Fenity relaxed back into the dirt.

He closed his eyes and tilted his head to the sun, but it didn't disguise that at least part of his focus remained solely on her. "Then I shall not tell you. For now, you'll be the gardener, who questionably dresses in fine gowns unsuitable for gardening, and I'll be the handsome, irresistible stranger."

"Well, you got the stranger part right, anyway." Both parts, actually.

"Ouch." He met her eyes and grinned, pushing a pile of dirt over her feet.

She shrieked and sidestepped away, laughing. "My guide is going to be cross with you." Their eyes met. He watched her with a bemused, almost affectionate expression. For the first time since arriving in Alberry, she felt at ease, but this was a dangerous game. She couldn't court someone else while competing for the prince's hand.

"Tell me, gardener, are you happy here? What has you seeking the solitude of the gardens so frequently?"

"Will you answer if I do?" she countered. "You certainly spend a lot of time outdoors as well." These were personal questions for two people who hadn't even exchanged names and shouldn't be getting to know each other in the first place. From what she'd picked up from the court etiquette Arinia tried to cram into her head, none of this was alright.

But she felt safe with him.

"I grew up here," he said, rocking back on his heels. "There are a lot of expectations placed on me and have been my whole life. Expectations I'm not allowed to circumvent. Leaving the castle helps me feel in control of my life. Connecting with the world around me reminds me there are bigger things than myself and personal circumstances." He focused on the trees in the distance. "I've never told anyone that before." He went quiet, as if waiting for her judgment.

But there was no judgment. Not from her. The Strife had thrust her into the same situation, and she already knew how horrible it was. Living your whole life that way...

The pain he tried to cover was clear, and everything in her wanted to make it go away. He deserved her honesty in return.

"I didn't grow up in this life, and I fear I'm not suited to it. The other females are cruel, and the ones who aren't have made it clear there are no friends in the Strife. Especially not with me, because my lack of training is going to land me in the bottom ten, if not very last place. And my parents deserve better than that." She sighed and her hands formed fists. "I'm really trying, but I can't change who I am, and it's hard to overcome my upbringing." She shook her head. "That sounds wrong. I loved my life and I plan to go back to it after this. I don't mind not knowing court etiquette and the proper way to paint a portrait. Except that it will hurt my parents."

"So you don't think you have a chance with the prince?" His expression was open and curious. "Being chosen as one of his ten favorites can help you stay off the bottom even if you fail the pillars."

"I haven't had the pleasure of meeting him. He's elusive, our prince. It's my understanding that our first meeting will be at the ball tomorrow." She gathered her courage. "Besides, it's hard to want to seek someone else, when..." Her cheeks heated. Giving her opinions freely had never been a problem, even to her admirers growing up, but this male made her feel more than that, and, well, maybe they could court once she lost the Strife.

"So you do find me handsome and irresistible." He grinned, making him even more beautiful.

"It's probably best you forget whatever you think I implied." She put her hands to her warm cheeks. "I'm sure I'm breaking a hundred rules right now."

His tone turned serious, and he placed a fist over his heart. "I won't forget, and I'm truly honored."

She couldn't help but ask. "Will you be at the ball? It would be nice to have a friend." Would one dance with him hurt?

He raised an eyebrow. "I'll save you the first dance." He gave a flourish of a bow that he'd probably done for the royals a thousand times, it looked so perfectly practiced. "Just don't forget your shoes."

Fenity stuck her tongue out at him. "Maybe I don't want to dance with you."

"I can see in your eyes that you do." He stepped purposely closer to her and stuck his face right in hers. "Or maybe it's me who desperately wants to dance with you." His warm breath caressed her cheek. He took up her hand and kissed it, soft lips on bare skin sending her heart skittering and heat traveling up her arm into her chest. "I'll see you tomorrow evening." He scooped up his belongings and walked barefoot back to the castle. His companion wordlessly fell into step beside him, nudging his shoulder with a grin on his face.

"And then you'll tell me your name?" she called after him, breathless and trying to pretend he hadn't affected her.

His answering laugh made her smile. He turned, walking backward. "Yes, gardener, I'll tell you my name. And by the way, that thing you implied you want me to forget? I feel the same way." He turned away and practically skipped until she lost sight of him around a wall.

A flutter, like sprites taking flight in her stomach and up to her heart, chased away the last of her misery. Maybe that was why she was here—to complete the Strife in the top group and get to know the kind lord.

Fenity tucked loose hair back into her braided twist, slipped back into her shoes, and headed into the castle, bidding goodbye to the sun and the dirt once more.

Tomorrow was the ball, and she'd get the prince to dance with her. Then she'd find the handsome, irresistible stranger.

CHAPTER 6

Fenity stood in her bathing room, hands on her hips through a soft robe while Arinia and the attendants waited for the dress reveal with bated breath. She'd been thoroughly scrubbed and perfumed, her hair already styled fully up with elaborate curls and tiny braids.

"Let's do this right." Arinia grinned, the excitement radiating from her. She clapped a hand over Fenity's eyes. "No peeking. Your dress is just through here."

Fenity couldn't help but give in to their excitement as they shuffled her blindly into the dressing room.

"Now, open your eyes." Arinia removed her hand. The attendants crowded around, clutching each other with eager smiles.

Fenity gasped. If she thought the day dresses were unnecessary, the ballroom dress was outright ridiculous. And exquisite. And beautiful.

Its shape supported by a mannequin, it featured the same shade of forest green they'd been outfitting her in, except overlaying the green was delicate gold netting with golden crystals.

A master tailor had sewn them in bunches from the top of the low-cut bodice right down to the hem. It sent the whole thing shimmering like treasure on the forest floor. But did the skirts have to be so voluminous? They puffed out, almost as wide as Fenity could stretch her arms. She would become lost in the layers if she didn't have six people waiting to help her put it on.

"It's gorgeous," Fenity said and meant it. "I love it."

Arinia clapped her hands in delight while the attendants let out squeals and relieved laughter. "Oh, I knew we'd win you over with this one." She lifted her chin, and the attendants hurried to remove the dress from the mannequin.

After fitting a hoop skirt over Fenity's hips, they lifted the dress over her head, twisting it in place while careful of her hair. One of them secured the ties at the back, cinching it way too tight, while another disappeared under the skirts and began fluffing them one at a time. Meryl was her name. Fenity watched, alarmed. Would she ever see Meryl again, or was she a sacrifice to the poofy skirt gods?

Fenity gave a small squeak when an icy hand grazed her legs, but then Meryl crawled out unharmed, if a bit disheveled.

"So, the feast is already well underway, but Strife contestants don't attend, of course. Not the opening feast." Arinia circled her, examining the quality of the attendants' work while they powdered and rouged and tied and tucked. "The contestants will parade through the room when announced and then proceed into the ballroom."

"So we don't get to eat?" Fenity's stomach grumbled.

"You're too busy to eat, and you want to fit in your dress."

Fenity scowled.

Arinia tossed up her arms. "Here." She grabbed a cookie from a nearby refreshment table and thrust it into Fenity's hand.

Fenity bit into the buttery sweetness, crumbs immediately cascading down her front. Two of the attendants gasped. Fenity rolled her eyes and casually dusted them away with her clean hand.

It was Arinia's turn to scowl.

"She's ready, ma'am." Meryl grinned, proud of their work.

Fenity spun slowly to the floor-length mirror. Her eyes flared, and she stepped unconsciously closer to her reflection—she hardly recognized the female from the forest. Her parents were going to love this.

Her makeup was just right this time—not too much. It made her eyes stand out and complemented the regalness of the dress. The narrow waist and lack of sleeves highlighted her toned muscles from all her days hunting and foraging. They swept up her hair with intricate braids pinned against curls and exposing her bare neck. She looked every bit like a princess in this fancy dress. Except for the cookie crumbs stuck to her lip—she quickly licked them away.

"Thank you all. This is sure to catch the prince's attention. I need all the help I can get." Just the slight turn of her hips sent the gold crystals sparkling.

"That's what we're here for." Arinia patted her arm in sympathy, then lifted it and dusted gold glitter over her skin. It rose in powdery puffs that smelled like flowers.

"Any last-minute advice?"

"Remember the dances we practiced. There will be food, but don't eat it." She pursed her lips. "Every contestant will dance with the prince. You'll know who's caught his eye already because they will be the first few he'll dance with." She finished dusting Fenity with scented glitter. "And have fun. This is a chance to let the prince get to know the real, albeit polished, version of you."

"What about when we aren't dancing with the prince—are

we allowed to dance with others?" Hopefully that didn't sound as eager as it seemed.

"Yes, of course. Remember, only one will marry the prince, but all of you are eligible females. The most important males in the kingdom will be vying for your attention, hoping you'll choose them when the Strife has ended."

Fenity smiled. That thought had made her want to revolt just a week ago. Males deeming the contestants worthy of their attention because of their status and nothing more? Lady Sarafine was proof enough that status and wealth were not a true measurement of a person's character.

But now, the thought of a certain male being allowed to 'vie for her attention' made her giddy.

Arinia left her at the back of a long line of Strife contestants, all waiting to parade through the feast. The females all wore the same large skirts, so broad they couldn't fit two across without brushing or crumpling against each other. They all, of course, ignored her. No one wanted to associate with someone who would drag them down, as Nisha had said. Fenity didn't spot her in the line, but the line stretched far to the doors. Fenity had been one of the last to arrive.

Night had fully settled in, darkening the windows and setting a romantic mood broken only by hushed conversations. The energy lights had dimmed to an orange glow, mimicking the flames from the sconces. But the subdued lighting couldn't mute the buzz of excitement in the air. They were about to be presented to the king and queen and their entire court, and then, they'd meet the prince.

Fenity breathed through her rising panic.

Her stomach rumbled as doors opened and the smells of the feast wafted her way. Roast meat and seasoned vegetables. Fresh, crackling bread.

The line moved slowly down the beamed hallway, skirts

and slippers rustling over woven carpet, poison bubbling from the mouths of scheming Strife contestants. Gossip ranging from how ugly certain females looked tonight, to how embarrassingly few warriors their parents had each pledged to the king. Though Fenity waited to join the more civil conversations, they kept their backs to her, so she kept quiet and thought through Arinia's instructions.

Enter when they announce her. Stop in the middle and curtsy for the king and queen. Make it to the ballroom where the prince will have his grand entrance after the feast.

Then she'd beeline for the refreshments. Or look for the handsome stranger. Both demanded her immediate attention and luckily distracted her from most of her nerves.

All those important eyes would be on her soon. Those gossiping, judging eyes who'd undoubtedly already placed bets on her odds in this Strife. They would have heard of her blunders and etiquette ineptitude, her inexperience. But she'd work hard to prove them wrong.

The contestant ahead of her in a dark purple dress, who the announcer called out as Lady Illeya Skyburn, crossed into the dining hall. It was almost her turn. Through the open double door, Fenity spied important courtiers dressed in all their finery, seated at tables piled high with silver platters of food. All their judgment waiting for her. She took a deep breath. It was just walking, nothing to it.

An attendant in palace livery called her name. "Lady Fenity Stormbrook of Southern Solice."

Head held high, she stepped into the room. Her slippered foot caught on an uneven stone, and she stumbled. She recovered quickly, but the door attendant rushed from beside her in anticipation of a fall and careened into her. They both tumbled to the floor, where he promptly disappeared somewhere in her billowing skirts.

The room gasped into stunned silence. This couldn't be happening. Her heart raced into a panic. Illeya glared at her mid-bow. The king and queen ignored the contestant and stared at Fenity with a mixture of horrified embarrassment and annoyed anger. Fenity kicked the attendant out from under her skirts and rose to her feet, but her skirts got hung up on each other, showing her bare legs underneath. Her breaths came too fast. Cheeks melting with embarrassment, she quickly righted them and lifted her chin.

Conversation roared to a start—along with plenty of laughter. The announcer said her name *again*—in case there was any confusion about who the Strife's biggest screw-up was—while the door attendant hobbled back to his post.

Fenity didn't focus on anyone as she passed through, letting her vision blur. She couldn't even look at her parents. And she'd been so excited to see their reaction to her beautiful attire. Had the handsome lord seen? If he was as important as he'd seemed, there was no doubt.

The enormous room held dozens of large, rectangular tables around the perimeter, all facing her fantastic display of exactly why she shouldn't be here and why they'd never pick her for queen. Her chances of getting herself out of the bottom half had just plummeted to zero, and it took everything in her not to let the welling tears slip and ruin Arinia's hard work. The rest of her concentrated on not sprinting right out of this nightmare, or worse—tripping again.

Would this seal her fate to the bottom ten?

She stopped before the royal table and executed the most perfect and graceful bow of her life. When she looked up, the king and queen's eyes said it all. They'd never pick her for their son.

With a sad smile, Fenity continued through the room, ignoring the judging eyes that had turned into judging voices

—as if her mistake was propriety's version of permission to speak their opinions outwardly, rather than the hushed whispers they'd reserved for the other contestants.

Blessedly, she crossed out of the dining hall, and the darkness of the near-empty ballroom swallowed her up and muted the courtier's harsh words.

She'd been in the ballroom before for dance lessons, but that was during the day. Now, the candelabras and chandeliers cast golden light to every corner, and the floor-to-impossibly tall-ceiling windows boasted night sky views filled with glittering stars.

But other than a brief flick of her eyes, there was no time to appreciate it. The room was empty except for the Strife contestants, staring at her, all huddled together to hear Fenity's latest blunder. Illeya stood in the middle beside Sarafine, clearly having told the others what Fenity had done. The lack of music and conversation suddenly made this the loudest room in the castle.

More contestants entered, just a few to go after Fenity, and joined their group, making a clear line between them. Thirty-nine on one side, Fenity on the other, all alone. Even Nisha had her arms crossed, a look of pity on her face.

Sarafine, of course, stepped forward. "We placed bets on how you'd mess this up. I won, but I didn't realize how spectacularly I'd win." She shook her head, brown curls swinging and irritation furrowing her brow. "You've stained the entire opening ball."

Fenity's cheeks burned. "I'm sure the attendant didn't mean to knock me down. I certainly didn't mean to make that kind of entrance. Why not ask after my well-being instead of being openly hostile?"

Sarafine's mouth dropped open, then quickly closed as she seethed. "You're fine. Your reputation, however..."

Some managed to look abashed, but not many.

Fenity turned her back on all of them and headed to the tables along the wall, lavished with food. She filled her plate, unseeing what she grabbed as tears marred her vision. Finally, a string quartet positioned in the corner, music began, and guests started piling into the room. The noise was almost enough to cover the contestants' gossiping and complaining.

Someone, maybe even a group of someones, used illusion energy and cast a sparkling night sky across the entire ceiling. Fenity watched, mesmerized. Her pulse raced at the fluttering of her own dormant energy, deep within her chest. She pushed it down, down, down—back where it belonged.

Her parents entered, and Fenity abandoned her untouched plate to duck behind a pillar. They sought her through the thickening crowd, but she couldn't face them yet. She'd let them down. Let herself down. She needed to endure this night, and things could be better tomorrow.

A herald announced the king and queen, and Fenity squeezed toward the front of the crowd. She curtsied with the rest of the court. No accidents this time. They took to their thrones on a dais at the head of the room. There wasn't an empty throne for the prince, but forty dances in one night would keep anyone busy.

Music and conversation swelled and filled the space that had grown even more majestic with the glittering ballgowns and tailored tunics. This was the opening of the Strife. No one could dance before the prince and he'd yet to arrive. Everyone had someone to talk to but her, it seemed. Even to fake a friendship, no one would bother. In fact, everyone seemed to avoid looking her straight in the eye, especially the other contestants who crossed her way. She'd lost track of her parents, thank goodness. Maybe if no one saw her with them, people wouldn't attach her bumbling ineptitude to them.

Would anyone notice if she left? They'd probably rejoice.

But, no. This was her chance to meet the prince. He was the only one who hadn't seen her trip and fall. And where was the handsome stranger? Even if he'd seen her, she wasn't giving up so easily.

The string quartet abruptly cut off, and a horn blasted through the room. The crowd drew a collective breath and pushed closer to the open doors at the other end of the room. Fenity stayed leaning against her favorite column, enjoying the cool air that rushed in to fill the space the crowd had vacated. What was the hurry? They guaranteed her a dance, but it certainly wouldn't be soon.

The tittering ramped up as the prince took the room. Fenity lifted onto her toes, but couldn't see around the crush of fine silks and organza.

King Sidian stood from his throne. "Prince Renic will open us with the first dance of the Strife."

Everyone applauded and turned their eager smiles toward the prince. Excitement thrummed through the room, almost as if the energies themselves were being manipulated. Fenity craned her neck, taking several steps away from her comforting column. Was that a crown sticking up between the crowding contestants?

Sarafine and Illeya pushed forward, each apparently sure of the prince's first pick.

"Our esteemed Prince Renic has chosen a contestant for the honor of receiving the first dance," the herald announced over the hushed room. "Fenity Stormbrook."

CHAPTER 7

Fenity's eyes went wide. The prince picked her for the first dance? Some perverse curiosity, perhaps? Or an extreme case of pity disguised as generosity?

Gasps of shock and outrage rippled over the room. Though she was surrounded by strangers, they all turned to her at once. They'd known exactly where she stood, ignoring her on purpose.

Fenity's silken slippers carried her forward, and the surprised crowd reluctantly parted for her. The shock turned hostile as she approached the Strife contestants on the edge of the dance floor. Sarafine and a few others openly blocked her path, a fae barrier of disbelief and anger, with crossed arms and hateful stare-downs.

What was it Arinia had said? The prince picked his favorite for the first dance. And if, at the end, she made the prince's top choice, she couldn't be placed in the bottom ten. So long as she kept up whatever had piqued the prince's interest in her—pity, curiosity—she might stand a chance.

Fenity nudged through, trying to pass Sarafine, but she

didn't budge. "What did you do to get him to pick you? You're nobody."

"Apparently not." Fenity forced a grin.

"Let her through," a smooth, male voice boomed out.

Sarafine and her cadre jumped and quickly backed out of the way.

Beneath a glinting silver crown stood a tall male with long, black hair and striking green eyes. He wore a blue-gray overcoat with silver embroidery at the cuffs and down the front, tailored just right over his broad shoulders and chest, with a cream tunic flaring out at the sleeves. His lips lifted into a smile she'd spent many hours daydreaming about. Her handsome, irresistible stranger.

"You," Fenity breathed. Her lips parted.

Prince Renic held out his hand with a shrug. "We are and are not who we pretend to be. Would the gardener like a dance?"

Fenity pinched her skirts and dropped into a practiced curtsey that would make Arinia proud. A new kind of heat brushed her smiling cheeks as she rose and took his hand. She wasn't even angry he'd withheld the truth—she'd done the same thing when they'd first met. They were both protecting their painful secrets, and she understood that need to her core. Especially in this place. If the lies had let them be themselves and help each other through difficulty, even for their brief interactions, then she loved the lies.

"I'd be honored." Fenity took his hand. His skin was warm and dry, his hold on her firm and sure. The only kindness in a hostile room. Like falling into a cozy bed at the end of a weary day. A warm fire to chase away the bitter cold.

She placed her hands where Arinia taught her, and the music began, but she hardly heard. Everything clicked into place as she recalled their interactions with new eyes.

"For the record, I never lied." Prince Renic led her around the empty dance floor with gentle pressures, reminding her what to do before the steps came. He didn't look around to see what others thought about his first choice, didn't bend an ear to the whispered gossip. He didn't even seem to notice that it was more than just the two of them in the room.

Neither did she.

"Oh, I know," Fenity said quickly. "You were very careful with your words. Very clever." He smiled, and it lit up his beautiful eyes. "I didn't lie either."

He quirked an eyebrow. "You're not the gardener."

Her dress billowed as he twirled her before pulling her close again. "I do garden. Or I used to. I'm fond of it."

He let out a deep guffaw that vibrated the space around them and penetrated her soul—a kind of unbound joy she hadn't witnessed since leaving her home in the Lirian Forest. Everyone else was so careful here.

"So then neither of us are liars." His face turned serious, and he closed the distance between them as he slowed their pace to match the changing music. His nearness warmed her, and she leaned into it, tightening her hold on him. "I'm glad to know we stand on equal footing as we begin our courtship."

Fenity swallowed. "Who says I want you to court me?" But her words came out in a weak whisper instead of the snarky sass she'd intended.

He grinned and leaned to murmur into her ear, his smooth jaw skimming hers. "That's why we're all here, isn't it?" They pivoted around the outskirts of the room. Still, no one else was dancing. The faces of the watching Strife contestants had turned dark and calculating. "Though if you don't desire to be here, I will not force you. Or any of the females. That is not my wish." His hold loosened, as if suddenly unsure of her desire to be here. "Perhaps it's time to invite the next contestant to dance."

"No!" She tugged him back toward her. "I want to be here. I wanted to be here because of you before I knew who you really are." His consideration of her choice was the final crack in the glass wall she'd built up around herself because of this place. He was the first person to even hint that she had a choice in all this. Not her parents, not her king, society, her competition. She wanted this. She wanted him.

His eyes softened. "I showed you who I really was before you knew me as the prince. Thank you for showing me who you are in return."

She was afraid of the answer, but she asked anyway. "So it wasn't pity for my fall that made you choose me?"

"You fell?" Concerned eyes scanned her body.

"An overly helpful guard knocked me down. Accidentally. You didn't hear? It happened in front of the entire court." His sincerity washed over her. He hadn't known. He hadn't chosen her out of pity.

He chuckled. "No, but I'm sure I will hear of it as soon as the next dance begins."

The song slowed, the last notes before the end. Fenity's heart picked up speed. This was it. She wouldn't get another dance with him this night, and who knew when she'd see him again? What if this was how he was with all the contestants? Showing his true self and winning them over with his princely charm? The other females already knew him and wanted him, whereas it had taken her until this moment to feel that way. The thought of him holding another female's hand made her blood boil irrationally.

"The first test starts tomorrow," he whispered suddenly in her ear. "Don't worry, it's not a pillar. My advice is to be yourself, especially now that you know who I am. I must spend time with all the contestants, but don't let that get to you." He bowed and kissed her hand as the song ended. "You were my first pick."

He let go and turned away before she could gather a reply. The other females swooped in from nowhere, and he picked one for the next dance—Sarafine, of course. The rest of them shuffled away, disheartened.

Fenity turned to do the same, and a host of finely dressed males waited with eager smiles.

"May I have the next dance?" one of the more eager ones said, holding out his hand.

Fenity took it before her brain caught up to her mouth. "Um."

The male gracefully led her to the dance floor where others were already pairing up. The rest of the males scattered in search of more Strife contestants. Fenity placed her hands like she had with Prince Renic, but the differences were immediate. Though handsome, this male's smile was disingenuous, someone putting on a show for her. His shoulders were not as broad, stature a little shorter, closer to her height. The way he moved her around the dance floor, he expected her to know the motions, almost discourteous compared to the way the prince had helped her along.

"I'm Lord Taleir of the Westwater Lands. Pleased to make your acquaintance, Lady Fenity." He pivoted, and she nearly tripped trying to adjust.

"Westwater lands? Your pata is Commander Skylin. My pata served under him against the invading goblins in the ten-year war." Well before Fenity was born.

"Your pata is a legend. It's about time they recognized him for it. I was glad to hear of his land appointment."

She beamed. "Thank you." Now if only she could keep from messing it up for Pata.

The song ended, and Lord Taleir gave a polite bow. "It was a pleasure. I hope we can do it again."

When he backed away, a new host of males already awaited. Fenity searched for the prince, but he was locked in the same cycle as she, with females circling him, waiting for him to choose his third partner of the night. From what she'd learned, the first choice was the most significant, but the order after that still meant a lot, even at this early stage. Illeya, in her dark purple dress, was third.

Fenity accepted the next male with little thought, letting the music and the lingering feel of Prince Renic's skin carry her emotions. There were too many things to worry about, so for now, she wouldn't worry about any of them. Not even Prince Renic across the room, laughing at something Illeya said.

His laugh cut off abruptly, and he lifted his face, eyes going straight to hers with a look of concern. Fenity gasped and focused back on her partner. He regaled her with stories of growing up with a sibling—rare for fae to have children at all, let alone children close enough in age to grow up together. Only truemates had that.

Her parents smiled and waved from a distance, trying to catch her eye, but they, too, were surrounded by a swarm of nobility, all vying for their attention now that their daughter had been redeemed.

Just as before, the males lined up to have the next dance. She tried her best to remember their names, but it was a lost cause. After a few more songs, she had mastered all the steps, and oh, how she loved to dance. She nearly forgot her partners, letting the feel of the music sweep her away. Too bad they wouldn't leave her alone so she could move around the room at leisure. It helped to forget the high rulers were only interested in her because of her pata's new holdings and her status in the Strife. It was as close to wild and free as she'd come since arriving here, the passion and emotion normally supplied by nature being replaced by the musical notes lifting her feet and her heart.

It tempered the sting of watching the prince with his own endless stream of partners.

Her partners seemed to notice her mood, some of them letting her lead, laughing along with her. A few of them frowned, tugging her in directions her body didn't want to go, trying to control her. She ended those dances early, using the break to rest and refresh.

Fenity accepted a crystal of elderberry punch from an attendant at the table, holding it with both hands to absorb its chill. Taking small sips, she savored the cold running down her throat. Dancing was tiring business.

"You know it was pity that made him choose you first, don't you?" Sarafine approached from behind, accepting a glass of punch.

Fenity suppressed a sigh. "Do you hate yourself so much that you must always try to make others hate themselves too?"

Sarafine glared daggers. "He knew about your disastrous scene and wanted to help." She feigned a casual shrug. "He's a good male—I know him *very* well—but it was a gesture of pity, nothing more."

Fenity narrowed her eyes. How well was *very* well? "If that story will help you feel better and make you leave me alone, then by all means, keep telling it." She turned her back and sipped her drink, but it had gone tasteless. She knew what he'd said and what she felt when she was near him. Did he feel the same?

Cold liquid splashed over the back of her neck and ran down her dress. Fenity gasped and spun around. Sarafine stood with her empty cup, looking as shocked as Fenity felt. She quickly fixed her face into a calculated smirk and crossed her arms. The attendant was the only one who seemed to see, but he didn't react, even to offer a towel.

"You threw your drink on me." Fenity couldn't believe it, even as the liquid seeped into the layers of her skirts and bled down her back into her underclothes.

Sarafine opened her mouth to say something snarky, but then her jaw snapped closed and a look close to panic crossed over her face. She thrust her empty glass aside as Prince Renic strode to the table, followed by a swarm of Strife contestants.

Prince Renic smiled when he noticed Fenity, but then froze with his arm reaching for a glass. He studied her. "What happened?" Concerned eyes trailed her body to the purple droplets dripping over her shoulders. The Strife contestants studied her as well, some already laughing as they'd concluded what had happened.

Sarafine pleaded with her eyes, but Fenity owed her nothing, and she wouldn't lie to one of the few people who'd been kind to her in this place. "It seems Lady Sarafine had an accident with her drink. I'm afraid it's now all over my back."

"You caught me in the middle of apologizing to Miss Fenity, Your Highness." Sarafine grabbed a towel from a servant and approached Fenity. "An unfortunate accident."

Prince Renic frowned in deep disapproval.

Fenity took the towel before Sarafine could touch her and dabbed purple from the back of her neck and shoulders. "It looks like my clumsiness is rubbing off on you." She reached for her back.

Sarafine's lips thinned.

"Let me." Prince Renic took the towel, and Fenity turned, revealing her bare back that was now undoubtedly streaked with purple. The prince wiped smoothly down her skin from neck to lower back. "That must have been a full glass," he accused.

Fenity shivered as his fingers grazed her skin. She turned to find Prince Renic's eyes creased with concern and Sarafine seething. "Thank you for your assistance, Your Highness. Unfortunately, my dress is ruined. I think I'll retire for the night." The formalness was for the watching contestants. She couldn't let them know they'd gotten to her.

Did Prince Renic notice the change in her?

She hated Sarafine for making her miss the rest of an incredible party, but she'd only embarrass herself and her parents further if she paraded around the ballroom in a stained dress. Besides, she'd accomplished the real reason for coming —to dance with the handsome lord.

He studied her, then nodded. "I understand. I'll bid you good evening, Lady Fenity." He gave a formal bow that matched his formal words and left for the dance floor with the next Strife contestant in tow.

Sarafine actually looked remorseful as Fenity passed her without comment. Probably remorseful at being caught. But if Prince Renic knew Sarafine *very* well, then he probably knew her character, too.

The eager males made it difficult to escape, but she finally managed. Exhaustion hit her upon returning to her rooms. She hadn't realized just how tiring dancing and scheming fae could be. Arinia mourned the dress but wasn't the least bit surprised by how it came to be.

Sleep came easily despite the prince's warning. The first contest was tomorrow.

CHAPTER 8

The sun was near to rising when the last dance ended, and Renic's bunched muscles relaxed. The torture had finally ended. After the first dozen contestants, he'd met all the political requirements and danced with a few of his own choices. Most important of them all was the first dance—Fenity Stormbrook.

She hadn't recognized him when they first met, one of the few times that had ever happened to him within his own home. He'd been completely free to be himself, with no preconceived expectations to rise to. And since she hadn't known he was the prince, there was no fawning or changing herself to please him.

And when she discovered who he was, she still didn't change to please him.

He bowed to the final contestant as she curtsied to him— Pernin, a lady of the court he'd seen growing up but had never connected with. Her holdings weren't important enough to make the king's list.

"Thank you for the dance." Dressed in dark orange, Pernin

offered her hand for a kiss but pouted when Renic used it to guide her off the dance floor instead.

"Good luck in the contest." It was anyone's guess how the pillars would go. He took one last sweeping look around the room, but the person he sought hadn't returned.

The contestants caught him watching Fenity many times—especially Sarafine. He pretended distraction, but his eyes always strayed back to her. The way she danced, laughing and carefree, so unlike the subdued movements of the rest of them. A wild spirit placed in the heart of a dying court, bringing light and air back into the castle.

There was no doubt Sarafine had doused that light on purpose. She wasn't usually so duplicitous, but the Strife changed people, or so he'd been told. Many lords and ladies had their eye on the throne. It was only the beginning of what his parents had raised him to expect.

With weary steps, he left the ballroom through the royal hall. Galan, his personal guard and closest confidant, fell in step slightly behind him.

"And how was your night?" Renic asked over his shoulder, navigating carpeted hallways past guards at their posts.

"Not as interesting as yours, I'm sure." Galan chuckled. "You hear a lot when people think no one's listening. I have to say, the way these ladies are already after you, you better prepare." His voice went high-pitched. "*He's so handsome. I'd dance with him any night. I'll do anything to be his queen. Anything.*" He laughed.

Renic stopped in his tracks, and Galan barreled right into his waiting elbow.

"Oof." Galan grabbed his stomach and laughed at Renic's grin.

"Yeah, well, you can have my place." Renic shoved him, chuckling, and picked up the pace to his rooms. He'd always known the Strife would be his future, a necessary part of ensuring a smooth transition in the kingdom's succession, and a way to maintain peace. The Strife assured that the next ruler was chosen fairly, giving equal chance to all eligible contenders.

Was it truly so equal if some were given better chances than others?

"No, thank you," Galan said, cutting into his thoughts. "Not even for all those females."

"No one's caught your eye, then?"

"Not yet, my prince."

They reached Renic's rooms, where a pair of guards opened the door. As usual, he waited while Galan checked the suite for threats. Twice his age, a highly trained warrior, and loyal to the core, they were more like brothers than friends. If tested, Renic had no doubt Galan would follow him even over the king's command. Renic was the only one he ever let his guard down around, and only when it was the two of them. Otherwise, he was alert and rarely smiled.

"All clear." Galan bowed goodbye and headed for his adjoining room.

"Thanks, Galan." Renic yawned. Morning dawned through heavily curtained windows, closer to purple than the light pink of day. He collapsed onto his bed, fully clothed, sinking into linens that smelled of flowers.

A knock on the door had him blinking awake. The sun hadn't changed.

Renic rubbed his eyes. "Enter."

Galan waved a note in his hands, yawning. "King Sidian has summoned you to his study."

Renic pulled a pillow over his face, groaning. "I politely decline." But he sat up, tossing the pillow aside. At least it was the study and not the throne room. Nothing good ever happened to anyone summoned there. "Get some sleep, Galan. The guards can escort me."

Renic left his rooms, mentally preparing himself for the long walk to his pata's wing of the castle. Of course, Galan fell in line behind him.

The guards bowed and let him in where he promptly collapsed into a leather chair in front of the hearth while Galan took a post inside the door. The fire hissed and popped, and Pata's chuckle rumbled from the chair beside him.

"I remember my opening ball well." The king wore blue silk with black stitching, his gold circlet resting on the table beside him. "I didn't have quite so many females to dance with as you did."

Renic wiped a hand over his face. "It was a long night, to be sure."

"I heard you did well, spending equal time with all the contestants. The high rulers are pleased."

"Thank you, Pata." Renic pried his eyes open, waiting for the true point of this summoning. "You were right about the contestants. They are already trying to gain the advantage over each other."

Pata smirked. "I warned you about that. Try not to get too caught up. What did you see?"

"Sarafine spilled a drink on Fenity which forced her to leave early."

Pata's mood darkened slightly. "Fenity from the south, Lord Stormbrook's daughter. He served me well, and the High Lord of those lands died in battle. I was glad to give the lordship to him." He frowned. "I didn't know he had a daughter of age."

Renic stayed silent, waiting to see where this would go.

"And she was your first pick, hmm? A high honor, and not what he discussed." His pata stared into the fire, absently reaching for a tankard on the table and sipping it. Honey mead, no doubt. A sweet drink with very little bite.

"I gave priority to everyone you asked, but I wanted the first pick."

Pata knocked back the rest of the drink. "This is your Strife, son. But our borders may soon be tested once again. Choosing a contestant must be about alliances as much as it is finding your queen. It's a balance. You'll get the feel for it." He reached out and patted Renic's shoulder. "But no more showing the Stormbrook female any favors. She's not a true contender here."

Renic shifted in his chair, resisting looking back at Galan. Nothing about the Strife was supposed to be preordained, and obeying his pata's meddling didn't feel right, even if the goblins were growing restless. "Thank you for your guidance, Pata."

Neither Galan nor he said a word on the way back to their rooms. There would be balance, but he also wouldn't forget whose Strife it was.

CHAPTER 9

Arinia entered Fenity's bedroom just after dawn. "All that talk about your dress, and you couldn't bother mentioning that you were *first picked?*" She tossed her arms in the air. "I had to find out from the gossip!"

Fenity looked up from the window, blinking.

So it wasn't a dream. "I assumed you knew. You know everything."

"Well, I know now." Her pursed lips reluctantly relaxed. "First picked! Well done, my petal. But now things will only be more difficult."

Fenity stood as attendants opened the rest of the tall curtains to streaming light. "I thought being in the prince's top ten made things less difficult."

"Oh, no." Arinia emerged from the dressing room carting a simple green dress. "Now you're the one to beat. You're the one everyone will be looking at, picking apart. Where you were once someone to scorn and forget, now you're a threat."

"Great." Fenity collapsed onto her bed, the pillow

billowing around her. It hadn't taken long to get used to the luxury of a soft bed.

"No sleeping. The Strife begins today, and all are to gather in the great hall." She shook the dress for emphasis, setting off a subtle shine in the silk.

After a trip to the bathing room, Arinia helped her into the comfortable dress.

A quick knock preceded the door bursting open. Her parents rushed in, all smiles.

"First picked!" Mata gushed. She wore a gown in a similar shade of green. "I didn't think you'd met the prince. How did you do it?"

"You've made us proud," Pata said, looking more polished than usual in his tailored tunic.

"We met. I just didn't know it was him."

Mata and Pata exchanged surprised looks while the attendants continued readying her, curling her hair and pushing slippers onto her feet.

"Apologies, my lord and lady, but Fenity must convene in the grand hall." Without looking, Arinia thrust a bowl of fruit and yogurt into Fenity's hands, then ushered her parents out of the room. Fenity gave an apologetic wave as the door closed behind them.

"Eat and walk. We can't be late." Arinia scanned her over, head to toe, nodded her approval, and then they swiftly left.

"What's happening in the grand hall?" She bit into the sweetness of the fruity perfection, leaning forward so nothing dripped on her.

"The art contest. The Strife always begins with something simple to ease the contestants into how things work. Prince Renic will choose his favorite."

Fenity choked. The paintings were part of a contest? Dread filled her gut, replacing her appetite. She'd done her best, but that class had been a disaster. It would be no surprise to find Uda had expunged her painting from the gallery.

"Count yourself lucky," Arinia said. "It's the tests we don't know about that are the most difficult."

Fenity paused. "Tests we don't know about? I thought at least *you* knew what they were."

Arinia ushered her along, undeterred by the panicked mess Fenity was quickly becoming. "There's always one pillar the contestants aren't told about. You won't know what it is or that you're being watched. I keep forgetting how much you don't know." Her lips thinned, but then she waved goodbye as other contestants veered off their own hallways, joining them in the long walk to the great hall.

Fenity walked behind them, feigning a calm she didn't feel. One of the five pillars was being silently tested. Which one? Not strength or poise. How would she know if she was being tested? She'd have to always be alert.

Some who'd ignored her before now smiled or made polite conversation. She shouldn't blame them—they risked just as much if they ended in the bottom half—but she did. Not one soul here had been real, avoiding her like the plague because they assumed she stood no chance. As tough as it was to admit, it hurt to be excluded because of circumstances beyond her control.

The echo of conversation preceded them through an archway twice her height. The grand hall lived up to its name —a giant room much longer than it was wide, with crystal chandeliers, marble floors, and windows letting in morning light and hints of the strange green garden.

Lined on both sides of the room, their paintings sat on full display supported by golden easels. Royals and courtiers sipped drinks and traversed the room in packs, studying and discussing the artwork. The contestants dispersed amongst them, forming their own packs and joined by the eager single lords. None of the females joined her—apparently being first-picked didn't exclude her from the humiliation they all knew was about to take place. Contrary to Uda's threat, she hadn't labeled the paintings with their names, but Fenity's was glaringly obvious, about halfway down the room on the right. The forest and creek were so abstract compared to the fine lines and distinct features of the other paintings.

There were already several people around it, whispering and pointing and looking over their shoulders back at her. She ignored them, pretending to study the other paintings while she moved about by herself. Whatever the lords had been seeking at the dance last night, they paid her no heed now. They avoided her like the rest—probably waiting to see how spectacularly she'd fail before deigning to speak to her again.

"Don't let this place dim your light, Fenity," Prince Renic said from beside her.

She jumped, hand over her heart. She'd been so caught up in ignoring the room, she hadn't noticed his entrance. The white-haired male from before—who must be his guard—stood to the side of the room, watching them.

He chuckled. "Sorry, but I saw you standing here all alone, studying my likeness." He paused. "I know why they stay away. I can see you wilting under the weight of it." He rubbed his neck as she studied him with wide-open eyes. "Just... don't let this place dim your light." At the beckoning of the king, the prince gave a nod and left to join him.

Fenity looked back at the painting. It was Prince Renic from the torso up, beautifully rendered though with dead eyes lacking any of the fire she'd just witnessed in him. She hadn't even realized she'd stopped at this painting, out of all the others.

A herald stepped to the middle of the room and bowed to

the royal family in their high-backed chairs brought in for this event. She stood far away from Prince Renic, further down the hall, but she swore every time she looked at him, he was looking at her.

Everyone hushed as the herald unrolled a yellowing parchment. "The Strife takes place to aid the heir in selecting a member among eligible nobility to marry, ultimately ruling beside them and securing the throne for future generations. It makes obvious what our eyes may not see through a series of challenges, each based upon one of the Five Pillars of Faedom. Each pillar carries the same weight, but the royal family's decision carries the heaviest." He re-rolled the parchment. "As part of the opening competition, Prince Renic examined the artwork and anonymously chose his top five. Similar to the winner of each pillar, the five winners will receive a reward." The crowd perked up at this. "Today's winners will receive one-on-one time with the prince."

The crowd cheered, and Fenity held her breath.

"The winners are Lady Sarafine. Lady Illeya. Lady Moona. Lady Nisha. And Lady Fenity."

Fenity's mouth dropped open. Her lips snapped shut at the sight of Prince Renic's bemused expression. Oh, he was definitely looking at her.

"We will remove the other portraits and label the winners, displayed for all to admire. Tomorrow, the First Pillar of Faedom commences."

Fenity sucked in a breath while the rest of the fae in the room applauded. The First Pillar was one she'd looked forward to celebrating in Solice's town square. She'd imagined listening to the gossip, watching the elders place bets on who would win, and viewing nightly reenactments of the magical feats. The fae who spoke of the last Strife said it was a grand time. She'd left her few friends behind when her pata became High Lord, but they had promised to meet up for the festival.

Instead of revelry, tomorrow would be her worst nightmare. Tomorrow it would all fall apart.

"Lady Sarafine," Prince Renic called out. "I believe your name was announced first." Behind him, the king and queen smiled approvingly as Sarafine made her way in front of them.

Fenity watched the prince through the crowd. Even without addressing her, his voice seemed to stand out, calling to her.

Before the royal family, Sarafine dropped into a disgustingly elegant curtsy, then simpered all the way to Prince Renic's proffered arm. As they left the hall for their one-on-one time, Sarafine looked over her shoulder and met Fenity's stare with a smirk before closing the distance between her and the prince.

Fenity rolled her eyes, and they landed right on a pack of lords waiting to talk to her. First picked *and* a winner of the art contest? Now she must truly be a consolation prize to be won.

She walked with the lords for a while, doing her best to get to know them and answer their questions politely. After all, she had vowed to do her best at this contest and that meant befriending the court. But after several turns of the room, she couldn't play along anymore and excused herself. Her thoughts were wrapped up in the prince and how she might not fail the energy test.

If the awarded time with the prince went in the announced order, she had time to try to do something about tomorrow. She couldn't fail the First Pillar.

Just as she'd hoped, her rooms were empty upon her return. Even still, she retreated to her bedroom and locked the door. She leaned against it, rubbing her face, heart beating erratically.

Was it worth this risk? Could she fail a pillar and stay out of the bottom ten? There were still four others, and they said each was given the same weight.

She shook her head and marched to the center of the room. She breathed deeply, willing her heart to calm. There *had* to be a way to display her energy other than its illegal form—anything to keep from claiming to be lacking. What prince would choose a powerless partner for their bride? What king would want heirs who might not inherit any energies?

The room spun. She couldn't believe what she was about to attempt.

Mata had warned her over and over since the day she knew what words were.

Do not access your energies.

Just like Fenity, her mata had energy, as did her mata before her, and hers before that. Only theirs was the dangerous kind. The kind they had to hide and never reveal except to warn the next generation. The kind the king killed for.

The ability to open portals.

No one questioned this law, or fought against the king for the right to use their energies, for one reason only. The prophecy. The curse placed by the humans long ago that promised the doom of all fae should they ever open a portal again.

Fenity shook her arms like she could shake off the fear crawling down her spine. Eighteen years of being taught to fear what she could do and avoid accessing her energy, but what if she could use it in another way? What if she could take that energy and use it for something else?

So long as she didn't open a portal, the wards wouldn't sound the alarm, alerting the entire fae population, and everyone would remain safe.

She hadn't been eighteen for long—maybe her energy

hadn't set yet. Maybe it wasn't too late. It was worth a try in order not to disgrace her parents and just maybe have a real chance at winning the Strife and winning the prince.

Fenity took a shaky breath and opened her mind to energy she'd never dared touch before. A tingling like the atmosphere charged before a storm erupted over her skin and warmed her insides. She gripped tight for control as the energy tried to pour through. Holding it back came easy—the only skill she'd learned to hone.

But this time, she had to let it loose.

Her hands formed fists as if manifesting her control. "Please work. Goddess of Nature, let me shape it to my will." She focused on something simple—a single blade of grass— took a deep, calming breath, and released the energy.

A haze erupted around her. An involuntary cry burst from her at the force flowing from her. Years of built-up energy rushed through the crack in the dam.

The air turned warm. The arched ceiling gave way to open air. Green grass tickled her bare legs and skimmed the hem of her fancy dress.

Her heart slammed into a sprint.

A portal. She'd opened a portal.

With a grunt of effort, like pushing a boulder into water exploding from a dam, she closed off the energy. The grass disappeared. The portal closed.

Fenity collapsed to the plaited rug, racking sobs bursting from her. She wiped sweat from her upper lip and stared wide-eyed at the door.

What had she done? The prophecy. The alarm. Any minute it would go off and they'd know what she'd done. They'd come for her. She opened her hearing, straining as far as she could, but her racing heart drowned all outside noises.

Shaking, she struggled to her feet and rushed to the window.

Nothing.

Outside, Prince Renic walked the garden, lazily strolling arm-in-arm with a contestant, looking utterly bored.

Other ladies of the Strife and hopeful lords relaxed nearby. They watched the prince or flirted with each other, all absorbed in their own activities—painting, reading, or sizing up the competition.

No one stared in horror up at her window. No one screamed and panicked. No guards took up arms to defend their world from the tragedy opening a portal was prophesied to release.

No alarm sounded in the distance.

Fenity dropped into a chair, hand gripped to her chest to keep her heart in place. She'd opened a portal, and no one knew.

Why hadn't the wards detected it? Was it all a lie? Or had she closed it too fast for them to detect it?

And where had she opened a portal to? She'd only meant to form a blade of grass.

She couldn't touch it again, not even to attempt the First Pillar. Without being able to wield her energy for anything but opening portals, using it meant only death. Death for her, and death for her family.

Tomorrow, she would fail the first challenge. In front of her parents, the prince, and the entire kingdom.

CHAPTER 10

"Mata, what am I going to do?" Fenity paced her parents' sitting room shortly after recovering from her brush with death. If anyone would know how to help her, it was Mata.

Her mata sat on a tall-backed chair tugging at the tight collar of her latest dress. A tiny reminder she wasn't born into this life either. Pata was at a meeting of the high rulers—King Sidian was taking advantage of having so many of them gathered at the castle.

"I'm going to look like a fool in front of the entire court. I'm going to fail this pillar." Panic closed off her throat as she looked into her mata's kind eyes. Her parents had worked hard to earn their place. Being ostracized because of their deficient daughter wouldn't just strip them of their new lands and put them back in the home they'd left. Everyone would shun them. All doors shut tight.

"We knew this would be a problem, my young one. Energy is always part of the pillars." Mata took a practiced sip of tea, one eye on the door for eavesdroppers. Their energy was dangerous at the best of times, lethal here in the heart of the kingdom. And Mata *never* spoke about it other than to warn Fenity never to use it.

"Why aren't you more worried?" Fenity paced by the untouched plate of refreshments Mata had requested—venison sandwiches and cookies encrusted with sugar crystals.

The alarm had never sounded, but as the hours ticked by, her nerves continued to fray. So close. She'd been so close to losing her life. Her mata's life.

"Because you are the prince's favorite." The teacup clinked against a porcelain plate painted with pink roses as Mata set it down. "First dance? Top five of the art contest? And rumor has it someone saw you flirting in the garden."

Fenity's cheeks heated. "I like him. A lot."

Mata smiled. "That pleases me. And that's why I'm so calm." She settled back in her chair as if emphasizing her point. "Continue to be in the prince's top picks, and it won't matter if you fail a pillar. Just be sure not to fail the others." Her eyes took on a misty look. "I raised you to be strong and independent. You've grown into someone remarkably capable, and I'm so proud of you. I know this isn't easy, none of it is. But you can do this."

"But there's no guarantee I won't fail the others and then I won't win." Fenity sagged into the matching chair, as much as her tight dress would allow her to sag.

Mata tilted her head. "I thought you had no interest in becoming queen."

"I didn't. I don't." She rubbed her temples. "There's something about the prince that makes me forget about what I used to want."

"Used to want?" Mata studied her as if seeing her daughter for the first time after a long journey apart. "Do you think—"

A quick knock, then a servant opened the door, letting Arinia into the room.

"It's time!" she announced, clasping her manicured hands together. "Your awarded time with His Highness has arrived." She surveyed Fenity's dress. "But you'll have to change."

Fenity smoothed the wrinkles caused by her slouching. "I'm dressed the same as the others waltzing through the garden." The castle's servants made them all perfect replicas of each other, just in different colors.

"You'll not be waltzing, dear. You're going riding."

A short while later, Fenity wore riding leathers, not a skirt or dress to be found. Following Arinia's instructions, she walk-ran all the way to the stables.

The sight stopped her short. Instead of horses, the prince had...

She gasped. "Unicorns!"

Prince Renic stood grinning, watching her half-hearted attempt to behave properly as she rushed to close the distance. Each hand held the reins of two beauties, one a solid black, and the other a shining white. They snorted and pawed the ground at her approach. Renic's guard was either absent or guarding from a distance.

The laugh Prince Renic was clearly holding back burst out of him. "I knew you'd appreciate this as much as I do."

Fenity stopped a polite distance away and bowed—not at the prince, but at the unicorns, each in turn. She hadn't seen a unicorn since she'd left her home in the woods, and she'd never dared to ride one before. They mostly kept to their lands in the Unicorn Sanctum, a protected piece of Asentia.

"This is Crucifan," Prince Renic said, raising the reins of the black unicorn. "And this is Opal. They are members of the castle guard. Opal will carry you—if you ask nicely." He winked.

"I can't believe this is real." She met his eyes. "This was just what my heart desired."

Prince Renic nodded his understanding, eyes creasing. "An escape and a piece of home."

Warmth flooded her chest, and she bowed again to the unicorns. "I am pleased to meet you, Opal. Will you bear me this day? I will try not to be a burden." She knew enough of unicorns to know they were intelligent beings, with hierarchies of their own, able to pass judgment on any fae they encountered.

Opal stepped closer, and Prince Renic dropped the reins. Fenity stuck out her hand, palm up, and the unicorn sniffed it. Slowly, Fenity caressed Opal's coat until she breathed easier under her care.

"Why am I not surprised?" Prince Renic's mouth raised in a lopsided smile.

Fenity grinned. So the prince wasn't a pampered dolt who knew nothing about the creatures they shared this world with.

"Thank you," she whispered to the mare, nuzzling her nose with her forehead, one eye on the sharp horn.

They both mounted, and Prince Renic sped away. Opal immediately bolted after them without a signal from Fenity. She scrambled to get a good grip with her thighs, leaning into the stirrups and adjusting to the speed.

They were flying.

She'd ridden horses before, but this was different. The strength as Opal stretched her legs and ate up the distance was like nothing else. She never ran ahead of Crucifan, always keeping at his side. The field blurred green beneath them, pale pink sky blossoming bigger the further they rode from the castle. Trees rose in the distance, and an immense weight freed itself from Fenity's chest. She laughed as the wind tore at her hair, which had been so meticulously stuck in a tight bun. She pulled at the pins until the hair burst from its binding, blowing long and free behind her.

Prince Renic laughed along with her, and when she snuck a peek at him, he was watching her. "We're almost there." He pointed ahead.

Fenity spotted a picnic waiting for them at the edge of the woods. The unicorns stopped short of the spread, panting and pawing at the ground. As soon as they dismounted, the unicorns rushed each other, nuzzling against one another.

"They're a mated pair, you know," Prince Renic said, meeting her eyes. "Now that they've found each other, they will never love another."

"Then I'm glad they found each other." Fenity held his gaze, drinking it up, afraid to blink and ruin this moment. Afraid to doubt his implication.

The moment stretched on as the seconds ticked by—him watching her, and her watching him. But it wasn't awkward. There was no urge to look away or interject some mundane conversation. Instead, she had to resist closing the distance to him. Her body nearly betrayed her. She almost moved toward him—to touch him? To take his hand? To wrap her arms around him?—but he spoke first.

"Are you hungry?" He waved his arm half-heartedly toward the spread.

"Starving, actually." She'd been too busy worrying for her life to eat anything all day. Though she'd rather stare at him for the rest of their time together.

She'd never felt this way before, so deep and immediate.

Prince Renic sat cross-legged on the blanket, leaving her plenty of room and a difficult choice. How close was too close to sit beside him? It wouldn't be proper to assume he felt anything for her as she did for him.

And there it was. That seed of doubt tried to worm into her

heart, but she shut the gate on it. It didn't exist. It was only there to poison her thoughts and open her soul to a cavernous hole filled with sadness and fear, pitted like fruit devoured by insects. But that wasn't who she was or who she wanted to be in this life.

Right now, she wanted to be with the prince, and not some proper distance apart from him. So, when he patted the blanket encouragingly, she sat right beside him, crisscrossing her own legs and not even adjusting when their knees touched.

Something like understanding mixed with appreciation flashed over Prince Renic. "I've been looking forward to our time all day." He filled two plates with meats, cheeses, fruit, and chocolates.

"Not too tired from entertaining so many contestants, then?" She bit into an apple slice to cover any hint of envy.

"Never." The word and his intensity caressed her spirit.

The unicorns grazed lazily while their riders nibbled their treats in companionable silence. If the prince was anything like her at all—and she suspected he was—then he, too, was listening to the sounds of the earth. The birds singing to each other in the trees, the breeze gently whispering through the grass, the buzz of insects going about their day without knowing or caring that a contest could make or break the rest of her life. And she was beginning to not mind at all that she'd had no choice.

Fenity set her plate aside and lay back on the blanket, appreciating how the grass cushioned her. She pillowed her arms behind her head and crossed her legs at the ankles. The prince hesitated only a moment before joining her, elbows touching, and they sighed in contentment in unison. Fenity couldn't help her laugh. Those immovable castle walls—how would she breathe when it was time to go back?

"I've never met a lady of the court like you before." From

the sound of his voice, he'd turned to face her, but she remained staring at the sky, studying the sparse clouds and basking in the cool shade of the trees.

If she turned her face to him, she just might kiss him—definitely not proper.

"I'm a gardener, remember? Not a lady of the court." Her mouth curved into a mischievous smile.

"And I'm a hunter, not a prince. Not the heir." He sighed, long and hard. "I want you to do well in this contest. I need you to."

"That might be a problem." Her focus stayed on the sky, hiding whatever reaction he'd give to the words she'd say next. "My energy... I won't be able to compete in the next Pillar of Faedom. I've already failed one of the five."

"You don't have energy?" The absolute devastation in his tone sent her hand down to grip his by his side. He knew, like she knew, what it meant to fail a pillar—especially this one. He knew how important it was to the kingdom.

He gripped her fingers, warm and safe, waiting for her to answer his question. But even as she felt she could trust him with the truth, her answer may put him in danger. It would certainly put her and her family in danger. Silently, she soaked up the feel of his skin while she still could as he rubbed his thumb over the back of her hand. She didn't want to lie to him.

"Will you look at me?" His baritone voice charged the air between them. The devastation in his tone transformed into grim understanding. Did he hear what she wasn't saying? Portal energy was rare because its bearers were hunted to extinction. It was far more likely she didn't have energy at all. "Please?"

Fenity blinked, then slowly turned. Their faces were inches apart. A tiny freckle stood out on his right cheek she hadn't noticed before. Thin silver streaks made his green eyes even more beautiful. She swallowed, discreetly breathing in the summer rain and honey blossom scent of him that made the world turn hazy at the edges, like a dream.

"What is this?" he asked, breathless, staring at her lips before dragging his eyes up to meet hers.

She sucked in a breath. He felt it too.

A faint, high-pitched giggling had her tilting her ear to the forest. She gasped. "Don't move," she whispered.

She knew that sound. Slowly, she lifted her head, catching movement from the corner of her eye. The unicorns watched the trees with interest. Fenity left the sanctuary of the blanket and tiptoed to the tree line.

The sprite was gone, but they'd left a gift—an acorn with a purple flower tied around its stem. Fenity cradled the gift in her palm, then replaced it with a bunch of grapes from the picnic.

"What are you doing?" Prince Renic chuckled, perplexed.

"I didn't realize sprites lived in these woods, so far away from where the fae sanctioned them."

"They don't. At least, they've never shown themselves to me." Something like awe entered his gaze as he studied the acorn in her palm.

"There you are," a grating voice called from a distance. A party of courtiers, Sarafine at the head, cantered toward them on horseback.

The unicorns retreated closer to the trees, and Fenity seethed, pocketing the gift from the sprites. She should have expected this.

Prince Renic wiped the disappointment from his face with practiced ease, smiling at the newcomers, which included three contestants and a handful of males. The party descended on the snacks as if they'd been laid out just for them.

Atop her horse, dressed in a fine red dress, Sarafine held her hand toward the prince for help down.

But Fenity was closer.

Fury passed over Sarafine's face as Fenity grabbed her hand and pulled her down from the saddle, steadying her. Sarafine ripped her arm away but smiled when she noticed the prince watching.

Prince Renic failed to hide his laugh behind his hand before becoming very interested in refilling his plate.

Sarafine stalked toward the blanket and placed a hand on Prince Renic's arm. The group immediately engaged in eating and laughing, stomping over the blanket and peace that existed just a moment ago. Fenity stood outside them once again.

Would Opal leave without Crucifan? Fenity stepped toward the pair, preferring their company anyway. Caressing Opal's soft mane, she tensed to mount, but a twig snapped behind her. She whirled to find the prince alone, the others still on the blanket.

"Leaving so soon?" His eyes were apologetic.

"Oh, let the forest dweller leave," a contestant mumbled in the background to a chorus of laughter.

Prince Renic acted like they didn't exist. "You don't seem the type to let them affect you."

"I don't belong in this world, Your Highness. I have to leave because I don't want to pretend that what they've done is okay. And somehow *I* would be in the wrong if I voiced my feelings." She paused. "It's funny, isn't it? Calling them out for their behavior makes me look bad, not them." She gripped the reins tighter. Every time she'd spoken up for what she believed to be right in this place, it had only hurt her. "So I should somehow accomplish retribution without naming the actual problem?" She shook her head. "That's not for me. I want tangible things I can touch. I want words that speak directly to the issue and actions that make sense."

"Renic. Call me Renic." His posture was brimming with apology, yet it wasn't his fault their time was ruined. Though he hadn't sent the others away, either. "I want those things too. But, you play the game well for someone who thinks they don't belong."

She wasn't upset with *him*. He certainly didn't owe her anything. As heir to the throne, *she* owed *him* her allegiance. Yet that didn't ease the sting of how he'd let his friends treat her and their time.

"I don't want to play, Prince Renic. I want something real." She mounted Opal, and the unicorn reluctantly allowed her to lead them away, racing back toward the castle with the courtiers' laughter chasing her the whole way.

The prince didn't follow her. She brushed off the irrational disappointment as the ever-present worm leached her hope away. When she returned to her rooms, the gift from the sprites was gone, fallen out of her pocket in her rush to leave the truth of this place behind.

CHAPTER 11

Renic lunged to grab Crucifan's reins. The male would follow his female to the ends of the earth, but it was obvious Fenity wanted to be alone. He'd hurt her. Deeply. What was supposed to be time alone to get to know this curious contestant had been ruined.

The unicorn resisted, but Renic coaxed him to stay after some pats and murmured pleas. He'd grown up around Crucifan and Opal. The king liked to believe they were his property, but Renic knew better. They only served where they pleased. It was more likely the pair were here to keep an eye on the world of fae, but Renic would never reveal his suspicion.

The mocking laughter of his so-called friends burst through his bubble as soon as Fenity rode out of sight. He spun, narrowing his eyes on them, but the laughter stopped, conversation taking its place. None of them would look him in the eye except Sarafine.

She held out a hand, beckoning, a ruby bracelet sparkling on her thin wrist. Somehow, Fenity in her simple riding clothes outshone Sarafine in her red, voluminous dress. "Come eat with us. You can't let this food go to waste."

He didn't move one inch closer. "I know what you did. You're lucky I don't expel you from the Strife this very moment for breaking a rule."

Silence as thick as sap gagged the group, with every face turning shocked expressions to Sarafine. Sarafine's cheeks pinked, but she lifted her chin. "And what rule is that, Your Highness?"

She was too proud to back down, even when called out. "Interfering with the contest. You—and the rest of you—" the group flinched, "knew this was my appointed time with Lady Fenity. She won her spot, just like you did. So why have you come?"

Fenity was right. It felt good to speak to how things were. To keep things real. But these were his peers, his court when he became king, and there was a delicate balance between revealing their treachery and maintaining their loyalty.

"It's not Sarafine's fault," Taleir said. He had the good sense to nudge Lady Merdin in the orange dress from his lap and stand. "It was my idea. It seemed funny before, but now I see it was just dumb. Please accept my apology." He bowed.

Sarafine kept a straight face, but Renic had played this game his whole life. The truth was written in their posture, past, and politics. This was all Sarafine's idea, a way to interfere with his interest in the one person he hadn't yet met of all forty contestants. Because her parents would accept nothing less than her total devotion to winning this contest. Taleir, like the other lords, was waiting around for the spoils. He'd already danced and flirted with almost every contestant, though he'd always had his eye on Sarafine, the shiniest of the colorful jewels the Strife displayed. Taleir would take the fall to stay in her good graces, and Sarafine would let him to keep herself in the prince's good graces.

And Renic would have to accept their flimsy, on-the-spot story to stay in the king's good graces.

"Thank you for your honesty, Taleir. You'll make a good advisor one day." Taleir beamed at the praise. "Try to do better. All of you." He cut a glance at Sarafine, who did nothing but pop a grape into her mouth. "Enjoy your picnic." He moved to mount Crucifan.

"Wait." Sarafine pushed off the blanket and motioned him away from the group.

Renic sighed and followed her. When they were far enough away to be discreet, Sarafine wrapped her arms around him, the distance closed between their bodies.

Renic tensed, averting his face when she tried to kiss him. "We can't. You know this." He'd courted her in secret before the start of the Strife. Or she'd courted him. But he'd ended it to give every contestant a fair chance.

Sarafine frowned but didn't fight back as he removed her hands from around his neck. "It's not fair. We're practically engaged, and all because of this pointless ritual, now I can no longer touch you?"

Renic rubbed a hand over his face. Where once he would have eagerly given in to her demands for a kiss, suddenly he didn't want it anymore. And it wasn't entirely because of the strict rules of the Strife.

"I will see this contest is done according to its rules and traditions. Every contestant will have equal chances to win."

"Why wasn't I your first pick for the ball?" Sarafine stuck her fists over the red silk on her hips. She'd been allowed to request a color when most weren't. "We talked about this. You were supposed to pick me. It's hard enough to not be together during such a time. You wounded me."

He almost reached for her hand. Almost. Sarafine never admitted anything others might see as weakness. "I'm sorry. Despite what we've shared, I'm duty-bound to see this done right. I shouldn't have made any promises."

"What, so you actually feel something for that forest dweller?" As his silence wore on, her scorn morphed into genuine worry. "I'm everything you could want in a queen. The king himself has said so."

"Every contestant will get their fair chance. Good luck with the rest of the Strife, Sarafine." He spurred Crucifan away from her, and the group didn't bother to wait until he was out of earshot before the gossiping began.

Sarafine's competitive nature drew him to her. But since the Strife began, it was more than competitive—she was obsessed with winning. Worst of all, he suspected it wasn't because she wanted to marry *him*. It was because she wanted to one day be queen.

Marriage. Renic wasn't even supposed to show interest in females before the Strife. Other than what his pata didn't know about, this was entirely new. And one of them would become his wife.

When he returned to the stables, Opal charged toward them. Renic barely dismounted before the unicorns embraced. A mated pair, similar to the truemate bond between fae.

Fenity was nowhere around. She'd made quick work of leaving as fast as possible. He couldn't play favorites, even if the contestants were dear friends. But despite his pata's warning, he'd have to make it up to Fenity. She'd lost her time with him, after all. And if he was being honest—as she liked to be— he'd lost his time with her too.

There was a vitality that surrounded her. It drew him in, made him want to seek her out, to know where she was and whose arms she was in. He needed to soothe her hurt and see her smile. He needed to *know* her.

Her painting stood out immediately to him. It wasn't the masterful work of a practiced talent. It was better. Unrestricted and wild, just like she was. They'd relaxed on the blanket, elbow to elbow, and when she'd finally faced him, it took all his self-control not to close the last few inches and taste her lips.

Sarafine hadn't even crossed his mind until showing up.

He didn't know what this was, but he had to have more of it.

CHAPTER 12

After a sleepless night full of dreams about drowning in red fabric and taunting voices, Fenity awoke covered in a full sweat. Today was the First Pillar. The energy test.

Mata, already dressed in her best, paced the room while Arinia and the attendants did their best to ready Fenity for her humiliation. Instead of gushing over her, the air was heavy with their pity. They all knew her secret—the one she wanted them to know, anyway—and they knew what was at stake.

"I'm afraid this will be a rather punishing day for you, my dear." Arinia squeezed a bulb attached to a glass jar and silver glitter that smelled of flowers dusted over Fenity's skin. "A stroke of bad luck, not having any energy." She pursed her lips.

"What's your energy?" Fenity couldn't help the annoyance in her tone. It disguised the fear.

"A small, but helpful one." Arinia squinted, and a small breeze blew Fenity's hair back. "You didn't notice your hair took hardly any time to dry?"

Fenity smiled at the way Arinia had made her energy useful to her chosen path. "An air affinity. I love it."

Arinia beamed. "Not so much that I can use the energy for more than this, but it's my special gift, and I'm glad to have it."

Fenity didn't doubt all the contestants had strong enough energy to bend it to their whims. Her own was certainly strong enough, if the world had allowed her to use it and learn to wield it properly. She would never blame her mata for that—it was for their safety—but resentment crept in anyway.

"How will this pillar be for me?" As dreadful as it was sure to be, knowing was better than not.

"Since you have no energy?" Arinia examined Fenity from head to slippered toe as the servants finished prodding and poofing. They'd outfitted her in a simple dress that boasted a lot of stretch with every bend and turn—much easier to move in than the usual tight, crystal-encrusted masterpieces. "It will be difficult. I can't tell you more than that, because the tests are never the same. There's no way to prepare for them."

Fenity gripped her shaking hands and met Mata's stare beside the window. Was there more than one way to fail the First Pillar? Was she in danger?

A bell chimed loudly from outside, making them all jump.

"My goodness, we're late!" Arinia shoved two servants aside and tugged Fenity out of the room. Fenity matched her pace, trying for one more look at Mata, but she was out of sight.

They hurried down the hall, the staircases, and down another hall before spotting some contestants making their way through the castle. With a push, Arinia let go of Fenity's arm and sagged against the wall, hand over her heart. "Follow them," she panted. "Do what they do. You can do this."

Mouth open, ready for the denial on her lips and the hundred questions she couldn't ask, she joined the back of the group that moved at a brisk pace. The contestant at the end with the burnt yellow dress was someone she hadn't spoken with much. One who stuck with the pack, but never joined in the jeers. Her auburn hair always contrasted with her dress. She ignored Fenity as if she hadn't just come running to catch up.

Fenity had no clue where the pillar took place—something else she should have asked Arinia. She spotted no guides, but someone must have led them. They crossed into parts of the castle she hadn't seen before, eventually leaving the castle entirely through a pair of doors in the back. Morning air brushed across her bare arms, and she rubbed them, still following the others. They turned onto a brick-paved street, and Fenity finally glimpsed the rest. A long line of all the colors of the rainbow stretched toward another building in the distance, where they disappeared through a set of doors.

She was the very last.

Shrouded in fog, the building looked newer than the castle, the stones not so dingy on their journey to the sky, smooth as they curved around and disappeared. Enormous glass windows lined the entire top, only visible with the magelights lit from within.

Fenity's silk slippers soaked through from the morning dew coating the road. Despite the long line, their pace remained steady, and soon she passed through the outer doors. The inside was warm, as if the building soaked up yesterday's sun and saved it for today. It took a moment for her eyes to adjust to the dimness as they traversed a dark hall. One by one, the contestants disappeared through an opening so bright she had to squint.

She couldn't see what was on the other side, and her throat closed with her panic. The reason became obvious as energy buzzed in her veins upon approach. They had spelled the doorway to not let the contestants see beyond it. There was no way of knowing what they were walking into.

She took a deep breath, like preparing to jump into a cold pond, and crossed through the energy shield. She stumbled into a room with thunderous applause. The shield had masked all sounds, too.

It was an arena, the biggest she'd ever seen. Oval-shaped, with tiered seating all the way around, filled with thousands of people. Though only well-dressed nobles—not an average citizen in sight. Apparently, only rich courtiers and families of influence were good enough to witness the event.

Actual pillars, twice her height and white with scalloped edges, graced the perimeter of the graveled arena. A tall wall separated them from the crowd, and the seating cascaded up from there. The royal family sat above them all on a glamorous balcony, banners of gold unfurled on either side, gold crowns gracing their heads. She unconsciously sought Prince Renic. He leaned against the balcony's railing, dark hair in a tail, though she couldn't see much as she followed the contestants. They wrapped around the perimeter, each stopping in front of a pillar. One for every contestant.

She spotted her parents among the other courtiers nearest to the royal balcony. Her mata had gone pale, but both of them smiled when she caught their eye.

When burnt-yellow female stopped in front of her pillar, Fenity took the next one, copying the others by standing in front of it on the inside of the arena. To her right, the person who must have been at the front of the line stared straight ahead. Red dress. A look of superiority. Lady Sarafine, of course. All the contestants faced each other, spaced around the massive area. The middle was open and bare, nothing but tiny white rocks that crunched underfoot.

The onlookers quieted their cheers enough that Fenity could hear her heart thundering.

From a platform directly below the royal balcony, a nameless herald—paunch with loose, draping silks—lifted his arms to renewed cheers. "His Majesty, King Sidian Arrowood of the Kingdom of Asentia, welcomes you to the First Pillar of Faedom!" Air energy must have bolstered his words, for they boomed through the space. "Our lovely would-be queens will each demonstrate the might of their energy. Disappoint the king, and well," he laughed, "you'll have to wait and see!"

The crowd roared their approval, but Fenity had gone shaky. The room spun, and she steadied herself with a hand behind on her pillar, breaking the formation the contestants had assumed. Was there a punishment for losing? Was she about to be sent home when she'd only just found a reason to stay?

She waited for a taunt from Sarafine, but none came. The female was too busy ignoring her, focused on some unseen point in the middle of the arena. Like she was concentrating really hard.

"The names will be drawn at random," the herald said with an oversized fake smile. "My liege." He gave a dramatized bow and flourished his hand toward the royal balcony.

Prince Renic crossed to a golden box Fenity could barely see from this angle. He drew a name and handed it to an attendant.

"Lady Mira Midfire of Oldinger," the attendant belted—someone Fenity hadn't met.

Across the arena, a female in a dark blue strapless dress stepped slowly away from her pillar, eyes darting from the king to the crowd and then back to a contestant she'd been next to—probably a friend.

"Do not tarry, Lady Mira," the herald snapped, all jovialness wiped from his round face. "We have a lot of contestants to get through."

Lady Mira nodded and half-jogged the rest of the way to the middle. She took a steadying breath that sent her silk bodice shimmering. Her nervousness was palpable, even from here. Maybe she had a small ability, or even no ability?

With a clap of Mira's hands above her head, a shockwave of energy exploded out from her. The gravel blasted away, right down to the bare floorboards. Fenity ducked, shielding her eyes from flying rocks. The screams of the onlookers abruptly cut off, replaced by a ringing in her ears.

Fenity gasped. She shot back to her feet, rubbing at her ears.

There was no sound. She couldn't hear a thing.

No one could. People were pawing out their ears, silent shouts in their outraged mouths. Contestants began sobbing. Rage simmered on Sarafine's face as the staticky buzz radiating around her warned she'd called her energy.

Smugness replaced Lady Mira's timidness. She waited until King Sidian stood, red-faced and pointing. Then she snapped her fingers, and all sounds resumed. Crying, screaming, cheering. The king spoke with wild hand gestures and his face split into a smile. Lady Mira was powerful indeed, and one to beat.

"Thank you, Lady Mira. That was quite awful," the herald said, a finger working at his ear. The crowd laughed with the release of their fear.

Fenity held her breath as the next name was called. It wasn't her. Nor was the next.

The demonstrations that followed ranged from simple spells, such as growing things, to more complex displays—like the one contestant who nearly set the building on fire. One female in pink cut her own arm open just to show the crown she could heal it.

When it was Nisha's turn, she strode confidently to the middle of the arena in a flowing yellow dress. Fenity couldn't remember what her energy was, but she felt the staticky buzz as it permeated the arena. Then all the heat in the air—in the ground, in her clothes, in her skin—leached away as if winter had suddenly descended upon them. Fenity rubbed her arms while the onlookers huddled together, breath fogging in front of them. Then just as quickly the warmth burst back into the room, making it feel hot by comparison.

Nisha controlled heat. She took a bow to loud, well-earned applause.

Each contestant that went only mounted Fenity's growing dread. Until it was her turn.

"Next, we will have Lady Fenity Stormbrook," the balcony attendant announced.

Fenity's breath caught in her throat. Her eyes went wide. All these people. Prince Renic. Lady Sarafine. And she was about to disgrace her parents in front of all of them.

Sarafine's gaze burned Fenity's back as she tentatively stepped forward. With shaking knees that trembled her dress and the impatient stare-down of the herald, she finally arrived at the middle of the arena where the floorboards were still bare.

She swallowed the heartbeat rising into her throat. The crowd murmured in a low buzz all around her. The other ladies of the Strife watched with rapt attention and curious, jealous eyes. King Sidian waved his hand that she was taking too long, and the herald shouted something at her. His words blended together and faded beneath the roaring in her ears.

Prince Renic nodded in hesitant encouragement, his features blurring as her vision tunneled. She didn't dare seek out her parents, or the tears she barely withheld would start flowing.

"I regret to inform His Majesty that I am unable to perform." Despite wanting to disappear into the ground, her voice was strong.

Shocked gasps burst around the arena.

"You have no energy?" the herald called out in disbelief.

Fenity shook her head, lips tight. She'd done her best not to lie, careful with her wording and responses. For whatever reason, she still didn't want to lie to Prince Renic.

"Then you have failed the most important Pillar of Faedom," King Sidian's voice boomed. "Let us hope you remain the only one." He glared around the arena, daring the remaining contestants to be found as unworthy.

The onlookers' hands clasped over their mouths, and their murmuring turned into lively conversations.

Fenity couldn't look at the prince as she hurried back to her pillar. She punished herself further by sneaking a look at Sarafine. But where she expected triumph and exaltation, she was met with unguarded curiosity.

Fenity stared at the ground as the next contestant was called forth. The rest of the demonstration passed agonizingly slowly. Even though she was no longer in the middle of the arena on display, she still felt all eyes on her. Still heard the whispering from all corners.

Failure. Not fit to be queen. Forest-dweller.

Fenity hardly paid attention until it was Sarafine's turn.

Sarafine didn't look at her as she took the middle. Without any movement—the raise of her arms or the twitch of her fingers—clouds formed above her, thickening and thickening in the middle of the arena until they burst down with rain. The storm raged in a perfect oval between Sarafine and the contestants, with a clearing in the middle keeping Sarafine nice and dry. Then the clouds expanded outward, the rain soaking everything in its path. Closer and closer to the other contestants and the edge of the arena. The front few rows of onlookers stood, eyes searching for a way to escape the deluge.

The rain barely touched the hems of the contestants' dresses when the downpour suddenly stopped, but instead of the clouds disappearing, Sarafine called on even more energy. A stream of light cast across the clouds, creating the most perfect rainbow over the entire arena. Sarafine had proven her mastery of manipulating energy to her whim with more than one ability simultaneously, a trait only gained by training from birth.

The crowd burst into relieved applause and laughter. The king laughed too, while the queen chatted with her attendants beside him. Sarafine bowed and took up her post again, still not meeting Fenity's eyes, not claiming the victory Fenity expected her to.

None of the other contestants could compare, most with weaker energy like Arinia's small wind ability. By the end, Fenity was the only one without a demonstration.

No one spoke to her as they filed back out of the arena to thunderous applause. None of it was for her, unless they'd enjoyed the spectacle of her humiliation. She'd sealed her fate.

She didn't dare seek Prince Renic or her parents. There was no way to top the disappointment she already felt in herself.

Now she had to wait for the winner to be announced. She'd endured, but what would the king have in store for disappointing him?

CHAPTER 13

From his cushioned throne set before a refreshment table overflowing with the finest delicacies, Renic watched Fenity stare at the arena floor, silently *begging* her to look at him as she filed out of the arena. Her shame was etched over her entire being, from the way her shoulders sagged, back hunched, to the way she kept her eyes down. She'd barely watched as the contestants lorded their abilities over her.

This pillar was important, of course, but not possessing energy didn't have to define her. From what he'd learned, she was more than this. So much more.

"That was riveting," Mata said, while Pata grunted non-committedly. She rose from her chair, golden dress rustling, while a host of courtiers followed her motions. "Did you enjoy the show, Renic? You know it was all for you."

"Very impressive." Renic had stolen glances at his mata during the displays. She'd been the one to compete for the prince's hand in the last competition, a century ago. He'd never asked her about it, but only because he'd grown up hearing all

99

about her glorious conquest. She'd won nearly every pillar, including the energy trial. Seeing what these females were going through—what they did to and said about each other—gave him a new appreciation for his mata. If she felt any lingering emotions from her trial, she hadn't shown it so far.

Pata, in a matching gold overcoat with detailed piping, ignored them and spoke, hands waving, with one of his top advisors, both pointing down at the contestants and laughing. The art contest had been Renic's choice, but the energy displays here today weren't subject to interpretation. Either the contestants were powerful, or they weren't.

"Are you ready, my prince?" Galan's subtle reminder that Renic wasn't supposed to be giving any one contestant more attention, especially this early in the Strife.

Renic ignored the subtle hint and turned back to seek Fenity. If he could only catch her eye, he would smile so she would know it was going to be okay.

But Fenity left the arena without looking back.

Truthfully, devastatingly, it really wasn't okay. She'd failed the First Pillar so spectacularly, she sat in the bottom of the bottom ten. Even with his favor, it would be near impossible for her to win the Strife. She'd have to work very hard.

"Let's go, son." Mata left on the arm of the king, as was custom. They would drop the act as soon as they were out of eyesight. Like all royals before them, his parents had married for the good of the kingdom, not for love. Just as he would.

Renic stepped away from the banister, waving away an overly poofed courtier who held out her arm to be escorted back to the castle. He wanted to be alone with his confusion. While the onlookers and contestants walked their own path, the royal family and those deemed most worthy as their company traveled the lesser-known underground passage.

Galan took the rear, even behind pata's regular guards, protecting their backs.

Separation was safer, his pata always said. In fact, it was almost his motto. Separation from the other races. Separation from his subjects. Separation of the rich and poor. The opposite of how Renic wanted things to be, and one of the few things he disagreed with.

Had Fenity grown up poor? She must have, living in the forest apart from the world.

But here she was.

Of all the contestants competing in the Strife, the simple fact was only one of them would win. That had been true his entire life, but seeing how it played out, how it affected real people and their real lives was entirely different from being told how it would go. Fenity had walked into his life and this contest entirely unprepared and uninformed. Yet there was something about her that made him root for her a little more than the rest. He didn't want to see her fail. He didn't want to see her punished, whatever his pata had in mind.

The others had performed as they were trained to, to the best of their abilities. He'd seen most of them use their energy many times. Though he hadn't realized just how powerful Sarafine had become. She'd shown the king exactly what he'd wanted to see, but so had several others.

They'd announce the winner—and the loser—at tomorrow's feast. Pata already looked like he'd decided without even consorting with him, as the rules said he should. Once the pillars were accounted for, just how much say would the king give him in choosing his future bride?

CHAPTER 14

Fenity made her way slowly to breakfast the next morning. They'd held it later than usual to allow the contestants to recover from the stress and energy use from the day before. Mata had hugged her, but mostly everyone gave her the space she needed after the soul-crushing defeat.

A group of contestants passed by in the hallway going the opposite direction—Sarafine and her usual crew. They laughed behind their hands, whispering to one another. Fenity ignored them—until she spied a familiar female in a pale-yellow dress. Nisha trailed the group.

Fenity gave her a small wave. "Good job yesterday. Your energy is incredibly powerful."

Nisha's lip curled in response.

Fenity turned away, pretending not to see, but her shoulders sagged. Nisha had once been so kind. Apparently, her new strategy to get ahead was to join the others in being cruel.

Who needs them? She hastened her steps to the dining hall.

A firm hand gripped the back of her green dress and yanked the strap hard. Fenity tripped sideways and they threw her into a wall. Her shoulder slammed into the wood, pain blooming. The dark purple female, Illeya—the one with earth energy—snarled in her face.

"So you think you're Prince Renic's favorite?" The shock of Illeya's anger was written over the other contestants' faces, but they made no move to stop their friend.

Fenity wrenched the fabric out of Illeya's grip, ripping it. The expensive silk draped down her bare shoulder. "What the hell?" She shoved Illeya, who stumbled before regaining her footing.

Some of the group—six in all—quickly lost their shocked looks, hands now forming fists. The buzz of energy coated the air, all of them ready to call upon their abilities.

"Best if you drop out now," Sarafine said. No hint of hostility, just a statement of fact. "You may have turned the prince's head, but the Strife will only become more treacherous."

Fenity hedged away from them. "I know you don't want me here, that I don't belong, but why be so mean? Why the anger?" She lifted a piece of her torn dress for emphasis. The fae at home didn't treat anyone like this. They shared knowledge and lifted each other up. "Do you think I'm going to quit because you don't like me?"

"You're right. We don't like you, and you don't belong. Drop out now, or losing the Strife won't be the worst of your consequences." Illeya sneered.

Fenity didn't miss the hint of surprise on Sarafine's face at the threat. Had they planned this ambush, or had Illeya's prejudices gotten the best of her?

"What are you even doing here? You can't win, forest dweller." Illeya tilted her chin to someone behind her. "Do it."

Nisha shoved her palm against Fenity's arm. The crackle of

energy barely registered before blistering heat seared her skin. Fenity ripped away at the same time Nisha stumbled back, jaw dropping. She left behind a red handprint ringed with blisters that *burned.*

Clenching her teeth through the pain, Fenity cast her eyes for something to use as a weapon. "You attacked me." She'd expected lies and deceit, but never this.

Don't act rashly. Brush it off. They don't matter. What they say and do doesn't matter.

But it did matter. This was just a small taste of what these powerful females were capable of. A warning. She couldn't let them get away with it.

Illeya stepped into Fenity's space, face close. Fenity didn't back down, hands forming fists. "Do you think you stand a chance with all the history between Sarafine and Prince Renic? Sarafine has all the qualities of a queen. The prince will never want an energy-less peasant. You are nothing compared to her."

Fenity widened her stance. "Better than an illiterate demon too inept to do anything but resort to violence to win. You wouldn't force weaker fae to do your bidding if I wasn't a threat."

Illeya screamed and lashed out. Fenity backed away, narrowly escaping her eyes being clawed out. Illeya's nails caught her chin, scraping and stinging. "How dare you?" She charged.

Instinct took over, years of fending off animal attacks. Fenity reared back her arm and punched Illeya in the face, knocking her back.

Sarafine grabbed Illeya's arms. "You're taking this too far," she hissed in her friend's ear.

Illeya's face contorted with fury. Energy crackled through the air. The ground shook beneath them. Illeya's earth energy.

"Get out of here!" Sarafine snapped, still holding Illeya back while the others stood in shock.

A crack split in the marble beneath Fenity's feet. Energy pushed against her skin, and her own rose to meet it. She bolted down the hall, Illeya snarling behind her. Her breaths came in pants as she raced toward her rooms. Guards and servants cried out in surprise as she flew by.

Her energy shoved against her, begging for release, begging to protect her against the threat she'd left behind. Her vision tunneled. Alone in her room, she slammed the door closed. *Not now. Keep it together.* Her panic couldn't control the adrenaline coursing through her even though the danger had passed.

The pounding rose to a roar in her ears. She wiped her chin, and blood smeared over her hand. With a shaking breath, her energy broke free of all bindings. The release of it—years of constantly flexing a muscle she hadn't realized was even there —was like flying. Pain and tension and stress all gone.

The room turned misty around her, then disappeared completely. Anger outweighed the fear that should have stopped her and forced her to tuck it all away, deep, deep, deep.

Green grass spread around her slippered feet. Real, with the earthy scents she craved. Her eyes went wide. She slammed the gate on her energy, closing the portal.

Where once stood a crystal chandelier and elaborate wood carvings, a sky erupted above her. Blue as the belly of a morning bird. As vast as the Embidian Sea.

Blue.

Where was her pink sky? Where had she gone?

This wasn't her world.

CHAPTER 15

The blue sky of this strange new world swirled around Fenity until she fell to her hands and knees. She clutched at the green grass. At least this was normal. This was real.

"Are you alright?" a male asked in an unplaceable accent.

Fenity scrambled to her feet, swaying. In the distance, just in front of a crop of trees on a dirt trail, stood a man outfitted in odd clothes—almost a dress, except with a hood and long sleeves in a deep purple color. Like Illeya's dress.

Before him stretched a clearing with a gently sloping hill covered in short grass. In the distance beyond him sat an enormous building, wide but not tall, with too many windows and hardly any stone. It all blurred together in her spinning vision.

He tilted his head in concern. The side of his face revealed rounded ears. Not fae.

Not fae. Human.

Fenity's heart galloped threefold, and she stumbled backward.

The human raised his hands. "It's okay. I'm not angry." His lips raised in a slight smile. "I won't call the guards."

Fenity turned and ran.

The human called out in surprise.

Her dress tangled in her legs as she picked up speed, racing down the hill. What had she done? At the bottom of the hill stood a tall fence made of metal bars, and beyond that appeared to be some kind of town, with buildings scattered amongst roads and trees. The fence was too high to scale, with no opening in sight.

Footsteps pounded behind her. She pulled energy to her, breaths panting and chest heaving.

But it wouldn't come. Had she used it up and now it had to replenish? Energy wasn't like an old friend who'd always been with her. She'd denied it her whole life, and now it wouldn't do her bidding when she needed it most. If she could get beyond the fence, there might be a place to hide until the energy returned.

"Wait!" the man called, somehow gaining on her. The distinct buzz and staticky feel of power summoned came from behind her. This human could control the energies.

Her slipper caught on something and she crashed hard to the ground, sliding further down the hill. Wind knocked from her lungs, she struggled to breathe, pushing up to her hands.

"Hey, are you hurt?" The man stooped down beside her. "You're bleeding." He gasped, backing up a step. "Your ears."

She crawled a few more feet before collapsing, shaking and coughing as air burned into her. Her elbows stung, scraped in the fall. Her chin still stung from where Illeya had scratched it. Her dress hung scandalously low, clinging to her shoulder by the one remaining strap.

It was better he killed her now. It was what she deserved.

She'd done the one thing her kind had been hunted to

near-extinction for. Opened a portal. It didn't matter she'd done it on accident. That only made it worse—she'd broken her promise to her mata and lost control.

The prophecy said this would happen. But it wasn't supposed to be her that unleashed doom upon her people. If he killed her now, maybe it could still be prevented.

Suddenly the Strife and her part in it didn't seem so big anymore. But she'd never see her parents or the prince again.

Fenity rolled onto her back and closed her eyes, shutting out the blinding blue sky. Even in the face of death, she couldn't watch it coming. There wasn't a level lower than this.

The static buzz began again as the human called his energy. This was it.

A mild heat built up along her arms, and slowly the sting of pain left her.

"Here," he said. She squinted up at him, and he held a square of cloth out to her. "I healed the worst of your scrapes, even an angry burn, but there's still some blood. You'll have a bruise."

She didn't take the cloth—hardly cared or even noticed the blood. "What do you want with me?" Why not just kill her now?

He dropped the cloth beside her but kept his distance. "You're on my property, so I could ask the same of you. How did you get past the guards?" He stared at her ears.

Fenity sat up slowly, heart and head still reeling. His property? "You own all this land? Are you a king?" The fence stretched on until she could no longer see it.

He burst out laughing, shaking his short, dark curls. "I'm a mage, but I guess I'm a rich one."

"And a human." She pulled up her dress.

"Human?" All humor vanished. His focus honed in on her,

and she struggled to her feet, ready to run again. "Yes, I am." The word trailed off. "And you're not. What are you?"

"I'm fae." She jutted her chin. "Your people cursed us long ago, promising our doom."

His lips parted in a small gasp. "You're not from this realm." He scanned her clothes. "You're far from home."

Her lips wobbled.

"I'm not going to hurt you. I'm not going to hurt your people. I only want to help." His kind eyes creased in sympathy.

She shook her head, swallowing back her tears. "It's too late. I've already started it."

"Started what?" He picked up the cloth from the grass and took hesitant steps toward her. "May I?"

She froze, fear locking her limbs. He cradled her wrist and dabbed blood from her arm. There was no pain as there was no longer a wound. His energy had done that.

"I wasn't supposed to come here," she said when he let go and stepped back with upraised hands. This was a dream, a horrible nightmare. Could she even return if and when her energy cooperated?

"How did you get here?"

"I opened a portal." She whispered it, because even worlds away, she couldn't shake the fear that admitting it out loud would get her killed.

His eyes went wide. "That magic doesn't exist here."

"I have to get home. I have to leave." She was pathetic. She'd let fear get the better of her and did the one thing she *knew* not to do—unleashed an ancient prophecy upon her people. And she couldn't keep her voice from shaking, her hands from trembling, her breaths from coming in rapid pants.

The human stepped back. "I have so many questions, but I understand if you have to go. Will you come back?" He watched her, waiting, the curiosity of a starving scholar in his countenance.

Fenity focused, pulling at her energy again like the other day.

Nothing.

"It won't come," she cried. "I can't make it work again." She needed to get away from this *human*. Oh, what had she done?

"Your magic? You probably depleted it if you've never traveled before. I can't imagine the enormous amount it would take to do something so incredible." He pushed a wisp of curly black hair from his forehead. "Look, I'm on the mage council. I know about these kinds of things. You're in a strange place with a strange being." He gestured toward her. "Clearly shaken up. You need to calm down and rest for a spell."

Fenity took deeper breaths, but her lungs didn't want to expand all the way, clenched tight as they were to hold in her tears and panic.

Why was the sky so blue?

Any second, this human would turn into the monster fae history had painted him to be. Humans had *cursed* the fae before finally being banished forever.

"I promise, I won't harm you or your people." He glanced back up the hill. "I have a picnic just down the path behind the mansion." He pointed. "Take some refreshment, sit for a spell, and it'll come back to you." He smiled in reassurance.

He didn't seem malicious. He could have killed her if he'd wanted—that was apparent from the amount of energy she'd sensed in him—but he was eager. Eager for her to agree, eager to ply her with questions. And he was right. She wasn't going anywhere if she couldn't calm down.

She gave a hesitant nod, and his eyes widened. He hadn't

expected her to agree. He led the way back up the hill—she'd come far in her mad dash—talking the whole way.

"This is my estate. I inherited it from my grandfather when he died a couple years ago. He raised me after my parents decided they couldn't afford the training for my magic. Though he didn't actually raise me. There were nannies for that. More like he sponsored me through school and my apprenticeship to become a full mage."

Surprisingly, even though she didn't understand half the words, the endless rambling helped steady her as they neared a blanketed area beneath two tall shade trees. Green, of course. All the trees here were green, not a hint of other colors. A basket similar to the one Prince Renic had used sat with plates and food.

Prince Renic. What would he think about this? The alarm would have tolled. Did they know what she'd done? Her fingernails dug into her palms.

"Please sit," the human said, slowly sitting as if showing her how it was done. "I'm sorry I'm talking so much. I'm nervous, truth be told."

She sat far away from him, nearest to the fence so she could run for it again if needed. Though he could stop her if he wanted. "Why nervous?"

"You knew who I was—a human, I mean—but I've never heard of your kind. No one here has. You're a new discovery. The gift of the Nether Realms is unprecedented. How do you do it? Can you teach me?"

"It's a blight in my world. Humans are a blight in my world." All the fear and hate drilled into her through school and culture wanted her to fear and hate this human, but she'd always seen things as they were. He wasn't a bad person.

"Because we cursed you?" He filled a plate with plain bread, hunks of orange cheese, and red berries of some kind, passing it to her, which she promptly ignored. He poured pink liquid, the shade of her sky, into a fancy cup painted with blue flowers. She ignored that as well. "Eating and drinking help too," he said quietly.

She tore a piece of bread and chewed, missing the herbs always baked into bread in her world. Her heart finally settled to a safe rhythm. "A long time ago, humans and fae lived amongst each other. We had our separate worlds, but travel was open between us. Humans grew too greedy, demanding more land and resources, until our two races eventually went to war. As the last portal closed, sealing the humans from our world, the human wizards banded together and cast a curse. The prophecy."

Her hands shook, spilling the pink liquid that had washed sweet and sour along her tongue. The human remained quiet, as if he didn't want to frighten her out of finishing her story. "Whenever a portal shall open again, a force will be unleashed upon the fae, through red flame and ash, and we shall be no more." A tear trailed its way down her cheek, and she let it. She no longer deserved the joy she sought so covetously in life.

He was barely breathing. "That is powerful magic. Ancient magic. Humans haven't had access to that power in a long time, casting collective curses." The awe was apparent in his voice, though she didn't look up from studying the dark blue blanket, focusing on the specks of dirt and blades of grass they'd tracked across it, and trying to hold herself together.

What good would falling apart do now?

"So you're fae. You exist only in children's tales now. Fae must be long-lived to remember where humans do not." In his eagerness, he'd edged closer, but strangely, she didn't mind.

She nodded. "Our elders are well over a thousand years old."

He grinned at the offering of new information. The way his

eyes lit up and crinkled in the corner could almost pass as handsome, if his ears weren't stunted and he wasn't wearing a dress. "You must have so many questions," he said. "I know I'm just bursting with them, but I don't want to overburden you. You've been through a lot."

She should have a lot of questions, but numbness extinguished all curiosity. It allowed her to feel better, almost safe, even. Contrary to everything she was taught, this human male had been honest and kind, and showed polite compassion though she was a foreigner trespassing on his land.

"Just one," she finally said. "What's your name?"

"Forgive me, I should have told you before. I'm Marek. Some know me as Master Marek, and soon-to-be High Master, once the vote goes through at the mage council next year." He held out his hand.

"I'm Fenity." His grip was firm and warm before he let go.

"A pleasure," he said, then glanced back toward his mansion.

"I'm going to try again." Fenity stood, brushing crumbs from her ruined dress. Arinia would have a fit—if the guards weren't waiting to execute her upon her return.

"Right." Marek pushed to his feet. "Of course. Because coming here was an accident?"

She nodded, though there was so much more to it than that. She concentrated, and this time, she sighed with relief at the trickle of energy. Dread chased away the relief. What would she be returning to? "Thank you for your kindness. I haven't seen much of it as of late."

"I know I'll probably never see you again, but you're welcome here anytime. I mean it. If you need a place to escape or an ear to listen. Maybe all those burning questions you wished you'd asked will need answers." He perked up. "Maybe you want help to master your magic. If so, I hope you'll come back."

She gave him a thin smile—the most she could muster—and opened a portal. It came easier this time, like it had already been at the surface instead of buried so far down. The world around her turned foggy, including Marek, who watched open-mouthed, eyes full of regret.

She thought of her dressing room back at the castle, hoping the portal would take her where she wanted. Expensive rugs and crown molding replaced grass and blue sky. She breathed a sigh of relief and let the energy go. Marek disappeared, replaced by her reflection in the dressing-room mirror.

She gasped. Her gown had slipped low on her chest, and she was smeared with dirt and grass stains. Blood speckled parts of her arms. The scrape remained on her chin, and her hair was pulled loose from its braided bun, sticking out in every direction.

But there were no alarms. No shouts from guards coming to take her life. No noise to suggest they knew what she'd done.

The door opened behind her, and she ducked for a place to hide, but there was none.

Mata.

Her mata took one look at her and quickly closed the door. "Where have you been, my young one?" Caution and fear swam in her eyes—emotion breaking through the lady she'd become—and Fenity glimpsed the mata she'd been when it was just the three of them in the woods, before all this madness of wealth and status.

The tears she'd held back now streamed down her face.

"Fenity. No." Mata covered her mouth with a gloved hand. Her face went pale.

"I'm sorry, Mata. So sorry." Fenity collapsed onto the

chaise, her body curling over her ruined dress. With Marek, she'd found momentary solace. She'd told him, but he didn't know the breadth of what she'd done. Couldn't.

But Mata knew. Mata came from a long line of females who knew. She had known fae who'd died for this ability, and even some who'd died to protect others from discovery.

And like the child Fenity was, she'd burst through generations of secrets big enough to get their entire bloodline wiped from existence.

Fenity's tears turned to racking sobs. They'd prepared their whole lives for this, for the day a portal opened and the prophecy came for them. Gather at the town square. Be ready to evacuate to the safe haven—an ancient fortress in Oldinger.

"It's okay." Mata bent to her side, rocking her. "No one else knows. Somehow, the wards didn't detect you. It'll be okay." She sounded as if she was trying to convince herself more than Fenity.

A commotion outside the dressing room made them jump. Several voices talking pleasantly. The handle jiggled, and Arinia stepped through.

Her mouth dropped open. "Sky above, what happened here?" Her attendants streamed in behind her, masks of shock on their faces.

"She tripped—" Mata began.

Fenity stood, swiping her face dry. "The other contestants. They don't like the attention I'm getting from the prince."

Arinia's brow furrowed in anger. "I told you things would get vicious. I didn't think it would happen so quickly." She clapped her hands, and the attendants recovered themselves, scrambling in and out of the room.

They ran a bath, filling the space with the scent of roses. Arinia yanked new clothing from the closet, followed by fluffy towels and a cart of tea and treats. Fenity's stomach rumbled.

Arinia held her hand, patting it while the attendants scurried about. "This competition is fierce. It's history in the making. And with these stakes comes desperation." Beside her, Mata squeezed her shoulder. "What comfort and respite we can offer, we will. Let us take care of you."

Nothing Arinia could say would penetrate the self-loathing and devastation welling inside her. She was a failure as a daughter, as a fae, and as a contestant. All for a curse laid down by humans long dead and her rare ability.

After a long soak in the warm bath, nibbling on mini cakes and desperately clinging to Mata's empty reassurances, she only felt mildly better. Then Arinia kindly informed her there was another ball this evening.

"I'm not going," Fenity said as the attendants dried her and brushed through her long hair.

Arinia's eyes creased. "I understand how you feel, but you must. You can't let those demons ruin the good thing you have going here. Show them you aren't afraid. And when His Highness dances with you again, they'll know they didn't win."

"You can't refuse the king," Mata said from a chair in the corner. She hadn't left the chamber, waiting patiently while Fenity bathed. Her eyes looked empty as she stared into the distance, subdued.

Whatever good thing she'd had going was long gone after losing the First Pillar, but Fenity breathed deep through her nose and nodded. The attendants took that as their cue to lace and powder, preparing her for another evening amongst the nobility. The wounds on her arms were gone, and someone covered the scrape on her chin and the bags under her eyes with makeup. It had been a long day of opening portals and dooming her people to a fiery fate.

Her eyes burned.

"And you were doing so well," Arinia exclaimed, studying

her. "Remember, the more they hate you, the better you're doing. Don't let them see your tears. But if they do, make sure you use it against them." She slipped a comb encrusted with green jewels into Fenity's fresh curls.

"Thank you. You've been so kind to me." And it didn't seem like it was only because she was getting paid, or because they'd reap the rewards if the king chose Fenity for the prince.

Arinia patted Fenity's neck, probably so as not to ruffle the green dress that clung to her like a second skin. "Time to face them."

The threat from the contestants seemed laughably small after what she'd done.

Mata stood. "I'd like a moment alone with my daughter."

Arinia and the attendants dipped their heads and left the room, closing the door behind them. Fenity resisted the impulse to see if her beating heart was visible through the tight dress.

"You got lucky." Mata's fear had given way to anger. "You can't let it happen again. You must control it." She stepped closer. "What if the wards had tripped? What if someone else had walked in on you?"

There was no way the king's warriors could trace the portal to her, that she knew of, if the alarms had sounded. And the same excuse that worked on Arinia would have worked on anyone. But Fenity didn't speak those thoughts out loud.

"I'll be careful. I'll control it." She held Mata's gaze until Mata nodded, satisfied, and finally let her leave for the ball. They'd been close before when it was just the two of them, Pata away fighting the battles that won him his new status. Now they grew further apart with Mata having less and less time to spend with her. Fenity's actions might have driven that wedge home.

To her relief, this ball didn't have the grand introductions like the first one—no risk of messing things up this time. Or less of a risk, anyway.

She took in the ballroom with newborn eyes. None of these things mattered anymore. The pretty décor with its energy-sculpted ice and glittering ribbons. The table overflowing with the fanciest food. Courtiers dressed in their finest watched her every move, waiting for Prince Renic so the dancing could begin.

Her world had become bigger than all that. Her world had become two worlds. Were there others? How many more were there? Did Marek know of them? Was that one of the burning questions he'd promised she'd find later?

Now that she'd opened a portal, would it cause more harm to see him again? She couldn't undo what had been done.

The crowd grew quiet, and everyone stared at her.

"Lady Fenity Stormbrook," the herald said with a hint of annoyance.

Oh! They'd been calling her name. Had the prince picked her for the first dance again?

She unclasped her hands and hurried through the barrier of people surrounding the empty dance floor.

The herald's voice rose again. "Please step forward to accept your punishment for failing the First Pillar of Faedom."

Fenity's heart lodged in her throat.

CHAPTER 16

Fenity stood alone in the middle of the dance floor, a sea of finely dressed courtiers lining the room, watching her and whispering. Laughing. The rich opulence of the flickering candlelight gleamed off the golden chandeliers, glittering crystal, and polished wood—mocking her. Refined décor to contrast her forest-dwelling, slovenly failure.

The shame of losing wouldn't sate their hunger? Now they would punish her for it, too.

As if the gossiping courtiers observing the full depth of her humiliation wasn't enough, the dais sat before her where the royal family looked down on her with varying expressions. King Sidian appeared bored, while Queen Lara frowned, not meeting her eyes. Prince Renic was the opposite. Even though Fenity refused to look at him, his constant gaze burned into her. It was almost strong enough to read his dismay. Either he knew exactly what was about to befall her and wanted to tell her, or he knew and didn't care. The way he shifted in his cushioned throne gave away nothing.

Or maybe he was bored, too.

"As is custom," the herald continued, wearing his own expression of disdain, "each pillar will have one winner and one loser, with the rest ranked between them. The winner will be rewarded, while the loser receives a punishment."

Fenity's palms sweat, but she didn't dare move. She fixed her gaze above and beyond the king's head, on an energy-made swirl of colorful light dancing on the far wall. The room blurred around her.

"Lady Fenity Stormbrook, as punishment for losing the First Pillar of Faedom, you will be given an impediment for an undisclosed future pillar. In addition, your sire, Lord Storm-brook, will pay an increase in taxes for the next year."

Fenity's lips parted, and the courtiers gave a collective gasp. Her parents were to be punished for her failure? She couldn't look at the prince, couldn't look at anyone. She would have won that pillar if they knew what she could do. Instead, they were laughing behind her.

"No further details will be disclosed presently. You are dismissed," the herald said. "Lady Sarafine Rivers, please come forward."

Sarafine appeared from the crowd as if she expected this, head high, arms swaying gracefully beneath the red lace enveloping them. She locked eyes with Fenity, triumph blaz-ing. Fenity may have won the first dance, but Sarafine won the First Pillar, and that counted for everything.

Fenity's parents were waiting for her at the edge of the dance floor, but she couldn't face them. They'd known this would be the outcome, but she'd still shamed them in more ways than one. With an apologetic grimace, she headed the opposite direction, swallowed up by the gossiping crowd.

"Lady Sarafine, for accomplishing the high honor of winning the First Pillar of Faedom, His Majesty bestows upon you a reward. A boon for a future pillar." Sarafine bowed low while the onlookers clapped. "In addition, the increase in taxes for Lord Stormbrook will go to your sire, Lord Rivers."

Fenity's jaw clenched tight. The nearby courtiers didn't laugh. Their shocked faces said it all. Her humiliation was complete.

She hurried to the exit.

"Prince Renic will now choose the contestant for the first dance of the evening," the herald said, energy carrying his voice over the murmuring guests.

Sarafine smiled and stepped toward the prince. The courtiers all parted for Fenity, as if she were a plague they wanted nothing to do with.

"Lady Fenity Stormbrook."

Fenity stopped and spun around. The prince had chosen her. After everything that happened?

Smoothing her dress and swiping at her eyes, she went back to the dance floor, ignoring the overly loud snide remarks. And ignoring Sarafine's narrowed, hate-filled eyes as she stepped aside.

Prince Renic stood alone in the middle, tall and broad-shouldered, hand upheld, brow darkened. When she placed her hand in his, the tightness in her chest eased. The music began, a trio of flutes producing slow notes rich in harmony, and Prince Renic pulled her in, feet moving to the beat.

"Why?" It was all she could say before her throat closed with emotion. The room was thick with everyone's thoughts. They may have been jealous of her success before, but now they questioned his pick, just as she did.

His hand pressed into the bare skin on her back, fingers flexing. His jaw ticked. "I couldn't bear to see them steal your light."

She closed her eyes, an odd but welcome peace giving her

momentary contentment. His face drew closer to hers as he pivoted them in a sweeping turn. It wasn't pity that made him choose her. She felt it deep in her soul—he'd *wanted* to. The fact that he had, despite her new-standing position in the Strife, meant everything. *Everything.*

"Thank you, Renic," she whispered, squeezing his hand as the courtiers swept past her vision. They didn't matter. Only this moment mattered.

He gave a quick inhale. "You said my name." He looked into her with wide-open green eyes, green like her comfort. He looked at her like she'd given him a gift. "Please, never call me prince again."

"What about Hunter?" She smirked.

Renic laughed. "Whatever you want, if it will keep that smile on your face." His lips suddenly formed a frown. "Will you forgive me for what happened at our picnic? I've thought of nothing else since I allowed them to interfere. They are to be my court. This dynamic is how I was raised." He leaned closer. "You woke me up, Fenity. I was complacent. You showed me it doesn't have to be that way. You make me want to be a better male."

Her heart swelled, lifting the corners of her mouth. "You do make it difficult to stay angry with you." She caught and held his gaze so he'd know what she was about to say was important. "I just want honesty. Thank you for giving it to me. Of course, I forgive you. Renic."

He swallowed, and his voice dropped low. "I can do honesty. For one, you make me feel things I've never felt before."

Fenity inhaled, breathing him in. "I feel the same way about you." So many words sprung to her head through her heart.

"Fenity." Lord Taleir waved to her from the side of the

dance floor as they moved past, breaking the spell.

Fenity's cheeks warmed in annoyance.

Renic's eyes danced with merriment, not the least bit bothered by the interruption. "Find someone else to entertain you?"

"Oh, him?" She glanced over her shoulder. "You don't have to worry about him. He's only more handsome and charming than you."

He nodded solemnly. "Wealthy, too, I suspect."

"Don't forget powerful." She batted her eyelashes.

Renic squeezed her waist and leaned closer to her ear. "I'll have to challenge him for your honor." He nearly growled.

Fenity's breath caught, and she pressed closer to him. They'd both taken a risk and hinted at the connection between them. And she already wanted more. "There are thirty-nine other ladies of the realm all clawing for a place at your side. Now you know how it feels."

He glanced at her lips. Then his eyes narrowed. "What happened to you?" He was looking at her chin. The scrape Illeya gave her.

"That was nothing." Her face dropped, trying to hide it.

His grip crushed hers. "Who did this to you?" His head swiveled, though even in anger, he led them gracefully around the dance floor, disguising his upset. "The other contestants, wasn't it?"

Fenity kept silent. She didn't owe the other contestants anything, but she was guiltier than all of them.

All playfulness gone, Renic seethed behind a mask of careful indifference. He'd lived the game of pretend a lot longer than she had. "Tell me who." His voice was stern, commanding, and his nostrils flared.

Before she could speak, the song ended, and the bolder ladies surrounded him—most of the ones who'd attacked her —but he didn't let her go. They stood in place too long while he warred with his emotions and what to do next. She tugged against his hold, not wanting to let go but wanting to protect him. He didn't need to be dragged into her mess, and she didn't need any extra attention on her.

The herald saved them.

"For his second dance of the evening," the herald's annoying voice boomed over them again, "Prince Renic chooses Lady Sarafine Rivers."

Renic still didn't let her go until Sarafine was practically on top of them. He squeezed Fenity's hands before he did, and she dipped her head in a proper bow. Sarafine glared daggers at her, and the court went abuzz with murmurs.

Fenity wouldn't get another chance to dance with him tonight, though he didn't have to dance with all of them anymore.

Emotions torn in too many directions, she caught her mata's eye across the room. The depth of the king's punishment crashed over her like a sudden summer storm. She followed her parents out into the quiet hall. The melodic music and the chattering cut off behind the closed door. The hallway was much brighter than the dim ballroom, too bright to hide her tears.

Though her pata wasn't the hugging type, she threw her arms around him anyway. "I'm so sorry. I humiliated you." Before Pata could utter a word, Fenity released him and hugged her mata.

Mata rubbed her back in soothing circles. "It's not your fault, young one," she whispered. "We're only sorry you had to endure it this way."

Pata put a strong hand on her shoulder. "We're good at enduring. There's nothing you could do that would make us any less proud of you." He knew and guarded her secret, of course. They weren't as close, since he'd been away on and off most of her childhood fighting battles for the king, but she loved him.

Her parents' words comforted her, but underneath them, they had their own battles to face. Gossip and politics to navigate behind closed doors where she couldn't venture. The increase in taxes and the threat of losing everything they'd worked for. She couldn't take on the burden of fretting on their behalf. She could only help them by doing her best going forward.

The next pillar began soon, and she did not know what was coming, but she couldn't let them down.

CHAPTER 17

Arinia let Fenity sleep in the next morning. When she finally roused, she opened her eyes to Arinia's bright eyes, face split into a big grin, just bursting to gossip.

Fenity found herself smiling, too. She tossed off the blanket and stretched, wincing at her sore muscles. Using so much energy had taken its toll. Despite the misery of the past couple of days, she felt... good. "Morning, Arinia."

That was all the invitation Arinia needed. "So, did you enjoy your dance with His Highness last night?" She playfully smacked Fenity's arm as they moved to the dining table for breakfast. "First picked again! It's so exciting. It's all the court can talk about. 'Why would the prince pick *her*?'" Arinia winked. "Why, indeed, hmm?"

Fenity shrugged and sipped her tea. The smile that wouldn't stay off her face had Arinia laughing and slapping her knee. The conversation with Renic—not Prince Renic—played over and over in her mind. He felt things for her. He cared about her safety. Well, the feeling was mutual.

"I don't know why he picked me, but I'm grateful." Fenity ate her sliced fruit and eggs topped with fresh herbs.

"I received some exciting news." Arinia clapped. "King Sidian will announce the next pillar in the dining hall today."

Fenity's stomach churned, and she dropped her fork. She took a deep breath. It was going to be okay. She couldn't think of it as another chance to fail. This could be her moment to shine.

Besides the energy pillar, the test for poise was the only other one they knew about—some ridiculousness about wearing queen's regalia. They were already well into the Strife, with only four more pillars before they announced the winner.

The king's promise loomed in the forefront of her mind. Which pillar would he choose, and what would the punishment be? Would she even know ahead of time?

The happy morning now marred by the nerves of the day's importance, Arinia and the attendants dressed her for the day. Green, of course. Like Renic's eyes.

The dress hugged her bust like all the others, then flowed out from her waist down to the floor. The beaded embellishments were just a darker shade so as not to be too flashy, over a wide neck with long, tight sleeves.

At least she could shelter in the enormous bottom if she needed to flee whatever this challenge may bring. She swished her hips back and forth, and the skirt swung like a bell. Maybe she could tie it up if she needed to run.

"You look lost in thought, dear." Arinia braided Fenity's hair with quick efficiency until Fenity lost all track of what was happening within the intricate swirls and sweeps of hair. "Thinking about those contestants who attacked you?"

"Just thinking about the challenge. And my punishment." Fenity shrugged, watching Arinia put the last pins in place through the reflection in the vanity mirror. The other attendants took her breakfast tray and left. "Do you know anything?"

"All I know is that they advised us to dress you formally." Not really a clue at all. They could cart them off in their formal dresses and dump them in the woods, then rank them by who made it back the most unscathed with their sanity still intact.

Fenity's lips twitched. She could only hope.

A bell chimed, and Arinia jumped. "That's the signal." She squeezed her shoulders. "Follow the others to the dining hall."

Fenity gave her an encouraging smile and followed the other contestants down the hall.

She should have been nervous, heart racing despite her mind trying to talk her body out of it. But she wasn't. With this challenge, all the contestants were on level ground. None of them knew what was coming or how to prepare—unless they somehow cheated, of course. Her thoughts went to Sarafine, who probably knew every lord and lady and even servant in the castle.

But it didn't matter. The enormity of what she'd already done put all the rest in shadow.

The contestants walked in groups now. They'd figured out who was worthy to spend their time with. Fenity walked alone.

She forcefully *shoved* the self-pity aside. This part of her life was only for a little while.

The contestants streamed into the dining hall, scattering. The room was completely empty except for three thrones upon a dais in front of the tall windows where King Sidian, Queen Lara, and Prince Renic sat.

Fenity couldn't look away from Renic as she took her spot on his side of the room, even when the other contestants shuffled away from her. And he watched her back. The intensity in his forest eyes made her belly go warm. If the others noticed, she didn't care.

Despite the circumstances, her lips curved up. One look from him and her focus narrowed from multiple worlds to just him and those all-seeing eyes. When the doors shut behind them, the king stood from his throne. There was no sign of the ever-present herald, but there were no courtiers either.

King Sidian smiled, gaze sweeping over them and back while everyone quieted. "Thank you all for coming. I will now introduce the next challenge. Today and for however long it takes, you will compete for the Third Pillar of Faedom: leadership."

What about the Second Pillar? Arinia said they don't always go in order. The ladies whispered with excitement. They were that much closer to finding out what was in store for them.

King Sidian paced the dais, hands clasped behind his back. Renic watched with curiosity, as if he was learning about the challenge, too. "Over time, we will invite the leaders of our world here to the castle. In rare circumstances, you may travel to them. You will meet with every significant race that shares our lands."

Some contestants gasped. "Even the trolls?" one asked.

"Everyone," the king repeated sternly. He brightened, forgetting that he was trying to pretend he was a friendly king, no doubt. "During their stay, you will have an audience with them, one on one. Those may last a few seconds or several hours. It depends on you and them."

"This can't be true," a female in a coral dress said nearby.

"They will test your merit as a worthy queen. After all, one of you will have dealings with them one day."

Interesting. She'd met other races through her pata and in her wanderings, but she'd never seen a troll before. They *ate* fae. And what about the goblins, with the constant hostility between their races? But it could be fun. A way to see the world without leaving the castle. What did the king mean by 'significant' races? Significant to who? So many were trapped here when humans were banished and the portals closed for good.

Queen Lara rose from her throne while the king sat. Her skirts, poofy like the contestants' except a shiny gold, rustled as she stepped forward. She took the contestants in, noting the groups and separations, eyes lingering on Fenity standing apart from the rest. "The first interviews begin today." Her face filled with whimsy. "Would you like to know which race is first?"

Fenity held her breath. The contestants clapped, unable to contain their excitement.

"We begin with the sprites." Queen Lara clasped her hands in front of her. "Enjoy the rest of this beautiful day. A castle attendant will notify you when it's your turn."

Fenity grinned. For a moment, she'd wondered if they would even include the sprites as a race of these lands, as wild and skittish as they were. She suspected they were here even before the fae, as they didn't keep to what was supposed to be their territory.

As the royal family departed, the contestants broke apart wearing various expressions, from appalled—some thought fae were too good to interact with other races—to afraid. Fenity was elated. This was a challenge she could excel at.

"What are you smiling about?" Illeya, in her purple dress, called out from the safety of her friend group.

"She's excited to see her family again. You know, the trolls." It was one of Sarafine's friends, Lady Moona in the light blue dress. Sarafine and Nisha smirked.

"Yeah, she'll fit right in with the other forest-dwellers." The quieter female in the bronze dress finally found the courage to show off to her friends. Merdin, in the orange dress, laughed.

"The universe is so much bigger than your pettiness and

small-mindedness," Fenity said, then examined her nails as if the state of their polish was more important than anything the females had to say. Because it was.

All of Sarafine's friends glared in outrage. Sarafine opened her mouth, then quickly closed it.

A comforting presence approached from Fenity's peripheral before he spoke, like a balm to her soul. "Are you the ones who attacked Lady Fenity?"

Fenity blinked up at him. She was *not* expecting that—the directness. Like he said, they were his future court.

Renic stared the group down. The white-haired guard stood further back, features livid. Sarafine disappeared quickly into the exiting throng.

The other five females froze, outrage replaced by fear.

Fenity's eyebrows rose. She'd never asked him to protect her. Never expected it. This was what the contest was about, wasn't it? Everyone competing for his attention in whatever way they deemed most effective.

Her hand wanted to reach out and take his, so she gripped her voluminous dress instead.

"Never, Your Highness," Illeya finally said. They all bowed low and stayed there, waiting for him to release them.

He bared his teeth at them, and they flinched. By now, it was just them in the room plus a few curious contestants lingering by the entrance. Even the king and queen had departed through a different door.

"You're fortunate Lady Fenity won't say who. You don't touch her, is that understood? Do you think hurting another contestant will win you favors with me? That is not how this game will be played." He sniffed. "You five will be lucky to make it out of the bottom ten. You disgrace your families. Go."

The females tripped over each other in their haste to depart, crying and shaking, and pushing the onlookers out of their way. Nisha was the last, looking back just before she crossed the threshold. When Fenity met her eyes, regret and sorrow turned to molten anger. They'd had such a strong start before she'd decided Fenity wasn't good enough for kindness.

"Fenity, I'd like to formally introduce my guard and friend, Galan." Renic gestured to the muscled male who dipped his head. "He was just leaving."

"It's nice to meet you." She held out her hand, but when Galan moved to take it, Renic frowned.

Galan dropped his hand and raised his eyebrows. "I'm honored, Lady Fenity." He bowed and swiftly left the room.

The door closed, and they were completely alone. Just Renic and her.

Fenity turned to him. "Galan is very loyal to you."

"He is." He watched her, slowly raising his arms, countenance radiating protectiveness and need. Need to touch her, need to make sure she was okay. She knew that need, because she felt the same.

She went to him, and it was like falling. They gripped each other's arms, foreheads touching. Then cheek slipping against cheek until their bodies pressed together in a warm embrace. Both times they'd danced, she'd wanted him to hold her this close, but of course he couldn't. Something had changed between them.

She breathed him in, rain and honeyblossom. "I didn't ask you to save me. But thank you."

"I didn't mean to step in. I heard the way they were speaking to you, and I nearly lost my mind." He pulled back to stare down at her. "You must promise to tell me if anyone ever harms you again. I can't live with the knowledge you'd let them treat you that way with no repercussions. It's *wrong*." His thumb skimmed her jaw, and she shivered.

"Only if you promise the same in return." She squeezed his

arms as he chuckled. "I mean it. I can't live with the thought of anyone hurting you." The courtiers were afraid to cross paths with him, afraid to lose his favor. That didn't mean they never would.

"There's something more at work here." His eyes dipped down to her lips, and his hand moved to the back of her bare neck, so tender. "Tell me you're here, not because I'm the prince and you want to win the Strife," he whispered, "but because you feel what I feel."

Her throat constricted. He was so sad, so terrified that she was using him, like all the other contestants would. She brought her hand to his face, fingertips resting along his strong jaw. "I felt what you feel when I thought you were a hunter, before I ever knew you were just a prince."

"Just a prince?" One side of his mouth quirked, and the furrow between his brow lessened. "And you, just a lady of the court." Tension flowed from his shoulders, and his focus went back to her mouth.

She licked her lips. The king had forced her into this contest against her will, and now there was nowhere else she'd rather be.

He cradled her face as he leaned down. She stood on the balls of her feet and sighed. This wouldn't be her first kiss, but the only kiss that counted. She'd never felt this way about someone before. She'd fallen hard, and she'd fallen fast. Here was safety. Here she could be herself.

Just before their lips met, a throat cleared. "Forgive me, Your Highness."

They jumped apart. An attendant stood at the door, eyes on the floor. Neither had heard him enter. Behind him, Galan turned away, hiding a slight smile.

"They are waiting for her," the attendant said with a note of embarrassment.

"Yes, I forgot. I chose you for the first interview. That's what I was coming to tell you."

Fenity's eyes widened. "The first?"

Renic took her hand. "I saw you in the field the other day. You're going to outshine them all. But first." He eased the door closed, shutting Galan and the surprised attendant out of the room. He pulled her back to him, or maybe she was already leaping.

Their bodies and mouths came together. Finally. But despite the burning inside her, his kisses were soft and sweet, fingers sliding over her skin until they plunged into her hair. Her arms wrapped around his broad frame, heart racing, breaths shallow as they found their rhythm. She was floating. He didn't use his tongue. Didn't force his way in, but the fire in his commanding lips, his breathing, the turn of his head and feel of his hands on her was enough to melt her into the floor.

Hallway light flooded over them as the door opened again. "You don't want to hurt her chances, Your Highness." Galan's eyes gleamed.

Renic placed his forehead against hers and nodded, breathless. "He's right. You must go. You can do this."

Fenity swallowed and reluctantly left, allowing the attendant to escort her away from Renic. He watched her go with a hunger in his eyes and a smile on his lips. Up staircases and down halls that seemed to wind in circles, they traveled to a part of the castle she'd never been. Her lips carried the feel of Renic's kiss the entire way, and she frequently glanced at the ground to make sure it was still beneath her feet. Her mind and body had not come down from the clouds, and she never wanted them to.

The whole world could likely see the truth written on her face.

A fluttering noise caught her attention as the attendant

finally stopped outside a tall set of double doors. Wood-carved fawns and birds decorated the edges. Two more attendants stood at attention on either side of the doors.

The fluttering sounded again, louder.

Wings.

The attendant reached to open the door for her.

"Wait." She held up a hand. Sprites were skittish creatures. It'd taken years of patience to gain their trust enough to be close to them. "I'll let myself in."

The attendant dipped his head and departed.

She edged toward the door, resting her hand against the smooth wood, listening. By the rustle of wings, there were several sprites in the room, but no sound of fae.

"My name is Fenity Stormbrook," she called out in a comforting tone. She paused at the sound of increased flapping, allowing it to settle before continuing. "With your permission, I will enter the room now. I will move slowly, and I bring nothing but kindness."

Sprites, in her experience, were beings that belonged to nature. Fenity believed with her whole heart that fae once did, too, before humans corrupted them and the fae adapted their lives to be like them. Her mata had raised her to be like their ancestors, belonging to nature. If the sprites were anything like her, they felt the walls closing in on them now, the desperate urge to flee to open spaces and safety. It was a testament to King Sidian's power that they'd come at all.

More fluttering and a high-pitched tapping came from beyond the doors, a *tap tap tap*. They were granting her permission.

At the last second, Fenity darted to a bouquet of fresh flowers on the table down the hall. Foxlace, breesia, hythica... Ah, yes. She plucked a strand of sage from the colorful vase. Sprites loved sage.

Fenity rattled the door handle, and a burst of fluttering came from inside. "I'm coming in now."

She slowly opened the door and entered the room, closing it softly behind her and holding the sage out. She took in as much as she could while keeping her eyes low. It was a small library of sorts, with a formal desk, tall windows, and several bookshelves around the perimeter. The shelves served the sprites well, as dozens perched along the edges, watching her and watching the group on the desk.

A male and female sprite stood on a stack of books wearing little golden crowns on their heads, wings still except for the occasional twitch. Surrounding them were their guards, sprites with mini swords and bows, all raised in warning.

The enormity of the situation filled Fenity's eyes with tears. She would have never had this chance if she hadn't been part of the Strife. Few ever laid eyes on the sprite rulers. They hadn't sent representatives but had come themselves.

"It is an honor to meet you, Your Majesties." Fenity curtsied low. Fluttering burst around the room, but Fenity kept still.

The queen gave a tiny nod, and the king tapped a scepter upon the book. Two of the guards flew to her hand and took the sage, bringing it back to their rulers. They didn't speak. Though they had their own language, Fenity didn't know it.

"Your cause is my cause, Your Majesties, and whether I become queen or not, I will respect where we come from and do all I can to preserve it." She winced as images of the human world flashed in her mind. She bowed her head to cover it. Her actions had already put them all in danger from whatever the prophecy would bring. Could she find the danger and fix it before it came to their world? She owed it to all of them to try.

The king rapped his scepter on the books again, quieting the fluttering sprites perched along the room. The queen took flight, coming closer until she stopped directly in front of Fenity. She hovered there, waiting.

Fenity's eyes stung again. She raised her hand slowly, without hope or expectation. The queen landed lightly on her palm, the barest of pressure with her slight weight. Her hair was a light enough shade of red to almost pass for pink, wavy past her shoulders beneath her crown. Barefoot, she wore a strapless dress of white flower petals. Her wings were beautiful, a shimmery green color, fluttering to keep her balance upon Fenity's shaking hand.

She was a wisp of a thing, but she seemed brave, meeting Fenity's eyes, being here so far away from her guard and mate. The sprite queen smiled—really smiled—and dug her hand into a pouch at her side. She produced a small seed which she dropped into Fenity's palm.

She took flight, waving her hands as she went, and in her place, a pink bloom budded from the seed, petals unfurling like pages of a book. It grew to the size of her palm as the queen took her place back on the desk.

A tear leaked down Fenity's cheek. What a precious gift. "Thank you," she whispered. "I'm honored." She bowed before them, then to each side of the room, paying her respects to all the sprites.

Movement caught her eye as she rose. The far wall had small holes cut into it. Behind it were the shadows of legs—fae legs. She was being watched. All the contestants would be watched.

The sprite king rapped his scepter again, and the door behind her opened.

"I'll never forget this." Fenity cradled the blossom as she took the sprites in one last time, then left, shutting the door behind her. She let out a shaky breath. That had been one of the best experiences of her life, nearly overshadowing Renic's kiss. She'd treasure the flower for as long as it lasted.

"You weren't in there long." Sarafine approached from down the hall with a different attendant than the one who'd escorted Fenity. "Looks like they didn't deem you worthy of their time."

Fenity closed her first over the flower. "Good luck," she said, choosing not to stoop to her level.

"Keep your luck. I've been doing this a lot longer than you." When her attendant reached to open the door, Sarafine didn't stop him.

Fenity opened her mouth to interfere—not for Sarafine's benefit, but because the sprites deserved respect—but Sarafine got there first, brushing past the attendant to waltz into the room.

The sprites exploded with a winged-flurry of activity before the attendant shut the door. Fenity gazed at the bloom, sadness weighing down the corners of her mouth. But this was the Strife. This was what the king expected to happen. The sprites could take care of themselves.

Their flower earned a special place on the windowsill in her bedroom, so every time she looked to the trees, she'd also see the reminder of the sprites' respect.

CHAPTER 18

B y the end of the week, word had traveled to the other contestants about approaching the sprites with caution. Some even took gifts to the king and queen, though the wrong kind—flowers that were poisonous to them, or gold they couldn't use. Fenity suspected the door guards had noted her success and sold the information. The idea had spread from there.

Days passed as she used her free time to study the rest of the races, and at the end of the week, they all gathered in the dining hall to hear an announcement. The sprites had chosen their winner. Fenity tried not to get her hopes up. She'd done her best, but even if she won, this was only one race out of many.

As before, servants cleared the dining room of tables leaving only a dais for the royal family. Except this time, the courtiers were present. The contestants gathered in front of the king and queen while noble members of the court and all the important fae of the realm ringed the room. Fenity's parents stood together somewhere far behind her.

Sarafine and her group stayed well away from Fenity after Renic's warning, but Fenity only cared about Renic. Besides a few glances from across the room at dinner, they hadn't talked since their kiss.

While they waited for the king to begin, Fenity watched Renic. He spoke with his mata, smiled politely at the females who called out his name, but his eyes always strayed back to hers. Fenity couldn't look away from him. If she was supposed to pretend she wasn't developing deep feelings for the prince, she was failing.

And if she was honest with herself, it was more than developing feelings. It was as if they'd always been there.

The herald, who seemed to be the only one allowed to make announcements on behalf of the king, stepped forward. His paunch stomach strained against his silky blue tunic. The gossiping, scheming contestants immediately shushed each other until everyone quieted down.

The herald gave a dramatic bow to the king and queen. "Welcome to all. I am pleased to announce that Queen Wisp and King Axis have chosen to rank all contestants. They have made their decisions for the Third Pillar of Faedom." The sprites were nowhere in sight, but they likely returned home as soon as they could. Fenity would have.

The herald unrolled a piece of parchment. "In order from most recommended by the sprites to least, the names are as follows." Fenity held her breath, fingernails digging into her palm. "Lady Fenity, Lady Maira, Lady Pria, Lady Daream..."

The herald continued on without taking a breath, but Fenity could hardly listen. *First.* The sprites had picked her as the winner. She was surely glowing with happiness.

Renic puffed out his chest with pride as the names droned on. She grinned back at him. She was proud of herself. Being an outcast 'forest dweller' wasn't such a bad thing.

Sarafine, not surprisingly, landed toward the middle, and the other females who'd been so vile to her were at the bottom. Sprites were exceptional judges of character, it was said. Even the contestants who'd copied Fenity's ideas had not succeeded —not without sincerity in their hearts.

The herald finally finished the list. "The top five winners will be awarded one-on-one time with the prince in order of rank. The bottom five will miss the next ball."

Her parents swarmed her from behind. After a quick congratulatory hug, they were off to celebrate their daughter's success with the other nobles.

Moona and Nisha, two of Sarafine's group who'd been in the bottom five, started crying. No doubt their parents were important figures in the court, but it hadn't protected them against failure this time. Fenity didn't feel one bit of guilt. Nisha had shown her true colors and had chosen the wrong side. Even with her advantages, it would be tough to crawl back from her failures.

Renic departed with his parents, but the promise of time with him made the walk back to her rooms feel lighter. Losing one pillar didn't have to be the end of everything.

Halfway down the hall to her rooms, Fenity stopped. Realization dawned. She actually *wanted* to win. She wanted to do her best to come out on top. And not only because of her parents or the threat of failure. But for herself. For Renic. And the good she could do for the people and races of this world.

The thought of Renic ending up with someone like Sarafine or one of her friends made her stomach churn.

Fenity's steps resumed with purpose. Whatever was in her power to win the Strife, she would use it. Whatever she could do to prepare for what was to come, she would do it. She marched right up to Arinia, who'd waited for her return. Arinia grinned ear to ear and began congratulating her on the win, but Fenity cut her off.

"The Second Pillar of Faedom—Poise. Tell me everything you know and how I can prepare."

Arinia's eyes sparkled. "There she is."

By that afternoon, Fenity stood in her bedroom, sweating under layers of thick clothes—a heavy dress with lots of underthings, and an enormous robe that wrapped over her shoulders and dragged the floor. Arms shaking, she held a round vase that had a good heft to it.

"Sorry, dear, but you'll have to hold it out like this." Arinia held her hands palms up and extended out. "In the last Strife, the contestants held the crown instead of wearing it."

Fenity nodded, soaking up the information. She raised her arms, making the vase immediately feel much heavier. "This doesn't seem too bad." Her muscles hadn't atrophied too much from her foraging and hunting days. She could hold an arrow nocked for a long time, waiting for prey to cross her path.

"It isn't yet," Arinia corrected. "Standing around in a dress may not seem difficult, but the queen's regalia is more than a dress. It's layers of heavy fabric and jewels, for hours and even days without rest."

Fenity nodded. "I can do it." It seemed like such a silly challenge compared to the others so far, but she wouldn't let the chance at an advantage go to waste. She didn't know how much time they had before the Second Pillar, but she'd do all she could to prepare. It was the only other challenge they knew about, anyway. She already planned to read up on the other races in the castle library.

"You have a few hours before your time with the prince. Let's see how far you get."

Fenity wiped sweat from her brow onto her shoulder, arms already heavy. "No problem."

Ten minutes later, Fenity's arms shook so badly, she nearly dropped the vase. "Is this thing valuable?" she puffed.

Arinia smirked. "No. I suspected this might happen. I'm glad you asked me for help before it was too late."

Fenity narrowed her eyes—partly out of annoyance, and partly to divert the sweat from trickling into them. "How do you know it's not already too late? And why didn't you suggest this earlier if you thought I could benefit from it?"

Arinia glanced at the attendants who were tidying the room. They retreated immediately. "I didn't suggest it because you didn't ask. King Sidian gave precise instructions, and none of us will sway for fear of the consequences. I can't help you beyond basic dress and etiquette, and the rules which you would know anyway if you'd grown up in this court. Unless you ask specifically."

Fenity's arms dropped, and the vase shattered. She didn't disguise the hurt that warped her expression. She trusted her guide. Arinia had been so kind and caring. But really, she'd withheld vital information from her. Did the others figure it out before Fenity did? Were they already preparing for what was to come?

"What else haven't you told me?" She threw off the heavy robe and put her hands on her hips to keep them from shaking.

"Don't look at me like I stole your last sweet. I like you—I really do. But I will always serve my king and kingdom first." She frowned like she truly regretted hurting Fenity—but maybe not. Fenity couldn't even trust her own judgment anymore. "There are things I haven't told you, but I can't until either the time is right or you ask the right questions. By order of the king."

"Is there anyone I can trust in this world?" Not the contestants she'd tried and failed to befriend, definitely not the king, and now not even Arinia.

Renic. She could trust him.

"I'm sorry, my lady." Arinia stooped to pick up the larger pieces of broken pottery.

"I'll take care of that. Right now, I think I need to be alone." Fenity removed more layers, letting them fall at her feet because her arms were too tired to hold them. "I may be behind, but I'm going to work at this every day."

"Oh, you're not behind," Arinia said, helping her remove the last layers of clothing until she was just in her simple green dress. "As far as I've gleaned, only one other has prepared as diligently as you."

"Let me guess."

"—Sarafine."

Fenity pinched her nose.

"I'm sorry you had to find out this way, that no one can be trusted here. In another life, things could be different between us. I hope you know I think of you as a friend, even if I'm forbidden from fully embracing you as one." Fenity stayed quiet while Arinia put away the items and headed toward the door. "I'll be back in a couple hours to help you dress for the prince."

Fenity listened to the silence. Arinia had warned her not to trust anyone, but her wide-open heart forgot to tread cautiously.

As soon as she was sure Arinia wouldn't return, Fenity bolted to her dressing room, locking the door this time. She could feel the vileness of this place, like a poison, seeping into her skin and locking within four impenetrable stone walls.

She grabbed at her chest, so tight her lungs might burst. When did this become her life? Chasing after an unattainable prince, dealing with fake, vicious courtiers, unable to trust anyone.

She'd been tossed around from here to there, doing what

was expected and trying to remain happy through it all. But she wasn't happy. '*What are you even doing here?*' Illeya had asked.

Because she had no choice!

Fenity's energy bubbled to the surface, the product of emotions she could no longer keep in check. When had she lost all control over her life? Was it the day she was born with this *curse* that ruled her every action? Never allowed to be truly free and truly herself? Because who was she while she held a big part of herself in check?

She slammed her hand against the door.

Who was she while she let those females treat her this way instead of doing everything she could to stick up for herself?

A coward. A weakling. Not someone she could be proud of. And yet there wasn't anything she could do but endure. For her parents. For her life.

But there was one thing she could do. One thing she could *learn* to control.

Mata had once explained that portal energy could take her anywhere she wanted to go, just like in the days of old before it was outlawed. It could also be shaped for other uses, though Mata had never wanted her to discover that detail. Too dangerous to try.

But there was one other person who seemed trustworthy, and he held the answers to all her burning questions. If Marek could help her master her energy, as he'd said, she'd have one more tool to win the Strife.

CHAPTER 19

For the tenth time that afternoon, Pata's annoyed glare reminded Renic to wipe the smile from his face. They sat at the long table in the council room, Pata on one side, him at the other, with the most powerful rulers in between, and the rest seated along the walls—including Fenity's pata. It was all the high rulers of the kingdom, one from every region, except for those too old to make the journey, or those occupied at the borders. With the roaring fire in the hearth combined with the guards and Galan, the room was stifling.

But Renic was warm for a different reason. The feel of Fenity's lips lingered on his skin, a heat he didn't want to wipe away. A joy he didn't ever want to let go.

"Prince Renic," Pata called across the table, eyes narrowed. "What are your thoughts about what Lord Rivers has brought before us?"

The most important fae in the world turned to him at once.

Renic's smile dropped, and he sat up straighter. Behind him, Galan coughed to cover a laugh. "Lord Rivers. Thank you for bringing this matter to our attention. The king and I are grateful."

Heads swiveled left and right. Pata's cheeks turned red with anger.

Galan leaned into his ear and whispered. "Lord Rivers has proposed to lend some of his warriors to defend the border against the goblins, encouraging the rest to do the same."

Renic cleared his throat. "I believe no harm can come from protecting our borders with additional warriors. With the reports we are hearing, the goblins are indeed growing bolder. Thank you for your counsel, Lord Rivers." A smooth recovery. He wasn't usually so unfocused.

"You honor me, Prince Renic." Lord Rivers, seated directly to Pata's right, dipped his head. He'd been much more respectful since his daughter, Sarafine, joined the Strife. "Next is a matter of the crown. The alderfae has presented another grievance on behalf of the people. They want inclusion in the Strife."

Lord Skyburn scoffed. "You already know His Majesty's answer."

Lord Rivers' lips thinned. "I know. But you also know any grievance the alderfae brings must be presented to the king. That is the law."

Pata watched, waiting for the high rulers to have their say. But Illeya's pata was right—the king was a firm believer in separation of crown and commoner, despite Renic's view. The people wanted to witness the events of the Strife, a contest that shaped the entire kingdom's history. They wanted it so much, their complaints compelled the alderfae—their eldest elder—to be involved. And they should be allowed. The castle's gates should be open even when they weren't in the middle of a Strife. King Sidian was king of the *fae*, and Renic was heir to the *fae* throne. They weren't here to serve the rich and royal, but all fae.

But his pata didn't see it that way.

The rulers continued to argue amongst themselves—some in favor of opening the Strife, most not—until the king raised his arm and they quieted.

"The Strife is a matter of royal bloodline and its continuation. It's commendable my subjects wish to celebrate this momentous occasion. They may do so in their own homes and villages." Pata turned to Lord Rivers. "Tell the alderfae that will be the final word in the matter."

Lord Rivers bowed. "Yes, Your Majesty."

"That will be all for today." The king stood, so Renic followed, and then all the rest as formality dictated. Any more business discussed would take place outside the council room as the lords and ladies maneuvered and took advantage of the large audiences the Strife provided.

Soon it was just the two of them, not even any guards.

"I apologize for my distraction, Pata. The Strife has my mind preoccupied." Better to get it out of the way before Pata had to ask for it. Besides, it wasn't up to his usual standards.

The king studied him for a long moment. "You need to take the goblin threat seriously. I've sheltered you from it, but a lot of planning has gone into how to handle their hostility."

Eons ago, when the initial land treaties were drawn, the goblins chose their location. Of course, that was before portals were outlawed and the goblins could travel to their home world. But their territory was pocked with swamps, if not jutting with uninhabitable, jagged cliffs. They wanted more, but the kingdom of Asentia wasn't prepared to grant them more.

Renic leaned back in his cushioned chair. "I know about

the attacks on the villages. I've heard the same reports you have."

"Not all of them. I want you to spend time at the border, to really see what we're up against and appreciate why I've made certain decisions." Pata drummed his fingers on the polished table.

"What decisions? And what about the Strife?" Was he to leave Fenity so soon? But his pata was right. It would do him good to be seen by the fae and learn about the goblin threat.

"There will be time between the pillars. This is important." Pata stood, ready to dismiss him.

"And you won't tell me what the pillars are?" He pretended to be preoccupied with scooting back his chair.

"No." The word vibrated the walls, the final say in the matter. "You will be trained in the rituals as they come, but that is all."

"Yes, Pata." Renic dipped his head and left. A host of advisors, including Lord Rivers, waited in the hall to take his place.

Renic headed for the stables, taking the roundabout way to avoid most of the contestants, Galan close behind. He'd seen most of them growing up, but it was as if the Strife had struck a new frenzy in them. A countdown to when their chance to be queen was over. Some more than others.

"I can feel you thinking," Renic said over his shoulder. He'd set an aggressive pace in case anyone got the idea to approach him.

Galan followed him out a side door into the gardens and down the path to the stables. "You're different with her."

Renic licked his lips. "I don't know how to explain it. I can't think of anyone or anything else."

"Hmm." Galan didn't say what they were both thinking.

"Keep your ears open, Galan. If you hear of any more plans against her, or anything that may harm her, I want to know."

There had already been several and were bound to be more if Renic couldn't hide his growing feelings.

"Yes, my prince."

The Strife was his chance to shine as a ruler, and he didn't want to fail. But the horses and outing awaiting them couldn't distract him from thoughts of her. Come what may, Fenity had to win.

CHAPTER 20

The fae possessed a beautiful gift to explore other worlds, a gift that was once revered before humans ruined it and kings slaughtered those who possessed it. Maybe the prophecy wasn't real. Maybe the wards set to alert the fae when a portal opened didn't really exist. Opening a portal hadn't caused destruction the first time Fenity had done it.

Marek said he could help her. So long as she didn't get caught, there was no harm in seeking escape and answers.

The energy came to Fenity faster this time, as if whatever blockade had built up from not using it her whole life was wearing down. She opened and closed it quickly, before the sound of any gongs reached her ears. Maybe that was the key. Opening and closing it too fast for the wards to detect. How long did she have? She hoped to never find out.

Gray clouds mercifully blocked out the blue sky, and these looked nearly the same as her clouds back home. But pouring rain drenched her nice dress and styled hair in seconds. She stood on the same sloping hill as last time, but the human mage was nowhere to be seen. Of course, he wouldn't be sitting around in the rain waiting for her to maybe turn up again.

She sludged through the grass that had turned muddy in patches, not minding the rain except that it was cold. And how was she going to explain another ruined dress to Arinia? Marek said he lived in the grand building with so many windows, so she set her course on it. It had been such a shock arriving in the human world that she hadn't looked around before, but now the thick rain blocked out all her surroundings and turned the house into a blur in the distance.

Finally, some semblance of a path took shape, and she followed the worn trail until it gave way to stepping stones and then a gravel path. Manicured bushes shaped into perfect squares led her into a courtyard. The path ended at glass doors set between even more windows.

It was too dark to see inside, and there wasn't a soul around. Her breath fogged in front of her as she sheltered under a lattice arbor with vines growing all over it.

This was dumb. She shook her head.

The door opened, nearly banging into her. Marek's surprised face met hers. "Fenity, you came back. My servants saw you coming." He opened the door wide. "Come in. You must be freezing."

She hurried in before she could question whether it was wise. Though it was just as easy to leave from inside as out.

They entered a dining area of sorts. It had one long table that ran the full length of the room, rather than smaller tables around the perimeter. The large windows let in gray light that didn't disguise the light green painted walls, like the leaves of a hythica flower.

Very strange.

Candles decorated the table along with burning sconces around the walls, but otherwise, it was a dim space and not much warmer than outside. Fenity shivered.

"Come, let's get you to the fire. I've ordered refreshments." Arm raised to guide her without touching her, he pointed toward the next room. He still wore the odd purple robe that looked even more like a dress the way he had tightened a belt around his middle. The humidity made his dark curls even curlier, highlighting his rounded ears even more.

Fenity took a steadying breath.

The next room was so different from the one before, it could have belonged in a different house. Panels of red adorned with darker red florals decorated the walls, complementing the red chairs and bookshelves of dark wood. Fenity gravitated toward the fire in the hearth, stretching her hands close to the delicious warmth and studying the portrait hanging above—a landscape that had turned black from soot and ash.

"Is that better?" Marek perched on the edge of a plush chair near the fire. A leather-bound book lay overturned on the small table beside him, like maybe he'd been reading when she arrived.

Fenity nodded. "I don't have much time. It took a while to find you." Now that she was standing still, her shaking hands betrayed her nerves. The weight of all it meant to be here pressed on her heart. "I almost didn't come."

He rubbed his hands on his knees. "Do you think you could come to the house next time? Is that even possible?"

She thought of the green dining room and nodded. "I think so. It seems to take me where I visualize going."

"That's so fascinating," Marek said, picking up the book and scribbling in it. It must have been a journal.

The questions filling her mind became so jumbled, she couldn't recall any of them. Except one. "Can you help me learn to control my energy?"

Marek paused in his scribbling. "Yes, of course we can try. Quick question, have you ever traveled to a different realm? Besides this one, of course."

"No. This is my first one." She peered closer at his book, reluctant to leave the warmth of the fire. "I don't know why I came here of all places, but our worlds were once connected, so maybe it was easy for the energy to find its way back here. What are you writing?"

He looked up, shaking the hair from his eyes. "Oh, simply documenting this magic. Like I said, the gift of the Nether Realms doesn't exist here. Can you do other things with your magic?"

"We call it energy. If trained before it sets, we can do other things, but most have one gift they are best at. I'm hoping mine isn't set yet and that you can teach me to shape it."

He scrunched his eyes in skepticism. "The strongest of us can evolve our magic as we train to shape it to our will, some more than others. So why can't we open portals?"

Fenity shrugged. "We don't know much because they execute anyone caught with the power." She shivered. That hadn't happened in a long time, so either they truly were a dying breed, or they had gotten very, very good at hiding it. "It's passed on from mata to daughter."

"Mother to daughter?" He scribbled frantically in his journal.

Fenity turned toward the fire, biting her tongue. She gave away too many secrets—if humans had forgotten so much. They were supposed to be the enemy, the reason her energy was forbidden, her family working hard to hide the secret. If it wasn't for their greed, there would still be travel between their worlds.

But this human, not even a noble but wealthier than one, didn't seem greedy. He'd offered all he had and sheltered her from the storm. She pushed the warning bells away. What could he do from here with anything she told him? Humans couldn't portal.

A cart rattled from down the hall. Fenity watched Marek, waiting for him to react, but he scribbled for several more seconds before he perked up, like it had taken longer for him to hear it.

"The refreshments." He jumped up and left, closing the door behind him. His words were muffled but audible. "Please do not disturb us. Miss Fenity is a guest here, but she has a deformity which she wishes not to be known."

Deformity?

"Of course, my lord." The burning curiosity was plain in the female's tone, but Marek was alone when he pushed the cart through, the hall dark and empty.

The cart was ladled with sugared biscuits and candy, sandwiches cut into triangles, and something that smelled sour, like pickled vegetables of different varieties. He poured steaming tea into two delicate glass cups on a silver tray.

"Tea?" he asked, using a silver spoon to stir sugar into his cup. "I'm sorry if it seems like I'm hiding you." He brought his fingers to his ear. "Humans aren't ready to know the truth you've brought here."

"And you are?" Was he going to help, or was he just being kind to fill his journal with the fae's secrets?

He reached for her hand. When she didn't uncurl her fingers, he patted her arm instead. His skin was soft and warm. "I'm more than ready. I want to get to know you, Fenity. And not because of your magic. You fascinate me. I want to know about your life. Your likes and dislikes. Once I know how your magic works, then I can help you learn to control it."

"What would happen if others found out about me?"

He shook his head. "Nothing good. They could become hostile in their fear of the unknown. The idea of other beings and other worlds existing is a child's fantasy. A stargazer's wildest theory."

"So why aren't you afraid?" She wasn't yet ready to hope he might be sincere.

"I'm not afraid because I trust you. I feel we were meant to be friends, like you came here for a reason. Remember, I'm a very high-seated member of the mage's council." He lifted his purple dress like that meant something. "As long as you're with me, you're safe. I won't let any harm come to you."

Her hands unthawed, and he passed her a cup of overly sweetened tea. The herbs tasted like home, woodsy and earthen.

"I believe you." Fenity didn't know why, but she trusted Marek. Maybe he was right, that she was here for a reason. She set down the cup, shaking her head when he gestured to the food. "I have to go."

His face fell in disappointment. "I truly am sorry."

"It's not you." She paused, debating. "I'm competing in an important contest. My daily routine is dictated and monitored fairly closely. If I stay here too long, they'll notice."

"Oh!" He set his cup down with a clatter. "Then, please, go. I don't want you to come to any harm over this."

Her lips raised into a smile. "Thank you. I haven't felt myself lately. I think the contest and all the constant unknowns are getting to me." She hadn't known true home in a long time. "But I've felt nothing but kindness and patience from you, so thank you. It's the escape I didn't know I needed.

Just promise me if I answer your questions, you'll help me with my energy."

Marek had been right. It was in her nature to explore, to cling to freedom and the truth of things. The truth about their world and reality was that history had hidden things from them. But it didn't matter. Here, she could forget the Strife, forget her role and the enormous weight on her shoulders. Here, she could be whoever she wanted.

"Of course. I'll do everything I can." The earnestness in his face tugged at her heart. He was almost handsome when his curls hid the tops of his ears.

She pulled at her energy, buzzing the room with it. He watched with fascination. With a quick wave, she left the odd red room, returning to her dressing room. The heat of his hearth was gone, leaving her skin chilled, but she was alone, and her dress was only slightly damp. She left the dressing room and rinsed her face in the bathing room.

Arinia burst inside just as Fenity was undoing the mess the rain had made of her hair. All the attendants trickled in with her. She gave Fenity a long, head-to-toe look before speaking. "There's been a change of plans. Your time with His Highness will have to wait." She snapped quick instructions to the attendants, who flew into action. "Did you fall into the bath? Never mind, doesn't matter."

Fenity had never seen them move so quickly, and before she knew it, she was wearing tight leggings and a tunic for travel with a tight green vest, her hair twisted up in a tight bun. Besides the vest, a green ribbon was tied in her hair.

"What's going on?" she asked amongst the flurry. More importantly, would she get to make up the lost time with Renic?

Arinia wrung her hands. "It's not unprecedented. Rulers

have been known to throw out a surprise or two to keep the competition lively."

"Are you trying to drive me mad with anticipation?" Fenity jammed her feet into leather boots and remained still as the attendants laced them.

"I can't say anything, is what I'm trying to say. The king will tell you everything."

Is that why her attendants hardly talked to her, even when she asked them simple questions? Because they might reveal things she wasn't supposed to know?

Fenity dawned a cloak, not quite rid of the chill from the rain, and followed the other contestants in the hall. They all wore outfits matching hers, except their vests and hair ribbons bore their individual colors. Who decided who got what color? Did everyone else get to pick and green was the only one left by the time Fenity arrived?

Some actually smiled at her this time, and a few said hello. Pity for losing the First Pillar? She smiled back but feared giving more effort than that. Arinia had proven it was unsafe to trust anyone here. Every single one of them stood against her after the Strife presentation when the guard had tripped her. No one wanted to help when she was brand new and floundering. Did they feel guilty now?

Instead of the dining hall, the females filed out the front to the courtyard. The wide-open space was paved with stone and ringed with decorative trees featuring big white blossoms out of season. It was probably someone's sole job to use their energy to force the flowers into bloom.

Once she made her way through the clustered contestants, she immediately spotted Renic beside his pata on a small platform. He wore a deep frown that had Fenity wrapping her arms around herself.

"I have a regrettable announcement concerning our Third

Pillar challenge." King Sidian folded his hands over his fancy embroidered tunic, jewels glinting in the afternoon sun. "The trolls have refused to send a representative to the palace. As they are the next race, you must now travel to them."

If the trolls weren't cooperative enough to come here, it was doubtful they'd be receptive to anyone going to their territory uninvited. The troll border was not close, but if it was a race to get there first, it would be her.

Several females whispered to each other, hands waving in a flurry, brows lifted in fear. Sarafine and her friends stood unbothered. Was that a smirk? Did she know something?

Fenity watched Renic who watched her.

Sarafine, in her burgundy leggings and matching tunic, glanced between the two of them, seething.

"Carriages await with provisions already packed by your personal attendants. As this is unexpected and potentially dangerous, you will go in pairs." Carriages? Pairs?

Some contestants grabbed each other's hands. Fenity's eyebrows shot up as three hands took hold of her arm, claiming her as their partner. She'd never spoken to any of them.

Fenity eased her arm from their grips. They didn't react except to edge closer, boxing her in and nudging each other aside. If going alone was an option, she'd choose that.

"The assignments are posted on the wall behind me." King Sidian pointed, and Fenity's shoulders drooped. "You may not trade. However, this will be no simple task. You may choose to remain behind, but you must be confident in your ranking with the other races. Losing this one will affect the end rankings."

Yeah, right. They wouldn't let a contestant win the leadership pillar who failed to exhibit the courage required of a queen.

Yet several contestants fell back. Trolls were violent,

temperamental creatures, but they still had a place in this realm. Why would anyone risk failing one of the pillars of faedom?

Sadly, Sarafine and her friends stayed in the contest, though a few looked torn about it. Worry was written all over Renic's face.

King Sidian adopted his usual irritated expression as everyone settled back down. "Find your partner, then proceed immediately to your assigned carriage." This was Renic's contest, his future. But the king didn't seem to care about that.

The contestants scrambled to see who their partners were. Fenity held back. She didn't want to know. Couldn't be anyone good. But if it was one of Sarafine's friends, she'd go it alone rather than let them sabotage her.

Renic stayed behind with Galan, while the king and his guards departed. He caught her eye and motioned her to the side. Heart stuttering, she skirted around the clamoring group and met him behind a sweet-smelling bush. They weren't entirely cut off from view of the others, but it was the closest thing to privacy they'd get. Galan dropped to a discreet distance.

Renic took her hands like it was the most natural thing in the world. Her melancholy instantly lifted. "I made sure you weren't paired with any of those spiteful females. I'm sorry about our one-on-one time. We can make it up after you get back."

"Good." She smiled warmly. "So you're not coming?"

"I have to stay here. Not by choice. We're having issues with the goblins again. Nothing for you to worry about." His eyes narrowed. "The thought of you facing the trolls alone... Well, let's just say my pata and I did not see eye-to-eye on this task." He sighed, squeezing her hands. "I'm not allowed to do anything that will put me at risk, or rather, put the heir at risk.

My parents have tried for years, decades, but I'm their only offspring." His eyes burned into hers. "They aren't truemates."

Truemates.

"Am I interrupting?" Sarafine came around the garden, staring pointedly at their nearness.

"Yes, actually," Fenity said.

Renic chortled but covered it up with his hand. "Never, Lady Sarafine."

Sarafine stuck her hands on her hips. "They put us together."

Of course they did. "Joy." Renic must not realize Sarafine was the lead of the spiteful females.

Sarafine glared and looked at Renic as if she expected him to defend her. He didn't.

"The carriages are ready to leave." Sarafine stomped away.

Renic's smile slipped as he watched her walk away. "She's under a lot of pressure. I hate to see her so distressed." He rubbed the back of his neck. "You really got on her bad side, didn't you?"

Fenity soured at the reminder Sarafine and Renic practically grew up together. "Not on purpose."

Renic let go of her hand. "Please be careful. The pillar isn't worth your life."

"I can take care of myself. But if you want me to make sure your friend returns unscathed, I'll do my best." She stepped back, then gasped as he gripped her chin, gently but commanding.

"Don't do anything rash. Bring yourself back."

"Okay." She nodded with wide eyes. How dangerous really was this task?

Fenity found her carriage, the first in a long, long line of gilded carriages, each pulled by a pair of horses. No guides. No attendants. Just two drivers and two trunks strapped to the back. If she had known anything about what would happen when she left the castle, she would have prepared. Weapons. Gifts for the trolls, maybe. Whatever she could procure. But she had no idea. That also meant none of the others did either.

Though, Fenity couldn't help but notice the dagger sheathed at Sarafine's waist as she sat on the opposite bench, as far away as she could.

Fenity had studied what she could of the races she was less familiar with. They used to believe trolls turned to stone in daylight, but that was just part of their energy. They could turn to stone at will in defense or sheer stubbornness when fae were trying to push them off their land. Fenity had laughed at the thought of mighty fae warriors standing around, waiting for the trolls to resume their normal forms so the battle could continue.

"Two days by carriage," Sarafine said, the volume of her voice making Fenity jump. "Have you ever traveled so far before?"

She ignored the implied jab. "Yes." To an entirely different world. And even before that, when her parents forced her to give up her forest home for the grand estate that was her pata's dream.

Fenity watched out the window as the manicured lawn and the handsome prince disappeared.

"You have no hope of winning, you know. Not without energy." Sarafine sounded like she was convincing herself of Fenity's chances more than Fenity.

But what if she was right? What if it didn't matter how well she did at the other pillars?

Fenity studied the battlements around the castle as the carriages traveled through the outer gates—tall, sheer, and formidable.

No books to read. No journal to write in. No sketch pad to

draw in. Just endless time with someone who hated her for reasons outside her control. Her head would fall off her shoulders staring out the window before she allowed Sarafine under her skin.

Mercifully, Sarafine didn't speak again. Afternoon slipped to dusk, and when the carriages finally stopped for the night, Fenity's neck screamed when she straightened it. She didn't allow her pain to show, keeping a blank face. Nor did she glance at Sarafine.

The contestants piled out of the carriages, stretching their arms and legs. They'd somehow found a stretch of road that fit all of them, over a dozen to carry the pairs who'd elected to compete.

The drivers distributed a small meal of dried meat, bread, and cheese, along with a leather water bottle, but that was all.

"And just where are we to sleep?" Illeya called out loudly from Sarafine's side.

The drivers ignored them, though their faces looked pinched, like they wanted to answer but were ordered not to.

"Is there no inn?"

"Or tents?"

Fenity smiled and bit into the dry sandwich she'd assembled. She and her mata had slept outside more often than inside. Sarafine could take the cramped carriage and be the one with a crick in her back. A night under a clear, open sky with a view of the bright stars and moons sounded heavenly.

A contestant in a carriage further back announced that their trunks included a large blanket. It was of fine quality and more than what she needed.

Sarafine snatched hers and made for the carriage. "Just stick to your side."

Fenity shook her head and headed toward the field beside

the road. Sarafine's boot scraped the dirt when she stopped, pivoting to find Fenity not blindly following her.

"Where are you going? We have to do this challenge together."

Fenity could practically hear the hands on her hips but didn't turn around to verify. "I'm going to get some peace and quiet. Carriage is all yours."

"Lady Sarafine," one of their drivers said. "As your reward for winning the First Pillar, King Sidian has granted you a private tent with your own sleeping quarters and prepared meals for the duration of our travel to and from the Troll Highlands."

"How kind of His Majesty." The smile in Sarafine's voice was directed toward Fenity, but she ignored it.

None of the other ladies opted for sleeping outdoors, seeking the comfort of their filigreed and cushioned carriages instead. When night set in, Fenity was the only one looking for a good patch of field to sleep on.

Would they notice if she left? She could sleep warm in her own bed tonight, right now, if she wished. But would they see or sense her departure? Or come looking for her, unable to find her? It wasn't worth the risk.

She soon found a small divot that would shelter her from the breeze. The grass was high here—the perfect mattress for her bedroll. She spread out her blanket, pulled her cloak tight around her, then snuggled in. Only when she nestled in the right position did she cross her hands behind her head, take a deep breath, and open her eyes to the sky.

Stars burst into her vision, like glittering dew drops, dotting the darkness from horizon to horizon. The twin moons, Prisanthony and Pirus, were cresting for their nightly adventures, so beautiful and bright away from the torches and lights of the castle. So much better than she remembered each time she'd gazed up at them from the window of her fancy rooms at the palace.

One day she'd get married under these stars.

Everything good happened under their watch. Renic's amused eyes as he laughed with her flashed in her mind. His set jaw as he felt anger on her behalf. His furrowed brow as he sought to protect her from harm.

Warm and content, no longer enclosed behind walls, sleep came easy.

CHAPTER 21

Eventually, the long line of carriages stopped just before the border between the Kingdom of Asentia and the Troll Highlands. On the fae side of the line, the branches were cut back and vegetation kept at bay, but on the other side, boulders littered what was once a road. Vegetation had overgrown in places, though they couldn't see far for the bends in the road as the elevation slowly climbed.

Fae didn't visit troll lands except to battle them over land and border disputes. Trolls weren't the wildest of the races inhabiting their world, but they were perhaps the densest.

The contestants piled out, rubbing their arms against the chill and staring beyond the fae lands with fear and trepidation. Fenity was the only one wearing a cloak—thank goodness for a rainy day in the human world to prompt her to bring one along.

From their trunks, the contestants each possessed a bag with a bedroll, waterskin, food, a map—though no compass— and a dagger and sheath.

"What's all this for?" the female in coral—what was her

name?—asked. She held the dagger's hilt with two fingers, like it might dirty her reputation to have any more contact with it. "The trolls are meeting us at the border, aren't they?"

Obviously not. If they were at the border, everyone would already know it.

A driver stepped on a flat boulder and cupped his hands around his mouth. "His Majesty sends instructions. You will enter the Troll Highlands unescorted." The daughters of the fae court burst into protest, but the driver didn't pause. "You have three days to make contact and return. The trolls will give you an object if you earn it. Remember, you must perform this task in your assigned pair. Anyone who wishes to withdraw may do so now. If your partner withdraws, you cannot win this pillar."

While he spoke, Fenity repacked her bag, arranging the items to best preserve the food, and strapped her dagger to her belt. Sarafine had nothing snarky to say as she followed her lead.

When the driver finished, he jumped off the pillar and all the drivers tended to the horses, ignoring the chaos they'd left behind. A few contestants dropped their packs in the dirt, folding their arms and groaning.

"I can't believe this. There'll be none of us left to marry the prince if we all get killed chasing trolls through the wilderness in a foreign land."

"I don't even know how to use a weapon, much less against a violent creature twice my height!"

"How are we supposed to even find them without a guide?"

"Ladies," Illeya called out. She wore her purple ribbon as a headband, decorating the brown waves she'd left hanging past her shoulders—increasing the likeliness of her hair getting snagged during a trek through the wilderness. She waved her arms until most of the contestants quieted, focusing on her.

Fenity retied her boots to be more secure. Forget them all. This task was hers.

"Ladies, please. Don't you remember? Some of us already stayed behind. They've already lost."

"So?" Merdin, in orange, asked from the front of the group.

Curiously, Sarafine wasn't joining her friends for once, hanging back away from everyone, though still keeping well away from Fenity. She braided her hazelnut hair behind her, tying it off with the red ribbon.

Illeya smiled. "Enough of us have dropped out that the bottom is taken. That means anyone who leaves now is already safe."

Huh? Coming in the middle was certainly better than the bottom, but that didn't make you *safe*. Losing was losing when it came to the pillars. No one would believe this drivel.

Fenity hoisted her pack.

The contestants glanced around at each other, and then the fear and uncertainty lifted from some of their faces, replaced by relief.

Fenity's eyebrows rose as several females dumped their packs and returned to the carriages, Illeya leading the way. Furious partners chased some of them down, arguing to stay. When the dust settled, only five pairs remained. As the carriages departed, Illeya, who'd been paired with Nisha, stepped out of her carriage with a smug look, and they became the sixth pair.

Interesting strategy.

Not that Fenity trusted Illeya at all before, but she'd definitely be vigilant about any poison the female uttered from now on.

Fenity didn't hesitate to rummage through the discarded packs, earning sneers of disgust from the others. She grabbed two extra bedrolls, two more daggers, two waterskins, and several packs of food. She returned to Sarafine and handed her the extras.

"They didn't give us enough food for three days, and I expect we'll need each second, leaving no time for foraging. Repack and let's go." Fenity set her bag on a boulder to stuff more food inside. At least they wouldn't run out of water— Sarafine could just use her energy to conjure rain again.

Sarafine's face darkened. "You're not in charge here. You don't tell me what to do. I outrank you."

Fenity closed her eyes and begged the gods for the patience not to toss Sarafine off a cliff the first chance she got and blame her death on the trolls. Way, way too tempting. "The castle was your territory. You said and did what you wanted to me, and there wasn't much I could say because you're right, there I am totally out of my depth. But here, this is *my* territory. Mine. And if you want to survive, you *will* listen to me." She pulled the bag's straps tight and hoisted it once again. "And we're the same rank, Sarafine. You've just held your position longer, which clearly doesn't mean dirt to the prince. So pack your bag and *let's go*."

Sarafine bared her teeth, fury as red as her dresses burning in her eyes. The distinct zing of energy singed the air. "Forest dweller," she burst out, then punched provisions in her pack like she was imagining punching something else—or someone else.

One of their drivers brushed by, picking up the discarded remains, adding to the already precarious bundle in his arms. The others did the same, collecting what none of the contestants deigned to discard themselves.

Fenity grabbed a dusty bag, handing it to one of them. "Thank you for your care these past days," she said. "It couldn't have been easy."

They glanced nervously at each other, as if fearing they

might get in trouble. They didn't talk, but one gave a small smile and the others nodded in acknowledgment.

What had the king done to scare these males like this? Was it really so severe a punishment for even speaking to the contestants? There was a whole side of King Sidian Fenity had never considered. How had Renic grown up with a pata like that?

Thanks to packing extra provisions, Fenity and Sarafine were the last to depart the fae lands. To Sarafine's credit, she didn't hesitate like the others when they stepped onto the troll road. She matched Fenity's long strides.

As they skirted around boulders and fallen limbs, Fenity recalled all she'd learned from her mata and in the library. Trolls stayed in family groups, sheltering in whatever was most convenient, as they didn't bother building things themselves. Their strength and thick skin made them impervious to most weather.

They needed to find a cave or building of some kind, probably near water. The map showed ancient towns connected by roads like the one they traveled. It had once been human land until the fae banished them and the trolls overtook it. There was a castle not too far away that likely used to house human royalty. If it was still standing, it might be a good place to find the trolls. Without conferring with Sarafine, Fenity used the map and the position of the sun and moons to point them in the right direction. They had a long walk ahead of them.

Fenity filled her lungs with sweet mountain air. Elder trees rose beside them, needles and branches littering the road. For a moment, it was almost like being in the woods at her old home —wild, untouched, billowing with life in every direction. Scents of dirt and crisp evergreen, distant mountain snow and decaying leaves. And the sounds—hundreds of trees singing their songs with each wisp of wind rustling their canopies. Did it get any better than this?

Her steps were nimble, silent over sticks and brush. At every bend in the overgrown road, the world gave them a beautiful new scene to behold—a rare empty field with flowers struggling to bloom, a burbling creek with rocks worn smooth, a glimpse below of the valley they'd arrived upon, so vast and green and wide.

And the ever-constant stomping of Sarafine, kicking rocks and snapping limbs like she'd never stepped foot off a paved path in her life. And the *sighing*. An average of once every twenty steps. Whatever Sarafine was waiting to say was so close to bursting, the sighing must have been the only way to release the pressure.

They didn't encounter any contestants, but the path veered several times with evidence of some of them going different directions. A thick, overturned tree trunk blocked the next bend.

"Let's rest here," Fenity said. They'd walked for hours without a break.

Sarafine collapsed onto the log, panting.

Is that why she'd been so quiet? She was saving her breath for hiking?

It was a gorgeous place for a rest, with a welcome break in the trees allowing a view of the distant mountains. Fenity hadn't spent much time in the mountains, and the climb was taxing.

Craving the restorative tea her mata used to make, she gathered small logs and built a steeple in a clearing in the road. Snapping a mushroom off the overturned tree and peeling back some bark, she rubbed them together until the friction sparked embers. With dry grass as tinder, she moved to start her fire.

A quick buzz of energy, and flames burst from her sticks. Fenity fell back on her rear, dropping her mushroom.

Sarafine picked at her nails. "My demonstration was water, but that's not my only skill. Most of us were trained to manipulate the energies before it was too late. You would know that if you'd done any research before you arrived. Just half a second of preparation could have saved you so much ignorance. It could have saved you from looking like a fool in front of the entire court. And that is why I have no sympathy for you."

Fenity dusted herself off, hands forming fists. "I don't want your sympathy. But I do want to clear something up. One minute, I was happy in the home I'd always known, with my future all planned out. The next, I was living a stranger's life in a new estate and parents who were suddenly trying to be someone they weren't. Barely a month into this new world, the king forced me into the Strife against my will. There was no warning. No time to prepare. And instead of sympathy and understanding, I find nothing but hostility and more people pretending to be something they're not. You're fake. The king's fake. Arinia's fake. My parents are fake. Everyone is fake except Renic."

Sarafine lifted her chin. "That's Prince Renic, or His Highness, to you."

Fenity met her stare over the crackling fire. "That's not what he told me."

Gods, she missed him.

"You'll never be good enough to deserve him." The words were dark and weighty, sludge-like, as if held in all day. This was what Sarafine had been thinking as they'd made the trek, what she didn't dare speak until now.

Fenity tilted her head. "Does love have to be deserved?"

Sarafine snapped her fingers, and the fire went out. "What do you mean 'love'?"

Fenity's cheeks warmed.

Love.

It was true. She loved Renic already, without hesitation, without falter. She watched the smoking remnants and didn't say a word.

Sarafine scowled, then drank long and hard from her waterskin.

"Try to ration that," Fenity said, sipping from her own, letting go of her craving for tea. "What if you're injured? You might not always have energy to summon more."

Sarafine recorked her water without looking up.

"I'm not trying to tell you what to do. I only know what I know, and I want to help." Mostly because she needed Sarafine to survive, and if Sarafine ran out of water, whose water would she drink next?

"I'm not an idiot. I can manage on my own." Sarafine hoisted her pack, ready to depart.

"That won't keep me from pointing things out you're doing wrong." She could help Sarafine, even if Sarafine had never helped her.

"So you think because you're a forest dweller and I'm a courtier that you know better than me? You don't know me or what I've been through, the training I've had for this contest since the day I was born. The pushing, and pushing, and never doing good enough and never saying or acting the right way." She snatched the map right out of Fenity's hands. "Watch and learn." She stomped down the path, leaving Fenity to follow.

Fenity let her lead, stunned into silence. Sarafine was right. Fenity didn't know a thing about her, not really. She liked the color red? Or maybe her parents made her pick that color to stand out.

Just as they made assumptions about her because of where she'd come from, Fenity had done the same to Sarafine. There had been pain in those words. A toughness buried. What would it have been like to be the opposite—instead of growing up not knowing she'd be a Strife contestant, what if she'd always known? How different would her life be if the entirety of her existence was shaped around winning the hand of some male?

No life at all.

And a family as powerful as Sarafine's would expect her to win. All that pressure.

"I'm sorry," Fenity said to Sarafine's back, catching up. Sarafine faltered but didn't abandon her determined stride, following the map perfectly without assistance. "You're right, I don't know you. I shouldn't have assumed that I did."

She knew better than to wait for the return apology Sarafine might have made if she wasn't too proud to admit she'd made the same mistake. She hated that she waited anyway.

Walking on in silence, they eventually neared the castle ruins by nightfall. In the distance, the crumbling remains rested at the base of a cliff, no sign of life except for the sharp shadows of a tall fire burning brightly from somewhere within the ruins and flickering off the mountainside. Dark shapes moved about, adding their shadows to the eerie display.

It had to be trolls.

Closer to them, a smaller fire burned. Fenity slowed their pace, cautious, until they recognized four of the contestants sitting around it. All Sarafine's friends. They stood as Fenity and Sarafine approached.

Illeya, Nisha, the female in bronze, and Merdin in orange. Sarafine immediately went to Illeya, and they embraced. The others sat, making room for Sarafine on a log.

No one scooted over for Fenity. They didn't even look at her.

"They've stomped around for as long as we've been here," Illeya said, voice lowered, hair full of leaves. "There's no guard, no one on watch. From the noises, it sounds like they've caught live prey and are feasting." She wrinkled her nose.

"Some kind of animal," Nisha added.

Fenity stood outside their circle, their backs to her and arms stretched toward the fire, its warmth too far to feel. "A fire isn't a good idea," she called out. Trolls weren't overly bright, but they could still see.

"Illeya thought it would be better to approach them in the morning," Merdin said, ignoring her. "And Tully found this yummy fruit."

"Good work." Sarafine patted Illeya's hand, then accepted a bite of fruit from the bronze contestant—Tully.

Fenity pulled her cloak closer around her. The air gusting off the mountain was especially cold now that the sun had fully set. There'd be no place by the fire for her tonight. Not this one.

She walked past the group, hoping it was Sarafine's guilty gaze she felt on her, but probably not. Waiting until morning was a good idea, as trolls were more docile in the daylight.

She crossed into the woods flanking the road. The breeze died down, blocked by the trees. It didn't take long to find a clearing between thick bushes to settle in. Wrapping both blankets around her—for warmth and to prevent getting stabbed by a stray twig—she kept her boots on and body alert. She dozed, still trying to convince herself the way they treated her didn't matter. All that pressure to win must take precedence over kindness.

A scream pierced the silence of the frigid night. Fenity shot to her feet before it fully registered.

"Help!" the female screamed. "Do something!"

Others let loose cries of anguish.

Fenity charged through the forest, leaves and rocks skittering underfoot. Tree limbs whipped past in a blur.

The contestants' fire had burned down to glowing embers. A little up the road, three of the contestants held Illeya back as she struggled to get away, screaming, reaching down the path.

Fenity gasped.

Sarafine's unconscious body was already halfway toward the castle ruins, a troll holding each leg, dragging her back to their lair.

CHAPTER 22

Energy crackled through the air from Sarafine's friends, yet none of them used it. Fenity's own energy responded uselessly as the trolls dragged Sarafine away.

"What happened?" Fenity gasped. "Why aren't you doing anything?" She sprinted toward the trolls, looking over her shoulder. She slowed when none of them followed and Sarafine disappeared into the castle ruins.

Illeya slumped to the ground, crying.

Nisha knelt beside her. "We were asleep. They knocked Sarafine out. They tried to take all of us, but we awoke and fought back. We were no longer easy prey." The path was a mess of broken limbs, puddles of mud, and scattered rocks, evidence of their efforts.

Merdin held a hand to her forehead, blood running between her fingers. "We tried to get her back, but our energy didn't slow them down."

"You should have been here," Illeya accused between sobs,

pointing at Fenity but staring at the ruins. "It should have been you."

Fenity tore a strip of cloth off her tunic and handed it to Merdin. "Let's go. There's still time to save her before they eat her." It might already be too late, but they had to try.

She took several steps away, but stopped and turned. No one followed.

"We can't go there," Nisha said. "We'll all be killed. They're just like we always thought, brutal and savage. They can't be reasoned with."

"This was a fool's challenge," Merdin said. "The king had to know we would fail."

"He wanted to cull the weak," Tully said, packing her bag. "Well, he won't cull me."

"I'll go," Illeya said, wiping her face. "We have to save Sarafine."

"No, we're leaving," Merdin said.

Illeya stared her down. "Not without Sarafine."

"The king said we have to stick together. You saw what just happened. We're nothing against them." Tully went for her pack.

Merdin took Illeya's arm. "We have to tell the prince. He won't stand for his number one candidate being captured. We'll tell the prince and come back."

Illeya met Fenity's eyes for the first time, and all the hate and jealousy and vengefulness were gone. In its place was someone scared and powerless. "You'll help her, right? Until we bring someone back?"

"She has to," Merdin said. "They're partners."

Fenity's lip curled. "You'd just get in the way. Go now, before they come back for the rest of you. They have your scent now."

"Come on." Merdin tugged Illeya's arm.

"I'm sorry. For everything." Illeya inched back with every tug. "Just save her."

Nisha and Tully had already retreated down the road. With a nod from Fenity, Illeya finally let Merdin lead her away, though she watched with growing dread until they rounded a bend out of sight.

Fenity kicked dirt on the remaining embers, fully extinguishing them. She'd warned them, but she could have tried harder—doused the fire herself, or begged them to set a watch. She sprinted toward the ruins, outlined now by the slow-rising sun, still far from morning, the sky a deep burgundy and dotted with stars.

There was no sign of the trolls, so she chose speed over caution, following the trail that led right to the front gate of the ruins—a flattened path formed by Sarafine's prone form dragged backward all that way. The remains of the gate hung in shredded wood and broken metal, and not much more. Beyond a courtyard reclaimed by the forest, the castle's roof had long collapsed, exposing columns and crumbling walls. No sign of the trolls, or Sarafine, though Fenity listened with all her might. A sour scent hung in the air.

The only sound was her rapid heartbeat racing in her ears and the happy chirping of morning birds.

This was ludicrous. What was she going to do against trolls? Her pata had taught her how to fight, but she was no sword master. She didn't even have a sword, just a small dagger. It would be easier to blame Sarafine's death on the trolls and move on in the contest.

Fenity took a deep breath and slipped inside the ruins.

The inside was somehow colder despite the walls blocking most of the wind. Compacted dirt and stray stones covered the ground. Whatever graced these once-grand halls had long since deteriorated.

The roaring fire she'd seen earlier was gone, with no beacon as she'd hoped, leaving only the thick scent of burning wood. But maybe that meant they hadn't eaten Sarafine. Fenity crept along dark, empty corridors, peeking over crumbling walls into vacant rooms, seeking Sarafine and trying to imagine how life had once graced these halls. Had it been a rich lord? A summer home for the human heir? Had there been tapestries and dancing and parties and rich furnishings? Maybe she'd never know.

There was no sound but her own breathing. No movement. She made her way toward the cliff side of the castle, following her memory of where the shadows had danced. She stopped cold at the sound.

Snoring flitted softly across the stone. No whispers. No cries for help. She leaned around a doorway, stone covered in lichen. Three trolls slept sprawled on a floor littered with bones. The stench of rotting flesh hit her like a slap. On the other side of the room, Sarafine lay in a heap on the cracked stone. Her chest rose and fell. Fenity breathed out a sigh of relief. Not dead.

Their forms towered over her, leathery skin in wrinkled hunks where it smushed together at the joints. It was impossible to tell their genders with their raggedy shorts and nothing else, bare-chested and bare-footed. Their colossal heads had hardly any hair, and dirt caked their bodies.

Squinting across the darkness, Fenity looked for injuries, examining Sarafine from head to toe. She gasped. A troll had a hand wrapped around Sarafine's ankle, like a child with a favored toy, asleep beside her.

How was she going to get Sarafine out? It wasn't like she could create a portal and whisk her to safety. Not unless she wanted to take a troll with her. And expose her secret.

Fenity held her breath and crept into the room. Even in

hard boots, her steps fell lithe and silent. The stench grew exponentially. Fenity retched. It hadn't been rotting meat. It was the trolls.

She tiptoed on, breathing through her mouth. Her pounding heart reminded her of her fear. This close, the trolls were enormous. She didn't want to consider what might happen if they awoke. Their bulky forms were easy to sidestep, and thank the moons they didn't stir. Hopping over loose stones, she finally reached Sarafine, kneeling beside her prone form. No blood, but a nasty welt had formed on her forehead, the tight skin swollen and shiny. Scrapes covered her arms from being dragged.

Fenity put a shaking hand over Sarafine's mouth—just in case. "Sarafine." She shook her. "You're okay. Wake up."

Sarafine mumbled, trying to turn over. The troll's grip locked her in place, so she kicked in her sleep, trying to free her leg.

"Be still," Fenity whispered as loud as she dared, pinning Sarafine's hips with both hands. She held her breath.

The troll didn't wake from its snoring slumber, but Fenity scarcely breathed until she was sure none of the others had awoken.

"Sarafine, wake up." She shook her shoulders, and Sarafine's eyes fluttered, but she didn't wake. "Goddess of creatures, help me."

One eye on the troll, Fenity swallowed bile and rested her hand against its hard, dirt-crusted skin. It didn't move, so she slowly pried its blood-caked fingers up, one by one.

When the last finger lifted from Sarafine's ankle, the troll snorted and rolled. Its hand lifted and clamped around Fenity's arm. Fenity squeaked, instinctively pulling against the iron grip. She froze, but the troll didn't open its eyes. It tucked its arm close, yanking Fenity down to its side, the tight grip crushing her arm.

Sarafine remained unconscious, now completely free from the troll.

Could this day get any worse? What was she going to do? The troll's huge hand completely encircled her upper arm.

"Sarafine." She couldn't move, but she gave a few strong tugs anyway. The troll didn't wake and her arm didn't budge. "Ugh." She was smarter than this.

Instincts sent her gaze shooting over her shoulder. A huge troll stood behind her, staring at her slack-jawed. She lay flat, closing her eyes and pretending to sleep. Would it remember they'd only captured one female? Her heart thumped wildly. Energy thrummed in her veins, but she couldn't portal away while in the grip of a troll. She couldn't leave Sarafine behind.

The troll nudged her legs with a bare foot, scooting them an inch. She didn't react, feigning unconsciousness. The troll sniffed around a few more times, shuffling his feet. Then its heavy footsteps retreated to the other side of the room.

Fenity waited for it to settle back into sleep, but then the shuffling returned. Something landed on her legs, and the troll grabbed her ankles. Fenity opened her eyes. A rope!

Her whole body shook.

Fenity kicked hard against the troll's grip, over and over, but it simply sneered at her. With her other arm pinned, she flailed wildly, every instinct warning her to escape, escape, escape. The rope wrapped tightly around her, binding her legs together.

"You think we no see," it rumbled. Its words came slowly, like each one required immense consideration. "Fae thinks trolls no see. But trolls see."

Fenity stared in fearful, wide-eyed silence. She'd read they spoke to each other in their grunting ways, but nothing hinted they spoke her language. Could it be reasoned with?

"I do see you," she said, voice shaking more than expected. "I'm sorry for entering uninvited. You took my partner."

The troll grabbed a second rope and tied it around Sarafine's ankles. She didn't stir. "You food now."

"King Sidian sent us to make peace with you. I can help your kind." She pulled her arm, earning a loud snore from the troll.

"No peace with wretched fae." The troll spit, and then its thick fingers curved into a fist. "You sleep now." It raised its arm.

"Don't!" Fenity tugged her energy toward her. The troll's fist came down on her head, and she dropped into uncon-sciousness.

CHAPTER 23

The parchment slipped from Renic's fingers. Galan put a hand on the hilt of his sword and rushed to the sitting-room window, looking for threats.

But there was no threat. Not to the castle, and not to him. It was Sarafine, and it was Fenity. Illeya sent the message via wind transfer at an enormous cost.

"They've been captured by trolls." Renic stood by the hearth, indecision locking his limbs.

Galan snatched up the letter, reading it.

Prince Renic,

You must hurry. Trolls captured our dear Sarafine last night. Please, I beg the crown's assistance. Lady Fenity is doing what she can, but what can she do against a horde of trolls? Please. You must come immediately.

Lady Illeya Skyburn

"My prince," Galan said slowly, "I'm sorry, but we'll never make it in time. And the king won't permit you to—"

Renic raised his arm. "My pata should never have sent them on this unwinnable quest. We're going." He moved toward the dressing room to pack but pivoted and made for the door instead. "We're going now. If anyone tries to stop us, you know what to do."

Galan rushed after him. "I implore you to think rationally. This is the Strife. You can't show favoritism, and you can't interfere."

"Sarafine is there. My pata will understand." He picked up the pace, rushing past the surprised castle guards.

Galan jogged to keep up. "You're the heir. If there are guards at the border, you won't be allowed to cross."

"Stop trying to protect me and protect *her*," he snarled. Nothing existed except finding them and ensuring their safety. No rationality. No politics. No permission. Just racing to Fenity as fast as he could until he saw her with his own eyes and held her once again.

CHAPTER 24

Grit glued Fenity's eyelids together when she awoke. Her head throbbed with a pounding that made her swallow back bile. She went to rub her eyes, but her hands were bound and tied to her ankles so she couldn't lift them. Prying open her eyes, she blinked into the sun now streaming from overhead. She lay within the ruins still, but the trolls were gone.

No, not gone. Their snores rattled nearby. They'd sheltered from the sunlight. She could portal out now and escape. Marek would help her.

"How did they find you?" Sarafine asked, voice low. Fenity jumped, pain cracking through her skull like a lightning strike.

Fenity rolled over to face her more fully, breathing through the agony. Sarafine sat up beside her, back against the wall, wrists and ankles bound just like Fenity's, head bowed like she was in pain.

"I tried to rescue you." Fenity would feel more embarrassed if the situation wasn't so dire. It would be days before the other contestants brought back help. If the king would even allow them any help.

Sarafine snorted. "This was doomed from the start, wasn't it?"

Fenity nodded, then winced. The troll had knocked her hard. "Use your energy. Get us out of these bindings."

"My fire isn't exact. I could burn you."

"Make a flame near me and I'll scoot close enough to singe the rope." Being burned was way better than being eaten.

Sarafine concentrated, the buzz of energy accompanying her efforts. A fire burst into life halfway between them. She must have fed it energy, for there was nothing but rocks for it to burn.

"We can both use it." Fenity wiggled toward the flame, alternating her legs and upper body until she'd wormed her way over. Sarafine did the same. To minimize the risk of burning herself, she positioned her ankles close to the flame first. Sarafine elected to do her hands, but that meant her whole upper body was close to the fire.

Sarafine hissed in pain, jerking away before the rope could catch fire. Fenity's ankles grew hot, too hot, excruciatingly hot. She bit her lip as a scream worked its way up her throat. Pulling her legs apart, tension stretched on the rope until it finally caught and snapped, falling to the ground. She whimpered. Her leggings had burned away and blisters ringed the side of her leg.

Fenity sat up, swaying. Dizziness spun the stone walls and crumbling wooden beams overhead. Fighting hard against the nausea, she angled the rope around her wrists toward the flames. Sarafine had yet to make any progress. Fenity reached for the knots.

A deafening roar sounded from the end of the room. The fire disappeared. Fenity shot to her feet, promptly falling over as the world spun on its axis. Three trolls charged out of their shady spot, roaring and drooling, racing to their prey.

"Run, Fenity!" Sarafine pulled her energy forward. Flames sprung up between them and the trolls. They screeched, coming to a stop. "I can't hold it for long. Go!" Sweat beaded her forehead.

"Not without you." Hands still bound, Fenity reached into her boot for her dagger. Gone.

"Watch out!"

The trolls took a running jump through the flames, murder in their eyes.

No time.

Fenity leaped to Sarafine's side, barely missing a swipe from the lead troll.

"You have to trust me now." She summoned her energy quicker than ever. She opened a portal just as the troll lunged for them, closing it in a flash.

They lay on Marek's red carpet, alone in his sitting room, the air warm, their surroundings immaculate.

"You!" Sarafine reeled, scooting as far as she could, wrists still bound to her ankles. "What have you done?"

Fenity reached for her, but Sarafine flinched away, eyes wide with naked fear and something that looked like guilt. Fenity raised her bound hands. "I know. I know everything you're thinking right now. But it's going to be alright."

"What have you done?!" she screamed into the carpet.

Fenity jerked her head up, sending pain pounding through her skull. "Shhh. You need to keep calm." Marek warned the servants to leave her alone, but what if he wasn't home? She spotted a letter opener on top of a pile of papers. Snatching it up, she hurried to Sarafine's side.

"Don't touch me!" Sarafine jerked away.

"Just let me cut you free." Fenity grabbed the rope. The

blade wasn't sharp at all, but she slowly cut through the bindings.

Sarafine rubbed her wrists and backed into a corner, taking in the room with her face drained of color. "Where are we?"

Fenity studied the room with new eyes. The furnishings were polished wood, the carpet a unique weave. The colors were overwhelming, the ceiling low and almost suffocating. It couldn't hope to pass for a room in the fae world.

"This is the only place I could think to come where we'd be safe." Fenity watched her like a caged animal.

"You're a portal opener."

"Yes."

"You told everyone you have no energy."

Fenity remained silent.

Sarafine lifted her chin, then winced, some of her fight returning. "It takes incredible energy to open a portal. Why not use it for something else?"

"I couldn't risk accessing it, not even to learn what I might do with it."

Suspicion turned to tentative understanding. "No, you wouldn't have any help or training growing up where you did, now would you?" She spoke mostly to herself, lost in thought, studying the foreign books lining the shelves.

Fenity didn't deny it, though the instinct to defend her mata was strong.

"The prophecy." Sarafine spun, eyes wide again. "How could you have done this? You've doomed us all."

"I couldn't let you die. I just reacted. I had to do something."

Sarafine raised her hand in front of her, as if she could shove the consequences of Fenity's choices away with sheer will. "Is not my life numbered among the fae? 'The doom of all fae' would probably include me too, don't you think?" She pointed. "But that wasn't your first time. You've been here before."

Fenity sighed in defeat. Why pretend she didn't do exactly what Sarafine said? "Nothing can excuse what I've done. I know that. I *have* been here before, after you and your friends attacked me."

Sarafine closed her mouth. The indignant expression fell from her face.

Footsteps clicked from the hall, but then stopped and turned the other way.

"We have to get back," Fenity said. "I'm prepared to face the consequences of my actions. Just... Let me say goodbye to my mata."

Mata.

They would know she had the ability, too.

Her eyes stung, and she covered her mouth. She'd traded both their lives for Sarafine's. The king would never let them live.

But could they run away? Live in the human world, maybe. Marek would help her.

"I won't tell anyone." Sarafine watched her. "So long as our people remain safe, I won't tell."

Fenity collapsed into an armchair, shaking. Her life. Her mata's life. They now rested in Sarafine's hands. If Sarafine thought she might lose the Strife, how far would she go to win?

But Fenity couldn't regret saving Sarafine from death at the hands of the trolls. Even knowing the trade, even now knowing it hadn't gained Sarafine's friendship or gratitude, she wouldn't change anything. She'd made a choice, and it was the right one.

"Thank you," Fenity whispered, words shaky. The gratitude didn't feel real because Sarafine could now use the information Fenity had given to save her life against her. And she didn't deserve Sarafine's silence—she'd opened a *portal* despite the prophecy and the consequences.

Fenity shook out her numb hands. "Let's go. The others left yesterday to get help. We don't want to be discovered missing if they come back."

Sarafine nodded, and Fenity took her hand, slick with sweat. Sarafine was well and truly scared, and hiding it well.

"Wait," Sarafine said. "You didn't answer my question. Where are we?"

"The human world."

Sarafine gasped, face going white, but whatever she'd planned to say cut off when Fenity opened a portal. Woods and a dirt road, air chilled from mountain cold. She closed it quickly and dropped Sarafine's hand. Examining her burns, she feigned casualness, when really she was straining with all her might to hear the distant peel of a gong alerting everyone to her failure.

Nothing.

The trees swayed unnaturally as Fenity's head injury reared its head.

"The alarm didn't sound." Sarafine stared at her wide-eyed. "Are the wards even real?"

"I hope to never find out."

They stood in the woods near where Fenity had slept. The blankets were scattered from her mad dash to the contestants' screams. She dug in her pack and found both waterskins, passing one to Sarafine. She took a long, long pull.

"What, no speech about conserving water?" Sarafine glared.

"We both know I can get more."

"Unless you're injured and can't access it." But Sarafine paled and peered through the trees at their surroundings.

"Keep using it and you're going to get caught. You're lucky our wards haven't detected you yet."

Fenity gathered the blankets. "Maybe they're a myth to scare those of us with the ability and keep us from using it. But I'm fast. I don't leave it open for long."

"And you don't think the trolls will talk about the fae who disappeared from their capture?" Sarafine stuck her hands on her hips.

Fenity swallowed hard. "Trolls are proud. They won't admit their prey escaped them." At least, she hoped.

"We didn't get a token for the king. We won't win the challenge."

"I'm not sure there's a way to win this challenge, besides surviving."

Sarafine's lips thinned. "I'll get my pack." She headed down the embankment toward where their fire had been. "We need to be long gone before nightfall."

"Illeya took your pack. I don't think she believed I'd succeed. But I have enough provisions for both of us."

Sarafine harrumphed. "Or you can just get us more, right?" She rolled her eyes but it didn't cover her uneasiness.

They started back down the trail, sun hanging low in the sky. Fenity fought to avoid limping as her boots rubbed against her blistered skin. The castle ruins were a shadow at their backs, and they unspokenly hurried their pace.

When night finally forced them to stop, Fenity shared her extra blanket and food. Sarafine mumbled something that sounded like thanks, which was more than Fenity would have received a few days ago.

It took much longer to travel back to the border, partly because of Fenity's burned leg, but mostly because she kept them off the roads and made them sleep in shifts. Sarafine didn't argue for once. They weren't safe so long as they were in troll territory, and they wouldn't be caught off their guard again.

Halfway through the next day, Sarafine stepped wrong on a loose rock. It rolled, and she went down. Hard. She cried out in pain, and Fenity rushed to her side.

"Are you alright?"

"I twisted my ankle." Sarafine wrapped her hand around the pain, face contorted with pain.

The sun was drooping, and Fenity didn't want to spend another night here. But she couldn't risk a portal to a location in the fae world.

"Can you walk?" She held out a hand.

Sarafine reluctantly accepted help to her feet, but one step on the hurt ankle had her crying out again.

Stars above. This was not good. "Okay, just rest a bit. You probably sprained it."

Sarafine eased back down, glaring at her leg as if she could scare it into complying.

After preparing a tea with herbs Fenity knew would ease the pain—which Sarafine balked at until Fenity threatened to leave her behind—she wrapped a torn strip of blanket tightly around her ankle. The swelling was too great to put her boot back on.

They lost another day letting Sarafine rest. When they traveled, she leaned heavily on Fenity, limping the entire way. It was slow, exhausting work, but it was downhill, and they didn't encounter any trolls. They didn't encounter any fae, either. No one came to rescue them.

Bleary-eyed and out of food and water, they finally approached the border after days of hard travel. All of Fenity's muscles ached, her head still throbbed, and her untreated burn oozed, but they were alive. They finally spotted the very tops of the gilded carriages between the trees.

"Can you hear me?" a male roared from down the road. "Fenity! Sarafine!" There was movement behind the boulders still obscuring the view.

Renic? She hurried their pace to a hiss of pain and a glare from Sarafine.

"Let go of me," Sarafine said. "I command you to let go."

"You can't hop by yourself." Fenity slowed back down.

They rounded an enormous boulder in the middle of the torn-up road, and there he was, flanked by two guards clad in palace attire. A third guard hovered behind him, dressed more casually—Galan with his long white hair. Sarafine's friends stood huddled together, wrapped in blankets by the carriages.

"Fenity!" Renic spotted them and moved to approach, but the guards blocked him with their arms.

"I'm sorry, Your Highness. King's orders."

He shoved them aside and leaped over the border to the troll lands—a dangerous place for the sole heir to the throne. Galan crossed with him but stayed near the border, alert.

Renic jogged closer, yet still so far away. "Lady Sarafine. What happened?"

"You're here." Fenity wanted to dump Sarafine on the rocky ground and run into his arms.

"You came for me," Sarafine said, tears spilling over. "The trolls captured me. You don't know how glad I am to see you."

Even Sarafine's poor performance couldn't disturb Fenity's joy. He was so close. She could almost touch him and remember he wasn't a dream.

Renic finally caught up to them. He took Sarafine's arm, and she promptly dropped her whole body and all her weight against the length of him.

"You're okay now." He anxiously scanned Fenity from head to toe, touching her arm as if checking she was whole. "They said you were in trouble, that you went to rescue Sarafine from the trolls."

"They captured me, too. But we got away." Fenity let him lead her, tucked close to his side, Sarafine hobbling on the other. The three of them ambled toward the protection of the fae lands. Galan studied her as he took up a position behind them, guarding their backs.

"Oh, Sarafine," Illeya said as soon as they crossed the border. Along with Nisha, she rushed to Sarafine's side, where Renic relinquished her, though Sarafine tried to hang on. No other contestants had returned.

Illeya held her, squeezing tight, until the guards and a healer arrived to assist Sarafine to the carriages.

"Ride with me," Renic said, arm still around Fenity. "I'm not convinced you're alright."

"I am, except for this burn." And a few other things. But she knew what he meant. She wouldn't be convinced he was alright until she could put her hands on him.

Renic smiled, but concern flooded his face. "I shouldn't have let you go."

Fenity's brow scrunched as Renic led her to a healer. "Let me? I *had* to go. I couldn't risk losing another contest."

Renic kept quiet while they were around the healer. "Walk with me, Galan." He and Galan left to check on the others, always staying within eyesight. The healer salved and bandaged her injuries, and then Renic helped her into his carriage. They hadn't brought many back—Renic's, and one for the contestants, servants, and guards.

After ordering Galan to remain with the drivers, Renic settled beside her on the cushioned bench. This carriage was much roomier than hers had been, with carved details of leaves and whorls painted in shimmering golds and silvers, all complementing the green, velvet bench.

Now that she was warm, safe, and doctored, exhaustion weighed down her eyelids. She could have died. Nearly had. She trembled from the weight of the past few days.

Renic leaned over his knees and pressed his palms over his eyes. "I should have warned you." Anxiety rolled off him, as if he'd held it in until away from prying eyes.

Fenity took his hand, gently pulling it from his face. "We haven't known each other for long, but you know me better than that. I'm strong. I knew what we were getting into. I knew the trolls were dangerous. And I'm perfectly fine." She lifted her arms to prove her point, but her sleeves slipped down, revealing raw rope burns.

"What is that?" Renic's countenance turned thunderous, eyes narrowed as she pulled her sleeves further down. "They tied you up?"

"All fine, remember?" She placed her hands on either side of his face, warm and smooth, pressing her forehead against his.

He swallowed.

Her mouth fell open, and she pulled back. "Sorry." Touching him felt as natural as breathing. But he wasn't hers. It was too easy to forget he was the prince.

Renic took back her hand and nuzzled her palm, eyes closed, lips grazing her skin. "The need to protect you is over-whelming." He lifted his face. "All the more reason I should have warned you."

"Warned me?" She watched as the muscles in his jaw twitched. "There is no token, is there?"

He shook his head. "King Makas has a token, but he'd never give it to a fae. Not in a million years. My pata would have known that even before sending everyone here."

"Then how can there be a winner?" Her eyes slid closed

without permission as Renic traced her arms with his fingertips.

"Pata wouldn't tell me. But he knows what he's doing. I know whoever wins the most races wins the Third Pillar."

Never enough answers to satisfy. She leaned her head on his shoulder, and he tucked her close. "How did you get here so fast?"

"I received Illeya's wind transfer. I raced here as fast as I could. Pata doesn't know I left. He'll be... unhappy when he hears. I'm not supposed to interfere with the pillars."

"You didn't though, did you?" He'd only crossed into the troll territory at the last moment. How long had they waited for their return?

"This time." The solemnness of his voice warmed her bones. "I don't intend to make the same mistake again." He squeezed her closer, and she breathed his honeyblossom scent, but then she sat up and faced him.

"You're supposed to use the Strife to meet your wife, Renic. What if that's not me? What if you spend your time dancing with me and protecting me, and you miss out on meeting the female you're supposed to be with?" He deserved happiness, even if it wasn't with her, but the questions turned her stomach. "What if I don't win?"

He cupped her cheek, green eyes holding hers. "I've already met the one I'm supposed to be with. Spending time with anyone else would be a waste of precious moments I could be spending with you."

Her heart melted. Her breaths shuddered in and out. She leaned forward and kissed him. Not the sweet kisses of before. Their mouths collided with hungry desperation, tongues slipping over each other, sending vibrations roaring through her body.

One hand pressed into her back, pulling her closer yet

never close enough. She plunged her fingers into his long hair, earning a gasp from him.

The need to touch him, to be near him, was tantamount to survival. She couldn't survive without food and water, and she couldn't survive without Renic. Finding him had been a gift—a beacon in the darkness—and she never wanted to let it go. She'd never get enough of him.

When the carriages stopped for the evening meal, their time together ended. Etiquette forced her to join the other contestants. The hostility rolling off Sarafine and the others told her all she needed to know—whatever ground she'd gained by saving Sarafine's life was gone. But they didn't speak to her, only to each other, and Fenity couldn't find the courage to ask why.

On the last night before returning to the castle, they stopped for the evening. Fenity found a suitable spot behind a crop of trees to relieve herself and was just about to drop her leggings when loud, crashing footsteps stopped her.

Fenity tensed and peeked around the trees. Lit by the light of the moon—Prisanthony was hiding this night, only Pirus with his half-hooded glow—Sarafine hobbled her way over, eyes narrowed in hostile determination, injured ankle bound so she couldn't bend her foot.

"Are you okay? Do you need help?" Fenity ignored Sarafine's hostility and stepped forward to help Sarafine lest she trip on a hidden bramble.

"What do you think you're doing?" Sarafine accused, coming close enough their foreheads almost touched. "What gives you the right to steal Prince Renic's time from the rest of us?"

Fenity's anger simmered to the surface, but she took a moment to hold her tongue. "You know the prince. Do you think he'd allow anyone to *steal* his time?"

"He's promised to me," she snapped. Her words reeked of jealousy.

"Impossible." Fenity's jaw unhinged. "This is the Strife. He's not promised to anyone."

"He didn't tell you we courted before the Strife?" Sarafine laughed, lip curled in a sneer. "For a moment, I almost respected you. But you're delusional if you think he's your happily ever after."

Fenity gasped as if slapped. It was too much. Too many times to endure the unwarranted punishment for a life she never asked for.

"Do you ever stop to listen to yourself?" Fenity shouted at her retreating back. "Why can't he be my happily ever after? Because I'm not *you*? Because I wasn't born to the same life as you?"

Sarafine spun around. "That's exactly what I think. Me and everyone else. You're not good enough for him."

"They think that because *you* told them to. Renic and I are exactly right for each other."

"They listen to me because the noble houses respect me, as they should a future queen." Sarafine lifted her chin. She didn't need to say what she implied—that they didn't respect Fenity, that she'd never be queen.

"He'll never choose you." Fenity's eyes burned. She hated how right Sarafine was. Sarafine's dark words cracked open the bubble of light Fenity had tried to hide in. The black spear stabbed all the way to her heart, leaving no place to run.

They didn't respect her. She wasn't meant to be queen. And Renic's affection wouldn't be enough.

"*He* doesn't have to choose me." Sarafine shook her head

and huffed through her nose, like an adult humoring the ignorance of a child, before hobbling away.

"Yes, he does." But the words sounded uncertain, left hanging on the wind.

What did that mean? Fenity sagged to the dusty ground. Renic had warned her the court would never accept her if she didn't do well at the pillars. Was that what she meant?

Sarafine was playing a game Fenity couldn't ever hope to win. But would she still keep her promise not to tell Fenity's secret?

CHAPTER 25

They arrived back at the castle at midday, and it seemed the entire court had turned out. The courtiers and the rest of the Strife contestants stood in a large bunch on one side of the front entrance, while the parents of the ones who'd returned stood on the other. Servants lined the road, bowing for their prince.

A servant opened the carriage door, and the contestants piled out, leaving Fenity to go last. Renic was already in the courtyard amongst the waiting crowd. While everyone cheered for him, Fenity quietly slipped out and made her way toward the castle.

Sarafine milked it for all she could, limping and leaning on Illeya and calling for Renic's aid. He didn't go to her.

"Fenity!" Mata and Pata rushed to her side from the crowd of watching courtiers. Mata's voluminous dress wrapped around Fenity's legs as she took her arm, scanning her over, not even caring how filthy her daughter was. "Thank the valley you're okay."

The panic in Mata's voice was the only thing keeping

Fenity from looking for Renic as the tall walls swallowed them up.

Pata led them inside, speaking in low tones. "A contestant didn't survive."

Fenity gasped. "No, who?"

"Lady Carlin," Pata said as they ascended the first set of stairs. "She wore the fuchsia color. They're from a small holding in the west. Her pata is a good male."

"King Sidian should never have invented such a dangerous test." Mata didn't let go, hurriedly leading them to their wing of the castle.

"Keep your voice down." Pata's gaze darted to the dark corners of the corridor. He lowered his own voice even more. "It was a hopeless mission."

Fenity nodded. "No one was going to win." Her parents had learned what she had.

"Not in the way you think," Mata muttered, face sour. Her posture said not to press for more.

"Don't worry about it now." Pata patted Fenity's arm. He remained silent until they stopped at her door. "You're back safe. Now get cleaned up. The king has called for a celebration feast with a formal announcement in only a few hours."

Would they have chosen the winner of the pillar so soon? Maybe a contestant succeeded in gaining a token from the trolls.

With one last lingering hug from Mata, her parents left as Fenity entered her suite. She was immediately engulfed in a crushing embrace accompanied by the nauseatingly powerful scent of dying roses.

"I was worried sick." Arinia held her back by the shoulders. "I couldn't tell you. That there was no way to win. And then we heard you rescued Lady Sarafine. I told you to be careful."

"I'm fine, just tired." Fenity stepped away and inhaled the

fresh air. "So you knew it was an impossible mission too, then?"

She wanted to feel betrayed, but Arinia had been clear there were things she couldn't divulge, even if she wanted to. It was a constant battle to remember she couldn't trust this kind, caring female. Not with her secrets, not with her wishes or desires or strategy. Everything could be repeated back to the king, or the other contestants, or anyone, if those were the rules Arinia had sworn to play by.

"I knew there was no way the trolls would treat with the fae. But you knew that too."

It was a longshot, certainly, but she'd been too naïve to think King Sidian would send them for no reason other than... What? To see who might succeed despite the odds?

"I had my suspicions. But I still had to go. I still had to try." Anything to win a place by Renic's side.

Arinia nodded, and something like pride gleamed in her eyes. "Your bath awaits, my lady." She swept her hand to the bathing room.

Fenity nearly moaned. A hot bath with clean, running water was about the only thing that made leaving her home in the woods bearable. After a healer tended her wounds—a nice female named Healer Fetam—Fenity eased her weary body into the tub.

The muscle-easing soak was cut short when the attendants came to prepare her for the feast. Without even a moment to inspect her latest green dress, Arinia ushered her to the dining hall. One thing was certain, she never wore the same dress twice. So much waste.

Seated at a long table that ran the perimeter, beside courtiers she didn't know, she kept her ears open for gossip. And her eyes open for guards to come arrest her. Would Sarafine keep her word?

Steam rose from her plate, filling her nose with the scents of exotic herbs and smoked meat. Her mouth watered.

The gossip was more of the same. All around the room, courtiers and contestants voiced their predictions of the king's announcement. Maybe he'd announce the next pillar. Maybe he'd declare the winner of the troll challenge. They stuffed their faces with the delicious food, but Fenity couldn't eat.

Renic had finally entered the hall with such despair in his expression, it took everything in her not to go to him. He sat on the opposite side of the room at the high table beside his pata —also not eating. Even across the room, his gaze burned into hers like he was trying to tell her something.

What had happened since their parting?

When most of the eating had slowed, King Sidian stood from his high-backed chair.

The room descended into silence, as if they'd been watching, waiting on him to make his move. Fenity had. Queen Lara stared up at her husband with an empty expression, while Renic rubbed his hands on his knees, trying and failing not to keep his eyes locked on her.

The need to touch and comfort him was overwhelming.

"Welcome back ladies of the Strife. Some of you have done us proud by bravely venturing into enemy territory and returning." King Sidian held his arms behind his back, gold-embroidered tunic and matching cape rustling as he came around the table to pace the middle of the room. "Some of you failed to rise to the challenge. And tragically, one of you lost her life." He let the silence linger. "Any loss of fae life is a tragedy, but we won't hold the trolls accountable. This time."

Right, everyone knew who was to blame. Fenity found her heart racing in anticipation.

The king pivoted and paced in the other direction. "But who's the winner here? The ones who knew it was too dangerous and remained safely behind? The ones who crossed over and then fled in the face of danger? Your prince will answer this riddle." He turned and puffed up his chest toward Renic.

Fenity's lips parted. The king would allow his son to finally speak?

Renic's chair scraped back as he rose. The despair was wiped from his face, but not his eyes. He looked the picture of handsome in his matching gold-embroidered tunic, tight over his broad chest. "The female who obeys her king will always overshadow one who doesn't. And your king commanded the Third Pillar to measure your leadership by conferring with the eligible races of this world."

A perfectly scripted and delivered speech.

King Sidian nodded. "But not all of you obeyed. Now, every fae knows the trolls do not compromise. Their hate of us runs deep. None of you obtained a token. On what merit, then, should we choose a winner?" He raised an eyebrow.

Renic swallowed. "The one who tried the hardest must win. The one who was the bravest. The one who obeyed her king to the fullest."

It was like watching a sick play. The king fed lines to his son, and those lines were delivered with the king's voice coming from Renic's mouth.

King Sidian turned to the courtiers who watched with eager smiles, and the contestants who watched with clenched teeth. "And how do we prove who that is?"

Fenity had been brave. She'd done everything she could to retrieve the token until there was nothing but survival.

"The one who lived and returned most injured. They, above all the rest, sacrificed the most in pursuit of obedience and loyalty." Renic's voice echoed in the stone box of a dining hall until muttering overtook it.

Fenity's nails dug into her palms. The person most injured without dying? Obedience? Is that what Queen Lara was to the king? Nothing but an obedient female to decorate his side?

Renic would *never* treat Fenity like that.

And this court? The way they seemed to care more about their own wealth than the actual people and creatures of this realm? They were just like the humans.

"My pata, His Majesty King Sidian, will now announce the winner." The paleness of Renic's skin sent Fenity's breaths to shaking.

King Sidian smiled around the room, making Fenity's skin crawl. The courtiers leaned forward.

"The winner of this segment of the Third Pillar of Faedom is Lady Sarafine." All the courtiers erupted into applause. King Sidian held his hand out to Sarafine, as if she was right in front of him, ready to accept it, when in fact she was across the room wearing a smug expression and hobbling to her feet.

Fenity slouched as hope drained out of her. She'd lost another challenge.

Sarafine finally limped her way to the king and took his hand, bowing. She hadn't been *that* injured. Fenity's lips thinned. Sarafine must have refused the healer upon their return.

He took her arm and helped her to the empty chair beside Renic. "For her reward, Lady Sarafine will continue the evening as His Highness's guest. No other contestants will dance with him at the ball." He straightened with a frown. "It grieves me to announce we have more than one contestant in the bottom spot. Many failed to even attempt entry into troll territory. For your punishment, you will miss tonight's ball. Also, your lands will incur a fine, and the money will go to Lady Sarafine's holdings."

Shocked gasps rang around the room. The king tricked them. Now their money would go to an already wealthy lord.

No one moved. The contestants who'd remained behind or returned after Illeya's manipulation shrunk behind their place settings, heads swiveling amongst each other.

King Sidian smacked the table. "Leave now."

Renic's eyes flared. He did *not* like this, though he did nothing to stop it.

Ladies in colorful dresses rose hesitantly all around the room. Blues and pinks, yellows and purples. So many of them had failed this challenge. They hurried from the dining hall, bottlenecking at the door, while the gossiping rose to a crescendo. Lords and ladies spoke in outraged tones. Only eleven contestants remained. There would have been twelve if not for the tragic death.

It was the shame of being called out that was the true punishment. And now their parents had to give money to Sarafine's.

When the time came to proceed to the ballroom for the dance, Fenity gave Renic a small smile and escaped to her room, where Arinia and the attendants were absent. Nothing good would come of watching Sarafine pull him close, run her hands over his chiseled chest, place her lips to his ear and whisper secrets he would hopefully only pretend to be interested in.

Fenity rubbed her arms and squeezed the despair away. She needed out of this suffocating prison. But she really needed Marek to teach her to control her energy. Only after securing the doors did she pull her energy and open a portal to the human realm.

CHAPTER 26

The lively melody of the string orchestra filled the ballroom, carried to the furthest corners with energy. At his pata's urging, Renic swept Sarafine around the room for the fifth dance of the night. The ice sculptures and displays of colored light swirling on the walls did nothing to lighten his mood as Sarafine pressed her body into his. Pata spared no expense on the grand spectacle that had become the Strife. No amount of energy or political maneuvering was too much. Renic knew that now.

Fenity should have won the troll contest. She was the brave one, running into danger to save another. From everything they'd learned, Sarafine would be dead if not for her.

But the king had convinced him otherwise, and like the young fool he was, he'd gone along with it. Whose Strife was this? But his pata was wise beyond Renic's years, and the true king. There were so many pieces at play, and Renic only knew of a fraction of them. He had to trust his pata was doing what was best for him and the kingdom.

But this was torture.

"Are you having a nice evening, Prince Renic?" Sarafine lovingly looked up into his eyes, pulling him closer, desperate for him to reciprocate.

"It's a beautiful night." Renic nodded and looked away. He didn't blame Fenity for leaving. The thought of her in another male's arms made his vision turn red.

Irrational. Primitive. And yet, uncontrollable.

He wouldn't even stop to wonder what had taken hold of him, because that would leave room for doubt. There was no doubt and there was no choice. He needed Fenity. Needed to be with her and protect her. Needed so much more than the Strife would allow.

"Looking for someone?" Sarafine cut into his thoughts.

He tore his gaze from the doorway. She wasn't coming back. "No, sorry." *Focus.* "You seem recovered from your ordeal. What was it like being in their territory?" The limp Sarafine had earlier was long gone, and she moved around the dance floor as gracefully as ever. Courtiers and the remaining contestants whirled around them. Renic felt their stares.

Sarafine shuddered, finally putting much-needed space between them. "It was awful. I thought I'd never see you again." Her long lashes fluttered.

Had she always been so obvious? There was nothing real about the attraction she pretended to feel. But attraction wasn't necessary for the heir to find a match. Not in the Strife.

"I'm glad you're safe. I'm grateful Lady Fenity saved you."

Sarafine's brow darkened, and she went silent for a few turns around the room.

Would this song ever end?

She seemed to shake herself. "Fenity is a good female, Renic. But she could never be queen."

Renic stopped dancing. "And why not?"

Sarafine looked to see who was watching as they stood still

in the middle of the dancing courtiers. "She doesn't know how to rule, and she's too busy clinging to her old life to learn. She'll never earn the court's respect, not after all she's done here. And the king prefers me."

His body tensed against the truth of her words—and the urge to deny them. "Thank you for the dance. I need some air." He turned and left for the garden doors, ignoring her shocked stare, grateful he'd held his tongue so well.

How dare she speak about Fenity that way? How dare she be so right?

A guard opened the door for him, but it was Galan who closed it, blocking out the noise of gossip mixed with music. Renic gulped down the chilly air, and it helped clear his head.

"What's wrong with me?" Renic asked without turning to face his friend. Wisps of clouds moved swiftly over the stars, and a soft breeze rustled the nearby bushes and trees, dark with shadow. "Why can't I focus on anything but her?"

Galan's footsteps shuffled over stone until he placed a hand on Renic's shoulder. "You know why."

He did. He did know why.

Galan squeezed and let go. "And if you're not careful, everyone in court will know, too."

Including the king. And Fenity would be in even more danger than the Strife already put her in.

Renic finally turned to his friend, and he wore a small smile. "What?"

"I'm happy for you."

"I have to see her, Galan."

"Then go to her. But don't get caught."

CHAPTER 27

When Fenity appeared in Marek's study, he was sitting in a plush armchair by a warm fire. He jumped, his journal and quill tumbling to the carpet. The staticky pinprick of energy burst outward from him before he saw her and clamped it down. He held a hand to his heart, eyes wide.

Fenity's lips twitched into a smile. "Sorry. I have to be fast, and I never know where you might be."

Movement caught her eye. A female servant at the side of the room gasped, dropping a glass that shattered on the ground.

"Out," Marek commanded roughly. The servant fled the room, and Marek rushed to Fenity. "Thank the gods you're okay. I came home and saw the blood. I didn't know what to think. What happened?"

That's right, they'd been bleeding and forgot to clean up the mess.

She smoothed her fancy dress. "I'm okay. My companion

was injured, but she's okay now." More than okay. "I'm sorry about the blood."

He rubbed the back of his neck. "My servants have had to turn more than a few blind eyes since you appeared."

"Do you think they'll tell? I mean, they're eventually going to figure out who I am." Especially now that she'd portaled in front of one of them. The danger of that didn't bother her like it should. If they tried to capture or study her, she'd leave this world and the fallout behind and never look back.

"I told them it's mage council business. Besides, I think they're a little afraid of me because I have magic—or energy, as you call it—and they don't."

He patted the armchair beside her, so she settled in, trying her hardest not to think of Sarafine wrapping her arms around Renic as they danced around the ballroom at this very moment.

"Is energy rare here? It's rarer *not* to have energy in the fae realm."

"Having a lot of it is rare. You see people with minor gifts a lot, so minor it's hard to tell if it's magic or just skill." He handed her a warm cup of tea. "You're dressed very nice today. You look beautiful."

She glanced down at her green beaded gown. "I left a cele-bration. I lost another contest in the Strife." She gripped her cup. "They weren't celebrating me."

"The Strife?" His eyes strayed to his journal still lying on the floor.

"It's a competition to choose the next queen." She trusted Marek. She did. But telling him more than strictly necessary made the hair on the back of her neck rise.

"And *you* are in this competition? You could be the next queen of the fae?" He blinked in surprise.

It sounded so grand and weighty when pared down like

that. Yes, she could be queen. But there was so much more to all of it than that. It was too much to explain, so she sipped her tea and nodded like his questions weren't the sum of her whole world—past, present, and future.

"Well, they should be celebrating you. What you can do— it's nothing short of a miracle. The things we could discover, the people we could be, the worlds we could visit!" He snatched up his journal and quill and resumed his scribbling.

She grimaced. "It's hard for me to see it that way. I've lived in fear of my gift my whole life. Even being here is a risk." She set down her cup and wrapped her arms around herself. "I miss my home in the forest. I'd give up this gift if I could go back to my old life, if it wasn't for..." She'd almost said his name in this place. "But speaking of my gift, I'm ready for you to help me expand it."

Marek didn't hear. "Can you show it to me? Your world? Can you take me there?" He watched her—a mixture of hope and hidden eagerness, like he feared spooking her by how badly he wanted this.

She tilted her head. Bring a human to her world? The risk. The consequences. "It's dark there now." What was the risk if she took him somewhere no one would be? She could do it. Easily. The prophecy said nothing about bringing a human to the fae world. "Maybe next time I visit, I could bring you back with me. You must promise to leave when I say it's time. So, about my energy?"

"I promise. Thank you, Fenity." He grinned and leaned forward like he might hug her. "Yes, let's work on your energy."

Footsteps clattered to the door, followed by a soft knock. "Lord Marek."

"I told you not to disturb me when my guest is here," he called out, eyebrows furrowing.

The male voice behind the door quivered with nerves,

words speeding up. "Master Aldridge is here. We asked him to wait, but he's—Oh, Master Aldridge. I—"

"He's in there, is he?" This male's voice rang with authority. The new energy from the hall was palpable.

Marek sprung up from his choice, eyes wide. "Get us out of here." He jumped to Fenity's side, grabbing her arm. She ignored the warmth of his hand and pulled at her energy. The room hummed with it.

The doorknob turned. Did this male mean to harm Marek? Fenity opened a portal to the one place she hoped no one would be. She sucked in a breath with the effort to close it just as the door swung open, and then they stood in a field.

She didn't even listen for the gongs this time. She'd learned their secret.

Trees lined the expansive field, their color absent without the sun. The last time she'd been here, this field was full of beautiful blooms, now dormant for the coming of winter.

Marek stared around the darkness, wide-eyed and panting. "I can't believe this. Thank you. I didn't think you'd really take me."

"Neither did I." Irritation coated her words. The cold air prickled her bare arms, her eyes quickly adjusting to the night. Prisanthony was slowly coming back to grace them with her pink light, and Pirus as well, so there was enough to see by. "Why did I?"

"That was Master Aldridge. He and I are in competition to become the next High Master of the mage council. The leader." Marek dragged his hands over his face. "An unannounced visit is unusual. I think one of my servants let slip something about you."

"What about me?" Her voice rose. Panic, anger, and fear all rolled into one.

Marek grimaced. "Just that I'm conferring with a new

mage from out of town. That's what I hope Aldridge thinks, anyway. He's been poking around, and I don't want him to see you or trap me into answering questions I don't know how to answer. At least not until the potion is complete." At her narrowed eyes, he kept speaking. "I'm working on a potion to disguise your ears. Or, at least, my apprentice is."

"You have an apprentice?"

Marek nodded. "All masters do. She runs my apothecary shop." He lightly touched Fenity's arm. His scent of old parchment and metallic energy filled her space. "It's illegal to practice magic without a license in my world. He might not ask to see yours, but there's too much at risk."

Fenity's nose scrunched up. "A license? That's barbaric. Does it cost money?"

Marek didn't hear her. He clutched his robe dress to him and stared, open-mouthed at the sky. "You have two moons."

She looked up. "How many do you have?"

"Just one." He didn't tear his gaze from the sky.

"Your moon must be so lonely." The thought of their Prisanthony without her Pirus dropped a cold stone in her heart, and she shivered in the night breeze.

"Is it safe to cast a magelight?" Marek scanned the treeline, edging closer with a clear itch to explore. She knew the feeling well.

"This is my half-sister's land, but the house is beyond sight over those hills. They won't see us." The energy built up around Marek. "Wait." Fenity grinned. "Let's move to the trees first. I think you'll enjoy it."

He cocked his head in confusion, but they trekked to the trees with only the light of the moons.

"Okay, go ahead." Fenity watched his face as he released the energy and a small sphere of glowing white light burst into existence beside them, floating at eye level.

When her eyes adjusted, Marek was staring at her with a warmth that had her shifting back, dress rustling. She jerked her chin to the trees, and he mercifully broke eye contact and gasped.

"They're not green." His jaw unhinged, and he stepped back, taking in the beauty before him. The closest tree boasted a canopy of deep topaz that faded to a light yellow toward the top. The lack of light muted the colors, but Marek's magelight seemed to grow with his joy as he spun to take in the colorful trees.

His light rose higher to see the pinks and oranges of a different tree. Fenity whipped her head back toward the hills. "Not any higher," she warned. "I couldn't explain my presence here. We're far away from where I'm supposed to be."

"It's incredible." Marek bent to scoop up a purple leaf from the ground. "I mean, of course our worlds wouldn't be the same, even if there are obvious cultural similarities from when we lived amongst each other." He pocketed the leaf.

"Yes." His light grew brighter still, and unease pooled in her stomach. "Marek, please lower your light." He carried on as if he hadn't heard, pocketing more fallen leaves of various colors. "Marek!"

He finally looked up.

"Lower your light."

"Oh, sorry." His magelight dimmed, drifting down from the canopy.

Fenity breathed a sigh of relief. "I need to get back to the castle. They'll notice if the ball ends and I'm not in my room."

"Yeah?" He scooped some dirt and added it to his pocket, chuckling. "I should have brought a bag. Next time. Your world is incredible."

Pride swelled her chest. "I love it here. This was just the

distraction I needed. It would have been anguish to sit in my room alone, wondering what Renic—"

Fenity spun to the distant hills. Horse hooves, racing their way at breakneck speed. "Someone's coming. We have to go." She called her energy to her, running back to Marek.

"I don't hear anything." He paused from examining a seed pod.

She halted her sprint and listened hard. The hoofbeats were close. They'd crest the hill any minute. "Extinguish that light!" She closed the distance to him, readying her energy. It was slower to come this time—this was her third portal in a short amount of time.

Marek's magelight went out just as she grabbed his hand.

Lantern light crested the distant hill. Marek tensed.

"We have to be fast." Fenity's heart pounded, energy rushing inward, then outward with the formation of a portal. He stepped closer to her as it shaped around her. The black night sky turned opaque and mixed with the orange glow of the cozy room.

The sharp-tipped horn and nose of a black unicorn preceded its rider over the hill before Fenity and Marek disappeared, back into the human world. General Ashryn, her half-sister's husband.

She realized too late that Marek's Master Aldridge might still be there. There was nothing she could do.

Panic clutching her throat, she scanned their surroundings. The red room was empty.

Fenity collapsed into an armchair, hand to her chest, vision spinning. She closed her eyes against the floral panels that seemed to tilt around the room, closer to her, and then back again, alternating and tilting at the same time.

"Fenity!" Marek shook her shoulders.

Her eyes popped open. She'd slumped down in the chair, but the floral panels were no longer trying to attack her.

"You passed out," Marek said, taking her hands. "What happened?"

"I did?" She withdrew a hand to rub her temples, closing her eyes again as a fresh wave of dizziness and nausea hit her. "I'm going to be sick."

Marek rushed away. There was a lot of banging before he shoved a cold bucket that smelled like ash into her hands. She vomited up what little she'd eaten of Sarafine's fancy celebration dinner. Marek retreated to the other side of the room until she was done, returning with a cold rag he placed on her forehead.

"It was the magic. You used too much."

"I think so." She held the rag to her face, cooling her heated skin until the dizziness abated. She tested her energy, and it wasn't completely gone.

"That's good. It will help you when we finally get to experiment. It's like a muscle that needs to exercise to become stronger." He rubbed his hands down his robe. "What was that on the hill back there?"

"My brother-in-law." She sipped at the cup of water Marek gave her. "I don't think he saw us." She prayed to the moons he hadn't. "He's the king's general. He's almost never home. I was stupid to forget he might be there—my sister had a baby. Lela. Males become very protective of their partners during pregnancy, and then their offspring after birth." Not even the opening of the Strife could have kept him away, but Lela was nearing her first year. He couldn't stay there much longer.

"I'm sure my eyes were deceiving me, but his horse had a horn—almost like a—"

"A unicorn? Yes, General Ashryn rides one of the most

powerful unicorns in the land. Bromlin. A gift from the king, though Bromlin chose his rider."

Marek took the opposite armchair. "Incredible. What other species does your world have?"

"Lots, as I'm sure your world does. We can compare our similarities and differences another day. I have to get back." It sounded more enthusiastic than she felt. She'd sleep sitting up in this uncomfortable armchair if she didn't need to return before passing out.

She set the rag down and pushed to her feet. Marek held a hand out, an offer of support in case she needed it. It was that hand that helped her find her strength—she didn't need his help.

"Fourth portal of the night," she said with a forced smile. "Going for a record here."

She drew the energy to her.

"Thank you for the adventure, and for showing me your beautiful world. We should do it again."

It was too risky to bring him back to her world. "Maybe we'll try a different world next time. *After* we work on my energy." She tried not to feel the mounting frustration that she'd risked visiting and was no closer to winning the Strife.

He chuckled. "Good idea."

With a push of energy that felt like swimming in tree sap, she portaled to her world, back into the dressing closet.

Fenity awoke from the floor at the rattle of a distant door. She'd passed out again. Stumbling, she unlocked the dressing room door just before Arinia opened it with widening eyes.

"You went for a walk through the garden, didn't you?" Arinia pointed to the dirt on her shoes.

Fenity was almost too tired to latch on to the perfect cover story Arinia had unknowingly handed her. She mustered her strength. "I lost another challenge. And I'm falling for the prince. I couldn't stand by and watch him with her." It was a safe admission, one that Arinia probably suspected anyway. She fumbled for the laces at her back. "I just need to sleep."

Arinia obliged, helping her remove the gown. "You're truly growing fond of the prince?"

"Very much so." She yawned.

"This is good. Very good. No male can resist a female who's attracted to him. It will help your chances."

Dress removed, Fenity stumbled to the bed, barely making it under the covers.

"We can work with this. Get some sleep."

Fenity was asleep before Arinia even left the room.

CHAPTER 28

It seemed Fenity's head had barely hit the pillow when a quiet but persistent knocking ripped her from sleep. Night still cast its dark, comforting blanket over the world, the room dim and tranquil. She rolled over, burying her face deeper into the soft pillow and pulling the fluffy quilt to her chin. Whoever knocked at her door soon gave up.

Then the doorknob rattled, and someone entered her room. Fenity's eyelids fluttered open, consciousness threatening to surface once again. A shadowed figure stood beside her, and before she was aware enough to start punching, Renic's scent washed over her, rising like a sudden summer rain.

A piece of her heart had returned.

"What are you doing?" The words came out a mumble. She tried to rise, but a gentle press of his hand on her shoulder had her lying back down on her side.

Her sleep-addled mind didn't give her room to doubt before she took his hand and pulled him down beside her, needing his nearness. The stolen moments between contests would never be enough.

He curled against her back, strong arms wrapping around her. He nuzzled her face and sighed into her neck. A new scent joined his. A waft of feminine perfume that wasn't hers. Her vision darkened.

"I needed to see you." His fingers brushed the length of her bare arm. "I'm so, so sorry, Fenity. You should have won. You were the bravest. It was torture, pretending everything was okay. Searching for you and not seeing you. Sarafine was so angry at my distraction."

She hated that Sarafine's name had entered the room with them, as strong as Sarafine's perfume masking his scent. But he was here, holding her. It was a bliss she never thought she deserved.

Would he be apologizing if he knew what she'd been up to this night?

He moved her hair aside and pressed his lips into the back of her bare neck. Everything was moving so fast, and it should have scared her. But it didn't. The sensation sent a trembling thrill down her body.

"Say something," he groaned. "Please. Forgive me. End this torture."

She pulled his arms tighter around her, relishing the feel of them—so different from all their embraces before, with only her thin nightshift and his tunic separating their skin instead of layers of formal dress. "There's nothing to forgive. This is the way it must be, right?" She'd ignore the perfume, and he'd ignore whatever scents must still cling to her from visiting the human world, and they'd grasp whatever time they had.

"It still hurts." His kisses moved up her ear, ending at the pointed tip. She shivered.

The pain of the evening was all but forgotten with his near-ness. The Strife. The ball. The court. Even the outside world didn't exist for them. No worlds did, except the one they'd created that only held the two of them.

"I need to say what we've been dancing around these past weeks." Renic's words broke the silence, soft and full of feeling.

Fenity's eyes shot open, pounding heart chasing away all sleepiness. She turned to fully face him, pretending she wasn't about to leap out of her skin. He looked so beautiful, face solemn and relaxed on her pillow, smooth skin bathed in moonlight, dark hair down around his face. The need to kiss his full lips was crushing.

She knew what he was going to say. It was the only explanation for what was happening between them. And she embraced it with open arms.

His hand took hers. "We're truemates."

She squeezed his fingers as her heart fluttered. "I know." Her words were a breathy gasp,

Truemate. He was her truemate, and she his.

She'd suspected it, hoped for it, longed for it, and yet a part of her wished it wasn't true. To be a truemate with the heir to the Kingdom of Asentia. What if she lost the Strife? Or did being the prince's truemate guarantee she won? The thought of someone else in her place—holding his hand at his side, conceiving his heirs—made the world turn red at the edges.

But what if she won?

She wrapped her arms around his middle, and he cupped her cheek, watching her, waiting for her to break the silence.

Fenity caressed his face in return, her fingertips starting at the point of his chin, her palm sweeping across his warm cheek, until her fingers spread into his hairline. "I can't describe the happiness it brings me to belong to you."

"And I belong to you." He smiled, and she saw through the relief he tried to hide, like a secret weight was lifted. He kissed her cheek, then trailed his mouth over her skin until their lips met.

Her restraint nearly collapsed as she placed her hands against his muscled back, deepening the kiss and pulling them closer together. It was so rare to find your truemate, not before spending a lifetime or more looking, if ever.

But that's what they were. From the moment they met, something drew them to each other. The need to protect him, to erase his pain and past hurts, was overpowering.

It wasn't just falling in love—they were *meant* for each other.

Instincts ruled their actions now, the way they moved, the way they kissed. There would never be a point where she'd tire of touching him, where there was such a thing as too close. Silks and shifts slid over skin, and they didn't have to speak to know what they wanted next. It was the bond of truemates, this connection they shared and these instincts that drove them forward. Everything else faded away as they joined in this precious moment, bound together.

Renic was her home now. Not the forest, not the keep, not the castle. *Him.*

Afterward, she dozed blissfully in and out while he held her and caressed her red hair until the sky lightened. "Renic," she whispered. "They can't find you here."

His eyes fluttered open, meeting hers with a warm smile. "Let them see."

"What will happen if they catch you?"

"I'm not sure. Pata instructed me not to spend time with the contestants unless part of an earned reward, but not the consequences."

She sat up beside him, frowning. "What about the Strife? Is it even necessary now?"

His brow creased, and he let loose a long, weary sigh. "My

pata won't cancel it." He stood to collect his things. "The Strife is tradition. The high rulers and allies would be outraged at losing their fair chance to put their daughters on the throne." His jaw clenched.

"But can someone else win if you've found your truemate?" Panic seized her lungs.

"No, of course not." But the hint of uncertainty sent her stomach churning. He must have noticed because he crossed the room and took her hands where she sat on the bed. "I don't want to lie to you. An heir has never found their truemate in the Strife. It's such a rare phenomenon, the Strife would never revolve around finding one. You must do well at the pillars... the court won't accept you if you don't."

She swallowed hard against the tightness his words brought. The light had left his eyes, and she couldn't have that. "You're wondering how to handle this, aren't you?" Fenity squeezed his fingers. The weight of the crown only added to his burdens. She couldn't begin to understand his perspective, but she wouldn't be another thing for him to carry.

He squeezed her fingers back. "Always." He glanced at the window with its mauvy glow of the rising sun.

"Time to pretend?" She held her breath.

"We can steal a few more moments." He guided them back to the bed, and she lay against his chest, content once more.

"You make a good pillow." She nuzzled his warm skin.

He chuckled and went back to running his fingers through her hair, brushing it back and away from her face. "We can't let anyone know of our bond. You would be in danger, and not just from the other contestants. Pata would think I was doing you favors, giving you information to help you win, throwing the contest. And he would be right." Renic pulled her tighter to him. "You have to win, Fen." He jolted her for emphasis. "I'll do exactly what they fear—I'll help you as much as I can. In secret."

"No." She shook her head against him. "That's not how I will win. I won't cheat."

"Good." The simple word rumbled through his chest.

The thought of being the future queen, trapped within the immovable stone walls, made her stomach quake. But she'd endure anything to be by his side.

"I know you have to go. Let me fall asleep first, at least." She wanted to lift her face to him. Kiss him. Love him. But her body was heavy with exhaustion.

"I almost forgot," he said. "Before the first dance, the herald announced the next contest. The Second Pillar of Faedom—poise. Did Arinia tell you? I think it was on purpose, so the contestants who missed the ball as their punishment wouldn't hear about it right away."

"The queen's regalia? What about the rest of the Third Pillar and the other races?" Panic punched the sleepiness from her mind. She'd trained in her spare time—wearing heavy dresses and balancing objects on her head—but had it been enough? "When?"

"In a month. The Third Pillar will continue alongside it with the other races, but Pata wanted to give the people time to grieve the loss of Lady Carlin in the troll trial."

Her heart skipped a beat. What if she couldn't balance the right way, or she couldn't last? All those females who'd prepared for this their whole lives, and she'd had mere weeks.

"Hey." His hands held her face. "You're stronger than them. It's just parading around in a formal dress. Nothing to it, okay?" He kissed the tip of her nose. "The best thing you can do now is rest. I'll stay until you fall asleep."

His warm presence was a reassurance behind her, but she stared wide-eyed into the dark room, well beyond sleep. She couldn't lose another contest. How could Renic justify picking her over the others if she failed even one more? The court—the kingdom—would be in outrage.

"Sleep, my love. Morning will soon be here. There's time yet." He traced his fingertips over her once more, down her arm, over her elbow, the smoothness gliding delicately over her skin, tickling slightly, but also soothing. Down to her hand and fingers, then up again, skimming the thin straps of her nightdress, up over her shoulder, her neck, up the side of her face and gently digging into her hair, then back down again. Slowly. Patiently.

Her eyelids grew heavy again. The worry slacked from her pinched face. Contented exhaustion reigned.

A sharp gasp pierced the room. "Prince Renic! Stars above. Nobody look. Everyone out!"

Doors banged, footsteps retreated. A heavy arm lifted from her body. Fenity's eyes finally opened, and she sat up with a yelp.

"You fell asleep!" Laughter burst from her lips at Renic's red cheeks and mussed hair. This was how she wanted to wake up every morning, in his arms and uncaring about their appearances or the world's judgments.

He smiled at her reaction, casual, totally at ease with being caught.

Arinia closed the sorcer door on the retreating attendants and threw her hands on her hips. "You know the rules, Your High-ness, no consorting with the contestants." Her voice came out a whispered hiss.

Renic held up his arms in surrender. "But you'll keep my

secrets, won't you my favorite 'Nia Nanny?'" He flashed a grin Fenity didn't recognize.

Nanny? Had Arinia tended him as a child, then?

"Oh, you knock that off. There's no charming your way out of this one. Maybe you don't care enough for this female not to get her expelled from the Strife, but I do."

Renic turned to Fenity. "You won over Arinia? You truly can achieve the impossible."

Arinia scowled. "This is serious. Servants talk. You're playing a dangerous game with her future just for a little fun on the side." She crossed her arms. "I taught you better."

The implication stung, even if Arinia was only trying to protect her. Is that what the world saw her as? Only good enough for a side quest, rather than the heroine of her own story?

Renic wiped the impressed smile off his face and crossed the room, taking Arinia's reluctant hands.

"It pleases me to no end that you're so fond of Fenity. I know now I can truly trust you to protect my truemate from the dangers of this court and contest."

Fenity held her breath. They weren't supposed to tell anyone.

Arinia's eyes shot to her, mouth falling open. "*True*mate?"

Fenity found her cheeks burning, but when Renic reached for her, she joined them at the door, taking his hand.

"Truly?" Arinia took them both in. "Young lovers can often confuse it for infatuation, you know."

"Truemates," Renic said, strong and confident. "Truly."

Fenity had never felt such pride.

Tears swam in the unshakeable female's eyes. "Oh, I'm so happy for you, my prince. So, so happy." Her hand shot to her mouth. "But then we must hurry. The Second Pillar of Faedom is next, and she's nowhere near ready."

Fenity's heart raced anew, nausea churning. She'd forgotten about that. Not to mention who knew when the Third Pillar would continue. Luckily, the exhaustion of the night before had eased.

Renic kissed both their cheeks and gave a shallow bow to Arinia. "Then I'll leave her in your capable hands. We ask that you keep this knowledge between us. I know I can trust you."

"Of course, Your Highness. Always." Arinia bowed low at the waist. "Probably best for the other attendants to not find you in here again. Let them think what I initially assumed."

Renic nodded. He kissed Fenity softly on the lips. "You were never just a fling. You will always be the one I devote my whole life to winning. I'll fight forever."

It was a magnanimous effort of will not to stand on tiptoe and steal more of his lips as he reached for the doorknob. "As will I."

Renic stood in the hall, staring into her with a depth that could swallow worlds, one side of his mouth tipped up in a way that told her he'd felt the weight of her simple words. She'd meant them. She'd never stop fighting to be with him.

Arinia shut the door, breaking the connection. "He couldn't have picked a better match, but he's right to want to keep it secret. Your enemies will only work harder to get rid of you if they find out."

Fenity blinked away her reverie. Arinia once said she couldn't be trusted. Now they had no choice. "You mean... kill me?"

Arinia frowned. "It wouldn't be the first time. It'll be up to you to keep your distance from him, you know. The males never stay away."

Fenity doubted she had that kind of self-control. Now that she'd found him, she didn't want to stay away from him either.

And it wasn't in her nature to pretend things were other than they were.

But if it would keep her safe long enough to win?

A knock broke into her thoughts, and Arinia let the attendants back into the room. Renic must have given them the all-clear.

"We have time to prepare, and I'll keep teaching you everything I know." Arinia called for more of the heavy dresses.

"Everything you're allowed to teach me, right?" Fenity asked in low tones. If the king had told them what to share, then she didn't want any spies hearing Arinia broke the rules. Let Renic worry about that part.

"Of course." Arinia nodded in understanding. She helped the attendants layer on the garments and gowns. "Now, we can't access the real queen's regalia, but these are almost as heavy. If you can stand with these, holding the crown out like we've worked on, you'll be just fine."

Fenity filled her lungs with determination and set to work. She had one month, and she'd use every moment.

CHAPTER 29

The night before the Second Pillar of Faedom, Fenity tossed and turned. She'd prepared as best she could, wearing the heavy garments, weight lifting, and running the gardens in between it all. She'd earned plenty of nasty looks and loud remarks from the contestants and courtiers. Apparently, exercising in public was frowned upon at the castle. Luckily, the muscle memory from her days hunting and foraging in the woods hadn't left.

Whatever. She wouldn't be at a disadvantage just to appease their made-up social rules.

The worst part about preparing at all hours was that she hardly saw Renic, only a glance or two across the room at dinners, and once in the garden. But advisors surrounded him, waving their arms and competing for his attention. His brow furrowed in deep concentration and worry, and he didn't see her before they entered the castle, out of sight. Whatever it was, it looked serious.

"Today is the day," Arinia said in a sing-song voice, throwing open the curtains.

Fenity's eyes flew open, heart immediately galloping. This was it. One out of five pillars, all wrapped up in a single event. She'd had no control over the outcome of the First Pillar, and honestly, her only goal had been not to embarrass her parents. Now, *everything* was riding on how well she performed. And winning was the only option.

Her parents wished her luck the night before, though they were oddly distracted. They wouldn't be in attendance. It was too hard on Mata to see Fenity suffer. And, truthfully, Fenity stood a better chance if she wasn't worried about them.

An attendant rolled a tall cart in. Hanging from it were the finest pieces of clothing Fenity had ever seen. The fabric shined, and the stitches were so tight as to be nearly invisible. They oozed wealth, and these were only the underlayers.

"The official regalia of the queen." Arinia beamed and pulled the cart toward the dressing room. "Some of it, anyway."

Numb, Fenity stood still while the attendants dressed her in a layer of undergarments, followed by a simple white silk shift with sleeves that skimmed the floor, and then a tight-fitting corset. There were already more layers than she ever cared to don, and this was just the start.

"The guides dress all contestants in this exact combination." Arinia circled her, finger to her chin, as she examined the attendant's work. They rouged her cheeks and swept her hair up off her neck. "Attendants will add more pieces once you enter the arena."

Fenity had trained for this. "Why is this the queen's regalia? What is the need for all these layers?" Her sticky skin squeezed under the different fabrics that seemed to grow tighter the longer she wore them. It was nothing like the garments she'd practiced in.

"It's tradition. It dates all the way back to when we shared this world with the humans." Arinia sprayed something in Fenity's hair that smelled sour.

"So it's a human custom, then? That explains the eccentricity of it."

"Know a lot about humans, do you?" Arinia waved the attendants away.

"Of course not." They didn't teach about humans in school, outside of the prophecy. She pretended her shift had suddenly developed a bunch of wrinkles that needed her immediate attention to smooth.

Arinia ushered her from the room and hurried her down the hall. There was no sign of the other contestants. How late were they? "You're noble now, my lady, and one day you'll be queen. You should know these things. The clothing represents the might of the queen and her right to rule. It is ceremonial, a symbol to our people of your position and power. As our people witness this event, the first time our future queen will don these clothes, it's the first time they can begin to see you on the throne." She huffed, out of breath from their pace. "Keep your head high, Lady Fenity. You've earned your prince, now you'll earn his subjects."

Outside, the air chilled Fenity to the bones, even through the layers of clothes. The gray sky threatened an early winter. They quickly hurried to the arena, still no contestants in sight. "Are we late?" Fenity picked up her pace, hunger pangs reminding her she'd forgotten to eat anything.

"No. The others must have been early." Worry leaked through her tone.

They finally caught up to them beside the arena.

"Oh, thank the valley." Arinia leaned against the side of the building where the last of the contestants trickled through a side door. Just like she'd said, they were all dressed the same— simple white shifts and white slippers, hair pinned up in the same rounded way, but with no adornments. Thirty-nine females all running around in their pajamas. "Hurry now. The king's servants take over from here. I'll see you on the inside."

"Thank you," Fenity said with warmth. "I couldn't do this without you."

"Remember, head high."

Fenity nodded and rushed to take her place at the back of the line, where the contestants studiously ignored her.

The stone walls blocked the chilling wind, and she instantly missed it. The hall was stifling, only wide enough to fit single-file, and it curved, so it was impossible to see ahead.

The last Strife occurred well before Fenity's birth, when King Sidian came of age. The celebrations in the towns were so grand, the memory still lived on. Especially as Prince Renic approached his Strife, the contests had been the only thing people talked about anytime Fenity and Mata reluctantly made it into town. Besides the heavy garments, Arinia said the females paraded around to be judged for their poise, queenly air, and mannerisms.

There was no action she could take, no strategic decision to make that might help her come out on top. She'd prepared the best she could. Either she'd be judged worthy, or she wouldn't. Enduring was the only option.

An open doorway loomed ahead, the brightness of the space beyond spilling into the dark hall and highlighting the contestants as they passed through. Fenity took a deep breath of comforting darkness. *Head high.* She passed through and entered the arena.

She was the last one, and cheers crescendoed around her, like they'd waited for them all to enter before unleashing their pent-up applause. The arena looked as it did before, with tiered seating filled to capacity. Except where before the pillars had been spaced around the gritty arena floor, now squares of flat stone marked their spots. Fenity followed the example and took her place upon the last remaining stone, just big enough for her slippered feet.

In the middle, spanning the full length of the arena, sparkling accessories and jewels lined multiple tables, and rack after rack held more white garments. One set for each contestant. A king's ransom of wealth and waste.

A herald, the same obnoxious one with the protruding belly as before, stood on the platform erected directly beneath the king's balcony. Banners of shining white and gold hung down the full height of the arena, flanking the platform. As the herald quieted the crowd, Fenity finally dared to raise her eyes to Renic. He stood at the edge, a glass in one hand, pretending disinterest in the events below.

But she knew him.

They'd dressed him in a white tunic and trousers with gold embroidery and accents. It fit snugly over his broad shoulders and muscled torso. They'd braided his hair back, and it suited him. His eyes were unreadable from this distance, her spot being as far away from the balcony as possible, but his stiff posture told her enough. He was watching her, and he was worried for her.

Fenity lifted her chin and averted her eyes. She wouldn't disappoint him.

"We gather today to honor the Second Pillar of Faedom— poise. But what is poise, and why is it so important in a leader?" With his belly leading the way, the herald paced his small platform, as if in deep reflection of his words. "Our future queen must have the confidence, steadiness, and composure to rule at our king's side." He stopped pacing and stared down the audience on both sides. "Would the goblins have retreated at the Battle of the Eastern Banks if our king had arrived weak and ill-prepared?" The crowd shouted and cheered. "Would our people have banished the humans from our land if our queen had cowered in their presence when the cursed prophecy was laid forth?"

"No!" The crowd rose to their feet, pumping their fists.

"No!" the herald repeated. "And so some may call this the most important challenge of them all. Our queen needs poise, for the good of all faedom, and so I say, let the challenge begin!" The resounding cheer shook through Fenity's chest.

King Sidian tipped his cup to the herald, beaming at the crowd from his gilded throne. Beside him, Queen Lara watched on, but Fenity couldn't read her. When the king motioned to his son, Renic reluctantly sat on the opposite side.

Servants dressed in white robes streamed from the open doorways around the arena. Five of them stopped at each station. Five for each contestant, then.

Fenity took a shaking breath, willing the nausea and nerves to settle. Why, oh why, had she not eaten breakfast?

She didn't recognize the attendants who approached her, each now bearing a different type of garment. It took two of them to carry one piece—a gold, sleeveless overlay. The urge to step back at their approach almost had her stumbling away. She already wore three layers of clothing and was ready to jump out of her tight, claustrophobic skin. How many more could they add?

The first was a white shift much like the one she already wore, but this one hung down to her ankles, its poofy sleeves tight at the wrists. Thankfully, it was silky and thin, billowing with her movements as the attendant worked it over her styled hair and pulled it down over her waist. Unlike the under-shift, this one hung looser, even more like a nightgown.

The next piece was an impossibly large hooped skirt, tied tight around her waist, and then a second skirt to cover the hoops, this one in thick, velvety white. Though oddly empty of embellishment down the front, the sides and back had embroidered panels of gold made up with golden braids and small, golden beads. She matched the arena décor.

She matched Renic.

He sat on the edge of his throne, while the king ate delicacies from a plate, reclined and comfortable. Her mouth filled with saliva, and her body jerked back and forth from laces tied and garments adjusted.

At least the wide hoop skirt allowed a breeze.

Next they laced a thick, sleeveless vest in the same velvety white and gold down her front, giving her figure back. Thicker gold shoes with a slight heel replaced her slippers, not entirely uncomfortable.

Sweat slipped down her skin, and she pulled at the tight collar squeezing her throat.

"Attention please," the herald's energy-carried voice boomed out. The conversing onlookers quieted. There was a smile on the herald's face that made Fenity want to run—a cruel twist to it. "During the First Pillar of Faedom, we unfortunately had one amongst us who could not perform." Fenity's heart leaped into her throat. Renic's face shot to his pata. "A punishment was promised, a disadvantage to be doled out at a future date. Lady Fenity, your punishment awaits." He raised a hand to the middle of the arena.

Her attendants held one last piece. Fenity's lungs seized. *Metal.* Like gold chainmail.

The attendants—all five of them together—lifted the metal dress over her head, twisting it just so over her body. When they let go, it was like a boulder dropped on top of her. Her knees nearly buckled.

It was nowhere near what she'd practiced with Arinia. Not by half.

The attendants didn't even look at her as they fastened the

gold to special hooks built into the skirt and bodice. Though sleeveless, the metal covered the entirety of her front and back, from her collarbone, draping down to the hem of the wide skirt.

They stepped back, circling her, making minor adjustments while the crowd clapped their approval and the contestants watched with mixed expressions. No one else wore this piece of the regalia.

How long could she last like this?

"Very nice," boomed the herald. "Very nice."

The completed look was radiant on the contestants. Magelight gleamed off the gold. The shape of the bodice made their waists look even smaller, and the poofy sleeves gave them each a dignified, regal air, while still elegant and feminine. The way the top squeezed their necks, with their hair pinned up, made them look taller.

For once, they were all dressed the same, in the same color, with only their mannerisms and past conduct to distinguish them. Trade the skirt for pants and they'd look like mighty female warriors ready for battle.

"Our contestants are nearly ready. But next comes my favorite part." The herald clapped his hands twice. "Bring on the jewels!"

The attendants must have been waiting for this call because as one, they moved from their frozen positions and approached the tables in the middle. They carried three over-sized black velvet trays back to each contestant. Fenity inhaled. Even since becoming a lady of the court, she'd never seen so much wealth.

Gold, jewels, rings, bracelets, earrings, and every manner of unnecessary adornment. Magelights hovered closer making the jewelry sparkle, reflecting rainbows of light over the attendants and contestants.

Fenity had always liked shiny things. Babbling creeks on a sunny day. Crystals embedded in rocks. The wings of a fluttering sprite.

These held hardly any appeal.

The crowd oohed and aahed, leaning closer with covetous eyes.

The attendants wasted no time layering it on her already overburdened body. Two golden bracelets for each wrist, some encrusted with jewels in all the contestants' colors. They clipped heavy earrings with tiny gems hanging down on thin gold chains to both her pointed ears. Four rings. A delicate golden anklet. And last, they fastened a thick rope of gold around her neck. Cold on her skin, an enormous diamond hung from the center, weighing it down.

Enough wealth to save the world.

Did the jewelry count as another layer? She was counting it. That made ten.

But the racks in the middle weren't empty.

The herald clapped again, and two attendants approached them.

"Oh no." Fenity groaned, sweat trickling down her back.

Huge, fluffy, fur-covered white robes with matching gold embroidery left the racks. It took two attendants to carry them. They wrapped the cloak around her shoulders and secured it with a thick gold clasp at her throat. It was so long, its hem rested on the ground. A small mercy, really. The weight of the cloak would have been her undoing.

"There is one final piece," the herald said. "My king, will you do the honors?" He bowed, and King Sidian was already ready and waiting—all part of the plan.

"These fine contestants please our prince and heir," King Sidian boomed from the balcony, though Fenity couldn't see the prince. Queen Lara stood at his side. "I give my blessing to add the last piece of this test." He waved an arm, and the attendants recognized their cue, stepping quickly back to the tables.

Another piece? Did they not realize her body was a flaming inferno beneath this thick robe and billions of layers?

She squeezed her eyes tight, focusing on her breathing. In through the mouth, out the nose. In through the mouth, out the nose. This was a test. The heat and weight and formalities were all a test. There'd be time later to melt down.

Loud applause erupted from the crowd.

When she opened her eyes, calmer than before, Renic stood before her.

"What?" She blinked.

His lips quirked to the side. "Lady Fenity," he boomed. "Please kneel."

Beside him, an attendant held a tray of black velvet, upon which sat a gold crown. Gems the colors of every contestant decorated each spire, with the middle spire adorned with a diamond that matched the necklace.

Had he already picked her to win? In front of all these people and the contestants?

No. Each contestant also had an attendant waiting with a matching crown. She was just the first in line since she'd arrived last.

Fenity bent her knees, limbs trembling with the effort under the heavy layers, and slowly lowered herself to the ground. The wide skirt with its giant hoops rose to meet her face, but she pinned it with her arms to her sides. Instead, it billowed neatly behind her—thank goodness. She went gracefully down, comforted by his presence.

Arinia told her they had to hold the crown in front of them. That's what they'd practiced. Already, something was different about this Strife than the last one.

Renic took the crown in two hands, and she bowed her

head as he placed it, nestled within her hair they must have styled for this purpose. The crown, with all its gold and jewels, sat heavy on her head, just one more weight to encumber her.

"You look beautiful," he whispered. "I'm so proud to call you mine." His voice dropped even lower, expression turning grim. "Stay on your stone. Don't lock your knees."

"I will." What about parading around the arena?

Renic straightened. His voice carried as he said, "Rise, Lady Fenity, a worthy bearer of the garments of the queen's Strife."

He offered her no hand up, as he might have done, clearly part of the test. But she pushed to her feet, keeping her balance despite the heavy gold and fabric.

Renic flashed a pleased smile, and then proceeded to the next contestant. His words were the same, going to each, one by one. The time ticked by so slowly, and the heat and discomfort chased away by his brief nearness wasted no time in returning. Fenity's eyelids drooped.

"It is done!"

Fenity gasped awake at the herald's words and the thundering of applause. Renic was gone, and all the contestants had been crowned. An ache had formed in her lower back. She smacked her dry mouth. The attendants left the middle of the arena, streaming past her on the way to the exits.

"I need water, please," she whispered as the first one passed by.

But he ignored her.

She nearly lunged for the last attendant as she hurried past. "Please, I've had nothing to eat or drink today."

The attendant paused, eyes on the ground. "None of the contestants have. It's forbidden." Then she hurried away.

Across the arena, she caught Sarafine watching her with an unreadable expression.

No food or water? How was that a test of poise? That

explained why Arinia hadn't offered breakfast. She wiped sweat from her brow, past caring about the inelegant gesture. Was she the only one who didn't know about this rule? She'd bet her mata's new jewel collection that at least some hadn't obeyed.

A horn sounded from below the balcony that awoke the crowd from their slumber and sent them cheering again. Skirts rustled as the matching contestants focused their attention on the herald.

King Sidian stood at the balcony's ledge, and Renic joined him shortly. The contrast between the two was stark. While they wore matching attire, the king was broader in shoulder and slightly thicker in girth, with a larger crown upon his head. And while the king's posture was one of ease, Renic gripped the banister, jaw clearly clenched, even from this distance.

"We humbly await your command, my king," the herald shouted, dropping into a deep, overly dramatic bow.

It was all a charade. Just a big show to appease the people and give them some semblance of control over who their next ruler might be. How much could it truly matter? Renic had made his choice.

But then why did he look so nervous?

Across the way, Sarafine turned to face the middle of the arena. Her posture became rigid, feet shuffling, and she held up her voluminous skirt.

Fenity watched closely, but not even Sarafine's friends mirrored her actions.

Did she know something?

But what?

"The Five Pillars of Faedom represent who we are and what we value as a people and in our rulers." King Sidian's voice carried through the arena, and the crowd quieted to listen. "Like a true pillar that supports a structure, these values hold up our society. That's important to remember. So we're implementing something new this Strife." The king spread his arms wide. "I introduce you to the Second Pillar of Faedom." The satisfied grin on his face and the way Renic suddenly leaned closer made Fenity's gut clench.

She faced the middle of the arena and copied Sarafine, gripping the layers of her skirts and the hem of her robe and raising them from the ground—so, so heavy with the chain-mail underneath.

The horn blared again, and a deep rumbling sounded from beneath them. The ground trembled. Fenity whipped her head from side to side, seeking the danger her instincts told her to expect. This was a test. Something new.

The trembling grew to shaking, and then all at once, her small platform moved. She gasped. Others screamed. They were columns—the same columns that had ringed the arena during the first test.

And they were rising from the ground.

CHAPTER 30

The columns lifted higher. Fenity threw out her elbows, barely maintaining her balance while gripping the garments. Others were not so lucky. When the weight of the heavy, gold-encrusted robe lifted off the ground, some toppled backward. They landed in a heap of hoops and scattered jewelry, the crowd laughing and pointing.

The female beside her quickly pushed to her feet and tried to climb back on the rising pillar, but the herald interrupted her with a booming announcement. "If you fall, if you falter, if you resign, you are not worthy, and will be eliminated from the Second Pillar of Faedom."

Still, the female kept trying. Without her color, Fenity hardly recognized her, but she was the one who wore coral. Her arms wrapped around the stone, face crumpled in desperate anguish. But the columns rose higher and higher, soon well above any achievable height to climb, especially so encumbered. The attendants gently led her away, collecting her discarded crown and errant jewels that had fallen in her tumble.

When the columns finally came to a stop, they towered above the crowd twice her height. Fenity dared to look around. The coral female wasn't the only one to fall victim to the weight of the garments and the surprise of rising through the air.

Twelve. Twelve columns stood tall and empty. Sarafine and her friends—Illeya, Merdin, Tully, Moona, and even Nisha—had all made it. The rest were crying, scowling with anger, or staring ahead stoically, in shock or deep in planning their survival strategy.

Fenity slowly eased her grip on the garments, testing their weight and its effect on her balance before fully letting go. Without the ground to support the extra fabric, it was as if the layers were trying to rip the skin from her bones down to the ground. Pulling, straining, her body contorted with gravity. Sweat dripped down her legs and pooled under her arms and chest.

The crowd loved it. Money exchanged hands and cheers intensified each time a contestant swayed or shifted—all courtly etiquette and propriety discarded.

Well, it wouldn't be her. She poked a tentative toe to the edges of her small pillar, ensuring she stood at its very center, just in case. Then she stood as tall as she could, chin held high, and posed as a phony queen.

Don't lock your knees.

Renic's words from before had her bending slightly, though what importance this held, she couldn't say. It was more comfortable, like the long hours she spent waiting for prey to cross her path. He watched her, hands still gripping the banister. The king and queen had left the balcony—probably too boring now that it had become a waiting game.

Fenity locked eyes with Renic, absorbing his silent strength and distracting herself from the ache in her back and the stifling heat.

The hours ticked by. Shadows moved across the arena with the shifting sun. Onlookers came and went, returning with food and drink. The savory smells simultaneously sent her mouth watering and her stomach churning.

An attendant offered Renic refreshment, but he shook his head, keeping his eyes on Fenity. He was in this with her.

A scream sounded across the arena. Fenity wrenched her gaze in time to see the contestant normally in pink toppling off her pillar. But she wasn't the one who screamed. She was unconscious as she fell. Her body landed in a sickening heap. Attendants rushed to revive her, then carried her from the arena.

A few moments later, two more contestants fell in the same unconscious manner—one right beside her. Fenity reached out, as if she could do anything but watch. The female woke up as she hit, crying out in agony.

What was happening? An onlooker with energy trying to hedge the bets? She scanned the crowd, but the excitement had kicked them into a frenzy, people rushing back to their seats, more money exchanging hands.

She looked to Renic for answers. Once he caught her eye, he slowly raised his knee above the banister and quickly tapped it before lowering it back down.

Don't lock your knees.

That was why the contestants were passing out. She ensured her knees were still bent.

An intensity drew her attention, and she found Sarafine scowling at her. The female shifted her gaze to Renic before looking away. She'd seen. She knew Renic had helped her.

How much longer could this go on? It had to end soon, and the winner would be whoever kept their poise the best, right?

Or was it really down to the last female standing? How sick was this?

The sun set fully, and only magelights and torches lit the space, orange light mixing with white, leaving dark shadows rippling over the columns.

"I can't do it," the female directly across from her called out. "Let me down. I'm going to fall." She swayed. The crowd cheered, almost willing her to tumble. Her pillar slowly lowered, and the female nearly went over the edge. She barely caught her balance, much to the crowd's disappointment, but she fell to her knees once safely on the ground. Two attendants helped her from the arena.

It was as if her actions gave the rest permission to do the same. Cries of mercy and relief rippled across the arena. Pillars lowered. Females crouched and clutched the edges for balance. Some didn't make it to the ground, toppling backward halfway down. Cheers mixed with cringes and collective gasps as so many quit at once. One in three had their pillars lowered and were escorted out, heads hanging in shame and exhaustion.

Fenity imagined what awaited them on the other side. Being stripped of these layers of inferno. Gulping down sweet, cold water. Throwing themselves on a pillow-top lounger, eating fruits and sandwiches while servants fanned their heated skin.

The temptation to follow their lead was real. She didn't have to look to know Renic was watching her, willing her not to give up. Her neck ached too much to turn and see. The weight of the golden crown grew worse and worse.

When the dust and crowd settled, Fenity counted the remaining contestants. Fourteen left out of thirty-nine.

And of course, Sarafine was one of them. Along with Nisha and Illeya.

It had been fine to pretend she was okay as the day wore

on. But now it was more than just her neck that ached. Her limbs trembled. The ache of hunger and thirst competed with her aching back. The heavy cape weighed her down, trying to topple her backward. The combined wretchedness of all of that was nothing compared to the chainmail sending constant pressure on her limbs as if trying to drive her into the very stone she stood upon.

Her tongue dragged like sandpaper through her dry mouth. Eventually, she had to admit the black spots floating in her peripheral were more than mere shadows, and definitely not a good sign. The room swayed if she moved her eyes too much, so she stared straight ahead.

Another contestant cried out and collapsed from her pillar. Fenity had lost count. Her misery was such that she secretly cheered with each one, bringing her that much closer to ripping out of this cage they called the queen's regalia. She vowed right then and there to never wear them again. Even if she became queen. They couldn't make her—could they? Well, if she had any say in it, this would never be part of the next Strife.

The room lightened, and she blinked, trying to make sense of it. Had she fallen asleep? She scanned the crowd, which had thinned considerably, leaving only those willing to face the discomfort of sleeping on a hard tier to keep their coveted seats.

A whole night had passed while she sweated and shook.

A horn sounded through the dead quiet of the arena. Fenity's body spasmed with shock. Her knees buckled. Before she could fall backward, she threw herself into a crouch and gripped the edge of the pillar.

Her heart pounded, adrenaline rising her from her stupor. Steadying herself, she achingly rose back to a stand as the herald spoke, his voice piercing the still-brightening night.

"At last, we have reached our final ten contestants. Our mighty king has invited our allies to the west to share in the rest of the festivities." He extended his puffy-sleeved arms out to both sides of the arena. The horn blared again, but she was ready this time.

The crowd murmured as torchlight appeared from each alcove around the top of the arena. Pounding footsteps echoed unseen down the hallways. From each archway, a warrior in battle armor emerged bearing a torch, and behind streamed lines of creatures Fenity had only seen recently in books. Gnomes. They looked like fae, only rounder and less than half as tall with longer and wider ears. While gnomes had good relations with the fae, each stuck to their own lands.

"We welcome the Westland Gnomes." The herald made a dramatic bow as the gnomes filed in, filling the back rows the fae had vacated for closer seats. They watched the fae as curiously as the fae watched them.

The females wore simple dresses layered with fabric and belted with various-sized bags. While the males wore looser robes and bulky boots, with daggers at their sides. Some wore hats that made them appear taller. All the fabrics were colors of the earth—greens, browns, deep blues, and pinks. There were no children, but the youngest among them had large, endearing eyes, as if they hadn't grown into them yet.

They stared in awe around the arena, some casting distrustful eyes at the royals on the balcony. But Fenity also caught a lot of them looking at her more than the other contestants.

This was the show they came to see, right? But there was nothing to distinguish her from the others. Even her red hair was mostly hidden under the exquisite crown and fluffy fur of her queen's robe—the same as all the females.

Soon, the trail of newcomers ended, and the excitement

died down. When nothing else happened, no other announcements, her shoulders drooped. She'd hoped the final ten would earn them some reprieve. A chance to rest and eat and drink.

Ten out of thirty-nine. She breathed deeply, chasing some of the nausea away. She could make it.

Fenity tilted her eyes to the balcony, and her dry mouth dropped open. Renic wasn't there. He'd been her rock. She'd just assumed he would never leave. Craning her neck, she whimpered with the sharp cramp, but spotted him. Seated further back beside the gnome king and queen. He spoke while they listened, staring ahead at the contestants. King Sidian and Queen Lara lounged in their thrones, ignoring the lot of them.

The remaining contestants seemed more composed with the watching gnomes. Where once they rolled their shoulders or bent to massage cramping muscles, now they stood still and poised as queens.

But the fae in the front rows...

Fenity tilted her head. Her skin pebbled despite being overheated.

The fae leaned forward as if a force pulled them toward the arena. Where they'd been half-asleep before, now their attention was hyper-focused, gazes alternating between the contestants, the herald, and the royal balcony.

Tension filled the air, thick as the sun's rays warming the space even more as it rose higher in the sky. The contestants felt it too. Heads swiveled now, knowing something was wrong but unable to find the source.

Sarafine. She'd known about every test before it came, somehow, as had her friends.

When Fenity met Sarafine's gaze, she stared right back. Her mouth curled into a confident smirk. She pulled her arms out from under the heavy robe and held them up at her sides. Waiting for something, something she knew was coming.

Fenity copied her. She risked a glance toward Renic, but just as her eyes found his, full of fear and foreboding, a horn blared from the herald's platform.

Excited yells roared out from the fae. They stood, reared back their arms, and lobbed projectiles into the arena.

Fruit, rolls, rotten vegetables, and unidentifiable things hurtled through the air toward the contestants.

Fenity's heartbeat tripled. The buzz of energy sparked all around the arena. Her muscles tensed as she braced herself. It was all she could do.

The melee rained down around her, splattering into the sandy ground, exploding against columns, but some found their mark. Something smashed into the side of her cape, putrid liquid splashing her arms.

A contestant screamed as she fell. Fenity couldn't turn to see who it was. More food and objects pelted into her back. The thickness of the robe and skirts, along with the chainmail, absorbed most of the impact, but with her back to the crowd, she couldn't anticipate where the next object might strike.

With a split-second thought, she spun around on the pedestal, facing the crowd more fully. The weight of the robe, now sodden with putrid juices, nearly dragged her off-balance, but since her arms were already free of the confines of the cape, she splayed them for balance.

The fae in front of her took her action as a challenge. Their throws became more precise. But now she could use her arms. A lord in fine dress flung a giant mushroom cap toward her middle. She lifted her arm like a shield, and it whacked into her bone. It hurt, but the impact didn't affect her balance.

Sweat dripped down her face as she played this sick game of keep-away, blocking moldy rolls and old food with her arms, pivoting to maintain her balance when they struck her legs, and dodging and weaving where she could.

The smell overpowered her, and she gagged.

Several more screams sounded around the arena, followed by the cheers of the fae. The gnomes watched the spectacle, seeming just as horrified as she was. Hands over mouths, wide eyes taking in the scene. This was why her parents hadn't come. Somehow, they'd known and had been too afraid to tell her. Thank the trees the fae weren't using any energy against the contestants. Who knew what powers these noble families possessed?

It was sick. This whole contest. The king. Renic for not speaking out about this. The females for what they allowed themselves to become—for cheating, conniving, working against each other. And, truth be told, she was sick with herself. How had it come to this? She'd quit here and now to prove a point if there wasn't so much on the line. Her family.

Her truemate.

A loud splat and a cheer drew Fenity's attention. Moona had used her energy to create a shield around herself. She stood, perfectly clean and unaffected, while food harmlessly struck and fell around her. The fae near her worked themselves into a frenzy, going for the unprotected podium instead, but it was too sturdy to be affected by rotten food.

Movement caught Fenity's eye. Her arm came up just in time to block a tomato from hitting her face. The juices exploded into her eyes. She cried out from the burning, vision immediately blurring. She rubbed pulp from her face, gagging at the putrid stench. Something large and hard slammed into her stomach. The air burst from her, and she threw her weight forward, barely avoiding being toppled backward. Something smacked into her head. The queen's crown flew, bouncing on the ground.

Fenity crouched, gripping the podium and blinking

stinging tears from her eyes. The fae turned feral. They'd found their weak mark.

Food of all kinds, and even small objects, hurled her way. She could only hang on and endure now. Slowly, she pivoted her hands and feet until she was facing away, her back once again bearing the impact.

Something hard slammed her in the back of the head, and she cried out. Stinging pain flared, and warm wetness seeped from her scalp.

A loud roar brought a whimper to her lips and a temporary halt to the flinging rubbish. She knew that voice, but she didn't dare raise her head and expose her face to the onslaught.

Across the way, Sarafine buzzed with energy, food turned to ash before her or was swept away by wind, though plenty still made it through.

Moona stood smug on her pedestal, rot and now rocks piling below. But then her eyes went wide, lips parting in horror. She lifted shaking arms, reaching forward, feeling for something. And then it became clear what had happened—her shield had failed, energy spent. The fae realized it too. Moona turned and ducked just as a potato hit her on the shoulder. Their frenzy renewed. It took mere moments before the onslaught pitched Moona forward off the pedestal. She landed on her side, hissing in pain.

The projectiles came to Fenity again. Hitting. Stinging. Flying past her or jolting the podium as they struck just below.

The arena spun. The yells blended into one long, endless sound.

Fenity's arms shook, trembling from gripping the podium so tightly. But she sat crouched. Frozen.

Something huge slammed into her shoulder blades. Her fingers slipped from the podium. Something else hit her side, and she toppled sideways. She lunged as she fell, arms splayed over the top of the podium. Her body hung on the side, poofy skirt billowing backward. The chainmail's weight dragged her shaking body and slippery fingers across the slick stone.

Fenity cried out. More fae had joined the others in front of her, and they hurled their spoils on her limp, unprotected body. Her arms. Her exposed side. Her head. She tucked her face into her shoulder and hung on for her life.

If she fell, she lost. Her garments were too heavy, muscles too weak to climb back up. A hard vegetable hit her in the head, and her hair sprung free of its golden pins.

Her hands slipped. The gnomes gasped. With a screech of effort, she gripped the podium's edge. How many times had she hung from tree limbs just like this? But this was nothing like her days in the forest.

A scream pierced the arena, followed by a thud and feral cheers.

The horn blared, its loudness somehow penetrating the frenzy. The onslaught stopped. Quiet descended.

Her podium began lowering to the ground.

Was it over? Had she won?

It didn't matter. Her grip gave out, and she dropped to the ground, collapsing to her side in blessed exhaustion among the piles of refuse and debris.

Her eyes slipped closed.

"People of Alberry, and our distinguished Westland Gnomes, we have reached a significant moment." The herald's words carried, muffled—like her ears had been stuffed with dragonlily seeds. "We have our final two contestants of the Second Pillar of Faedom!"

No. No, it can't be.

"Lady Fenity Stormbrook of Solice, and Lady Sarafine Rivers of Alberry!"

The last two? What did that mean? Two winners?

Her limbs wouldn't quit spasming.

But the herald wasn't done. "As decreed by King Sidian, they will now be dressed for the decisive battle—a duel to proclaim the victor."

CHAPTER 31

*W*hat? Fenity pushed up from the filthy floor. *A duel.*

Across the arena, Sarafine didn't look much better, covered in debris and bleeding from several cuts, but she stood with perfect posture, as regal as a queen could be, covered in rotting filth.

But her face—she was as surprised as Fenity over the news. What determined who won? If one of them killed the other?

Further proof of King Sidian's twisted mind.

Arinia dropped to Fenity's side, hauling her to her feet along with some of her regular attendants. "Let's hurry. You only have as long as it takes to sweep the arena of debris."

Fenity tried to walk, but her legs wouldn't move right. So much standing in such a small square with no food or water, and her legs were impossibly weak. Her whole body screamed in pain. She wiped sweat off her brow, and her billowed sleeves came back red.

She finally risked a look at the balcony. Renic wasn't there.

But the gnome king and queen were. They watched her with a mix of horror and pity. They held her gaze until the tunnel's darkness overtook her.

Her head lolled onto Arinia's shoulder. The sound of cheering slowly lessened the deeper they went. But the stench followed her, clinging to her soiled queen's garments. A fortune in fine linens, someone's life work, ruined for the court's entertainment.

They turned into a room, bright compared to the sparse sconces lighting the hallway. It was a sitting room with chairs and chaises, and a large floral-patterned rug in the middle.

And Renic.

Like a fire lit from within, Fenity's entire world seemed brighter.

"Fenity." He froze, brow crumpling, and then rushed to her. She collapsed against him, holding in her tears. "I'm sorry, so sorry." He didn't react to her food-caked clothes or the putrid smell, but caressed her hair, pulling chunks of debris from the lengths. "I couldn't protect you. I've never felt so helpless. So insignificant."

"Prince Renic, our champion needs to sit." Arinia pulled up a chair, but Fenity didn't move. "And some discretion?" she added in a low whisper.

Renic shook his head, holding her tighter. Beyond him, Galan stepped into the room, standing guard beside the door. Was that worry in his tight shoulders?

"Not your fault. I told you not to reveal anything," Fenity whispered. How much had he known? From his surprised face, not all of it. He hadn't done anything to stop it, but what could he have done? "You are my safe place. I never want to leave."

The slosh of water had her prying her eyes open and lifting her face from Renic's chest. She couldn't snatch the cup from

Arinia's hand fast enough. Never had she known such thirst, such need for water. The forest always provided, if one knew where to look.

She gulped it down. It was cold, and bitter, and everything. But it wasn't enough. "More please." She shoved the cup toward Arinia, then collapsed into a chair.

"In a bit, love, in a bit. Don't make yourself sick." Arinia took the empty cup and waved her arm. "We must prepare you."

Her attendants, who waited discreetly by the wall, surrounded her. They gushed and congratulated, a rare thing for them to speak to her. But she could only stare into Renic's eyes. They pulled and tugged, straps and ribbons and layers coming free, slipping over her head and shimmying down her body. Gold piled up on a cart beside her.

The raging inferno held in place by the chainmail and all the crushing garments abated by degrees with each layer gone. Breathing came easier. Air rushed in, chilling her blazing, sweaty skin.

Renic passed her bits of food she ate but didn't taste.

"My prince, we discussed this," Arinia said, approaching with some bandages. "It's not safe for her if this gets out."

Understanding broke through Fenity's fatigued mind. He wasn't supposed to be here. And he'd come anyway.

"If this gets out, I'll know whose fault it is." Renic glared at the attendants until they paused in their de-dressing and bowed their heads. Galan stepped from the wall, hand on the hilt of his sword.

"You know they will never tell. I hand-picked them for their discretion." Arinia sounded hurt at the implication, but she'd said it before herself. They didn't owe their loyalty to Renic.

Arinia dripped something on Fenity's head that made her

hiss and recoil. Renic stomped closer, but Fenity was too weak to chastise him.

"Easy, my prince. This cut needs sewing or she can't fight." Arinia took a needle and thread and began stitching Fenity's cut. Oddly, it didn't sting as much.

"These drops and the healing herbs in that water ought to help, at least enough to get you through this battle."

No healer this time, then.

Her words sunk dread into Fenity's stomach, knotting it. "Was that real? Do I really have to battle Sarafine? Her energy is *powerful*." Could Fenity keep from portaling if it came down to protecting her life? Die at Sarafine's hand, or execution for opening a portal. And execute her mata, too. No. She couldn't allow that to happen.

Her mind flashed to Marek and his safe estate, a different world where they didn't pit contestants against each other to compete for one male's hand.

"Historically, energy isn't allowed in duels," Renic said, passing her another morsel of food. "I doubt Sarafine has any left, anyway. She used it to keep herself upright during the final ten."

Fenity gripped the food instead of eating it —bread baked with cheese and fresh herbs. "What kind of contest is this, Renic? How does any of this prove poise or worthiness of your hand?" Her anger woke her up. Gave her strength.

Arinia finished bandaging up her head and moved to some smaller scrapes. Bare-sleeved and wiped of filth and juices, the blooming bruises all over her body were like a second skin.

"I didn't know about the battle." A muscle ticked in Renic's jaw. "My pata has been keeping things from me." He glanced at Galan, some silent exchange.

"But did you know about the plan for the so-called courtiers to pelt their daughters and future queen with trash, injuring us, making us bleed?" She didn't hold back the bite in her tone.

Misery shrouded him. "No. The high rulers have been eager to sway the outcome. Pata said this safely allowed them to. He didn't tell me in time to stop—"

"And can't you see why he didn't?" Arinia interrupted, not stopping her ministrations. "Even if King Sidian couldn't have predicted you'd find your truemate in this contest, you've grown up with most of those females. Their families spent their lives making sure you were close, that you were friends, so that one day, when the Strife came, they'd have the advantage. Would a good prince keep things like duels and danger from his friends?"

Renic's eyes narrowed. Fenity could see his mind realigning his entire childhood as nothing but a staged parody. She gripped his hand.

Arinia's lips thinned in sympathy. "Our queen needs to be strong and diplomatic. She must pass the five pillars *on her own* and prove herself worthy, otherwise what's the point of the Strife?"

Renic shook his head. Fenity could tell he wanted to deny Arinia's words, just like she did. But they couldn't.

Her thoughts were all muddled. Should the prince have the right to choose, his judgment being the final and only say in who was worthy to be a queen? Or were all these tests necessary to save the faedom from a weak ruler and perhaps weak heirs?

Arinia pulled her to a stand, and an attendant brought a mirror. They'd stripped away the outer layers of skirts, sleeves, capes, and jewels, leaving mostly clean garments underneath. The thick clothing offered protection and was still overly fancy in the white and embroidered gold. It was almost a warrior's garb.

"King Sidian thought this a punishment. Now it will be a benefit." Arinia motioned to the attendants. With Galan's help, they lifted the clean chainmail back over Fenity's head, instantly weighing her down and sending her knees shaking. Arinia secured a leather belt around her waist. Without the cape and hoopskirt, the weight was bearable.

Sturdy boots laced up her calves replaced the embroidered shoes. They carefully combed her hair, leaving it down in loose, soft curls. Fenity used a strip of leather to tie it out of the way. Thank the stars, no more pins. An attendant buckled a sheath to her side, and Galan presented a sword to Renic. Not his sword.

Fenity's eyes went wide.

Renic weighed the long silver weapon in his hands, then gave it a couple of swipes. The sword whistled through the air with the speed of his expert swings. He handed it to her, immediately weighing down her arms. It took three tries to get it into the sheath. This was no mere practice sword. No blunted edges or sheared tip. This was designed to kill.

Renic exchanged a glance with Galan that bordered on fear. "You've never handled a sword?"

"My pata didn't see the need to train me after I became proficient with a bow and knife."

"A knife?" Renic reached into his boot and pulled out a small dagger. He tried to hand it to her, but Arinia stopped him.

"No, my prince. She's only allowed the herb water, the small meal, and a sword."

Fenity shook her head. "This is insane. What if I refuse this barbaric and pointless duel?"

A horn blared in the distance. A door guard poked his head in, bowing when he saw the prince. "Time to go, your ladyship."

Fenity's heart beat into her skull. "I can't win this. How do I win?" Sarafine would have trained with the sword. She'd trained in everything.

"With your strongest asset," Arinia said, ushering her out the door and away from a grief-locked prince. "Your mind."

"You can do this, Fenity." Renic forced confidence into his words, but Galan kept him from following. He couldn't risk getting caught. She hadn't held him one last time. She hadn't told him she loved him.

Fenity shook her head, pushing all thoughts from it except for one foot in front of the other and how she was going to win this battle.

Sarafine may have trained with a sword, but she was weak, too. She'd spent her energy to get this far. Maybe that meant she was even *weaker*. Being spent of both strength and energy had to be a disadvantage. Fenity had slept like the dead after expending all her energy portaling Marek around.

What else? There was sand. She had to be better at moving over sand and uneven terrain than Sarafine was.

"Good luck, my dear." Arinia stopped at the tunnel's entrance, tears and dread shining in her eyes.

Fenity didn't miss a beat. She didn't let the exhaustion drag her down like she wanted. Didn't let the dulled pain of an aching, injured body show.

She walked out of that tunnel with her chin high and the crowd roaring. She hated all of them. They hurt her for sport. Her life and well-being meant nothing to them, short of how much coin they could make from her failure. But she wasn't here for them. They were the king's pets. For the rest of the fae world and the races not allowed here, for the others like her, forced to hide their true selves—this was for them. She'd fight so the next queen wouldn't be someone who'd forget them.

Directly across from her, Sarafine held herself in the same

way, looking confident in her matching attire, though no chainmail. Her bare arms sported fewer bruises. The arena was cleared of rubbish and fresh sand covered most of the remaining rancid juices. The columns had been raised back up.

Good. She could use them.

They both stopped in the middle of the arena, keeping well apart. The horn blared again, and the cheers and exchange of money subsided.

"A duel to proclaim the victor," the herald announced. His giddiness was like a cloak around him. "No energy. No mercy. The unyielding contestant will win the Second Pillar of Faedom." He raised his arms, and the crowd roared their approval, their blood lust not satisfied by simply throwing rotten food.

A servant approached the railing by the herald's platform, motioning him over. With a scowl, the herald leaned over while the servant whispered something in his ear. The satisfied smile returned. Fenity's palms began to sweat.

"Before we begin," the herald's voice boomed, "some adjustments must be made."

Royal attendants spilled from a doorway—the same team who'd dressed her before. They only approached Fenity, keeping clear of Sarafine. Fenity tensed. With efficient speed, they lifted the chainmail off and refastened the belt.

They carried the chainmail away to thunderous applause while Fenity glared up at the king. He didn't even look at her, conversing with his son, while Renic tried to pay attention to him. There was no doubt King Sidian realized his punishment had turned beneficial to her, so he'd changed the rules to suit his whim.

Fine. Now, when she won, no one could say she had an advantage. If she won.

Sarafine widened her stance, her face narrowed in single-minded focus. Fenity swallowed hard. Was she about to die? Would Sarafine give her a chance to yield?

Were her parents here, praying to the gods to spare her life? Was Renic doing the same, watching over her from the balcony above?

She squeezed her eyes shut. *Focus.*

The horn blared again. Sarafine drew her sword, raised the tip level with her body, and began circling Fenity in a slight crouch. There was nothing but determination in her calculating eyes. This was the moment she'd trained for, been raised for. The moment to win. The moment her family likely had ingrained in her to take with both hands and squeeze until the life drained from everything else around her.

There would be no hesitation from Sarafine. No quarter. No doubts about her current task—no matter how insane this whole thing was.

So Fenity couldn't allow doubt and hesitation either. It was just like hunting back home—she could do this. She drew her heavy sword and held it up, mimicking Sarafine's stance. Her tired muscles strained in protest. Maybe Sarafine would burn the last of her strength circling and never attacking.

With a yell, Sarafine charged and attacked. Fenity blocked with a slight shift of her elbow but stumbled back a step. The power of the blow vibrated through her sword and into her arm, numbing her bones.

Quick as lightning, Sarafine spun and swung to Fenity's newly exposed side. Fenity cried out and somehow blocked the hit with a contortion of her arms and body. Sarafine was like the large forest cat she'd stumbled upon once, circling her, fangs exposed to rip out her throat.

And just like that predator, Sarafine didn't stop. With Fenity's arms and body now off-balance, she jabbed at her middle.

Fenity jumped back, and the sword sliced through layers of fabric.

The hits came so fast, Fenity could only move—not think. Her mind detached from her movements. Her body moved on pure survival instinct with what her pata taught her of knife fighting. Block. Block. Spin and run away. Pivot. Jump sideways. Block again. Despite it all, her body was bleeding from several shallow cuts she had no time to examine.

She breathed, letting her limbs take over and willing her brain to stay out of it. She'd been *good* with a knife, but her pata had stopped training her with the sword after the basics, and this wasn't the same. If she paused to think ahead, the cuts would be worse than shallow and she'd die.

No matter what she did, she couldn't gain an advantage. Sarafine was slowly bleeding her to death. When should she yield?

Her boots scrunched over loose sand. Her panting breaths whistled in and out in time with her movements. Block. Bend. Jab. Retreat. Sweat and blood flung with her pivots. The crowd was a constant roar in the background.

Her back hit something hard, and she ducked as Sarafine's sword swung at her neck. The weapon glanced off the column, leaving a chunk missing from the ornamentation.

Fenity lunged, putting the column between her and her enemy. Her mind caught up with her, exhaustion weighing the tip of the sword to the ground. She was soaked in sweat. Blood dripped from even more cuts on her arms and sides she didn't remember receiving. They stung. Faces blurred in the background.

But Sarafine was clear as day, panting, free of blood, but not advancing for once.

This couldn't go on. As strong as Fenity was from all her days in the forest, Sarafine was better trained. Fenity couldn't just block hits all day, or eventually Sarafine would win on pure skill.

She had to end it before her strength failed, which wouldn't be long. It was time to try something Sarafine wouldn't expect.

And hope it didn't get her killed.

CHAPTER 32

On the other side of the column, Sarafine caught her breath.

Fenity tightened her shaking grip on the sword's hilt. It was now or never. "Even if you win this pillar, you still lose." She stepped closer, carefully keeping the pillar between them.

Sarafine chuckled—a tired, humorless thing. "So you've accepted you can't beat me and have switched tactics, hmm? I admit, I thought you would have done so sooner." She lifted her sword, sidestepping so she could meet Fenity's eyes. "Please, enlighten me how I'll still lose even after I kill you."

Kill?

"You're going to love this." Fenity lowered her voice to a quiet whisper, much too quiet for the cheering spectators to hear. "Renic and I are truemates."

The smirk dropped from Sarafine's lips.

Fenity smiled, putting all the vileness she felt toward Sarafine behind it. "He'll never belong to you. He can never love you, now that he's found me. Now that we have found each other. He won't choose you. Kill me, and he'll pine for me the rest of his days."

Shocked calculation flooded Sarafine's features, as she likely thought back through all their interactions, the times she'd caught them together, the moments Sarafine knew they'd been with each other.

Sarafine's sword arm finally trembled. The doubt wormed its way in, rocking her confidence. Fenity had promised Renic not to tell, but this was the one card she had to throw Sarafine off her game.

When Sarafine looked to the balcony to confirm what Fenity already knew—Renic gripping the edge, body, mind, and soul fixated on Fenity and this bloody battle—Fenity charged.

Sarafine blocked, but this time her sword gave under the weight of the attack. Fenity had memorized Sarafine's pattern, otherwise the next jab would have gutted her. She jumped back, smacking the strike to the side, then she struck. Her sword sliced into Sarafine's shoulder, splitting her skin open. Sarafine cried out, stumbling away with her sword raised to block whatever Fenity might do next.

Fenity's stomach roiled. She gaped at the blood streaming down Sarafine's non-dominant arm. This wasn't right. Nothing about this was right.

She couldn't hurt this female. And Sarafine would never yield.

"Sarafine." Fenity swallowed bile. "I don't want this. You're a worthy female. We don't have to kill each other. Let's call a truce." Ridiculous. Wasteful. Pointless. She nearly screamed her frustration.

Sarafine's face hardened. "You don't believe you stand a chance of winning, do you? A stray forest dweller soiling our palace with her dirty manners and untrained flailings?" She attacked, harder and faster than before.

Fenity could only defend, feet scrambling back as she blocked, pivoted, took the hits, until her back hit the arena wall. She hadn't expected it to be there. The surprise ruined her rhythm. Sarafine's jab struck her stomach. Deep.

A cry ripped from Fenity's mouth. Skin split. Blood gushed. Pain bloomed with a burst that flashed white stars in her eyes. Her energy rushed to the surface, but she barely held it at bay.

Sarafine left no time to regroup before she swung the sword, quick as lightning, for Fenity's neck.

Fenity threw herself to the ground just in time. A scream of pain ripped from her lips. Sarafine's sword slammed into the stone wall. And burst out of Sarafine's grip.

The sword skidded over the sand, and Sarafine lunged for it.

Fenity didn't give her that chance. She launched herself, slamming her injured body into her enemy. Sarafine came down hard on her back, Fenity on top of her. Black spots bloomed in Fenity's vision.

Sarafine immediately grappled.

Fenity shoved her sword against her throat. "Yield!"

The crowd's roar nearly drowned her out. But they didn't matter. It was just Fenity and Sarafine.

Sarafine stilled, rage simmering in her eyes. "Do it, then. Take your victory. You'll bleed out soon enough."

Fenity didn't dare move her focus to check. She didn't need to. The lightheadedness and sudden absence of pain told her all she needed.

Sarafine pushed her neck into the blade, drawing a line of blood. "Now my parents can live with the guilt over what they've forced me to become."

Fenity's eyes softened, and she moved the sword back a hair. "Your life is more than the Strife. It's more than your parents' expectations and the pressures of the court. You deserve to live it, even if it won't be as queen." Her words were soft, but she didn't slacken her grip. "No one has to die. Let's call a truce."

Sarafine scoffed. "You've already won. Yielding now will only further humiliate me and my family." She bucked, forcing Fenity to further ease back the sword to avoid injuring her. "Just do it! You hear them. They scream for blood. Do it or I'll tell everyone what you are."

The fae were on their feet, pumping their arms, baring teeth with their shouting. Behind them, the gnomes watched with open mouths and terrified eyes.

Fenity shut her eyes as dizziness assaulted her. Her belly ached beyond agony, but she still didn't see what kind of damage had been done. If she didn't know about it, it couldn't cripple her now when she needed every bit of courage.

"So be it." Planting her feet on either side of Sarafine, she hauled her up, screaming through the pain in her stomach. Gripping Sarafine from behind, she held the sword to her throat with a shaking arm. The sword was so, so heavy. An elbow to the gut and Sarafine wouldn't have to wait for her to bleed out.

But Sarafine didn't struggle as Fenity led them to the middle of the arena. In the balcony, King Sidian, Queen Lara, and the gnome king and queen joined Renic at the railing, ready to witness the closing scene of the show. Because that was all this was.

Renic's beautiful face had drained of color. His fear was plain to see, even from this distance. He felt everything she felt.

"My king," Fenity shouted. The fae quieted in expectation. "As Lady Sarafine, in her bravery, refuses to yield, I beg your mercy upon this daughter of the court." Sarafine growled in outrage. The fae booed and cheered in equal measure. "She is my equal, and I cannot take her life any more than I can take my own." She nearly screamed to be heard over the noise. "I will do as you, Her Majesty, and His Highness will."

She used the sword as a cane, the tip in the gravel, then bowed as her knees buckled, pulling Sarafine with her. Sarafine glared, eyes roving for her discarded sword, but she didn't go for it.

It was all lies. She wouldn't kill Sarafine no matter what King Sidian decided. And if Sarafine attacked her, she'd win handily. But Fenity had brought Renic into the king's decision for a reason. His opinion could sway the outcome. Fenity kept her head bowed, not daring to see what transpired above. An alarming amount of red pooled beneath her knees. Without looking, she pressed her hand tightly over her wound, a whimper escaping.

Around her, the fae gave their own opinion, but the cheers of agreement were overtaking the boos of disapproval. Despite their ferocity, they hadn't come here to witness death today. Would the king listen to his court?

Sarafine seethed, one hand covering her own bleeding wound on her shoulder. "All you've done is make yourself look weak."

"It wouldn't be necessary if you'd just yield. But if it works, I've saved your life." *And my soul.*

The horn blared, and the crowd quieted. Fenity slowly raised her head. King Sidian stood at the balcony railing alone. The rest of the royals had taken their seats, and Fenity could only see the tops of their heads from this vantage.

The king raised his arms, and the last of the fae quieted. The gnomes' terror had given way to pointing and talking amongst each other. They were as invested as the rest of them.

Fenity held her breath. She remained *very* conscious of the sword in her grip in case the king ordered them to continue fighting. She didn't want to hurt Sarafine, but she wouldn't forfeit her chance to win a pillar either.

"Lady Sarafine's unwillingness to yield is an admirable trait in a queen and a direct reflection of impeccable poise. As is offering mercy to a righteous opponent." King Sidian's gaze swept over his people. "A bit of luck goes a long way, too." He finally focused his attention on Fenity, and with a wave of his arm, retreated to his throne.

Fenity's breath caught. What did that mean? The room spun around them. Sarafine exchanged a blank look with her.

A horn blared, and the herald took his place at the podium below the balcony. "The winner of the Second Pillar of Faedom is Lady Fenity Stormbrook."

Gold glitter and colorful confetti burst around the arena with the staticky feel of energy driving it into the crowd. The fae erupted into cheers, the gnomes clapping politely behind them. Attendants poured through the openings.

Relief shot through Fenity's limbs, sapping the last of her energy. It took every scrap and the aid of the sword just to stand and pretend one last moment of poise. She'd won. She'd won the Second Pillar.

And all she wanted was to collapse. Despite the pressure she held to her stomach, blood flowed from the wound at a rate that made her heart trip over itself.

"This doesn't make us friends." Sarafine stumbled to her feet. It was as if she was ashamed to let someone in, someone as low-born as Fenity. Or maybe she really saw Fenity's mercy as weakness even if it was to save her life. But Sarafine had shown her mercy, too, or Fenity never would have won.

"I saved you from the trolls, and you kept my secret." A stab of pain halted her words. "Now I've saved your life again, even if it was from your own stubborn pride. Consider it a life-debt, if that makes you feel better about it. I may need something from you one day. You'll remember this and be bound to pay it." A favor owed by someone as powerful as Sarafine would be a priceless thing. Besides, when she became Renic's bride, Sarafine would be part of her court. Best to have her on her side, rather than an enemy.

The attendants reached them then, and Sarafine left with only one quick nod.

"Well done, my love, well done." Arinia wrapped a helping arm around her.

"No, not yet." Fenity pulled away. Hand pressed into her pulsating stomach, cuts still bleeding on her arms—and who knew where else— she walked on her own, chin high, back to the tunnel. She was well out of sight of the onlookers and the king when she fell against the wall, then slid down to the ground. The black spots bloomed larger.

Arinia and the other hovering attendants rushed to her side. "Healer!" Arinia cried out.

A female approached wearing close-fitted white fabric with long sleeves, the healer who'd tended her burns before. She placed a hand on Fenity's forehead, then wrapped a hasty bandage around her middle, causing Fenity to whimper. "Carry her to her rooms. It's a miracle she's still conscious."

"I'll take her." Renic's voice pierced through her pain-filled haze. He lifted her—gentle and mindful—before anyone could even bow at his presence.

She was home. Nothing bad would happen with his arms around her. His gait was quick and even, doing his best to hurry and not jostle her. Even so, it hurt. Her rooms were a long way from the arena. She dozed in and out, now that her body was no longer alert for danger. It was a good sign the healer thought she could recover in her room instead of the infirmary.

Fenity awoke with a cry as Renic placed her on the bed. The change in position pulled on her wounds. Arinia ushered out all the worried attendants who'd followed, including Galan. Fenity glimpsed her parents' anxious faces before the door shut and it was just the healer and Renic.

"Your Highness," the healer said sternly, almost as if she was bracing for an argument. "I must undress her ladyship. Don't worry, she's in capable hands."

Renic stiffened. "You're the best healer in the palace, Fetam, which is why I summoned you. But I'm not leaving."

Fetam bowed her head.

Fenity reached for his hand, and he gripped hers back like a lifeline. He didn't let go as Fetam tended her arms using healing energy instead of stitches, but his face turned pale, jaw clenched and ticking. He looked ready to do battle.

She'd heard truemates couldn't handle their partner in danger or in pain, that it could drive them to unnecessary or extreme measures. He needed a distraction before Fetam got to the worst of her wounds.

"Ren—Prince Renic, I'll be fine. Would you mind keeping my parents and Arinia company while Healer Fetam sees to my wounds?" As much as his comforting presence helped, his being here was going to become less and less explainable to the courts. Their secret had too many eyes on it already.

"I—what? But..." Renic glanced from her to Fetam to the door. "If that is what you wish."

"I'll be alright." She squeezed his hand again before letting go.

Fetam had brewed a bitter tea she now lifted to Fenity's cracked lips. "I'll summon you as soon as she's rested."

Renic gave them a tight smile, but reluctantly left the room, unease etched on his features.

Fetam didn't remark on his behavior as Fenity expected her

to. She quickly began removing garments, cutting some away when necessary, easing the layers from Fenity's wrecked body.

Fenity gasped, and wooziness assaulted her when she finally saw her stomach wound. It was deep, closer to her right side and higher than she thought. Blood newly bubbled, oozing onto the expensive bedding. She lay back on the pillow and closed her eyes, focusing on breathing, the rush of air in and out—not the pain, not the blood.

"Good," Fetam said, placing her hand on her forehead. "It's okay to sleep. If you were a typical patient, I would bandage most of these wounds to heal in their own time. Not this wound, though. This wound would have ultimately been fatal. Even so, contestants of the Strife get a healer's full abilities. You'll feel better soon."

Fenity's eyelids cracked open as energy pulled from the air around her and from within Fetam. Its warmth and life called to her own, but exhaustion kept it in check. A feeling like a nearby lightning strike but longer and without pain flowed from Fetam's palm to Fenity's body. She couldn't keep track as it split in different directions, seeking her injuries and healing as it went.

When the pain of each healed cut ceased to exist, Fenity relaxed further into the bed. It didn't hurt like she'd feared. The absence of each cut and bruise made her realize just how injured she truly was. And it was the pain still keeping her conscious. Her abdomen was last, and it was only partially healed when sweet oblivion took her.

CHAPTER 33

Fenity woke with a start, hand going to her now-absent wound. The room was darker, lit by soft sconces and candelabras. Someone had changed the bed linens and dressed her in a loose sleeping gown.

Fetam sat on an armchair beside the bed. Otherwise, the room was empty. Her head lifted from where it rested on her arm, and she handed Fenity a cup of lukewarm tea.

Fenity drank it eagerly, amazed at being alive. Sarafine tried to kill her, and nearly succeeded.

"You fought well, from what I heard. Your injuries healed with little trouble. A couple days of rest, hydration, and nourishment, and you'll feel even better." Fetam took the cup and handed her a biscuit. "Your parents and Arinia sat with you a while, but it's late. I sent them to sleep." She yawned, and Fenity nearly asked about Renic. Had he been here too? "There's a reason I waited for you to awaken. You're likely not even aware." She swallowed and sat closer, scooting to the edge of the chair.

Fenity's pulse jumped. "What?"

"You're pregnant."

Fenity blinked. Her hand went to her mouth, open with shock. "That's impossible." Fae took years to conceive. *Years.* Even truemates didn't conceive so fast, or at least she thought they didn't. "Pregnant?" She beseeched Fetam, who gave a firm nod of confirmation. Fenity's hand dropped from her mouth to her healed abdomen. "Stars, my injury. The baby—" She couldn't finish the sentence.

Fetam took her hand. "The baby is safe. Healthy. The blade missed your womb." Her voice was soothing, reassuring. "I assume you know who the sire is. If you had a mate or true-mate before the Strife, even if you weren't yet bound, you didn't have to compete. I hope your parents told you that." Fenity shook her head, but Fetam went on. "Regardless, I'm sure you're aware I can't allow you to continue to compete."

Fenity ripped her hand away. Shock struck her like an arrow. "I have to compete." She threw off the covers and rose to her feet. The room spun, but she gripped the headboard and waved Fetam's assistance away.

"Please sit. Let's talk about this." Fetam put light pressure on Fenity's arm, coaxing her to the chair.

Fenity shook her off. "You can't keep me from competing. I have to." Pregnancy didn't mean she couldn't continue. Her own mata was proof of that, working hard while Pata was often gone to battle.

"You know our customs. Even if the rules of the Strife permitted it, matas with child are sacred. The king, the court... no one would allow it. You can't even be an eligible contestant if you've borne a child before." Her expression pinched into pity, voice turning even gentler. "And Prince Renic won't choose a female impregnated by another male."

The dizziness cleared. Fenity let go of the bed and stood to her full height, which rose above Fetam. "Renic and I are true-mates. The child is his."

A child. *Renic's* child. *Her* child. *Their* child.

Fenity ignored Fetam, with her wide eyes and silent shock, and sat heavily on the edge of the bed. She'd imagined having a child with Renic one day, but she'd never thought it'd be this soon. What if she still lost the Strife? What if...

Fenity went still.

Would King Sidian get rid of Fenity so Renic could marry whoever won the strife?

Fenity's hands curled into fists, and her arms wrapped around her abdomen.

"Does King Sidian know you're truemates?" Fetam's words were heavy, as if she had reached the same realization.

"No. And no one can know about the baby. Not even Renic. He would pull me from the Strife to keep me safe, even if it meant I'd lose." He'd only worry about her. Give away their secret. She shook her head. "I'm not dropping out of the competition."

"The competition is dangerous. You might be injured again."

"Do you know what else is to come?" Fenity lifted her gaze.

"No, and I couldn't tell you if I did. But you're going to become ill. And how will you hide your progression?" Fetam raised a hand toward Fenity's middle.

"I'll figure it out." It was like the battle to the death on the arena floor all over again. She had to win at all costs. Fenity took Fetam's hands. "You don't owe me anything. You don't even know me. But, I'm begging you to keep my secret. You know what might happen if someone found out. Don't tell the king. Don't tell the prince. Please. My child must live. I must win my place at Renic's side." Her mind flung wildly for a way to convince this palace healer to lie to her king. "I can reward you once I'm queen."

"Lady Fenity..." Fetam glanced at the door.

"Please!" Tears leaked from Fenity's eyes. Desperate tears. She could run, flee now while the secret was still safe. She wouldn't have Renic, but her baby would be safe. She wouldn't even have to run—a portal to Marek or her sister's house near Diatem, and she'd be far away from the king's reach.

"Shhh." Fetam wrapped her in a hug. "I won't say anything. And I won't keep you from competing. But only if you allow me to monitor your health and progress."

"Thank you. Thank you." Fenity's whole body shook.

Fetam coaxed her into lying down. "I hate what the Strife does to you young females. The healers have treated more than battle wounds already. I've raised two daughters, and I wouldn't wish this upon them even for the chance at the prince's hand, even to become queen."

Fenity sighed long and hard. "Thank you for understanding. You must think I'm making a horrible decision."

Fetam frowned at the floor. "Unfortunately, I don't. This is the second Strife I've witnessed, and it follows all the old traditions. Traditions King Sidian won't idly let go. No one leaves, there's only one winner, and the king can change things to suit his whim." She hesitated. "Are you sure it's Prince Renic's? There's no one else it could be?"

Fenity's body tightened. "There's never been anyone else."

Fetam placed her hand on Fenity's forehead. "Then you *must* be truemates for it to have taken so easily. Rest now. I'll watch over you. I'll not speak a word." Her energy spiked, radiating into Fenity's body. She couldn't speak as sleep took her.

Fenity awoke with a warm arm over her and night still around her—two comforting embraces. Fetam's chair was empty. Fenity turned over, coming face to face with a sleeping prince. All the worry and fear from before was wiped away as his large eyes and perfect lips relaxed with sleep. His confident swagger and tender expressions were gone, too. It was just Renic, peaceful and content, snuggled into her, arm wrapped around her, with only the wind whistling against the windows, the crackle of a fire he must have lit in the hearth while she slept, and his soft breaths to fill the empty space. She pushed a lock of his hair back, and he nuzzled her palm in his sleep.

Pregnant. It was surreal. She carried their child, and it would kill her not to tell him. It would kill her when he found out she knew and kept it from him.

But it would kill her to have this child taken from her, or lose the chance to win his hand in the Strife. He wouldn't let her compete if he knew the truth.

She hoped he would understand one day.

Lying and playing their games wasn't her, but she would become what she needed to protect their baby. Her goals remained the same: win the Strife, earn Renic's hand, and live happily ever after.

If only it were so simple.

Renic's eyes fluttered open. He stared into her, a thousand emotions playing in his gaze, then he smiled and pulled her closer. "Fetam did a good job." Her long hair muffled his words. "Not even a scar."

She stiffened. "You looked?"

He ran his hand down her side, rising with the curve of her hips. "You have no idea how worried I've been. I was ready to tear down the palace walls to get to you. I could have sprouted wings and flown right off that balcony to save you from Sarafine's skill, and the gods wouldn't have been able to stop me. That's how close I came to losing my mind. Only Galan kept me from rushing into the arena and revealing our secret." He pressed his face into her neck. "So, yes, I looked. I had to make sure you were okay."

"I'm okay," she whispered, wrapping her arms around him, sinking her fingers into his hair and his back. "I'm okay as long as I have you."

"You'll always have me. I'll always protect you."

She pulled back just before he kissed her. Not always. He hadn't protected her in the arena. "You can't protect me from everything. This is *your* Strife. You didn't want Sarafine and me to fight, yet you had to allow it."

His inquisitive brow turned dark. "This is my Strife in that I will marry the winner, and I have some say in who that will be after the pillars are accounted for. But the king dictates what happens with the contests, as have the kings and queens before him." He wiped a hand over his face. "I begged my pata not to end it that way, but he wanted his spectacle. It's not up to me to allow or forbid what happens in the Strife. No inter-ference, remember?" His voice lowered to a whisper so soft it magnified the importance of his words. "If the validity of the winner is called into question, it could start a war. It has before."

She'd heard about that. A female had been the heir. The male who'd won her hand had won fairly, but the other rulers didn't like his family. They started rumors that he'd cheated, until too many believed the gossip, and fighting erupted. In the end, the only way to stop the war was to choose a new winner.

"I will win fairly. Then we won't have to whisper anymore. We won't have to hide anymore." She lifted her face and kissed him, sweetly at first. The kisses quickly turned hungry, desperate to forget everything but the two of them. Fear and longing collided, and emotions turned into want and need.

Their breaths came in pants, tongues dancing and hands roving.

Their hearts and bodies knew what their minds wouldn't speak—that this couldn't last. They would be caught or separated. He'd have to leave her to spend time with the other contestants who might try to kiss him or sleep with him. Nothing good ever lasted, so they would take this moment for what they could.

The room had turned a dark mauve with the slowly rising sun when his voice startled her awake. "How am I supposed to leave you here and pretend I don't feel *everything* for you? I can't even take my eyes off you in a crowded room." He lay on his back, shirtless, arms folded behind his head. "I've always been good at the game—the one where I pretend that what I want and feel don't matter. But you've shown me that it truly does. Just the thought of continuing it—doing everything my pata expects of me, ignoring you and my feelings for you—kills me."

She couldn't help but run her fingertips over his muscled chest. "It kills me, too. When Sarafine won the right to remain by your side for the evening." Her mouth clamped shut against the pain that bubbled to the surface. Visiting Marek had distracted her, but nothing could erase the feeling of betrayal. "And every time the king favors her over me."

"I know." He took her hand and guided her to lie against his chest. His heart beat strong and steady. "But I know my pata. Running isn't an option. He'd hunt us down, and I don't wish to abandon my role as heir."

Fenity knew one way King Sidian wouldn't find them. But she'd keep that secret to her grave if it meant protecting those she loved. "I don't want you to abandon your duties, Renic. I know it will be hard—agonizing, even—but we can persevere."

"Yes, we can." He caressed her hair. "But only if I do a

better job hiding my feelings for you." He smirked. "How about a deal? No more duels to the death, and I'll *try* not to turn overly anxious and give us away."

"Sounds good to me." She wanted to return his banter, but no wit would come. There very well could be more deaths before the contest's end.

"Hey." Quicker than she could react, he had her on her back, hovering over her, face close enough to kiss. "We can do this. Just a little longer, okay?" He kissed her nose.

"Okay." She smiled. "Wait, before you leave and I don't see you again for a while, I need to tell you something important."

The humor slipped from his features, and he sat beside her, giving his full attention. "What is it?"

She raised up next to him and took his hands. There was no reservation. No hesitation. "I love you." The words were so frail, too small to encompass everything she meant by them.

He inhaled. "I love you, too, Fenity. With all that I am." He leaned forward and claimed her lips, gently, lovingly, before pulling back. "But why did that feel like goodbye?"

"I don't want something to happen and I never took the chance to say it. That's all I could think about in the arena. That I might never get to tell you."

"But I knew." He held her to him. "I've known from the moment I met you. Just like you know."

"I do know." There was no denying his love, even before he spoke it.

He squeezed her once, then his weight left the bed. The rising sun meant it was time for him to go—time to pretend they weren't the only two people in the world, and that the world wasn't burning down around them.

"When will I see you again?" She sat up, watching him, memorizing him.

He paused, sadness touching his eyes. "I don't know. I can't often come here without raising suspicion. Too many eyes in this castle." He perked up. "But, you won the Second Pillar. That will grant you an award."

Renic tossed on a jacket and smoothed his hair. "For now, just rest. Fetam has taken a liking to you and insisted on overseeing your recovery. She's demanded at least two days' rest. For Sarafine too."

Fenity didn't know how to feel about her rival. Court and parental expectations, a hard upbringing and a hard life aside, everyone was in control of their own actions. Sarafine had shown her true colors time and time again.

Voices sounded down the hall. Renic's eyes went wide, and he hurried to the door. "Never thought I'd be sneaking around my own palace. You're one troublesome gardener." He winked, and she laughed and blew him a kiss as he slipped out of the room. It was okay to steal joy where she could. It was the only way to make the agony of being apart from him bearable.

A soft knock sounded at her door, and then her parents entered.

"You're awake." Mata's eyes filled with tears, and she wrapped Fenity up in a hug. This was the home she'd grown up in, her mata's love and wildness. Not the stuffy dresses and manners they'd somehow found themselves in. Yet she wouldn't change a thing—it was how she'd found her Renic.

Pata hung back, though his relief was plain. "We are so proud of you, young one."

She didn't feel young, but to them she was. "Did you know the Strife would be like this?" The words came out more accusatory than she meant.

"It's always like this," Pata said at the same time Mata said, "There was no choice. All un-bound courtly females of age must compete."

"No. It's okay. I'm glad to be here. I'm glad I can honor you."

Arinia entered the room, stopping short in front of her attendants when she saw Fenity's parents.

Mata gave her a squeeze, then rose and straightened her immaculate dress. "Take care of yourself, my love. We'll check in on you as often as we can."

"I love you." They weren't words she often said, but she'd learned there may not always be another chance.

"We love you too." Mata clasped hands with Pata, and they left, moving aside for Arinia to enter.

But instead of going to the closet for today's pick of green dress, Arinia gave her attendants new orders. They dusted, laid out fresh linens, and drew a lavender bath. Servants brought food and drinks in on trays. No dress.

"You're to rest and replenish today. And many more days, should you ignore the order and return to training too early." Arinia filled a plate with fruits and cakes. "You're not missing anything. King Sidian ordered a rest for all contestants. That pillar was livelier than anyone but the king expected it to be, I'm thinking. The healers have been very busy." She glanced at the attendants and gave Fenity a knowing look. "King Sidian and the heir are still entertaining the gnome royals, King Tirkist and Queen Depriess, so they are quite busy as well."

Fenity relaxed under Arinia's and the attendants' care, luxuriating in their pampering and replenishing her strength with food and warm honey milk. In the soothing bath, the attendants washed her hair, firm fingers massaging her scalp until Fenity nearly moaned. They directed her when to sit up or lift her arm, ensuring every part was clean and scented with floral soap. With hooded eyes, she complied, sleepily allowing them to care for her.

A long afternoon nap and a hearty meal of biscuits and

roasted vegetables improved her mood. But when Arinia retired for the evening and it was clear Renic wasn't coming, restlessness got the better of her.

Her injuries had healed, and she'd rested enough. It was time to visit another world and demand to learn how to control her energy. It was more important now than ever.

CHAPTER 34

Renic stopped in the hall, well away from the warriors guarding the king's private dining room. He rubbed his eyes with one hand, the other bracing against the wall.

"My prince?" Galan stepped closer, the buckles on his leather armor clinking. "King Sidian is waiting."

"I don't think I can do this, Galan. How can I entertain the goblin royals when Fenity almost died?" His voice nearly erupted out of his control. "I need to be with her."

Galan's mouth turned down in sympathy. "That's your heart taking over your rational mind. She didn't almost die. And she's being well taken care of by people you trust, remember?"

Renic nodded, latching on to the words. He took a shaky breath. Fenity was safe. He couldn't protect her if he didn't continue with the Strife and its rules. "I'm a mess." His chuckle wasn't believable, even to him.

"You're doing admirably."

Muffled voices sounded through the wall. "Lara, this is my

Strife, but I'm allowing you a say in the fifth pillar. That must be enough for you."

Renic met Galan's wide eyes. Pata and Mata. Renic crouched closer to the wall and pretended to re-lace his boot.

His mata was even harder to hear. "I thought this was our son's Strife." Movement and muffled conversation Renic couldn't make out. "I won't interfere, but let it be their vote. Grant me this one thing."

"I don't like it."

"Prince Renic," a door guard called out. Yamin—known for his extreme loyalty to the king. "His Majesty requests your presence."

Renic slowly stood. He took measured, casual steps to the door, as Yamin turned forward, jaw clenching.

That wasn't good. Yamin had caught them eavesdropping.

The king's private dining room was big enough to hold at least fifty courtiers and dignitaries. Today, a single table graced the middle, featuring silver platters and candelabras. The air smelled of fresh bread and buttered herbs.

Real candlelight instead of magelight bounced shadows over the paintings around the room. The paintings made this Renic's least favorite room in the castle. Visiting courtiers always got the tour. It started with the first painting depicting the races of this world living in harmony with the humans, moving on to the sunder when humans grew too greedy. Their parting curse upon the world. Until reaching the last painting —portal openers on the run, executed in mass. And it hadn't stopped. The beheading of innocents still haunted his dreams.

Renic never ate here unless forced.

King Tirkist and Queen Depriess dipped their heads to Renic as he bowed to them and sat at the table. The gnome king and queen sat on special pillows to raise them to the table's height. They wore dark green clothing of fine make and crowns made of interwoven sticks with scattered, glimmering jewels. With Galan guarding the door and his parents not yet arrived, it was only the three of them in the room besides the servants.

"Is Lady Fenity recovered?" the gnome queen asked in a higher-pitched voice. "My people were worried for her. She and the others were very brave."

Renic smiled warmly. "She is well and healed, thank you. We have the best healers in the kingdom tending to our contestants."

King Tirkist nodded. "Good, good. We did not expect that level of hostility from the fae."

Neither had he. Galan had forcibly restrained Renic to stop him from demanding answers from the king. Why allow such brutality during a test for *poise*?

But his pata's purpose had been served. The gnomes saw firsthand the energy and might of the most powerful fae. If they had any ideas of joining the goblin incursion, they were now second-guessing them.

Pata and Mata entered the room from a side door, arm in arm. Renic stood and bowed to them.

The door opened behind them, and Sarafine stepped through, bowing low in a red silk dress.

What in the moons was she doing here?

"Just in time." Pata smiled and gestured to the empty seat beside Renic.

Renic glared, silently questioning his pata, but his efforts went ignored.

"Thank you for inviting me, Your Majesty."

The gnome king and queen exchanged a glance.

As soon as they were all seated and served, Sarafine turned to them. "It is an honor to meet you, King Tirkist and Queen Depriess. I've studied your people extensively and have applied your values to my life. Such as the importance of being honest in my dealings."

What a manipulative liar. Sarafine had studied the gnomes, but it was only so she'd know how to behave in this very moment.

Renic stuffed a smothered mushroom in his mouth and focused on keeping his face blank. He did *not* turn to look at Galan by the door.

"It pleases us to hear that, Lady Sarafine." Queen Depriess took her king's hand.

The rest of the meal unfolded into the biggest farce yet, with his pata talking up Sarafine's accomplishments, and Sarafine sweet-talking the gnomes.

Renic considered himself an expert in pretending the world around him wasn't burning around him, but this was one of the biggest tests yet. His mata stayed as quiet as him. When dinner finally ended, Renic rose to excuse himself.

"Son, see that Lady Sarafine arrives safely to her rooms." Pata's tone was friendly, but his expression dared Renic to argue.

"Yes, Pata." He bowed around the room and held an arm out to Sarafine. *Play the game.*

Mata rose from the table. "I'd like a private word before you go." She waved him to the side door, and when Pata didn't protest, he followed.

Mata closed the door behind him and wrapped him in a hug, her strong floral perfume itching his nose.

Renic blinked his surprise. His mata had always been the more supportive of his parents, but never overly affectionate.

"I see you, my son. I know things you don't think I know." She pulled back and smoothed his tunic.

"What do you know?" Renic swallowed. It would be easy

for her to find out he'd spent time with Fenity, but did she know they were truemates?

She smiled before patting his chest and stepping away. "I've been reflecting on my own experiences in the Strife. I wouldn't change anything, but you are my precious son. It took no time at all for you to get so grown, and I only want you to be happy." She paused. "So be careful. There's only so much I can do." Before he could reply, she held open the door to the dining room where Pata and Sarafine waited for them.

"Oh, and son," she whispered. "Try not to worry about the goblins. Your council meetings sound dire, but Sidian knows what he's doing. We'll have the warriors we need."

His mask slipped back into place. "Thank you for your counsel, Mata." His mind spun in a dozen directions as he unwillingly took Sarafine's arm under the king's scrutiny.

Was the queen trying to undermine her king? How much did she truly know about Fenity, and how had she found out? And the goblins—was Pata making plans without him?

"How are you?" Sarafine cut into his thoughts halfway down the hall. Night had fallen while they dined, moonlight streaming from the windows with magelight in between. "We haven't had much time to talk since the Strife began."

Renic dropped her arm now that his pata couldn't see. "How did you secure an invitation to the king's private dining room in the middle of the Strife?" He didn't have to pretend her actions were okay when it was just the two of them.

"I'm trying to stay friends, Renic. We used to be so close, and I miss that." She pouted and reached for his hand, but he pulled it away, halting.

"I don't believe we were ever close. I don't believe you're here for me or our friendship. Only my title." Everyone had wanted to use him his whole life, even those who were supposed to protect him.

"Don't say something you might regret if I win. Would it be so bad? I'd make a good queen for you and our people." Her hazelnut curls tumbled over her bare shoulder as she tried to touch him again.

But again, he stepped back. She was a stranger to him. "If you were ever my friend, even for a moment, don't destroy the integrity of the Strife. A true queen would want to win fairly."

Her lips parted and her cheeks flushed. "I am winning fairly." She raised her chin.

Renic nodded, not believing the lie. "You know the castle better than most. You can see yourself to your rooms."

She stiffened. "Yes, Your Highness."

He walked away, Galan's unfaltering footsteps following him. His pata had warned him people would try to use him. He just never realized Pata would be one of them.

CHAPTER 35

Fenity slipped into her dressing room—the safest place to portal, with no outside walls to the hallway or other contestants' rooms. Plus, the clothing muffled any noises, and it had a lock.

Discarding her night slip, she picked one of the plainer green outfits—something suitable for energy training. Soft, skin-hugging pants with a cream-colored tunic featuring matching dark-green embroidery in a pretty leaf pattern. She tucked it in and paired it with a leather belt and supple leather boots, braiding her hair back. Remembering the cold, she donned a green cape, clasping it at her neck.

Was the outfit and cape necessary for visiting Marek's study? No. But winning the Second Pillar had proved she was capable of more than she thought. She couldn't stand lying around in bed being stuffed with food. If learning to control her energy from Marek took them out of the study, she would be ready.

At the last minute, she found a dagger and slipped it into her boot.

She pulled at her energy. Its warmth rose within her like an old friend. Thinking about the study, she opened a portal and closed it as quickly as she could—and gasped. Inside, the hearth warmed the space with a crackling fire, but outside, the windows lining the dining room revealed pure white. She crossed around the long table to them, breath fogging the glass. Snow blanketed the land, covered the green trees, and fell like cotton balls from a gray sky.

"Do you not have snow in the fae world?" Marek's voice made her jump and spin around. He stood in the doorway, hands up. "Sorry." He chuckled and approached her.

"Yes, but it doesn't fall this heavy where I live. Lived. Too many trees." She returned his smile and stared back out the window. "How do you always know when I'm here?"

"I set a ward to alert me when magic is performed here." He watched for her reaction.

"Oh. I guess that makes sense." She shifted on her feet, uncomfortable with his nearness. He was trying to cheer her up, but she couldn't shake this feeling of wrongness for being with another male. They were friends, but she'd never told him about Renic. But with the way he was staring at her, maybe she should.

"How's the contest going?"

"I almost died a couple days ago." She shrugged, like pretending it was nothing might make it so. "No one came to see me besides my parents." And Renic.

She hadn't realized that bothered her until saying it out loud.

His alarmed eyes slowly dimmed. "I would have visited if I could."

She shrugged again, this time pushing away the irritating stinging in her eyes. "The other contestants have never liked me. I don't fit in there. But I won the Second Pillar. So it's okay.

It's a lot more challenging than I thought it would be. But that's why I'm here—I need you to train me. But please, tell me something about you first."

Marek slowly nodded, seeing her change of subject for what it was. "There's a strong rumor that our High Master has taken ill. If he passes, there will be a vote to replace him. I think I mentioned my odds are favorable. It's a position for life, and I want it so badly I can taste it. There's so much good I could do in the world with my gifts. When I'm not home, I'm at the council building, swaying whomever I can reach to vote for me."

"Then I wish you luck." They didn't have a mage council in the fae world, but she understood hierarchy and the vie for power. "And what do you do when you're home?"

"There's not much to do around here when we're snow-bound." Marek rubbed the back of his neck. "When spring comes, I'll show you into town. I'm almost done with a potion to disguise your ears as human—reversible, of course. No one will look twice, and we can explore to our hearts' content. There's a traveling market that comes by. Lots of vendors and food. Those troupe performances can be fun, if you like theater."

"That sounds nice." How could she tell him she probably wouldn't be here by the time human spring came? The contest would be over soon, and she'd be busy learning how to be a queen.

No need to tell him now. She shivered and pulled her cape around her. "So, do you have time to train me now?" It was freeing discussing her energy with a friend who knew her secret and didn't judge her for it.

"Oh, of course. I've trained apprentices in my time." He glanced at the snow outside. "Though I usually start outdoors, in case you lose control. Do you feel up to portaling?" The eagerness in his eyes was plain.

"Where do you want to go?" She didn't know of many places she hadn't already shown him. Except home, her real home near Solice in the border woods of Sprite Forest. But they couldn't risk going there.

"Somewhere warm." He grinned, motioning her back to the study and closer to the fire.

She stepped away from the cold window with the beautiful, blowing snow. "Alright. But we only have this one try. If I don't make any progress with my energy, this will be the last time I can visit, I'm afraid. The contest is becoming more intense, and I won't be able to return often, if ever." In truth, the risk of what she'd lose by being caught now outweighed what she gained if Marek couldn't truly help her. This was a last-ditch effort.

Marek went silent for long enough that she finally looked at him. He hid the hurt with a soft smile. "What can I say? I thought we were friends." He picked lint off his purple dress.

"We are," she hurried to assure him. "You're a good person. I just can't make any promises."

"I'll miss you. I..." He stopped, though he wanted to say more, and she was grateful he did.

"I'll do my best." She smiled and lifted her tone, hoping to raise both their spirits. "Let's go train some place warm."

He nodded, so she stared into the fire, thinking of warmth, and the reds and oranges of the flames, sand and heat. When she held out her hand, he took it.

The energy came slower this time, sluggish from her recent bout with death, but she pushed through it. It built until she finally had enough to open a portal, but she'd have to be fast—it wouldn't stay open long.

She opened and closed it before it could sputter out. She

dropped Marek's hand as dry heat slammed into her, but the surprise of it barely cut through her exhaustion as she bowed over, retching into the sand.

I'm a fool.

She dropped to the ground, one hand on her stomach, one hand over the headache blooming behind her eyes. She couldn't even look to make sure Marek was okay, or why he was so silent. Deep breaths rushed in and out, while hot sand scraped through her leggings, and hot air whipped across her face. The nausea slowly subsided.

"Is this the fae world?" Marek's voice shook, his fear so clear she finally looked up. He spun around, staring at the sky in disbelief.

The world around them was stark and barren. Sand, and rock, and husks of trees. Looming above the wasteland was a red sky that cast the landscape in a ruby haze. Like the soft cotton balls of snow they'd left behind, ash fell from the sky in intermittent clumps and wisps before being blasted off by the next gust of hot wind.

Horror washed over her, reigniting the nausea. Sweat beaded and dripped down her collar. Where had she brought them? "This is no world I know. We need to leave. Immediately." How could she have been so careless? Her energy wasn't some theater performance where nothing bad happened and she'd be okay no matter what, just portaling across the universe to strange worlds with no consequences.

"No, wait." Marek held up a hand, still staring around the barren, blistering landscape. "There's no one here. We can explore a little while, can't we?"

"No. It's too dangerous." Fenity pulled at her energy, but only a trickle came. Not near enough to open a portal. *Oh no.* "I don't have enough. I'm too drained." She smacked her dry mouth, worry settling into her bones.

Marek dropped his pleased smile. "It'll refill." He reached down and helped her to stand. She closed her eyes to the tilting red sky. "There's a road here. We'll follow it a bit until you feel better."

He led her, and she stumbled along, half of her wanting to find some place to hide from the blistering heat until her energy recuperated, and the other half too exhausted to protest. Even if this might be her only chance to explore another world, warning bells were clanging so loud, the pain in her head was near blinding.

The road they now traversed was nothing more than a disturbance of the sand where many had trodden. It disappeared into a mirage on the horizon where the scorching heat rose in shimmering waves, marring the red haze.

"This is a bad idea," she said, pulling her arm from his grip, but still keeping up with his pace. "We don't know anything about the inhabitants of this land. Human? Fae? Something else?" The footprints were too windblown to discern. She strained her eyes and hearing, but all she heard was gusting wind. She couldn't even think about the possibility of being trapped here for long, with no supplies or water—dressed for cold weather in a scorching place—or it became even harder to breathe.

Strong. She needed to be strong.

Something smacked into the ground behind them, scattering rocks. They both jumped.

A black, oily arrow stuck out of the sand, with black fletching.

"What the..." Marek reached for it.

Fenity pulled him back. "Run!"

A dark figure rose from a hill on the horizon and nocked another arrow. Fenity burst down the path, but Marek's brow furrowed in anger. His energy coalesced, and when the next arrow flew, it slammed into a shield of some kind instead of driving home through Marek's eye socket.

Two more figures rose from the hill. Then three more. They were black outlines from this distance, but the vileness emanating from them turned her stomach.

Fenity pulled at her energy, but the trickle that answered still wasn't enough. "There's too many. Move!"

He followed her in a run, just keeping up with her speed. They had to find somewhere to hide until her energy replenished. She whirled at the thuds sounding behind her.

"Don't look back." Marek's brow furrowed in concentration. Arrow after arrow struck against his shield as they moved, harmlessly falling to the sand.

The dark figures descended the hill, but they moved slowly, in no hurry to catch up.

Sweat poured down her face, stinging her eyes. Soon they outpaced the arrows, slowing to a jog, but not stopping.

"We can't keep this up." The heat made her want to curl into a ball right on the road. "We need rest."

Marek's energy dissipated along with his shield as he dropped it. "I see black spots." He swiped at the air.

Fenity cursed, looking around for anything to shelter behind. "There, a boulder. We'll have to face them, but maybe we can buy enough time for my energy to return."

They trudged to the large boulder some paces off the dirt road. It was twice her height, the gritty surface blasted by sand and wind, and offered a blissful patch of shade. The temperature dropped in its embrace, and they hunched, panting and soaking up the hot wind as it pelted their sweating bodies. Fenity ditched her cape and grabbed the dagger from her boot.

"You're right." Marek panted, leaning around the boulder to see behind them. "This was dumb." His energy spiked. "The four fastest are almost here."

"I know. The other two are sneaking around the opposite way." Their heavy footsteps through the sand were unmistakable. She cocked her ear. "They'll attack at the same time."

A calmness settled over her. The killing calm. She knew it well. It always came before an attack in the forest, whether she was taking down game for their meals or defending against an animal attack. It cleared her mind, and she forgot her headache, thirst, and the burning heat.

"They're here," she whispered.

Marek raised his shield as four creatures approached from the left, arrows nocked and aimed true. Fenity gagged at the stench and the sight. She'd never seen beings like these. Beneath the black robes, they were fae, if fae were left to rot and waste away. Bones with hairless skin, black scaled armor. Red, empty eyes. Their lipless mouths open in a permanent sneer that frightened Fenity to her marrow.

Demons.

She'd brought them to the demon world.

A child's tale of nightmares and shadows. If it was real, then...

"Red flame and ash," she whispered as the demons drew closer. "The prophecy."

Fenity wielded her dagger in shaking hands, tearing at her energy. *Please.* She nearly sobbed. *Please heed me.*

The demons released their arrows, and when they struck Marek's shield, they attacked. Charging, they pulled thick, black swords that looked heavy enough to outweigh the demons themselves, yet they wielded them with ease.

Their backs to the boulder, Marek pulled even more energy. The staticky feel buzzed through her skin with incredible strength. A sword of blue flame appeared in his hands, but the demons didn't hesitate. Two brought their swords down upon him, while the other two broke for her. Marek blocked one, sending globules of flames flying. He sent a different form of energy toward the other, knocking the demon to the ground without even touching it.

Anger coursed under her skin, but it wasn't anger for this enemy trying to end her. It was anger at herself. *Red flame and ash.* This was all her fault.

That anger steadied her hand as the lead demon jabbed at her middle. She wouldn't let her baby grow up in a world destroyed by a prophecy she unleashed.

She pivoted back, remembering her mata's words—words spoken long before she'd become just another member of the king's court. *If you throw your weapon, you lose it.* Mata had been talking about wild animals, but the advice was sound. The demons were more like animals than fae—vacant, expressionless eyes. Stiff but solid and powerful swipes. No communication she could discern, just growls and grunts.

Fenity jumped aside with the demon's next jab, slicing it across the arm. Her dagger met bone, and the demon didn't flinch. Her second opponent charged. She couldn't let them attack two on one.

"Fenity!" Marek yelled as his energy spiked. Air slammed the demon closest to her, knocking it back and distracting the other.

She dodged the second demon's misplaced strike and jammed her dagger into its neck. The demon fell, ripping the blade from her grip, lodged in its bone.

The first demon charged again. She doubled over, dodging a powerful swing.

Another staticky burst of energy erupted from Marek, and blue fire engulfed his demons.

They didn't care. Shaking off the momentary stun, they charged, flames scorching their robes and thin skin.

Fenity's back hit the boulder. Her demon approached, head

cocked as if it knew her end had come. She was weaponless. Vulnerable.

But not helpless.

The other demon's sword lay discarded in the sand. The timing had to be perfect for an opening to roll and grab it.

The sound of grinding rock overhead pricked the edges of her hearing. Shadows rose from above.

The other two demons.

Her opponent stopped advancing. She risked a peek above. The two demons stood, each holding a large rock above their heads.

"Look up!" she screamed.

Mid-strike, Marek ripped his gaze above, just as a rock smashed into his head. He crumpled to the ground.

"Marek!" Fenity jumped to the side, but a rock the size of her head clipped her shoulder. She cried out in pain.

Marek's demons stepped toward her, then collapsed, the blue flames finally burning far enough. She lunged, grabbing one of their heavy swords. She tugged at her energy, but only a trickle met her call. This was not how she would end.

She leaped, dodging another rock that would have destroyed her sword arm, and faced her demon. Lifting the sword in a shaking arm, she pointed it straight at its heart. "This is your end. Not mine."

It reared back its lipless face and roared. Keeping one eye on the rocks raining around her, she swung for the demon. Adjusting for its blocks, she entered the dance she'd learned from her bout with Sarafine. The demon left an opening, and she lunged for it. At the last second, a rock sailed toward her, forcing her to back away.

She screamed her frustration and her strikes came more quickly. Sweat slipped down her arms and pooled in her palms, making the grip on her sword precarious. She pivoted around the demon, striking and blocking, waiting for it to make another mistake.

There.

Its arm dropped with the follow-through of a missed hit, and she lunged, her sword sinking into its side.

A lethal hit.

The demon fell to its knees, and a rock slammed into her back. Her vision went white, then black around the edges, but she kept her feet. She surged into a sprint to put distance between her and the boulder, but a rock cracked her in the skull. The last thing she saw was the horizon rising to meet the red sky before everything went black.

CHAPTER 36

Fenity awoke to a sharp kick to her feet. Her eyes flew open, and she squirmed away from her attacker over gritty stone, hands bound behind her and head pounding. The demon watched her worm her way to the back of the small, windowless room. Torchlight barely filtered into the small, dark room from behind a door made of bars. A dungeon.

The door was open, but the demon—this one in a red cape instead of a black robe—stood between her and freedom.

"It's okay," Marek said, voice hoarse. She jumped at his presence in the corner of the cell. His hands were bound behind him, too. The manacle's strange gold color glinted in the torchlight when he shifted, wincing. "They would have killed us if they were going to."

His words pounded in her skull, pain flaring to life from several places along her body. How badly was she injured? She gasped. The baby. How long had she been here? Was her absence noticed?

She pulled at her energy—and screamed. Pain unlike

anything she'd ever experienced erupted over her entire body. She convulsed on the ground, tears flowing as the pain ebbed away.

"Fenity!" Marek scooted toward her, but the demon snarled a warning. "What happened?" he asked as her sobs subsided.

"I don't know." She tried to get her shaking breaths under control. "I tried to use my energy." They'd done something to her while she was unconscious.

The demon approached her. Did it understand them?

The demon gripped her upper arm and pulled her to her feet as if she weighed no more than a twig. Fenity jerked away, muscles weak, but the demon tightened its grip until its claws pierced her skin.

"Where are you taking me?" She kicked and tugged, but she might as well have been attacking the stone wall. Panic crushed her lungs.

A second demon grabbed Marek, but he didn't resist. Why wasn't he using his energy? Was he out? Maybe they'd suppressed his too. As the aftereffects of the pain subsided, she noted the windowless hall, the relative coolness of the air compared to the inferno outside. They were underground, or deep inside whatever passed for a castle in this place. With bound hands and no energy, the odds weren't good they'd make it far if they tried to escape on foot. He'd apparently been awake longer than her. Maybe he'd worked that out for himself.

And maybe the demons understood them, if Marek wasn't forming a plan out loud.

They twisted around barren halls, decorated only with sporadic cracked plaster where once it might have been a splendid dwelling. Too much sand had made it inside, making the bare stones gritty no matter where they walked.

No furniture. No tapestries. Just crude torches and broken doorways.

A strange rumbling echoed through the air. Fenity couldn't place it until they passed an open archway and dozens of demons in black stood watching them, like they'd been waiting for her to cross this way.

And every bit of the walk, she sought a way out. A window. A door. A crack in the wall so big she might get her bearings on the outside world.

Nothing.

"Marek. We—" Her demon growled and shoved her to the ground. With her hands behind her back and no way to catch her fall, her injured shoulder cracked against the stone.

"Fenity!" Marek's energy flared for attack, then immediately abated, leaving him unharmed.

Fenity struggled to her feet. They didn't want to reach wherever the demons were taking them—she felt that truth down to her bones. Before the demon reached her, she took off sprinting. It lunged and grabbed her by the back of the neck and held tight. It pushed her further down the hall while she snarled her fury.

Soon they entered a wide room that echoed with its emptiness and blinded her with its darkness. And something else.

There was a wrongness here, lurking in the deepest shadows. Her knees trembled.

The demons dumped them in the dirt and took positions as guards beside the doorway.

Another bare, stone room, like being in an oversized crypt. Except...

"We don't often have outsiders. Not in eons." A deep rumbling emanated from the far side of the room, so guttural she shouldn't have understood. But she did. And it made her want to run for her life.

She lifted her eyes and took in the large throne upon the dais and the demon king upon it. King Theron. He was real.

His black, feathered wings shifted as he stood, scant torch-light reflecting off his skin—no, scales. Small red scales on his face and across his bare chest. Black, depthless eyes, pointed ears, and a pair of menacing horns made up the sum of the fae's nightmares turned real. And he was prowling closer.

Marek bowed to his knees, prostrating himself on the floor as much as his bound hands allowed. Fear-slicked sweat rolled down Fenity's spine as she fought the impulse to do the same, mind tearing in two. This wasn't her ruler. They had to go. *Now*.

"A fae and a human mage." The deep rumbling froze her in her tracks. He stopped halfway to them, not far enough. "How did you get here." A command to be answered.

Fenity clamped her lips together and searched for her energy. It was there, hidden in the back of her mind, just out of reach, behind the pounding pain from multiple injuries and the fear that threatened to pull her under. Crouching in the shadow of a demon king.

This was it. This was the consequence of her reckless actions. King Theron, destroyer of worlds, king of the demon world of fire and ash, traitor to the fae.

The *end* of the fae.

"Yes." His rumble was punctuated by a slight uptick in his lips. "You should fear me. You and the one in your womb." He inhaled deeply through his nose.

Marek lifted his head to look at her.

"I can't scent your energy. But the females carry it." He stalked forward, hand raising. "Only the most powerful among you can travel here."

What did evil want with her gift? He would use her to destroy her people.

"I opened the portal," Marek said, voice so breathless he had to repeat himself.

"Impossible!" Theron swiped at open air, and dust fluttered from the ceiling.

Fenity locked her mind and facial features in place.

"Humans are capable of more than you think." Marek raised to a stand, but his hands shook just as badly as hers, making the golden manacles clink.

"Then I'll give you a gift first, human." Though King Theron made no sound or movement, two demons rushed to flank Marek.

Before Marek could react, they gripped his arms, holding him in place. One of them produced a key and unlocked Marek's manacles.

King Theron's powerful legs closed the distance so fast Fenity didn't have time to scream. He shoved his palm to Marek's forehead. A red light glowed where their skin connected, and Marek's eyes rolled back in his head.

He was dying. Theron was killing him.

Helpless. Weak. If she fought, she'd die too. But it should have been her. It was her curse that had brought them here. He'd sacrificed himself for her and her child, because he was her friend.

The warmth and love of Marek's gift, and her rising anger at his mistreatment, eased back the fear. Energy nudged against her, but she didn't reach for it. Theron cocked his head, sensing her. She quickly switched her focus to all they stood to lose should she fail.

When Theron lifted his hand, Marek fell to his knees, panting. He didn't call his energy, nor did he fight when the demons locked the manacles back into place.

Fenity tried and failed not to recognize what she'd just learned. The king couldn't use his energy against them while they wore the manacles. They were spelled. It had to be what caused her pain before. She'd have mere seconds once they removed hers.

Fenity crouched to Marek's side. "Are you alright?" She needed to be closer to her friend.

The demons growled, hauling her up and back a few paces. King Theron watched her closely. His black, knowing stare pierced her mind. Her knees trembled, heart galloping.

She had to be quick.

The demons stuck the key in the lock. Theron raised his palm to her forehead, so close she felt his heat even in the hot room. His hulking form towered over her, his shadow like a blanket of fear. He traced a clawed finger down her cheek. Her mind went white with fear.

One manacle clicked open, dropping from her wrist. Fenity's breaths shook.

When the metallic scrape of the turning key and a soft click reached her focused hearing, she didn't wait for the manacles to fall before she dropped deadweight to the ground. She slammed the manacles against the ground, popping them open.

Her energy rushed forth like a burst dam. King Theron lunged for her with incredible speed, but she snatched the key and threw herself toward Marek, rolling. The portal was open before she even reached him.

King Theron's claws raked her back, pain searing. She closed it, leaving him and that hellscape behind. His howl of fury cut off, but his rumbling laughter followed her to the fae world.

CHAPTER 37

On knees and forearms sunk into the thick dressing room rug, Fenity panted, her vision swinging from red to black as she fought to remain conscious. Early morning light poured beneath the crack in the door, wall sconces still burning low with energy. How long had she been gone?

No screams. No alarms. No rushing of feet in search of a missing contestant.

"Where are we?" a male said.

Fenity screamed, lurching to her feet.

Marek tried to raise his bound hands, eyes wide, yet strangely empty. "It's me. You didn't take me home."

Her heart dropped back into her chest but lurched again with fear. "They will have heard me. You must hide!" Her stomach roiled as pain and exhaustion flared.

"Where?" He took in the hanging gowns and outfits of green.

She unlocked the door, then stopped cold at her reflection in the mirror. Her braid was half unraveled, clothes torn and caked in dirt and blood, face a mess of bruises, and her back *stung*. Nearly rivaling the pounding pain in her head. She turned, examining her back over her aching shoulder. Blood dripped from four long gashes. "How am I going to hide this?"

Footsteps sounded down the hall. Fenity threw open the dressing room doors and bounded toward her bed. "Under here!" She motioned Marek under the bed. "If we're caught, we're both dead."

How would she explain this? They were already as good as dead.

"Wait." The energy built around Marek.

"No, don't!" What was he trying to do?

The footsteps grew closer.

"You have to stop. They'll sense it." Her brow crumpled as she glanced at the door, expecting it to fly open any minute.

His manacles vibrated, but nothing happened.

"I have the key! Just hide." Fenity shoved the key into his bound hands. He cut off his energy and threw himself under the bed. Fenity jumped under the blanket, pulling it up to her chin just as the door opened and Arinia rushed in with a pair of guards.

Guards!

"Fenity, my petal." The magelight sconces lit up at Arinia's presence. "We heard a scream." Her eyes widened slightly, taking in the mussed hair and bruises that weren't there earlier. Arinia reached for her hand and lowered herself to sit on the edge of the bed.

The guards, wearing palace uniforms and sharp swords in their belts, split up, searching the room for danger. One of them approached the window directly by the bed, looking outside at the morning light-drenched courtyard and checking behind the curtains.

The words came out in a rush. "I had a nightmare and fell

out of bed. I hit my head on the table. Can you fetch Healer Fetam?"

Arinia straightened, concern replacing suspicion. "It's no wonder after what you've been through. I'll fetch her at once."

A female guard paused near the door to the dressing room, looking down. Fenity froze when she saw what grabbed her attention. A splatter of blood. The guard reached for it.

The guard by the window stooped to look under the bed.

"It's alright," Arinia said to the guards with a relieved smile. She gestured them toward the door. "Just a bad dream."

Fenity held her breath.

The guard by the window stood before looking, but the female guard cocked her head. She lifted her eyes to Fenity.

"My head is bleeding," Fenity said, heart in her throat. "I need a healer."

"Let us be off," the male guard said. The female's suspicious eyes moved past her.

"I saw Healer Fetam just a moment ago in the hall below us. I'll send her at once." Whether Arinia believed Fenity or not, she didn't question her. Neither did the guards.

Fenity waited until long after Arinia and the guards left to sip from the cup in her shaking hands, knowing she'd lose all self-control. Sure enough, as soon as the first drop hit her lips, the intense thirst she'd suppressed with the pain roared to life. She drank the entire cup dry, wishing for a hundred more.

"Marek, have some wat—" She cut herself off at the knock at the door. "Come in."

Fetam entered the room dressed in white just like before, as if she didn't sleep but worked through the night caring for the sick and injured. She shut the door, then paused, eyes narrowing slightly. "What have you done to my hard work?" She approached the bed, setting down a satchel that clinked with whatever was inside. "You didn't hit your head. *Something* hit your head."

Fenity prayed she wouldn't be able to detect Marek as well as she'd detected her injuries. "Yes, and my back has some scrapes. I was—"

Fetam stopped her with an upraised hand. "I don't need to know. Unless you need to bring a matter to the king?" She raised her eyebrow, but Fenity shook her head. Fetam pulled out a vial and unstoppered it, mixing the liquid with water in her empty cup. "This is the Strife. The contestants are ruthless —to each other and to themselves during training. You're not the first early morning call I've received. You won't be the last." She lowered her voice. "But you must take better care of yourself if you want this pregnancy to last. No unnecessary risks."

Fenity's cheeks heated as she drank the bitter liquid. She gave a silent nod. Fetam was right. This wasn't who she was. How did her life end up such a mess?

The drink settled her racing heart, relaxing her bunched-up muscles and easing some of the tension coiling her mind.

"Now, let's see to those injuries." Fetam helped Fenity remove her clothing, asking no questions about why she wore travel clothes—boots and everything. Fenity tried not to look down each time Fetam approached the bed. When Fetam set her satchel on the ground and occasionally reached for a new vial or bandage, Fetam gave her a funny look and told her to calm her heart.

Fetam soothed bruises and minor cuts Fenity didn't even remember receiving, pausing when she reached Fenity's head. "Whatever hit you must have been large." She clicked her tongue and healed the open wound. The pounding headache and spinning room slowly eased.

Fetam saved the gashes on her back for last, and they took the longest. "There was a dark presence to those, almost like a curse or a poison. They didn't want to heal. I've never seen it before." Fetam swayed from exhaustion, stumbling to hand Fenity a nightshift. "It was almost as if the energy in them resisted mine." She panted, holding a hand to her heart. "But I won in the end." She leveled a look. "I know you don't want to bring this to the king, but if you receive that kind of injury from another contestant again, I will insist upon it. If you weren't truemates with the heir, I wouldn't be giving you this courtesy."

So Fetam thought a female had attacked her.

"Thank you, Healer Fetam." Fenity couldn't express her gratitude enough. "Once again, you've saved me. Saved us." She held a hand over her belly.

"Let's check on that little one." A warm smile replaced Fetam's stern composure as she laid a hand over Fenity's abdomen. Warmth radiated from her hand like a gentle embrace. "All is well. Your ordeal has not disturbed the baby's growth," Fetam said after a brief minute. "You should have rested. I'm afraid I can't extend your recovery time any further without divulging your new injuries." She poured a vial into Fenity's cup and watched her drink it before wearily collecting her scattered supplies.

"I understand." Fenity's body sagged with relief. If she'd harmed her baby…

The empty vial rolled from the bed and hit the carpet with a thud. Fetam bent to pick it up.

"Any other advice you can give me?" Fenity hurried to ask.

Fetam kept her eyes up as she retrieved the bottle. "Rest as often as you can. Frequent small meals or snacks instead of a few large ones will help with sickness, as will the draughts I've been bringing you." She closed up her satchel. "Try not to get injured, but if you can't avoid it, don't get stabbed or fall on your stomach."

"Thank you. Truly."

Fetam gave a small smile and a bow before leaving, closing the door behind her. Fenity's eyes drooped heavily.

A rustling under the bed had her sitting up.

Marek wiggled his way out from under the bed and finished removing his manacles before pocketing them and the key. "That was close. I thought we would get caught."

"Me too. Do you want some water?" She handed him her empty cup, but he shook his head. How was he not mad with thirst? Her body drooped like a weight.

"Congratulations on your baby," Marek said. "Is Renic the father?"

Fenity blinked at the protectiveness that flared inside her. She didn't want to tell Marek a thing about her baby or Renic. They were hers.

"I need to get you home before morning comes." The words slurred slightly. Did she have the strength for two more portals? She felt physically fine after Fetam's healing, but mentally, she was beyond exhausted. Did she have the energy?

Did she have a choice?

"Must we go so soon?" He hesitated. "King Theron showed me how powerful I am, but he also showed me that no matter how much magic I learn, I'll never be able to do what you do and open a portal."

For some reason, relief burst over her. She'd almost forgotten about the demon king and his spell. Was that what he'd done? Examined Marek to explore the extent of his human energy? "The longer we wait, the more likely they'll catch us." She threw back the blanket, not caring her legs were bare beneath her short nightshift, though just that simple movement stole her strength.

What had Fetam given her?

Marek didn't seem to care about her state of dress, either.

He barely looked at her, or any other part of her through the opaque gown. "Maybe we could go back there. There's still so much to learn." His eyes filled with hope.

"What? To the demon world? No, never." She nearly hissed and had to work at keeping quiet. "We'll never go back there. We barely escaped." But they did escape. She was home. She was safe.

"Never say never." At her look of disgust, he shrugged and gave a lopsided smile.

"Come on. I'm taking you back." Her anger at his stupidity gave her the boost she needed to leave her tiredness momentarily behind. After opening her hearing to ensure no one was nearby, she summoned the dredges of her energy. It came like a bird trying to fly through mud. What if she couldn't open a second one to return home?

But no, there was enough, as slow in coming as it was. She opened and closed a portal, this time to the human world. They stood in his study, dark and quiet, with the fire long burned out. Cold air stole the warmth from her skin. The rich carpet poked at her bare feet.

"I'm going to miss you," Marek said, not letting go of her hand. His face was pale, eyes too wide to pass as excitement.

Fenity pulled her hand away. "I don't like it either, but I have more than myself to think about."

His eyes dropped to her stomach. "If your prince denies you, if your king abandons you, if your people turn against you, you'll always have a place here." Sadness and sincerity coated his words.

"Thank you. That means a lot." She gave him a smile and checked her energy reserves. It would be enough.

Marek never got the chance to teach her to shape her energy in other ways, but now she was out of time.

He watched with eyes almost like greed as she opened and

closed a portal home with the energy she'd held at bay. Unable to muster the strength to even cover herself under the blanket, she collapsed into bed and slept.

What felt like five minutes later, someone shook her shoulder. "Wake up, my lady."

"I'll splash some water," a female said.

"No," Arinia snapped. "Look, she's waking."

Fenity blinked to a blurry room, surrounded by her team of attendants wearing equal looks of concern. Sunlight streamed through the windows.

She was safe. This wasn't the demon world. This wasn't King Theron's dungeon. She never had to go back there again. She was safe. Exhausted, but safe.

"Drink this. Healer's orders." Arinia placed a warm mug in her hand.

Fenity gulped it down despite the bitter taste barely disguised by a dollop of flower nectar, the expensive kind. If Fetam gave the order, it was something her baby needed.

The tonic roused her, though she could have slept for another week.

Arinia nodded, taking the cup and replacing it with a biscuit with honey sandwiched within the layers. "Good. The king has called an assembly."

Full and content, Fenity half-dozed through her hasty bath and dressing, not paying attention to what she wore. The prophecy was contained. She was safe. She'd see Renic soon. She'd never open another portal again. Even if it meant never saying a proper goodbye to Marek.

The only thing keeping her from genuine comfort was not knowing what the king would throw at them next. Anything could be in store when they walked into that room. There were still two unknown pillars left, and three races to go on the Third Pillar of Faedom—gnomes, unicorns, and goblins. Though it was unlikely they'd meet with the goblins considering the recent border disputes. Another fight for her life this soon was the last thing she needed.

She left for the hallway and found her parents waiting by the door, relief on their faces. It was her first time leaving her rooms since the fight with Sarafine—that they knew of. Fenity's chest tightened at her mata's warm smile. She'd come this close to never seeing her parents again. Her mata sighed contentedly when Fenity hugged her extra tight before joining the contestants on their way to the ballroom.

The long walk was as monotonous as it was anticipation-filled. She was already ready to leave this absurd contest behind and move on with her life with Renic. How much longer could it go on? The elders said the previous Strife lasted six months.

The steel of resolve quickened her stride. She'd survived the demon world. She could last that long, if Renic was the prize at the end. The prize she'd never known to ask for.

When all the contestants and nosy members of the court assembled in the ballroom, the room was packed. Fenity stood to the side, allowing the marble column carved with floral reliefs to steady her rising nausea. The last few days had worn down every part of her. She pressed her hot cheek against its cool stone when she thought no one was looking. The dais at the front supported five thrones, but they were empty. Five, not three, which was unusual. And two of them were small, as if for children. Everyone milled and chatted, waiting for the royals to arrive.

No one chatted with her. Even after winning the Second Pillar mere days ago, they *still* wanted nothing to do with her.

She tried to talk to a few of the quieter ones, but the conversations quickly died as they returned to speaking with their friends.

And maybe it didn't help that even now, she stood away from them, ignoring the males clamoring for the contestants' attention. Definitely ignoring Sarafine in the middle of the room. Regal, laughing with her usual group as if she hadn't just nearly died for the king's whims.

The truth was, of course she was supposed to be playing their game. Her popularity amongst the court and in the eyes of the king might as well be a Sixth Pillar of Faedom for as important as it surely was to be in the king's good graces. But she hated the game. Almost as much as she'd hate herself if she changed who she was and pretended to be part of a world she never wanted anything to do with.

Until now.

This was Renic's world. And he was *her* world. And this would be her world, too.

"Fenity." Nisha cut into her thoughts. Fenity covered her surprise and turned. Nisha stood alone, dressed in a pale-yellow gown cut low enough that Fenity averted her eyes.

Nisha glanced at Sarafine and the group, red blooming on her cheeks, but they weren't paying attention. "I wanted to see if you were alright." She swallowed. "I wanted to say I'm sorry."

A thousand replies flew to the tip of Fenity's tongue—*of course you're sorry, now that you know I won't be in the bottom ten*—but she gave herself a moment to sort through them. She didn't know Nisha's past. What it had taken to be here, what she'd sacrificed for the chance at a future with the prince. What it would mean if she failed. Nisha played the game and bet on the wrong person. Fenity wouldn't have bet on herself, either.

But she wouldn't have done to Nisha what Nisha had done to her. No one with integrity would have.

"We could have been loyal friends, you know." Fenity smiled sadly down at her. "I really could have used a friend."

Nisha's mouth quivered. "I've become someone I don't even recognize. And it was all for nothing. I wish I had been deserving of your friendship." She looked down at her folded hands, eyeing Sarafine's group again. "I don't know how to make it right."

"Find new friends. Those are poison. They will only drag you down. Not everyone here is so underhanded." She put a hand on Nisha's arm. "I'm not perfect either, not even close. I forgive you, Nisha."

Nisha's lips parted, and she threw her arms around Fenity. There was so much in that hug—apology, relief, gratitude, and buried pain. When Nisha walked away, she didn't go back to Sarafine's circle.

Fenity smiled and resisted resting against the column. Pregnancy exhaustion was not something she'd ever considered when contemplating the Strife's trials.

A herald, the same sadistic one from the arena, stepped forward from the back of the room, stopping beside the thrones. The room plunged into silence.

"I present to you the royal family, and gnome King Tirkist and Queen Depriess."

King Sidian and Queen Lara took their seats first, but Fenity only saw Renic. *Her* Renic. He threw her a dimple-popping smile, gaze trying and failing to sweep across the room and instead staying locked on her as he took his seat and the gnomes took theirs. He looked especially attractive in a silky, beige tunic with tight sleeves and a green vest, hair tied back but for two thin braids on either side of his face. More gnomes followed them through the back entry, gathering behind the dais. The gnome court?

The herald bowed at the waist and backed that way until he stood further to the side. Fenity shuddered as images of stifling clothing and rotten vegetables flashed through her mind.

All the royals sat except King Sidian. He smiled over his court and contestants. To some, he might have appeared kind. But to Fenity, he was slick with oil and scheming. "First, I'd like to thank King Tirkist for his time here. It has been most productive."

What about Queen Depriess? According to what Fenity had read, the gnome court functioned as a unit, with both king and queen having equal power, unlike the fae court where the heir to the bloodline reigned supreme, male or female. Just because Queen Lara was complicit in her role as ornamentation, didn't mean that was how all courts functioned.

King Sidian went on. "The gnomes have chosen their contestant for the Third Pillar of Faedom. Though, of course, the majority winner of each race is the one who takes the pillar."

Fenity tilted her head. The gnomes had chosen a winner without even meeting the contestants. She'd seen them around the castle—had they been judging them in other ways?

Everyone shifted, conversations erupting. A group moved in front of her, and Fenity craned her neck to see Renic. Did he have any idea how this would go? His smile from before either meant good news, or that he didn't know anything.

He was looking at Sarafine, who was looking too smug for comfort. She'd lost the Second Pillar right in front of the gnomes. A race that valued integrity and hard work above all. Did she really expect to win?

King Tirkist stood and cleared his throat. "Queen Depriess

and I thank King Sidian and the fae of Alberry for welcoming us at such a historical moment." His voice was higher pitched and quieter than that of a fae, and he paced slightly as he spoke, barely audible above the speculating around the room. "While we did not visit with all the contestants, we've seen enough and are ready to announce our favored candidate." He waited until the excitement died down.

Renic shifted uneasily on his throne. Was he nervous she wouldn't win?

Something like anger flashed in King Tirkist's eyes as he gave a quick glance to King Sidian, but it was gone too fast to be sure. "Our chosen candidate for the Strife is someone who's demonstrated strength as well as restraint. Poise as well as skill. We choose Lady Sarafine Rivers."

What? Fenity's mouth fell open.

Cheers erupted around the room. Anyone who'd hedged closer to Fenity, thinking she'd be the definite winner, now rushed for the privilege to touch Sarafine.

Renic's entire being remained exceptionally blank, like stone carved by an artist whose only instructions were to capture no emotion at all.

She was that much closer to losing the Third Pillar, and he knew better than anyone what that would mean. She could lose the Strife.

The gnome king scanned the room until his eyes rested on hers, holding them. Was that sorrow she sensed? Regret?

Nausea returned full force, and Fenity sprinted for the exit before she lost her breakfast all over the ballroom floor. No one noticed her puking into a potted plant out in the hallway. No one but the door guards, and they didn't seem to care.

She'd lost again.

CHAPTER 38

When Fenity's nausea and disbelief finally cleared, she found herself in the gardens, an icy wind prickling her skin, the last of the flowers finally having succumbed to the cold. Even the deadness around her was preferred to indoors. This time of year, she should be foraging for early winter berries, rotating the drying herbs, and fortifying their hut for harsher weather. She was no stranger to cold, and she embraced its blissful numbness, letting it match the feelings in her heart.

She hadn't lost yet. And she'd still be Renic's pick, which counted for something.

Endure. Endure. Endure.

She just had to endure.

What would Sarafine's award be this time? A date with the prince? Maybe the king would propose on Renic's behalf right now. Fenity hadn't even received her reward for winning an entire pillar.

"Gah." She roughly scrubbed her wet face, stomping ahead on the frozen path. It was more than the contest that was diseased. It was this place, these people. Like a fungus festering in her heart and destroying her ability to think clearly.

She needed the forest.

Portaling was out of the question. Instead, she ran. Long skirts clenched in one hand, she sprinted past manicured trees and bushes, past courtiers bundled on cozy benches, until she passed through a break in the hedges. An open field crunched with frost under her slippered feet, and still she ran, until she reached the nearest crop of trees, well away from the palace walls.

She touched them, instantly feeling better. Instantly feeling like herself. She was turning into one of *them*. Thinking of only herself. Ruled by her emotions. Ruled by the desire for the prince's hand. Willing to do almost *anything* to win, and devastated when she didn't.

Would they think she'd totally lost her mind if she asked to shelter in the woods instead of her exquisite and unnecessary suite of rooms?

Yes, probably.

"This isn't the life I want for you, little one," she whispered, sagging back against the thick trunk of a leaning tree. "We'll make this a better place, you and I."

A twig snapped, making her jump and drop her hand from her belly. The unicorns. "Crucifan. Opal. You startled me." She curtsied low, eyes down until Opal pawed at the ground.

Fenity held out her hand, and Opal pushed her nose into it until Fenity scratched her forehead around her horn, careful to avoid touching it. She'd read they were sensitive. "I didn't expect to see you. I'm sorry I don't have any treats."

Crucifan watched her touch his mate with close scrutiny but allowed it.

"What brings you here, anyway?" Wary of Opal's horn, she

moved to scratch her neck. "I'd be home in a heartbeat if I were you." She'd never been to the Unicorn Sanctum—the land long ago dedicated to their race by a much wiser king than their current one—few had. But she'd love to go one day.

Opal jerked her head back at the sound of horses whinnying and the clatter of carriage wheels over a cobbled road. Crucifan's ears flicked back.

Fenity peeked around the trees. She hadn't been far from the road after all. A lone carriage approached the outer wall, driven by servants. Sarafine's signature red dress shimmered through the window.

Fenity's heart clenched. There beside her, on the side closest to Fenity, was Renic. They were the only two in the carriage. Sarafine was laughing, face close to his, one hand on his shoulder. When they passed Fenity's crop of trees, he turned toward the window, and his eyes went right to her. Unmasked devastation fell over his features, and a thousand words he wanted to say almost came tumbling out of his open mouth.

But then Sarafine spotted her, no doubt drawn by the unicorns still standing stoically behind her like the solid support Fenity sorely needed. Sarafine's face turned dark, and she said something Fenity couldn't make out, which drew Renic's attention from the window just long enough for them to pass out of sight through the outer wall. The gate shut behind them.

A fun trip to town for the two young lovers who'd be betrothed and married one day soon?

A nose bumped Fenity's back, and she turned from her self-pity to find Crucifan's judging eyes. Did he know she was Renic's truemate? Did he sense that within her? Or did he sense Renic's child within her womb?

Whatever he was trying to tell her, she took it as the

comfort she needed. The reminder not to give up hope as he allowed her to scratch his forehead next.

"Thank you both," she whispered. "It's not over yet."

Fenity re-entered the palace with new resolve. Hem and shoes soaked with melted frost, body shivering away the last of the lingering cold, she asked around until she located Arinia's room one wing over on the bottom floor.

This part of the palace was plainer—clearly not designed to impress foreign guests—with small windows, simple wall sconces, and carpet runners years past needing replacing.

Was she allowed to be here? After all, the guides and attendants of the Strife were bound by strict and secret rules to serve only the king. Maybe befriending a contestant violated the inner sanctity of those.

Who cares?

Fenity knocked loud and proud on the simple wood door the guard had told her belonged to Arinia.

Arinia answered, eyes going wide, and a male beside her ducked out of sight. "My lady. Are you well?" She took in the state of Fenity's dress and frowned.

Stars. "Sorry. I didn't think you'd be busy." Yet again, more proof she was turning into *them*. Of course Arinia had a life outside of forcing Fenity into fancy dresses. "I can come back."

"No, no. My son was just leaving." She pulled the door open all the way. "Please, come in."

The male strapped on a metal breastplate and grabbed a pack from the floor. He was older than her, that much was clear. He nodded his head in respect. "Lady Fenity. My mata sings your praises."

Heat tinged Fenity's cheeks as she entered the simple

room. A single bed with a small table and two chairs, a partition in the corner for dressing. It was plain compared to the fine clothes and fancy hairdos Arinia liked to wear. Had she ever asked Arinia about her life? How did she not know about her son, or that he was a warrior in the king's army? A high honor indeed.

Maybe she *was* more like them than she realized.

"Lady Fenity, this is Atraius." Arinia's proud smile prodded Fenity in the softest part of her heart. "He brought me flowers." She pointed to a small wooden cup with a sprig of white foxlace gracing the small dining table.

"I don't mean to rush you away. Please, what I need couldn't be a fraction as important as time with your mata." She edged toward the door. Warriors didn't see their family much. She would know. This was the most she'd seen Pata in ages, and he was only allowed to be here because she was a contestant.

"They've called us to another goblin attack. I was saying my goodbyes." He embraced Arinia in a long hug.

Fenity covered her mouth.

He left with a smile, and Arinia shut the door behind him, eyes shining. "Don't you fret none. I've said goodbye to him a hundred times, and he always returns. He's a good warrior, and a good son."

A goblin attack. There was so much to running a kingdom she didn't even know about.

"So, you've come all this way and ruined another dress. How can I assist you?"

Fenity blinked. Why had she come again? Oh, right. "There are two pillars left. I need your help figuring out what they are so I can win them." If she could even guess in the vicinity, she could get a leg up instead of always being one step behind everyone else.

Arinia gave a nod of approval, though her eyes turned cautious. "Do you have any theories?"

Fenity sat on the sturdy, if plain, wooden chair—it reminded her of her true home in the woods. Arinia set to making them tea in the small hearth.

"Well, aside from leadership, which has yet to be decided, there's compassion and integrity left. The two unknowns." Fenity drummed her fingers on the clean table. "How does a queen show compassion? Maybe by doing something for the people?" But King Sidian didn't seem to care about them. "Or a project to reach out to an ally in need? Like organizing a ball to improve relations within our kingdom or perhaps with the neighboring races." But that would fall under leadership, probably.

"Now you're thinking like a queen." Arinia handed her a cup, and the gingermint eased some nausea that had crept up. Fetam wasn't lying about feeling sick all the time. She'd need to get more of that tonic.

"Do you think I could be right?" So far, the pillars had all been extreme and vicious. Maybe that meant a change of pace for the next one.

Arinia simply smiled and shrugged. "What about integrity? Do you have any theories on that one?"

"You don't have an opinion? Or even a suggestion?" That must mean... "Are you not allowed to deliberate with me?"

Arinia didn't speak but gave a subtle shake of her head.

"Oh." Fenity studied her cup, cracked in the handle and plain white. She'd become used to the too-fragile-to-be-practical painted porcelain.

Wait. Her lips parted. Did Arinia know what the pillars were then?

She glanced up to Arinia's firm eyes and even firmer nod.

She knew. Arinia knew what the pillars were, and she

wasn't allowed to tell. And her actions meant someone might be listening to this very conversation.

Did all the guides know? Is that how Sarafine knew things about the pillars before everyone else?

Fenity swallowed and measured her next words and actions carefully. "Is that how Sarafine...?" she mouthed, rather than even risk a whisper.

Arinia nodded with her eyes.

The cup shook in Fenity's hands, anger bunching her nerves. No matter if Sarafine had bribed her attendants or there was something greater at work, it all added up to ensure Fenity did not win this competition.

"Did you hear me, my lady? I asked if you had any theories about the Fifth Pillar of Faedom, integrity." Arinia's voice was pleasant, loud compared to their silent conversation.

Fenity struggled to keep anger from shaking her voice. "Yes, the Fifth Pillar. Integrity." She took a deep breath. "To me, integrity means doing what is right, even if it's not popular. Though that's not really the way of the court, is it?" They did what was popular for them and their court, not what was right for fae as a whole. She sipped her tea. "It will be King Sidian who sets the parameters on what qualifies as honor. So... maybe some kind of individual test for that."

"In other words, you have no ideas." Arinia gave her a smile, and it was almost piteous.

"Right." Because she'd just stated the obvious. That was what the pillars were, tests for each attribute.

But why the pity? Because Sarafine was always several steps ahead of her in every way? Or maybe the contest was rigged. And either Arinia knew or she suspected.

"The king and Sarafine?" Fenity mouthed. It was clear the king favored Sarafine—maybe he was allowing her to cheat.

Arinia froze but said nothing. Then her eyes flicked once

toward the flowers her son had brought. Her face crumpled with worry and apology.

This was more than just loyalty to the king. Something was preventing Arinia from speaking.

Fenity's body locked. Arinia's son. Was the king threatening him? Did all the guides carry this same burden to keep the king's secrets? And every time Fenity pushed for more, she was further endangering them.

"I've overstayed my welcome." Fenity hopped up and gathered the teacups, taking them to the washbasin.

"Never." Arinia smiled with relief, her demeanor clearing. "In fact, it's nearly time to dress for dinner."

Fenity could hardly think of sitting through another feast. Not after all she'd learned. Another endless, wasteful affair where she was ignored by the contestants, side-eyed by the king, and tortured by not being able to touch—or even speak to—Renic. And this evening would have the added fun of watching Sarafine commandeer his attention from her honored position right beside him.

"Can't wait," she said flatly.

Arinia laughed and walked her to the door. "I'll be up shortly."

Fenity paused just before leaving. "I hope you know you're not a servant to me. Even though you are bound by king's decree and you say I can't trust you, I still do. I understand there are things beyond your control. Your life has value, and what you do here has value. I know that. I'm sorry if it seems like I forgot you had a life before I came." She blinked against her wavering eyesight. "I know I'm not doing any of this the way it's supposed to be done. I know I'm missing so many things. But I couldn't do this without you."

Arinia placed a warm hand against her cheek, her own eyes shining. "You're doing everything your own way, my dear.

That's why you should win." She pulled her into a tight hug. "We're rooting for you. Just keep learning, adapting, and being true to yourself," she whispered. "It'll all work out in the end."

Fenity nodded and headed to her rooms. When she and Renic ruled the throne, they would change the world. Loyalty would be inspired, not threatened. And good fae would have a voice, whether rich or poor, powerful or energyless.

The trip to Arinia's only taught her just how much she was still in the dark, and yet, her steps felt lighter. Her heart ached a little less.

CHAPTER 39

Late at night, after the feast had ended, Renic finally came to her. As soon as his warm body joined hers under the blankets, she awoke from a restless sleep, and the bitterness of enduring the evening melted away. As predicted, Sarafine had the place of honor beside him, while Fenity was relegated to a table near the servant's entrance of the room. She invited Nisha to join her, but the lead servant of the hall wouldn't allow them to switch seats. The constant coming and going of trays and rattling dishes made it hard to even hear the music playing in the corner.

But that was nothing compared to watching Sarafine place her hands all over Renic the entire evening. His arm. His shoulder. His hand. Even his chest at one point as she laughed at something he said and playfully shoved against him. Every time he'd locked eyes with Sarafine, Fenity had to grip her skirts to keep from smashing her plate or opening a portal just to get them to stop. The male they'd placed next to her was friendly enough, and she truly felt bad that she couldn't pay more attention to his attempts at conversation. He gave up around the fourth time she asked him to repeat his question.

So maybe she was *partly* to blame for her lack-of-friend situation.

"I'm sorry." Renic sighed into her hair, holding her from behind. "If I'm to protect you and our secret, I can't deny the winner their reward. But I know how hard today was for me, so I can only imagine how difficult it was for you."

"I just want to forget it. But I'm still awaiting my reward for the Second Pillar." His presence made everything right, like the bad never happened.

Except...

"Did your pata coerce the gnomes to choose Sarafine?"

Renic stiffened. "Yes," he whispered.

Fenity turned in his arms until she faced him. "So it's true."

He caressed her cheek. "I will always tell you the truth."

"Why didn't you warn me?" She'd won the pillar right in front of the gnomes. If there was another chance to win their vote, she would have known about it.

But she'd asked Renic not to help her cheat.

"I didn't know. After the announcement, I approached him and he didn't deny it." His hand left her face and clenched into a fist.

Her heart split into a million pieces. "I can't win." The gnome king and queen had wanted to pick her, but King Sidian intervened. There was no way to compete against a king.

"Yes, you can. You must."

Fenity sat up, throwing the covers off her heated body. But that wasn't enough. She hopped out of bed and paced through her anger. Her words came out in a hiss. "The *king* paid—or threatened or whatever—the vote of an entire race so that I would lose! What does this contest even mean if he controls the outcome?" Anger assaulted her, so strong it gave way to silent tears. Was nothing in her control? She could work as hard as she ever had and still it wouldn't make a difference?

Renic perched on the edge of the bed but didn't interrupt her pacing. Deep sadness graced his beautiful brow. "You're forgetting something very important."

"What?" she snapped.

"It's my bride. I will choose who I marry. And I choose you."

She stopped pacing, and he was right there to absorb the emotion she wore on her sleeve, holding her close. "But you said it yourself. Even choosing me won't be enough."

He was silent for way too long.

"We can change things, Fen. The courtiers only care for themselves. My own parents are more concerned about keeping their borders intact than they are about the people living within them. But you and I will change all that. We will be the ones to cleanse this court of their disassociation with reality."

We can change the world.

She pulled him closer, squeezing tight. She wanted it so badly. But nothing was ever so simple. King Sidian was actively working to help Sarafine win. And there was nothing Fenity could do about it.

"I can't wait to change things for the better by your side." She wrapped a hand behind his neck and tilted her head. He gave her what she so desperately wanted and kissed her.

Stars above, the taste of him. She'd never get her fill. Their lips danced, breaths mingling and tongues teasing. Just when she thought she might burst, Renic pulled back and smiled. He kissed her lips. Once. Twice.

"Come." He led her to the bed. "You need rest. I can stay for a little while."

Not all night, she knew. They couldn't be caught together again. He lay down beside her, holding her again from behind.

"I think I know what the Fifth Pillar is," he whispered, so quietly she almost thought she was dreaming.

"Don't tell me." Her eyes flew open and her heart sped, nearly drowning out his reply.

"I have to. My pata—"

Fenity clamped her hands over his mouth. "No. I can't judge others for cheating, then cheat myself."

He mumbled something and gently pried her hands away. "A theory then. I heard my pata call it the royal choice. That means my choice. I get to choose who has the integrity of a queen. That gives my say more weight when I choose you."

Fenity's hope burst and died. Royal choice could mean anything. Would King Sidian really let Renic choose? The Strife had turned into prince against king instead of who would be the best queen. And she had no idea why.

Several weeks passed without incident and without news. It seemed the court had their fill of drama, for a little while anyway. The gnomes departed, and Fenity was sad she never got the chance to meet them. They'd kept to themselves, staying outside the castle and not even attending meals.

Fenity used the time to study how to be a good queen, rest, and adjust to her changing body. Nausea. Sleepiness that hit without warning. She'd be in an etiquette lesson with Arinia and it was as if her eyes would close of their own free will.

"Their names are not 'older female in the steel-gray frock' and 'crabby contestant in the burnt-orange dress.'" Arinia rolled her eyes. "It's Lady Cameira and Lady Pernin."

Arinia quietly blamed Renic for keeping her up, but Fenity

hadn't seen him. He hadn't had time for visits. The goblin attack at the border kept him in strategy meetings—likely the real reason the Strife was at a temporary standstill.

Fenity missed him fiercely, but it was easier to hide her nausea and fatigue when he wasn't around. Her belly was still too small to see, but there was a hard bulge when she gently pressed with her hands. If she could feel it, he probably could too. Not much longer—the contest would end and she could finally tell him.

What a sweet day that would be. Females were supposed to be cared for and supported by their truemates. Not these secrets and midnight trysts, sneaking around like criminals.

It was easy to feel lonely in this boxed-up world, and since she couldn't risk visiting Marek, she decided she'd eat breakfast in the dining hall with the others for a change. And she made a promise to herself. If anyone tried to talk to her, she'd give them her full attention and best effort.

Entering the dining hall, a lot of contestants gave her weird looks from where they sat at the tables, already eating or waiting for breakfast. Whispered conversations broke out amongst certain groups. It was like the first day all over again.

But just like then, it didn't bother her. Maybe she needed their favor when she became queen, but she wouldn't sell herself or change who she was for them. Plus, now she had Renic. And she wasn't the nobody they thought she was. She'd won the Second Pillar of Faedom. Without cheating.

She looked for a single friendly face in the room. Nisha wasn't there, and no one met her eyes except a servant standing by the wall, who smiled and looked away.

Fine then.

Fenity walked to the empty chair closest to the servant and sat facing her. "It's so nice to see a kind face. I'm Fenity." She extended her hand, and the servant took it automatically.

"Sinda." She gave a quick curtsy. "Can I get your breakfast?"

"If it's not too much trouble. It still feels odd not doing things for myself, but that's not allowed here."

Sinda smiled and retreated to the kitchen. She returned with an array of delicious items, but the smell of eggs made Fenity gag. She pushed them away, and Sinda quickly discarded them. "You're the kind one. You helped my friend when she spilled the drinks."

"Oh, that was no trouble." If there was a way to be remembered, she'd choose kindness. Sinda replied with a deep blush, so Fenity kept talking. "There are so many rules here to learn. For instance, I'd love to invite you to sit and dine with me, but I'm sure we'd both get in trouble."

"That's true, m'lady. But, if I may, we like you better without the rules." Sinda's gaze darted to the side, then she curtsied again and hurried away.

There were two contestants one table over. Lady Mira in the dark blue with the powerful sound energy, and Lady Daream in the gold—she'd been one of the sprites' top picks. Fenity took a deep breath and approached them, plate in hand. "Mind if I join you?"

They exchanged looks before Lady Daream smiled. "Of course."

Fenity sat beside Lady Daream while Lady Mira pushed food around her plate across from them. "I wanted to apologize if I've seemed reserved. Honestly, I wasn't prepared for how things would be at court and I let it make me resentful."

"I made the same mistake when I first joined court as a youth," Daream said, kindness etched in every feature. "I expected the court members to be... better fae, I suppose. So it really disappointed me when I found out they were just like everyone else. It turned me bitter for a long time."

Mira's energy waxed and waned with the push of her fork through her berries. "What Daream is trying to say is, the quicker you accept that the court is just as corrupt as the rest of the world, the better you'll fit in. But you're doing alright."

"I'm just trying my best, like the rest of us. But you've both made an impression on me. Mira, your energy is unparalleled. And Daream, the sprites are good judges of character. I hope you'll both give me a second chance to prove I'm worthy to be here."

The contestants shared a long look before standing. Daream spoke for both of them. "You wouldn't be here if you weren't worthy, but we'd love to get to know you better, Fenity."

Mira gave a more hesitant smile, but it was progress.

Fenity finished and left for lessons with Arinia, leaving the noise of the dining room and heading deeper into the castle.

"You're disappointing us, Sarafine." A female's voice whipped out from around the corner.

Fenity froze.

"I'm doing fine on my own, Mata. You didn't have to do that." Sarafine's voice.

Fenity eased back down the hall, footsteps soft.

"Of course we did." A male's voice, quiet but just as harsh. "You lost the Second Pillar. You! You serve only one purpose in this world, and that is to win the Strife. He needs those troops, and you needed to win."

"I don't want to win like this."

"You can't lose another pillar." Her mata's voice quieted. "I heard a rumor Prince Renic will pick that woodland female. After all your time together, he should be wooing you. Why isn't he looking at you? You must sway him by any means. We must win the Strife."

"I'm trying."

"Try harder," the male said. "We can only do so much. You have every advantage. Don't return home if you lose."

Their footsteps moved this way, and Fenity jumped. There was nowhere to hide. The nearest door was too far down the hall.

She backed as far as she dared, then walked forward normally. When Sarafine's parents rounded the corner dressed in splendor to rival the king, they paused, lips curling in masks of disgust. Fenity ignored them and continued as if she'd been walking by and hadn't paused to hear every word.

So they were the ones who swayed the gnomes through the king, somehow. And they hated her. And they knew Renic would choose her.

Great.

Fenity hurried away. She knew the pressure for Sarafine to win was great, but she could never have imagined the consequences. They'd exile their own kin for a play at the throne.

It took longer than it should have to arrive at her rooms because she had to commit to the path she'd taken in front of Sarafine's parents. Then she got lost. She ended up exiting the castle out of some random back door in order to finally get her bearings. The cold should have felt biting, but it grounded her.

She turned down her hall to find Arinia pacing, the other attendants standing outside the door, wringing their hands.

Arinia gasped when she spotted her. "You were supposed to return as soon as you ate!" She met her in the hall and led her by the shoulders back the way she'd come.

"What's wrong?" Arinia was always a little high-strung, but this was more than that.

"The king summoned everyone to the courtyard. They've already left." Their footsteps turned to quick jogs. "I didn't have time to prep you."

"Do you know why?" Fenity took the lead. Finding her way out of this place was definitely something she'd memorized.

"The unicorns have made their choice."

Fenity nearly stumbled.

"Go," Arinia said. "You're faster."

Fenity left her behind, hurrying down the winding stairs of the castle tower, watching her steps and keeping one hand braced on the wall. This tower would take her closest to the main door. Panting, she burst into the courtyard, earning glares and eyerolls from the nearest contestants. It seemed she was the last to arrive.

Manicured trees and bushes, and the backs of a rainbow of gowns were all she could see. She slowed her pace to a regal walk and made her way forward. Beyond a fountain still spraying water despite the chilled air, the courtyard opened up into the flat land she loved to walk barefoot. On one side of the yard, a set of stone steps led to a landing at the base of another part of the castle. The royal family perched in thrones brought just for the occasion, with the courtiers standing behind and fanned out beside them.

Strife contestants ringed the rest of the field. Mira and Daream stood beside each other near Nisha, and all three gave her a smile or polite nod. The contestants wore thick wraps against the cold, but Fenity hadn't had time to collect hers. In the middle stood Opal and Crucifan. The power and beauty emanating from them, especially as a mated pair, could not be denied.

The herald wore a thick coat and was booming something about the privilege of having the unicorns here, and the graciousness of his majesty to allow the contestants access to such magnificent creatures. One eye on Renic—who'd found her the moment she arrived—Fenity crossed behind the contestants until she found an open spot to stand on the far side of the field.

"Decided to join us?" Sarafine quipped.

Fenity broke her gaze from Renic. "Sarafine." The harshness she wanted to put into the name was absent, making it sound kind instead. Maybe she needed kindness in her life.

Sarafine scowled.

Fenity sighed to herself. She wouldn't be the person Mata raised her to be if she let the Strife prevent her from being a decent person.

"I want to apologize for not being kinder to you," Fenity said quietly. It was just the two of them on this corner, with the nearest contestant on Sarafine's other side, but she didn't want anyone overhearing. "I understand now why this contest means so much to you."

Sarafine froze. "You don't know anything."

"Maybe." She knew that Sarafine carried the secret to destroy her and hadn't used it.

Fenity let it go and focused ahead.

"The unicorns will now choose their winner for the Third Pillar of Faedom!" The herald ended his proclamation with upraised arms, and the courtiers and contestants cheered.

Fenity's palms sweat. There was no reason for them to choose her, but she wanted it badly. And not just because of the Strife. To have the respect of the unicorns, let alone their leaders, would be the ultimate gift.

The courtyard held its breath.

Crucifan and Opal embraced, nuzzling against each other, then separated. Fenity didn't want to watch which direction they headed, but it was too mesmerizing to look away. Their powerful, untamed muscles flexed as they walked. Their hair shimmered in the sun that broke through the clouds.

Crucifan stopped in the middle, facing away from Fenity.

Opal, however, pivoted. Head lowered, she plodded straight toward Fenity and Sarafine's corner. The courtiers gasped. Sarafine grinned and raised her chin. Then Opal stopped.

Crucifan paced forward, his sure hoofbeats taking him to the contestants on the opposite side, near the royal dais. The females there stood taller, eyeing one another as if trying to gauge who it might be. Nisha was among them, her meekness almost convincing.

But Crucifan paced right by them. He approached the stairs, then jumped them in a single bound. Everyone on the dais reared back in shock, the courtiers screaming and falling over themselves. King Sidian stayed seated, but his brow furrowed in anger. Besides Fenity's parents, Renic was the only one who didn't act afraid, waving off the guards who tried to intervene. Crucifan ignored the overly dramatic chaos around him and slowly approached the prince. Renic stood and bowed deeply before him.

Crucifan lipped at his hand, clearly wanting Renic up. Renic knew it, too. Under King Sidian's watchful eye, he stood and followed Crucifan down the stairs and back to the middle of the field, where they stopped beside each other.

The contestants whispered amongst each other. Was this supposed to happen? The king and queen passed around uncomfortable smiles.

Opal resumed her unhurried pace, still heading in Fenity's direction. The white mare could just as easily have been aiming for Sarafine. Fenity stood still, carefully not meeting the unicorn's gaze head-on. The contestants Opal already bypassed protested loudly, and Sarafine threw glances at Fenity the closer Opal came.

Fenity didn't breathe. She couldn't let hope win. What if it wasn't her?

Opal closed the distance, walking a line that cut right between Fenity and Sarafine, so close it was impossible to tell. Opal stopped between the two of them.

The cold disappeared. The murmurs and accusations disappeared. Sarafine and her pain disappeared.

It was just her and Opal. And when the unicorn pushed her nose into Fenity's waiting palm, her heart flooded with warmth. She finally raised her eyes. Renic was already watching her, his pride and love waiting for her. But not surprise. He hadn't doubted for a moment.

Ignoring Sarafine's gaping mouth, Fenity followed Opal's prodding and trailed her to the middle. The two unicorns stood on the outside, facing the royal dais, with Fenity and Renic between them. He played his part well, with a kind smile and a healthy distance separating them.

The urge to grab his hand was nearly her undoing. Even arms apart, she felt his heat and his love.

The courtiers clapped politely as the herald stepped forward. "Crucifan and Opal, leaders of Unicorn Sanctum, have made their decision for the Third Pillar of Faedom. Lady Fenity Stormbrook!"

The contestants did not clap. The courtiers gave smattering applause while Fenity's parents cheered the loudest, glaring at their peers.

Crucifan whinnied, the sound piercing the field, and suddenly Opal reared, horn reaching for the sky, forelegs kicking the air. Fenity stumbled back at the same time Crucifan sidestepped into Renic, pushing him into her.

Renic caught her. She fell easily into his arms in a dip that had him staring down into her eyes.

"Are you alright?"

A nervous laugh burst from her lips. "I feel like this was

designed." The moment was nearly over, but she'd soak him up while she could.

He returned her smile. "I knew they'd pick you." His gaze dropped to her lips.

Guards rushed toward them, no doubt to save the heir from the wild beasts. Crucifan and Opal burst into a gallop, contestants diving out of the way as they rushed out of the circle.

Renic righted them and stepped away, his careful mask slipping into place. "Congratulations, Lady Fenity."

"Thank you, Your Highness." She bowed, and he walked back toward the dais as if he wasn't taking part of her heart with him.

King Sidian motioned a courtier over to him, and Fenity recognized him at once. Sarafine's pata. She'd seen him advise the king before. He was a lord just like Fenity's pata, but his lands were part of Alberry, and clearly, the king favored him.

Lord Rivers nodded to the king, whispering back. Fenity shifted on her feet.

Renic's eyes darkened infinitesimally. He heard the exchange.

Lord Rivers stepped back, and King Sidian rose from his throne. "Thank you, ladies of the Strife. With the goblins' latest hostility, they are excluded from the Third Pillar of Faedom. We will announce the winner of the entire pillar at the feast this evening."

Fenity couldn't help but narrow her eyes, thankful she didn't do worse. The king had ignored her win completely, without even congratulating her or giving her an award. Just like when she'd won the Second Pillar.

Renic didn't react except to follow his pata's lead and vacate the dais with the rest of the courtiers.

Winning the unicorns' vote didn't win her the pillar, but

they were the last of the races included in the challenge. The last of the races King Sidian deemed important enough to include, anyway. The fairies, for example, were too feral to outsiders to be included. Fenity had never seen a fairy, only shadows of them, and she wasn't sure she wanted to.

The contestants cleared out as well, leaving Fenity standing in the field feeling like an idiot, like she'd missed the instructions again. The freezing wind blew past, reminding her she was cold, so without pomp or circumstance, or promise of her earned reward, she pinched the lengths of her skirts and made her way inside over the cold ground.

Most contestants headed to the dining hall for lunch, but Fenity's nausea was too great, so she slipped away from the throng, taking the same winding stairs she'd used earlier. One hand on her belly, she wound her way around.

Was her awarded time still to come? Sarafine's had been almost immediately after she'd won the last time. Would King Sidian keep it from her? Arinia would know.

"What was that?" Sarafine's harsh voice echoed up the stone stairs, and Fenity turned to see her rounding the spiral. Light from the latticed windows hit Sarafine's dress, making the space glow red around her.

Fenity dropped the hand from her belly. "What do you want, Sarafine?" She continued the climb, eyes peeled for a place to throw up if the nausea attacked again.

"I saw the way he looked at you," Sarafine accused, following. "He has feelings for you, doesn't he?"

"I wasn't lying when I said we're truemates." She passed the landing for the floor directly beneath hers and kept climbing.

But Sarafine had stopped.

Fenity looked over her shoulder to see Sarafine, back against the gray stones, distress on her face. "You can't win.

He'll never choose you." But the words came out breathless and panicked.

Fenity walked back down to meet her. "Your parents will still love you, even if you lose. It's okay to lose sometimes."

"Not this." Sarafine swallowed, eyes darting. "It's not safe for you. Haven't you noticed it's only you and I winning this competition?"

Sarafine was the top contender among the contestants. Fenity was the odd one out, winning only by sheer luck and Renic's love. But why couldn't the others win? Was there some unspoken pact Fenity wasn't aware of because she wasn't one of them? Something that led to Sarafine winning the Strife?

"Why?" Fenity demanded. She couldn't stand the thought that her wins were because the others had stepped aside for Sarafine. No. She wouldn't believe it.

Sarafine lowered her voice to barely a whisper. "The contestant that died in the troll trial, Lady Carlin?" Sarafine swallowed hard, her confident composure unraveled. "She successfully retrieved a token from King Makas. Her partner was with her when she stole it. Lady Carlin should have won, but she died, and no one really saw how. If her partner had, she's not saying anything."

Fenity stopped breathing. Who was Carlin's partner? "Your parents, would they—"

"I don't know. I'm a piece in their game. Maybe." Sarafine pushed off the wall, some of her armor slipping back into place. "Stay out of the way and you'll be safe."

Sarafine didn't wait for a response. She descended the stairs, leaving Fenity alone. Sarafine had to be making it up, implying something terrible about the contest. Manipulating her.

But... no one else had won a pillar yet. And Sarafine's parents had convinced the gnomes—the only race susceptible to manipulation—to vote for Sarafine. And what Arinia had implied about how Sarafine knew the pillars ahead of time.

Would she really be in danger if she continued to try to win? Her hand drifted back to her stomach. She could compete in the Strife to be with Renic. She could face the court's disapproval, even the king and queen. She could stand the ire from all the ladies of the realm, but how could she prepare for danger to come from all sides?

Her slow steps eventually brought her to her rooms, her body numb from more than just the cold.

CHAPTER 40

Still numb from the cold and Sarafine's warning, Fenity entered her rooms. The second Arinia embraced her in congratulations for winning, she backed away with a gasp. "You're freezing! I should have thought to give you a shawl." She led Fenity further into the entryway. "Quick, draw a warm bath. Here, drink this." Arinia placed a comforting cup of hot tea into her hands, causing them to burn with pins and needles. She really was numb, inside and out.

The bath burned too, at first, then thawed her frozen limbs. They dressed her in a warm nightshift and hurried her into bed with extra blankets heated by energy. Warm and snuggled deep like in a burrow, there was a knock at the door.

Arinia answered it. "Oh good, you're here." She moved aside, and Fetam stepped into the bedroom, bag in her hand and a comforting smile on her lips.

"I heard you might have been exposed to the cold too long." Fetam set her bag on the side table.

Fenity sat up. "It was nothing to trouble you about, Healer Fetam. I'm fine now."

"Let's check you out, just in case." Fetam gave her a weighted look.

Arinia gave a satisfied nod and left with the other attendants.

When the door closed, Fenity lay back. "I'm truly okay, though I could use something for the nausea."

Fetam poured a draught that smelled strongly of ginger into her cup, then added a dollop of nectar from the side table. Fenity sipped at it, already feeling better.

"You're right, there's nothing wrong with you," Fetam said with a hand on her forehead. "But let's check on the little one." Fenity lay down, and Fetam shifted her attention to her abdomen. Fenity held her breath. "She's doing well. I can already sense her energy."

Tears sprung to Fenity's eyes. "She?" A female?

"Oh, yes. I didn't mean to tell you without your permission." Fetam removed her hand. "Your daughter is very clear to me, so it only came naturally to address her so. I'm sorry."

"My daughter." Fenity covered her mouth. Suddenly, the baby wasn't just an idea or a dream, but a real person who'd be in her arms in a few short months. And a daughter. Would she have dark hair like Renic or red like hers?

She'd have this curse too. It would be okay. Fenity would find someone to teach her how to control it.

"Congratulations. I have daughters as well." Fetam repacked her bag, leaving more of the draught behind. "Long grown now, of course. Take care of her."

"I will," Fenity barely managed to say.

After Fetam left, it was easy to push her cares away and sleep, safe under Arinia's watchful eye. She awoke, warm, rested, and comforted, with Arinia's kind face telling her it was time to prepare for the feast.

"Give me your best dress, Arinia."

"Yes, my lady." Arinia and her attendants were eager to comply, happy Fenity seemed to care what she wore for once. The dress she picked was beautiful. A huge gown with skirts like a bell. Green, of course, but pale green, with dark green crystals sewn into it, thick at the waist, then tapering off toward the bottom, like the start of a rainstorm. The corset was a bit tight, especially over her chest, but when Fenity protested from the pain, Arinia expertly loosened the strings in the right places. The dress looked nice with gossamer sleeves that added sparkle and a good plunge down the front that left nothing to the imagination.

While they fixed her hair into a half-up twist of curls and braids, Fenity's mind wandered. Who would be the winner of the Third Pillar? Sarafine had won the trolls, and somehow the gnomes. But Fenity won the sprites and the unicorns. The goblins would have been the tiebreaker, but the king had barred them. They'd only ranked them in the first sprite trial, but not the others. Had something changed between then and now?

Could contestants tie for a pillar? If not, who got the deciding vote?

Fenity didn't want to know the answers.

So far, only two pillars had winners. Sarafine won the First Pillar—strength—with her energy display. Fenity won the second—poise. That meant they were tied, right?

"You look incredible." Arinia clapped her hand over her mouth, breaking into Fenity's deep thoughts.

She stood, and Arinia led her to the floor-length gilded mirror as the attendants oohed and aahed over their work.

Fenity's eyes went round as she took it all in. The wide layers of the gown's skirts made her waist look thin. Matching green crystals sparked in her braids and curls, dangling like vines from her ears and neck. The makeup gave her a slight flush, more like her old self before she felt so tired all the time. Coal lined her eyes, making the blue stand out even more.

"Stars above, you're artists." Fenity touched her cheek to make sure it was really her. She looked like a queen. And yet, it *was* still her.

The attendants chuckled, and Arinia beamed. "Make us proud, Lady Fenity."

"I'll do my best." The parts she could control, anyway.

Fenity earned many side glances of envy as she and the other contestants made their way to the ballroom. All of their dresses were beautiful, but there was something special about Fenity's. She looked good and carried it with more confidence than usual.

Whatever it was, she'd take it. It helped disguise the fluttering nerves and rising nausea. Uncertainty lay ahead, though if she was waging coin like the other courtiers, she wouldn't bet on herself tonight.

The scene in the ballroom looked just like it had when Sarafine was announced as the gnomes' winner, except it was decorated for the dance to follow the feast. The royal dais sat higher than everyone, with courtiers and contestants filling the room. Large swaths of iridescent fabric hung from the ceiling and draped around the windows. Energy orbs floated near them, casting different colors around the room. The candelabras hadn't been lit, and the refreshment table sat empty—details to finish once everyone moved to the dining hall for the feast.

Fenity felt many pairs of eyes rake over her and linger as she made her way forward. It was easy to pretend they didn't exist. She would be as close to Renic as possible, with none standing between them.

She finally broke through the crowd, spotting him. His eyes

lit up in delight, then he took in her attire, and his jaw fell open.

"Wow," he mouthed. He leaned forward like he might leap from the dais.

She laughed out loud. "This old thing?" She pinched the top sparkly layer of her skirts and dropped it like it was rags when in fact it was the most elaborate gown she'd ever seen— aside from the queen's regalia that she vowed never to wear again. She couldn't help but notice his tunic color tonight —green.

Sarafine causally stepped past her, breaking their line of sight. Her crimson skirt brushed Fenity's, just as wide and voluminous as hers. They were dressed nearly identically. Sarafine's dress lacked the crystals, and the bodice was way more revealing, with deep plunges both in front and back, and no lace to conceal any bare skin. Sexier and more sophisti- cated. Somehow the crystals Fenity loved a moment ago seemed childish now.

What was happening to her? Sarafine hadn't even needed to say anything to make her feel inferior.

The matching dresses couldn't have been a coincidence. Had one of Fenity's attendants told Sarafine? Or maybe her parents had cornered the dressmaker—more proof of their influence in the Strife.

The rest of Sarafine's group joined her in the front, over- taking Fenity's spot. Renic's attention stayed on Fenity, not even glancing at Sarafine.

Fenity straightened her shoulders and raised her chin. She was right, and Renic was right. She was in control of her feel- ings and no one else's opinions should sway her own.

Fenity swished her hips a bit, and the dress shimmered so beautifully in the light of the orbs, she could only imagine what her jewelry and hair looked like. Renic's lips spread into a grin.

Stars, he was handsome.

"Announcing King Sidian and Queen Lara," the herald said before bowing deeply. The buttons on his blue vest strained near to bursting.

Everyone bowed as Queen Lara took her throne beside the prince, while King Sidian stepped to the front of the dais. Fenity tried to read Renic for any hint he knew how this would go, but he watched the king, body tensed as if waiting to find out with the rest of them.

Fenity fought back the rising nausea.

"The queen and I have reached a decision regarding the Third Pillar of Faedom." The queen and who? "The goblins have chosen our volatile time of the Strife to claim land that rightfully belongs to the fae. While we're at odds with them now, it won't always be so. Peace will be restored, but in the meantime, they can't have a say over one of our foundational pillars. As we currently have a tie amongst the remaining races, the rulers represented here cast their vote anonymously this afternoon."

A murmur swept through the crowd. A vote? Pata hadn't told her. But she hadn't seen her parents since they'd departed the courtyard earlier. Fenity's heart beat in her ears. She swept her gaze, looking for them, but didn't see them in the massive crowd.

Her eyes landed on the king, and his gaze pierced right through her, leaving her cold. "The final tally was thirty-one to nine. Lady Sarafine, I'm proud to announce you are the winner of the Third Pillar of Faedom."

Renic's brow rose in shock, then melted in sadness before he locked his mask in place.

Fenity had no such control. Energy flowed through her, fast

and powerful, reacting to her emotions. Heads turned her way. They sensed it.

Courtiers and contestants clapped loudly—it was the gnome defeat all over again. Except this was a *pillar*. She'd lost an entire pillar in a popularity contest the king knew she'd never win.

The energy raised the hair on her arms.

Fenity grabbed around her middle, holding herself and taking deep, shaking breaths. Contestants moved away, drawn to Sarafine and her win, though some still eyed her and those around her. Fenity shoved the energy down, down, down, until it eventually dampened.

Renic's mask slipped, concern showing through for just a moment as he watched her nearly fall apart, hyperventilating and alone. But her energy stayed under control.

King Sidian eased back in his throne, a pleased look on his face, and the herald took his place. "Our deepest congratulations to Lady Sarafine. If you will all make your way to the dining hall, I've ordered a celebratory feast." He gestured to the side of the room that flowed into the dining hall.

After the royal family, Sarafine led the way, as if she was already one of them. Her voluminous crimson skirts were a beacon for all to follow and fawn.

Fenity nearly ran the opposite direction, away from the corruption. One thought kept her following Sarafine like one of her lackeys—she'd won the unicorns' vote. She was owed her prize. So maybe she'd be the one by Renic tonight. The one to touch him as much as she wanted. The one to dance with him exclusively for an entire evening.

Servants stood at the door directing the contestants and courtiers where to sit. Fenity's eyes went right to the head table.

Sarafine already sat beside Renic, in the exact spot as before, trying to distract him with entertaining conversation.

"Right over here, Lady Fenity," a servant said, motioning her to the same corner she'd endured last time, where the dirty dishes went.

"I'm supposed to be over there." She pointed to Renic, who watched her even though the king was trying to speak to him. "I won the unicorn vote."

The servant fidgeted and checked a list Fenity hadn't noticed. "My orders are to seat you over there." He pointed, then gulped. "I'm sorry, my lady."

Fenity forced a smile. "My mistake." She took her old seat. The same male as before greeted her politely but didn't engage in conversation this time. Fenity picked at her food. She watched Renic ignore Sarafine by addressing his other neighbor. Fenity endured seven courses of Sarafine touching Renic and staring adoringly into his eyes.

Because the dance was next, and maybe, just maybe, then it'd be her turn.

When the feast finally ended, Fenity could barely keep her eyes open. She filed back into the ballroom at the back of the crowd with the rest of the Strife losers. As soon as her skirts cleared the door, she maneuvered her way forward to find Renic.

"The winner of the Third Pillar reserves the honor of the first dance," the herald announced from somewhere in the corner. Fenity thought hard about portaling him to the human world and letting them have him. Sarafine too.

It was supposed to be the prince's choice at these dances. She sipped on some sparkling juice to settle her stomach, while the musicians began a slow ballad from the dais cleared of thrones. As usual, the king and queen did not attend the ball. Fenity ignored the perimeter of contestants around the beautiful dancing couple. The room really was breathtaking when decorated for the ball. With the sun down, and the moons still rising, the colors glowed, walls now flickering with candlelight making everything sparkle. Like her dress.

The song wound to a close, and Fenity made her way to the open floor. Her turn.

The song ended, and the next one began. Everyone paired up and took to the dance floor, filling it with colors that matched the hanging fabrics. But Sarafine and Renic didn't separate.

Was Sarafine claiming her prize now? Before Fenity claimed her own? And wasn't it up to the king or Renic what the prize was?

Well, Fenity wouldn't allow it. Not today. She bunched her skirts in her fists and marched right through the dance floor, moving to intercept as they came twirling back her way.

Renic saw her first and brought them to a stop. The other dancers had to adjust the normal pattern to avoid running them over.

"Mind if I cut in?" Fenity asked automatically, then shook her head. "I mean, I'm cutting in."

Renic reached for her, but Sarafine's brow darkened, and she stepped between them. "Let's not make a scene. I won the pillar. I win the night."

"Prince Renic chooses who he dances with, not you." She couldn't keep the hate out of her words like Sarafine had. Sarafine might have shown compassion in the stairwell, but she'd had years to practice being fake and poisonous.

"King Sidian chooses, actually, and he chose me." Sarafine turned her back, ready to resume dancing with Renic.

"It's only one dance, Sarafine." Renic's jaw ticked. "Do me this favor?"

"It's not up to you this time." Sarafine blinked up at him. "Your pata—"

"I'm sorry, but Lady Fenity is right. I choose." Renic's words, though even keel and perfectly peaceful, snapped like a whip, full of an authority bestowed upon him by the strength of the fae and his mighty heritage. Sarafine blanched as he stepped right past her and took Fenity's hands into the correct pose for the current dance. "We will continue our evening momentarily, Lady Sarafine." Then he whisked them away, leaving a stunned Sarafine, her cheeks matching her dress.

Fenity grinned up at him, an enormous weight lifting from her shoulders. "For a moment, I thought I'd charged across the dance floor only to be turned away."

"I'll never turn you away." He stared down into her eyes, face stern and serious, body still leading them effortlessly around the room in time to the music. "I'm sorry you had to chase me. My pata did award Sarafine the evening with me, though he didn't announce it. I thought by honoring his wish, we'd avoid his scrutiny."

"I'm tired of shying away from his scrutiny. And I'll always chase you." She gripped his hands in three quick squeezes.

I. Love. You.

His mouth parted in surprise, and then he did it back. Squeeze. Squeeze. Squeeze. *I. Love. You.*

"Not much longer," he said, eyes dipping to her lips. "Rumor is the winner of the fourth pillar comes down to a vote. A fair vote."

Compassion. "A vote?" She'd assumed the secret test would be a surprise they'd have to endure somehow. Like they'd wake up one morning and be thrown into goblin territory to negotiate a truce. "For what?" Would the courtiers get another chance to ensure she didn't win?

"I don't know who's doing the tallying, or what the parameters are. I tried to pry, and it got back to my pata." He winced. "It did not go well."

"He doesn't want me to win." Her voice sounded hollow. "I see it in the way he looks sometimes."

"He doesn't know you like I do. Not yet. He wants what is best for our people, and he doesn't know that it's you." But Renic frowned as if unsure of his claim.

The song drifted to a close, and panic seized her lungs. "Is this all I get for winning the unicorns' vote?" Where was her trip to town, her seat beside him at the banquet?

Renic lowered his voice. "My pata ordered me and the courtiers to act as if that didn't happen. The Second Pillar, too. With Sarafine winning the pillar so soon after, he thinks it would be confusing to award you a prize, too." He ground his teeth, and a muscle ticked in his jaw. "It's not fair. It's not right. It goes directly against tradition—the townsfolk were expecting to see you and have raised concerns that have gone ignored. But I'm hindered from doing *anything* while we keep us secret."

Fenity couldn't reply. The song ended, and Sarafine was right there to take her place. Renic squeezed her hands three times before letting go. It did little to ease the sting as Renic's hands found Sarafine's. They fit so beautifully together.

Fenity dragged her feet to the edge of the dance floor, but it was an effort—her heart had turned leaden, weighing her down and threatening to topple her.

He *had* to know what Sarafine was doing. Everyone did. But, he had to let her, didn't he? Because this was the Strife, and no one could know they were truemates, just like no one could know she was pregnant, or it would put a target on her back. He was playing the game, and she was standing there staring at him—at every move his hands made to hold Sarafine, and every glance he took to her face and away. If anyone was paying a shred of attention, it would be obvious Fenity wasn't in this just for the title.

And suddenly, this was the last place she wanted to be. So, she stopped waiting for him to find her in the crowd—because he shouldn't—and left the ballroom. At least they'd had their one dance. And he loved her.

The urge to portal to the human world and tell Marek all about it was overwhelming. What would he be doing right now? Probably writing a book about everything they'd seen and learned from the demon world. She shuddered.

Sleep came fitfully that night.

CHAPTER 41

Renic was right. Rumors of a vote began circulating the very next day—Nisha overheard some servants mentioning it. Even so, several days passed before everyone was called to gather at the arena that evening. Fenity spent the time resting and quizzing Arinia about the duties of a queen—represent the common people, foster alliances between races, lead the equinox ceremonies, oversee the health of flora and fauna, and much, much more.

Now, Fenity tried to get answers about the tally as Arinia dressed her for the summoning—a more subdued, but still detailed, green dress—but Arinia was being especially tight-lipped. Which meant she knew what was going to happen and wouldn't—or couldn't—say. Fenity read her like an open book —Arinia wanted to tell her what she knew, but she'd be violating the king's rules. And endangering her son.

Where before this meant she couldn't be trusted, now Fenity understood and loved that about her. An honest, kind person, not swayable in her values—and she valued family.

Fenity couldn't shake the feeling that she was walking into

a trap. Why announce the winner in the arena instead of the ballroom like the other times? It was too easy to picture—they'd arrive, dressed up and waiting to find out who won, and then King Sidian would unleash a host of snakes or something, and they'd have to fight for their lives and see who survived.

Why not? This was his playground, and they played by his rules.

Arinia only half-heartedly argued when Fenity strapped a dagger and sheath around her thigh—which only solidified the snake attack theory.

There were only two bright spots in the whole affair. One, she'd be that much closer to the end of the Strife. Arinia had made subtle remarks about her eating too many cakes, as she had to let out most of the dresses now. Her belly was becoming more pronounced by the day, and hiding it would become a problem if this went on much longer.

Two, she'd finally see Renic. Despite roaming the halls pretending to be lost but secretly trying to catch Renic on the move, she hadn't seen him. And he hadn't come to her.

Carrying this secret alone was hard enough, but his absence made her feel the loneliest of all. She didn't know where he was or how to find him. What if something happened and she needed him? Arinia claimed not to know either. When she wasn't—probably pointlessly—studying to be queen, Fenity spent her free time coming up with the most outrageous things her mind could punish her with. Maybe his pata had forced him to marry Sarafine in secret. Maybe he died, and the king was too upset to announce it—Fenity had actually cried herself to sleep with that one. Luckily, Fetam told her the mood swings were a healthy sign.

Fenity had dined with her parents several times. It was a good temporary distraction, and they all agreed they were ready to go home. Though they each probably had different definitions of what that was. Pata to their new lands in the south. Mata to their old home in the forest. Fenity to Renic's arms.

When the time came to head to the arena, Arinia and the attendants shooed Fenity out. Just like sheep, the contestants followed the familiar path through the castle and into the frigid air. A blanket of snow covered the grounds, reminding her of the human world. It glistened like the queen's jewels against white silk all over the courtyard and sprawling lawn. It hadn't been disturbed except where cleared from the paths. Because who would leave the cleanliness of the walkway to explore the snow?

Fenity stomped a foot into it as she walked. The satisfaction of marring the perfection only left her with a cold, wet foot. But she smiled at the strange looks she got and rubbed her arms for warmth until they finally arrived at the arena.

The contestants had to wait in large, plain rooms for a long time, though no one ever explained why. The most popular rumor among them was that the king had not yet arrived, so everything was on hold.

The few benches were taken, so Fenity rested against a wall, storing her strength for whatever awaited them in the arena. Talking to the nearest contestants helped distract her from her racing heart.

"Have any of you heard what this is about?" Fenity asked Lady Arlen and Lady Pria.

"No, nothing." Pria shook her head and launched into all the theories she'd heard.

Sarafine and her group sat on the other side of the room, whispering behind their hands and casting glances toward Fenity. It could have been her imagination, but it seemed Sarafine stood a little aside from them, whispering less than the others. Did they already know what the pillar was? Probably. They weren't outfitted any different from her, so there were no clues to be deduced about what was to come.

Nisha did not stand with them. Interesting. She'd found a new group, some of the quieter middles who no one paid much attention to, but were probably safe from Renic's bottom ten.

At least Fenity was safe from the bottom ten and her parents didn't have to worry. They hadn't acted concerned when Fenity failed the energy test, but they had to be relieved now. Pillar winners didn't fall into the bottom.

When Nisha caught Fenity looking, she gave a timid smile and a small motion for her to join them. Fenity smiled back and excused herself from Pria's company. Nisha lit up, while her companions gave warm welcomes. Their circle's conversation was an exact mirror of the one she'd left. Everyone was worried about what would happen next.

And for the first time, Fenity felt like she belonged, like she was one of them instead of a forest dweller who didn't belong. This could be her world, too.

The joy slipped away when the gravity of it sank in—their doom might await on the other side. It had nearly happened before in the arena, for all of them.

Despite the undercurrent of anxiety, the contestants continued to mingle and chatter as if this were a social tea party instead of a precursor to the next challenge. They were all just doing their best to ride out the unknown, just like her. Finally, when Fenity thought she might jump out of her skin, an attendant in palace livery directed them to the arena. They filed out, down the hall in single file. Nisha squeezed her hand before taking her place in line.

The crowd erupted into cheers as the contestants filed in, and Fenity did a double take. While there were plenty of courtiers, servants filled most of the seats—contestant attendants, palace guards, and all the individuals who worked the castle and its many needs every day.

Arinia and her attendants had front-row seats, and they cheered and waved when Fenity finally saw them. Something lurched in her heart, and she smiled up at them. Maybe she wasn't as alone as she thought.

The same columns stood tall around the perimeter, and as before, each contestant stopped before one. Sweat beaded on Fenity's palms as memories thrashed in her mind. The heavy garments, the rotten food, the fight for her life.

She stopped in front of the next open pillar, far enough away to look up into the balcony and see the royal thrones. Her eyes went right to Renic. He was there, safe and sound, seated beside the king and queen. They watched the parade of rainbow dresses filter in. Renic was so small from this far away, but he looked right at her, never taking his eyes away.

It gave her the courage to face whatever awaited them this evening.

When the contestants stopped coming, the herald stepped to the front of his platform and raised his thick arms, quieting the spectators.

Fenity swallowed the lump in her throat. Here's where they found out their fate.

"Your Royal Majesties, lords and ladies, and good fae of Alberry. It is my honor to welcome you to the Fourth Pillar of Faedom." The crowd cheered again. "We know our Fourth Pillar represents compassion, and who better to measure the compassion of a queen than our very own Queen Lara?" He raised his hands to her, then bowed low.

To Fenity's surprise, Queen Lara stood from her throne and stepped to the front of the balcony. Fenity had never seen her speak in public, always letting King Sidian address the kingdom. She held her breath, waiting for what the queen would say.

While her cream-colored silk dress was anything but simple, with its layers of lace and embroidery, it was nothing like the queen's regalia they'd worn for the Second Pillar. Her hair was pinned up with a crown, leaving her neck free to show off the jeweled necklace graced with all the colors of the contestants.

She looked over the crowd and the contestants, looking every bit the confident leader her husband was. "Compassion, some would argue, is the most important of the pillars." King Sidian frowned from his throne. "And also the most overlooked of them. Helping those who are suffering, easing the burdens of others with our assistance. Feeling and understanding the trials others face. These are coveted qualities in someone worthy of being queen of the fae." She paused, smiling. The servants around the room smiled with her. "So, we've been watching you. All of you. His majesty and I, your prince, your attendants. The servant who prepared your breakfast plates. The maids listening in the hall. The guards observing at the door."

The contestants were too far apart to speak to each other, but Fenity saw fear in a lot of eyes.

She thought back to her treatment of everyone she'd encountered at the castle. She'd tried to be kind, treating them like she wished to be treated. But had that been the case the entire time? This place had tried to change her, making her less patient and more selfish. Did she mess up along the way?

"Not only that, but we performed little tests to see how you'd react, how you would treat those beneath your station."

Fenity didn't consider anyone beneath her station. It was pure luck she was here at all.

This pillar could not have been the king's idea. He didn't give a flying fairy about those less than him.

But when had she been tested?

Queen Lara went on. "Did a servant ever need your aid? Did anything unfortunate ever happen to one in front of you? How did you react? Did you deign to help?"

The servant who'd tripped in front of Fenity on her first day. She'd spilled all those drinks, and only Fenity had helped her clean up the mess.

"Your treatment of others is a measure of your compassion, and a very fitting measure of your worthiness to be queen."

Sarafine raised her chin from across the arena. She wasn't nervous at all.

"So, who decided the winner of the Fourth Pillar of Faedom? The palace workers did. Their votes have been tallied, and their voices have been heard." She accepted an envelope sealed with wax and opened it, skimming the contents. "I'm pleased to announce that Lady Fenity Stormbrook is the winner of the Fourth Pillar of Faedom."

What?

Queen Lara smiled wide, looking truly pleased, while Renic jumped from his throne before quickly sitting again, clapping politely. The king snatched the paper out of the queen's hands, but Fenity's attention was broken by the thunderous applause and stomping of feet from all the palace workers. None louder than Arinia and her attendants.

She'd won another pillar. Her eyes stung with tears, and gratitude carried her to the middle of the arena. She bowed to each side of the workers gathered to witness the result of their votes. They only clapped louder for her, and the tears sprung and flowed freely. She'd stuck to her values, remained true to herself and what it meant to treat people with kindness, and while that may have hurt her chances in every other aspect, in this one, it mattered.

"Thank you," she whispered, extending her hand from her heart to Arinia, whose eyes shone.

The herald raised his arms to quiet the crowd, and Fenity returned to her column. She'd won.

"Congratulations to our winner," the herald said. "She will receive her prize tomorrow."

Queen Lara raised her arms. "As is tradition, we also have a contestant who placed very last." Her face pinched in consternation. "While we expect competitiveness and even a degree of ruthlessness in the Strife, this individual has gone beyond what is acceptable, using her attendants, manipulating them into spying and worse, and also passing on vital secrets to her closest companions. If someone near her needed help, she ignored them every time."

Sarafine's face remained statue still as the crowd and contestants murmured. Somehow, she'd been caught. Renic and the king watched on.

Queen Lara waited until the noise died down. "Lady Moona Waters, the lack of compassion displayed in the Strife has placed you last. Expect your punishment soon." The queen pivoted back to her throne like the crack of a whip.

Moona? She was the one helping the rest of Sarafine's group? Fenity sought the female in the light blue dress, the one who the sprites had placed in the bottom five, the one who'd always snubbed Fenity. She stood on the opposite side of the arena, but her shock was unmistakable. Though it was impossible to tell if it was genuine.

The herald took over, speaking over the crowd. "Only one more pillar to go, and the Strife will come to a close. We bid you all good evening." He bowed, the crowd cheered, and the contestants filed back out.

Fenity floated out, barely feeling the ground beneath her feet. She'd won a pillar. That put her and Sarafine tied, with only the Fifth Pillar left—Integrity.

"You're more conniving than I thought," Moona hissed from behind her as they stepped through the hall. "Did you pay them off?" she asked. "Promise them riches if you become queen?"

The other contestants watched but didn't intervene.

Fenity ignored her and picked up the pace, pushing past contestants clogging the hall.

That was exactly how Sarafine won her pillars. Moona's spying and the king's assistance, but she wasn't crazy enough to make things worse, especially since she might end up publicly accusing the king of manipulating his own son's Strife.

"Walk away, then. You're good at that. Maybe sleep with the prince again and see if you can win the next pillar too." Her energy buzzed as she cast a shield around herself.

Fenity froze. The contestants gasped.

How much did Moona know—and anyone else she might have told? If she'd been spying, did she know about the baby?

Fenity slowly turned to face Moona. Her pale skin was mottled red with anger, arms rigid at her sides. The hall had turned leaf-falling quiet. No one moved.

Before Fenity could think of a way to undo the damage done, Sarafine stepped in front of Moona and grabbed her arms. "You lost, my friend. Don't make it worse by spouting rumors."

"But..." The anger drained from Moona's face as she beseeched Sarafine.

"Let's get out of here." Sarafine led Moona through the hall while the contestants watched in silence. Illeya trailed them, but the others in their group didn't follow.

"Did she really sleep with Prince Renic?" someone whispered nearby.

Fenity hurried away. She burst outside into the frosty air. The cold shock immediately chased the vileness of Moona away. All elation from winning had vanished. She needed Renic.

The walk cleared her head, and when she returned to her rooms, Arinia, her parents, and attendants were waiting for her with a mini-celebration—all manner of treats and several different kinds of tea.

"Did you know I would win?" Fenity asked Arinia as they embraced.

"No, but I had a hunch and wanted to be prepared." Arinia grinned and gripped Fenity's hands.

Their small group replayed the events of the pillar and the contestants' reactions. "Did you see Lady Illeya's face? I thought her eyes would fall out of her head," Alinne, one of her most outspoken attendants, said.

"We're so proud of you," Mata said, one hand on Pata's arm.

They dined on tasty treats for the rest of the evening. It was perfect, except it was missing someone.

Tomorrow couldn't come soon enough.

CHAPTER 42

Fenity arose with the sun after a restless night fighting a losing battle with the need to pee and waiting for Renic to come to her room. He never did.

Luckily, she didn't have to wait long before Arinia came to help her dress, bringing breakfast to quell the pangs that always led to nausea if not quickly sated.

"Do you know what my prize is?" Fenity asked through a yawn, a honeyed biscuit in her hand. She sat at the vanity mirror, an attendant shaping her hair and unsnarling it from tossing and turning all night.

"I believe his highness is taking you on a private tour outside the palace grounds." Arinia held up a green dress, shook her head, then held up another one that might have been an exact copy of the first for all Fenity could tell. Arinia nodded at that one, handing it to an attendant to prepare.

Could she stay in this robe all day once she was married to Renic?

He wouldn't mind.

A tour sounded heavenly. A trip off the grounds *anywhere*,

actually. She hadn't been away since taking Marek back to the human world. And to have alone time with Renic?

"That's better." Arinia smiled at her through the mirror. "You've won the heart of the people, Fenity, and the heart of our heir. Now you must win the heart of the court. Enjoy your prize, but be prepared to fight when you return."

To fight? Was Arinia telling her more than she should?

"The rulers already had a chance to vote for me, and they didn't. But I'll do everything I can." Is that what it took to win the fifth and final pillar? She'd learned their etiquette, dressed and acted like them, proved herself in the pillars. And her parents' holdings were no small thing, Pata's conquests known across the kingdom. What else did the court want?

An attendant cleared his throat, and Fenity glanced up to see a guard at the door. "Time to go, Lady Fenity."

Fenity looked down at her robe and squeaked. But Arinia simply clapped her hands. In no time, the attendants dressed her. With boots on, and a shawl for warmth, she headed out the door. Arinia waved goodbye with a big smile but didn't join her.

Fenity followed the solemn guard. Rich sunrise light burst through the windows and cast long shadows down the hall. When they reached the hall to turn toward the front where carriages picked up passengers, the guard turned left instead. Fenity stopped. "The courtyard is this way." Unease snaked down her spine. She hadn't memorized the exit routes for no reason. Was this a trick? Something of Sarafine's doing?

"Before your outing, you're needed in the throne room. Please, follow me." The guard continued down the hall without making sure she followed. But he was heading in the right direction if their destination was the throne room.

Fenity swallowed hard and forced her legs to move. Were

they about to take her reward away? Or was this a surprise Strife challenge?

The halls were clear of contestants, too early for most of them. Only servants passed her, giving her open nods of respect and kind smiles. She returned them, trying to convey her gratitude for their hand in her win, but nerves made her mouth waver each time.

The throne doors were open when she arrived but slammed closed behind her. The noise echoed in the tall space, and Fenity nearly gasped. She'd never been to the throne room, but its splendor outshone the rest of the castle. The room was all marble veneer and carved reliefs, with a ceiling easily ten times her height, no windows but plenty of magelights. Guards manned every door around the perimeter, but otherwise, the room was devoid of any courtiers or staff.

At the very back, directly across from the main doors, stairs led to a dais topped with thrones so ornate they must have been worth a fortune, taking many trees to carve. Seated at the largest throne was King Sidian.

So this was why she was here. At his behest.

She walked toward him—the trip taking forever as her heartbeat increased with every step. He watched her, eyes dark. She bowed low when she finally reached the bottom of the stairs and waited for him to speak—waited for him to reveal his hand.

For the longest time, he didn't say a word. So long, she wondered if there was some important step she'd missed. Was she supposed to kiss his ring or some other etiquette thing Arinia probably told her about during one of their earliest lessons when she wasn't paying attention?

"Do you think you're worthy to one day be queen?"

His words made her jump, and they echoed around the space, though he wasn't loud.

She rose from her bow and opened her mouth to reply.

"No." He cut her off, impatience and ire written all over his face. "I want a genuine answer, so speak carefully."

Fenity swallowed. King Sidian had powerful energy and had learned to shape it as most fae who possessed such strength, though his expertise lay in offensive energy. He didn't wield any now, though. He didn't need to.

The qualities of the five pillars. Strength. Poise. Leadership. Compassion. Integrity. Did she have those things? That's what he was after.

Yes, she did.

"Yes." Her voice came out more confident than she thought it might. "I may not be perfect, and I may not have won all the pillars, but that doesn't mean I'm not worthy."

"That is exactly what it means." He raised his hand. To dismiss her?

"I also believe the measure of my worthiness as queen is how I will serve my kingdom and people. I grew up a commoner, but I see that as a strength, not a weakness. I relate to them, these people who make up the majority of our kingdom. I know their plight, how some of them starve come winter without the proper tools and education." She took a steadying breath, but he didn't interrupt her. "I love your son, Your Majesty. Whether I win the Strife or not, I'm already devoted to him—his goals, his needs—until my dying breath."

"Love." He grunted, then did a double take at whatever he saw in her face. The king studied her as if seeing her in a new light. "Are you the one who possesses no energy?" He raised an eyebrow.

Fenity opened her mouth, then shut it. She'd begged Marek to teach her. She'd tried in the quiet hours of the night to shape her energy to her will, to do anything but open another portal, but it was set, and it wouldn't budge. "Yes. But I've developed strength in other areas to compensate."

His eyes darkened again. "Hmm. You may go."

She wanted to explain, to plead for his son's hand and convince him her weaknesses were strengths, but his narrowing gaze warned her not to. She bowed and retreated, traitorous heart still thumping, hoping she'd said the right things.

That was an interview. And if the king had a say in the winner of the Fifth Pillar, if the royal choice was his, this might be her one chance to prove herself.

She stopped halfway down the aisle and turned. The king watched her, his buzzing energy beginning to swirl. "I'm worthy of being queen of the fae and at Prince Renic's side. The contestants and courtiers, they don't understand this world is bigger than their grapple for power. The rest of the kingdom needs a voice, and I can be that voice."

She needed to be by Renic's side, but there was so much good she could do in this world. Instead of one school near her hometown to teach people about gardening and surviving, she could open a hundred across the kingdom.

King Sidian didn't say a word, but Fenity jumped and spun around at the sound of approaching guards. They reached for her arms, ready to toss her out of the throne room, but she pulled out of their reach.

"I'm going," she snarled and left without looking back.

Outside the throne room, the same guard escorted her to the courtyard. They passed by a lady on her hands and knees, a scrub brush in her hands. Two servants stood nearby, overseeing the work as the contestant in blue scrubbed the floor. Moona. Her punishment.

Tears slid down Moona's face, but Fenity looked away

before catching her eyes. To her, hard labor—something Fenity did every day growing up—would be the ultimate humiliation.

At the bottom of the palace steps, all newly shoveled of snow, sat a lavish carriage. And Renic stood in front of it, eyes and smile lighting up when he saw her. The urge to run and fall into his arms was almost too much to bear. He must have seen the trouble on her face—his smile turned to worry as he helped her into the carriage.

Fenity couldn't shake the feeling she had failed an important test and was spending her last moments with him.

It was just the two of them in the carriage, with one driver sitting beside Galan outside. When Renic shut the door, she gave in to her impulses, throwing herself against him.

Home.

"Everything okay, love?" His arms circled her, squeezing, giving her exactly what she needed, while his smooth face nuzzled the top of her head. "We finally get our outing."

The carriage jolted as the horses pulled it forward.

"The king interviewed me. He only asked me two questions. If I think I'm worthy to be queen, and if I have any energy."

He pulled back, his concern mirroring hers. "I'm supposed to be present for the interviews. They were to start tomorrow. I planned to tell you."

Worry furrowed his brow as he glanced out the window as they crossed through the tunnel in the outer wall that traveled beneath the battlements. Why would the king do it without him?

The gate was open, probably just for them, and the clip-clop of the horses' hooves echoed off the bridge as they crossed the Amelyn River. Water trickled over rocks way down below, and it filled the silence as they held hands, thoughts darkened.

A group of soldiers on horseback slipped through the gate,

following them. So they wouldn't be entirely alone on this outing. Protection for the heir.

"Do you think he's interviewing everyone without you while you're away, then?"

"It appears so." He drummed his fingers on her knee. "But why interview you and send you to tell me about it? He has no reason to hide things from me, unless he believes my top ten don't align with his and the court's wishes."

"Does he know I'm in your top ten?"

"No." He smoothed her hair back, looking deep into her eyes. "But clearly he suspects."

"If he didn't before, he does now." She winced. "I told him I love you. I told him I'm devoted to you until my dying breath."

Renic's troubled face split into another one of his breath-taking smiles, changing his entire being into radiating delight. "You do, do you? You're very brave, you know that." He brought her hand up, kissing her knuckles. "Until my dying breath," he whispered. "And forever."

She was pleasantly preoccupied with his lips until a rise in elevation threw her off balance, making her laugh and look out the window. They were traveling uphill.

"Where are we going, exactly?" She wanted to ask if this was the route he brought Sarafine but didn't want to sour anything by mentioning her name.

"It's a surprise." He pulled her against him, back resting against his chest.

"I've missed this. Missed you." It had been too long since he'd last visited.

She was surprised when she admired their bubble of joy it didn't physically glow. Surely it radiated their love in blinding shafts of light that burst through the windows and announced to the world they were truemates.

He squeezed her. "The goblins have purposely chosen now

to dispute the border. We had hoped they could be appeased with talks and a show of might, but they persist. This is the first conflict in my lifetime they haven't quelled with negotiations, so my pata is treating it like a teaching opportunity. I haven't enjoyed the Strife as I was promised."

"I hope it's resolved quickly, then." His lack of worry put her heart at ease, and soon the lull of the carriage had her dozing.

She blinked awake when the carriage halted and the rocking stopped. "Oh, no." She sat up to his smiling face. "Oh, why did you let me sleep?" The sun had shifted—it'd been at least an hour or so. "All that wasted time."

"Not to me." His voice was low and husky, and she got the sense he'd loved having her sleep cuddled into him, vulnerable and completely under his protection.

"Mated males." She rolled her eyes, loving that he loved it too.

He grinned. "Ready for your surprise?"

The driver opened the carriage door, and Renic hopped down first, holding up an eager hand. Fenity didn't second-guess. She gripped his warm fingers and stepped out of the carriage.

After finding her footing in the snow, Fenity looked up and gasped. Trees surrounded them on all sides, pillows of white on their branches making them creak and crackle with the wind. The scent of earth and bark surrounded her despite the cold trying to leach life from the woods.

"You needed this as much as I did. I knew it'd make you happy." He dropped her hand and spun in a slow circle, arms out wide. He took a deep breath of fresh air, free of the refuse of the palace. Free of the politics and oppression. Free of the poison and expectations. "Go ahead." He nodded at her.

Fenity glanced at the driver and Galan, but they were busy

tending the horses. The guards were nowhere in sight, though she heard them and their horses nearby.

She took a deep breath, cold air filling her lungs. It came out as a breathless laugh as she mimicked him, spinning in circles beneath a canopy of trees and pink sky.

Renic grabbed her hand and kissed her. He led her to a path she hadn't noticed. It was brighter that way, and she followed him, curious. She blinked at the view that caught her breath.

"Is that—"

"Oldinger Fortress." He watched her, joy etched on his face.

They stood at the top of a cliff overlooking a valley, and the fortress sat shrouded in haze in the distance. It was a place of refuge for the fae. Once, they had gathered there as a last stand against the humans before they were sundered from this world. Now it stood as a refuge in case a portal ever opened, igniting the prophecy.

Fenity shuddered. Would the fae retreat there one day soon because of what she'd done?

"Are you cold?" He snapped his fingers, and a servant retrieved a thick fur from the carriage. Renic wrapped it around her.

She smiled, trying to reassure him, but she couldn't peel her eyes from the fortress—so far away, yet stark in the surrounding landscape. A wide moat encircled the thick, gray stone and tall towers, visible even from this distance. It was enormous, but it had to be, to protect as many fae as possible. From her and what she'd done. *Fire and ash.*

"Fen?" Renic cocked his head, hand outstretched.

Behind him at the edge of the trees, Galan watched her with his head tilted, studying her.

Fenity accepted Renic's hand, shaking herself. "Is this where you bring all your truemates?" She batted her eyelashes, willing him to let her change the subject.

He barked out a laugh. "Yes, of course."

"Where did you take Sarafine?" She regretted the question as soon as his smile fell.

"Not here." He cupped her hands, rubbing the chill from them. "*You* are my truemate. You. And I know you feel what I feel. That no one else will ever matter. No one else could ever compare, ever come between what we have." He pushed his forehead into their joined hands, voice breaking, breathing ragged. "If you died tomorrow, that would be it for me. There would be no moving on. There could never be someone to fill the void you left."

"But you have a duty to the throne."

"Damn my duty," he nearly shouted. "My duty is to you. Don't you see? You are my purpose above everything, and no amount of time or distance, threat or obligation can ever change that."

"But what if I lose? What if Sarafine wins?" The words barely left her mouth, but he'd heard just the same.

"I won't let that happen." He pressed his warm hand to her cold cheek. "We will have a lifetime of moments like this, where I can show you the world and treat you like the queen you'll one day be."

But could he prevent it?

She pushed her fingers through his hair and pulled his face to hers. Their lips met, and that was it. The world, their worries, the past, present, and future disappeared beneath the burning passion and the never-ending need for his love and nearness.

He'd given her the woods—her place of contentment—when all along he was her contentment, and all she needed was him.

CHAPTER 43

The charge in the air when they arrived back at the palace was undeniable. Servants and workers ran about, more than usual in the blustering cold, and it had Renic shooting worried glances between Fenity and the palace grounds.

"Galan?" Renic called out the window.

"On it, Your Highness." There was a jolt and a distant thump as boots hit stone, then Galan jogged to the nearest palace guards.

Arinia was waiting for them at the foot of the stairs when they stopped.

"What's going on?" Renic demanded when they exited the carriage.

Arinia wrapped a comforting arm around Fenity. "The king has announced a meeting at the feast. We all agree he will announce the winner of the Fifth Pillar."

Renic's mouth fell open. He met Fenity's eyes. "I'll get to the bottom of this." He lowered his voice to a whisper only she could hear. "I'm not supposed to warn you. He told me he'd disqualify anyone I told."

"Don't say anything then."

He winced but nodded. Just before he left them standing by the carriage, he squeezed her hand three times and whispered into her ear, "Don't eat in the dining hall tonight. You must trust me." Galan followed on his heels, speaking rapidly.

Fenity blinked after him.

"Everything alright?" Arinia rubbed her hands together.

Fenity faced her. "Were the other contestants interviewed today?"

"Yes." Her tone told Fenity she wasn't happy as they entered the castle which gave immediate relief from the biting air.

Renic hadn't been present at the interviews. How was he to choose his favored ten if not given the chance to ask his own questions? Unless King Sidian never intended to give him a chance.

But the king didn't marry whoever won the Strife. Renic did.

If the king knew they were truemates, would that make a difference? Maybe they should tell him before he picked a winner without consulting Renic first.

"Come, let's rest and get you changed for the feast." Arinia led the way back to their wing of the castle.

Rest after a carriage ride? Who had she become that it sounded like an amazing suggestion? Renic said not to eat at the feast. "I think I'll eat in my room this evening."

Arinia glanced over at her. "Are you sure that's wise? The king will make his announcement and all must attend."

Right, the announcement. "You're right." She'd go and have nothing to eat.

Arinia sighed with relief, making Fenity tip her head at the loyal guide. She knew something she wasn't supposed to say.

Behind the safety of the closed doors to her rooms, Fenity turned to her. They only had a few minutes before the other attendants would arrive to help her change. "What can you tell me about the feast? Something's going to happen, isn't it?"

Arinia's mouth dropped open. "N-nothing." She glanced back at the door. "I promise, he only wants you there for the announcement." She jumped forward and snatched Fenity's hands, dropping her voice. "Don't push this. There are things I can't tell you, or my son's life is at risk. *Please*." Her voice rose again. "Would you like to rest before dressing?"

Fenity gaped with horror. So it was true. The king would murder one of his elite warriors to keep his servants in check. And they were listening or capable of listening right now? Just like in Arinia's room.

Arinia's face crumpled with worry, hands upraised, silently pleading.

"A rest sounds wonderful." Fenity's voice came out squawky but discernible. She patted Arinia's hands, a promise and commiseration.

Arinia nodded with relief. "I agree. It's been a long day." She turned Fenity around to untie her laces. Her whisper came back. "They aren't always listening—it could be a lie—but the king warned us they would be, so we comply. No one's willing to sacrifice their family to test it."

Fenity thought about all the things someone with the right energy for hearing might have learned from her rooms. Marek. Renic. Portals. Pregnancy. It had to be a bluff, or she would have been executed long ago. But Arinia was right, caution was best.

"I trust you." She kept her voice low like Arinia as the top loosened, making breathing easier and giving her stomach some much-needed room.

"I told you not to trust me at the start, remember? But I will continue to watch over you in every way I can. Trust that I won't betray you." Arinia helped her step out of the dress. "You have secrets you can't tell me, even though I can still trust you, right? So trust that. We can have secrets and still lean on one another."

So many secrets.

At Arinia's urging, Fenity crawled into bed in her underclothes, intending on mulling over all the new information as she waited to dress for the feast, but instead she fell fast asleep.

Arinia had to shake her awake and hurry to dress her so she wouldn't be late.

The delicious smells in the dining hall sent Fenity's stomach rumbling. If only she'd had time to beg for snacks. She was starving. She sipped at her water, tried to speak to her neighbors, and watched every door for Renic to enter and take his seat. Her parents had joined the feast, sitting near the other lords and ladies across the room. Queen Lara was absent, too. Only the king presided tonight, courtiers and contestants stuffing themselves with delicious meats slathered in sauce, roasted vegetables, crackling bread, and course after course of dips and bite-sized morsels that had her tablemates moaning. Fenity remained strong, sipping at her fruit water, drooling, and waiting impatiently for the king's announcement.

Instead of a vast variety of desserts, servants wheeled out a special cake that sent the contestants clapping. Ten-tiered, with mini royal crests made of molded chocolate. Clear sugar lanterns with magelights glowing inside hung from every layer, swinging with the movement of the cart. The servants rolled it to the middle of the open space, and the king stood from his table, smiling.

"Prince Renic, will you join us?" King Sidian announced to the room, and everyone quieted.

Fenity's pulse skittered.

Renic finally entered the dining hall, and the contestants whispered to each other while Galan remained by the doorway. Renic was dressed in his crisp finery, but the storm surrounding him was unmistakable. He didn't even attempt to smile as the room bowed for him.

King Sidian gestured to the servants who began serving the cake. But only to the contestants. The courtiers received a different dessert—mini versions of the same cake, with tiny tiers and a single sugar lantern. They gobbled it up, sighing with bliss. All Renic could do was cast glances at Fenity with his stormy eyes and hidden rage. When a servant placed a piece before her, its chocolate and vanilla scents made her stomach flip in nauseating ways. Renic subtly shook his head. She didn't eat it but crumbled it with her fork and took fake bites in case anyone was watching.

"A special dessert for our special contestants." King Sidian chuckled. "After carefully studying you and considering all you've accomplished—or not—during the pillars so far, Prince Renic is ready to announce his choices for the favorite ten." He nodded to the side and sat back on his throne.

So, not the winner of the Fifth Pillar then. But the tension in the room made it clear this was nearly as important. Traditionally, they couldn't win the Strife and not be in the top ten. The winner would be among the names called tonight. That is, if the king hadn't manipulated this too.

Courtiers leaned forward in their chairs. Forks clinked against plates of half-eaten cakes. The air felt heavy and heated with apprehension.

Fenity's favorite herald cleared his throat and took a spot in the middle, beside the rapidly dwindling cake. He unrolled the parchment from a golden case, flashing it around the room overly dramatically.

"It pleases me to announce His Highness, Prince Renic Arrowood, heir to the throne of the Kingdom of Asentia, has announced his favorite ten of the Strife. These chosen contestants are to be commended for their display of all five pillars of faedom, strength, poise, leadership, compassion, and integrity. They and their families have earned the respect of the fae court, and all the privileges that entails." He paused, eyes trailing the room in a clear effort to build suspense.

"The names are as follows; Lady Sarafine Rivers, Lady Illeya Skyburn, Lady Tully Windin, Lady Daream Drifturn, Lady Merdin Oakton, Lady Mira Midfire, Lady Verna Bloomshadow, Lady Cameria Seedman, Lady Arlen Edgefield, and Lady Fenity Stormbrook."

Several of the contestants burst into tears—any lingering hopes they had for winning the Strife dashed. But the sounds were muted. Sarafine and all her friends—the ones who'd hurt Fenity, the ones Renic vowed would be at the bottom—they made it to the top ten. All except Moona. Some of them had even refused to compete in the troll trial. They didn't represent the values of a good queen at all.

Renic's stormy eyes turned to devastation when Fenity finally looked at him. He'd had no hand in this. The king picked these top ten, only adding Fenity at the end because how could he leave her off and save face when she'd won two pillars?

Fenity watched Sarafine's friends congratulate each other, and it all became clear. They were daughters of the king's most influential rulers, commanding the most warriors, land, and resources.

A red haze slid over her vision. Her rapid heart drowned out the clinking of forks and obligatory congratulations. She was about to do something she shouldn't, and she couldn't stop. Didn't *want* to stop. How *dare* they do this to Renic?

Everyone bowed and scraped to the king, because he was the king, but no one stopped to ask why. And his foul deeds were never questioned, not even by his own son.

She stood with her glass of fruit water and clanked her fork loudly against it, nearly cracking the glass. Like a ripple effect, the quiet began in her corner and extended out until it finally reached the celebrating contestants and the king.

Renic swallowed hard. King Sidian narrowed his eyes in warning. Sarafine hushed her friends who hadn't paid attention to the quieting room and sipped at her drink, eyes guarded but curious. Her mata reached for her pata's arm, lips parted in concern.

Fenity didn't give herself time to second guess.

"Thank you, Your Majesty. I would like to take a moment and congratulate all contestants on making it this far in the Strife. It's not been easy, as we all know. All of you have prepared your entire lives for this. Though I don't share your background and privileges, I do share your love for our beloved prince and our fae values." She took a shaky breath. "Which is why I must speak out about the injustice being done here."

King Sidian motioned two guards over and whispered something. Renic shot from his seat, and Galan immediately left his place behind him and circled the room toward her. Queen Lara watched with barely concealed concern.

Fenity spoke faster as the guards made their way toward her. "Prince Renic will be an incredible king because he represents the values he holds dear in all his thoughts, actions, and choices. But he did not choose these ten, at least not completely as we were told, and as our future king, his voice should be heard."

The courtiers' gossip burst out loud enough to drown her

words, and the guards reached her ahead of Galan. She didn't regret one moment as gratitude and love radiated from her Renic, though there was fear, too. Even as the guards took her upper arms and tugged her away from her uneaten cake, and her pata held her mata back from rushing to her.

"Stop." Renic's chair scraped back. The room rippled with his command. The guards with their hands on his truemate halted, glancing uncertainly between him and the king. They didn't know Galan waited behind them, ready to fight on Renic's behalf.

This precious, loving, brave female. She knew no fear. Fenity had figured out exactly what happened, though he kept it from her for this very reason. Her sense of right wouldn't let her look the other way when someone was hurting him, as his pata was doing now.

He hadn't been brave enough to stand up to the king, but she was.

And now the room was looking at him. The grinding of the king's teeth was audible.

The problem was, Renic understood why his pata had taken the choice from him. He'd been tutored since birth to one day become king, and this was how it worked. The king needed powerful rulers to support him, and the Strife was one way to align them. Just like the bottom ten was designed to cull the weakest rulers.

Did that make it right? Of course not, but if Pata had explained it and made Renic part of the decision-making process, he ultimately would have agreed with the final list, even if he didn't like it. Even if he'd told some of these females they wouldn't make it.

Wrong and right didn't come as black and white as his trusting, loving Fenity believed. And he never wanted her to change.

"Lady Fenity, thank you for your kind words. We all agree you've graciously exemplified the values of the Strife throughout this contest, as have many contestants." He paused. How could he appease the court and his pata without disgracing Fenity, who mattered above all else? "The top ten is an honored place to be—"

His pata stood, motions rigid. "Prince Renic approves the top ten, of course. I would never take a choice from him that is rightfully his. Now, this evening has concluded. Please return to your rooms immediately. We have a big day prepared for you tomorrow." He clapped Renic on the back.

Big day? Another secret announcement he knew nothing about? The guards had let Fenity go, which boded well for them seeing the dawn of another day. Fenity watched him, unaware that all eyes were on her, ranging from respect from those who didn't make the top ten, to hostility from those who did.

He wanted nothing more than to go to her, but he couldn't. She left out one doorway—Galan following to ensure her safety—and him another, and it was the wrongest thing in the world.

Once in the royal hall and free of the eyes and ears of the court, Pata turned on him. "Did you put her up to that?" He pointed his large finger in Renic's face, energy buzzing from his rising anger.

"No," Renic said, keeping his voice down. "But I'm glad she did it. She did what I should have. Even if I agree with your reasoning, you shouldn't have taken the choice from me."

Pata's face turned red, but his voice stayed calm. "If you agree, then why does the choice matter?"

"It's my future wife, my future kingdom. If this is the one thing I possess to influence that, I should have been involved. You've trained me for this. I will do what's right for our people."

Pata glared at him for too long, but Renic knew him. He was thinking, weighing, considering.

"I agree, except that you're too close to this female from the woods who has no connections and no energy."

Renic's own rage had him narrowing his eyes. "She is everything I want in a wife, and if she was going to make the top ten anyway, then why did it matter?" Pata's words thrown back at him.

Pata finally stepped away, his energy banking. He might be used to his subjects and servants bending to his will, but he was also a rational king.

"The fate of the contest will be tipped by the next pillar. I want you to think about the merit of each potential winner, so you are prepared no matter who wins. Use the wits that make you a great ruler, the ones that made you not disagree with my actions in front of the entire court, unlike your chosen contestant."

Renic's fingers curled inward. "It's down to Fenity and Sarafine. Is my preference going to be taken into consideration?"

"Of course it is."

He couldn't tell his pata the truth. That he'd waste away to a shell of the ruler he might be one day if forced to give up Fenity and marry Sarafine. Even if his pata suspected half of his feelings for Fenity, he didn't know the truth. If he knew they were truemates and didn't want her to win, he'd work that much harder to eliminate her from the Strife. Maybe worse.

So he loosened his bunched muscles and dipped his head. "Thank you for your counsel."

His pata touched his arm, then left him in the hall alone. From the sounds of the dining hall, the court had retired and the servants now cleared away dishes and uneaten food. Renic didn't know what they did to the meal, but at dinner he overheard a conversation about a special cake and only contestants receiving it. It was good Fenity didn't eat anything, just in case, even if she'd watched the food longingly all evening.

Renic had been very careful not to be seen entering her rooms or spending too much time with her. He thought he'd had his pata fooled about his attachment, but apparently not. Fenity's confession would have only solidified what his pata suspected. At least their real secret was safe. His pata had been especially good at keeping secrets from him, maneuvering away from all his subtle questioning and outright denying even his bolder inquiries.

He had no idea what to expect from the Fifth Pillar. And even less clue how to help Fenity.

Back in his rooms, he couldn't do anything but pace, one eye on the door, and both ears listening for whatever might be coming tonight. Anything ingested would be fast-acting. After an eternity of waiting, Galan finally burst through the door, eyes wide.

"What's happened?" Renic held his breath.

"The contestants are being taken from their rooms."

"All of them?"

Galan nodded, breathless. "They are being kidnapped in their sleep."

CHAPTER 44

After stuffing her face with leftover fruit and pastries in her room, Fenity paced restlessly despite the heavy exhaustion that weighed on her. Now that her temper had flared out, maybe speaking against the king in front of the entire court and all the contestants wasn't wise. The way Renic kept looking at her, then at the king, it was clear she'd put him in a horrible position trying to be respectful to both.

It was the unspoken apology begging to leave her lips that kept her from sleep. Instead of dreaming, she planned an entire speech explaining how sorry she was for calling the king out like that. Even though she wasn't wrong, the timing was. There had to be a way to be queen and play the game on her terms without compromising her values.

Too much time passed, and Renic never came. She donned a thin nightshift to battle the stifling heat of the room despite the cold weather outside and tried to sleep.

Arinia entered her rooms in the dead of night.

"What's going on?" Fenity yawned and rolled over, pulling the blanket up to her chin.

Arinia gasped, stopping halfway to the dressing room. "You didn't eat the cake."

Fenity sat up. "The king poisoned the cake." She dropped a hand to her bulging stomach, even more thankful now for listening to Renic. He'd known something was wrong with the food.

Arinia's mouth parted in distress, and she glanced back at the doors. "You're supposed to be in a deep sleep, one you won't wake up from for several hours. They sent me to dress you before the guards collect you."

Fenity threw off the blanket, feet hitting the floor. "Collect me for what?" Anger chased away her weariness.

"Shh!" Arinia waved both arms, looking at the door again. "If you're not asleep, I have to tell the king. We'll dress you, then pretend to sleep. Don't wake up no matter what, not for several hours."

"Where are they taking me?" Had she finally proved to be too much of a threat and they were sending her home? Or perhaps speaking against the king had branded her a traitor and they would execute her.

"I don't know." Arinia returned with sturdy pants, a tunic, and vest. "All the contestants are being taken away. I think it's the Fifth Pillar."

"The Fifth Pillar." Integrity. So it wasn't Renic's choice. What kind of test for integrity had them drugged and kidnapped in the middle of the night?

She dressed quickly, adding a knife to her boot.

Arinia's voice was barely audible. "Get back in bed. Don't let them know you are awake. As far as I know, all the others ate the cake as the king commanded. I don't want to know what he'll do if he finds out you didn't." She headed to the door.

Fenity climbed back on the bed, heart hammering. How would she ever convince them she was sleeping?

"Good luck," Arinia whispered. Fenity closed her eyes to the sound of the door swinging open. "She's ready."

Two distinct pairs of footsteps entered, armor clinking, and approached the side of the bed. Fenity tried to even out her breathing, but her breaths came fast, responding to her racing heart.

The guards didn't notice. They wasted no time hefting her from the bed, two hands under her knees, two under her armpits. The urge to twist out of their grip and stab someone was way too strong.

Resisting the temptation to peek, even just a little, was nearly impossible. For a while, it was clear they headed to the front door, but then they made too many turns for her to know. It was only the intermittent brightness of magelights and wall sconces, and the sound of other guards likely carrying other contestants.

The cold air made it clear when they reached the outside, and Fenity was grateful for her cloak. She smelled horses and heard the occasional rattle of wagon wheels. Then guards shouted orders.

"His Majesty said this lot goes in this wagon, then the rest divided up after that, nine or ten contestants each," a guard said.

With that, Fenity's guards headed for a wagon. But suddenly they stopped, jostling her as they both bowed.

"My prince," the one with her arms said.

Renic. Renic had come.

"Where are you taking her?" he asked—no, demanded.

A pause. "We aren't to say, by order of the king."

Someone grabbed her hand from where she'd let it hang limp. The warmth and electricity behind it told her exactly who it was.

"And I'm ordering you to tell me. Now."

"We don't know—the drivers know—but they won't say."

Renic's voice dropped low. "If any harm befalls her—" He cut off the threat. "Lucky for you all, Fenity is more than capable of handling herself, no matter where you're taking her." She'd never heard that tone from him before. It spoke of the true depth of the truemate bond and the instinct to protect.

"Yes, Your Highness." The two guards bowed deep.

Just before Renic let go of her hand, he gave three distinct squeezes. She returned them without breaking her ruse. His amused chuckle followed her to the wagons.

They lay her down on the hard boards, half on top of another contestant.

"She's the last one." On squeaky hinges, the door swung to close.

"Wait. You didn't check her."

Hands gently patted up her legs and over her bodice, thankfully careful not to touch anywhere they shouldn't. Then they tugged her boots off.

"Found one." The guard's voice sounded pleased. "What are these attendants thinking, trying to slip their contestants knives?"

"They're thinking they want to win the pillar and their share of the betting pool. Plus the king's prize." He laughed, then stopped. "Wait, this is Lady Fenity. She's going to be queen, I'm sure of it."

They put her boots back on, gentler than they removed them, and then the door closed. Dust scattered over her, tickling her nose and driving her mad with the need to scratch.

But she didn't dare move, not even once the wagons were loaded and the horses pulled them away.

After an hour of moving, Fenity finally risked it and opened her eyes. There was just enough light from the moons streaming in the barred windows to know she was the only one awake, and the guards hadn't joined them in the wagon. Even with their hair obscuring some of their faces, the colors they wore gave them away.

And Sarafine's distinct red lay along the side. Ten females most definitely did not fit comfortably lying down, and she was lucky to have been the last so someone wasn't laid on top of her, burying her like they were each other.

The wagon walls and bodies made it warm despite the cold, but there were no other supplies. Food, water, or even a place to relieve themselves. Where could they possibly be going in separate wagons? Her sleep-deprived, pregnant mind wouldn't focus. She fell asleep without giving her body permission to do so.

She woke to loud thwacks striking the wagon.

Arrows.

CHAPTER 45

The drivers cried out as arrows struck them. Shouts rang from the wagons behind them, and their entire party halted. Fenity dropped the sleeping act and rushed to the window. None of the other contestants woke up.

Outside was chaos. Barely any soldiers had accompanied them, only the drivers. They unsheathed their swords, calling what magic they possessed to defend the wagons, but they were no match for the black arrows sailing toward them.

Even with the moons, it was too dark in the shadows of the trees to see who was attacking. This wasn't part of the Strife. King Sidian would never murder his own warriors to test the contestants. Would he?

Then she heard them. Yelling and the pounding of feet over dirt and rocks. She craned her neck.

The charge came into view, and Fenity gasped.

Goblins.

At least a hundred of them.

She'd know their forms anywhere, though she'd never seen one in person. Shorter, green-tinted skin, longer, wider ears, and clothing that only covered the most important parts, and thick leather armor slung over that. Tattoos covered their arms and even some of their faces. Mata had once told her it was to mark their clans and feats of battle. They charged with short-swords raised, battle cry piercing the night. They halted, realizing there was no one left to fight. Swords clanged in the distance—one lone fae left to fight, but it quickly cut off.

Fenity dropped as a goblin turned her way. This was obviously to get to the king. Somehow, they'd known about the contestants being moved this night for the final pillar. A spy?

"Get the dampeners," a female said in a gravelly voice. "We're dead if they wake up before we're ready."

"Sarafine." Fenity shook her shoulder hard, but she didn't move, not even a stir. She shook some of the other females too —Illeya, Tully, Nisha—but none of them moved.

"We only need the one. The red one," a male growled. "We're calling down the wrath of the fae if we take all their females."

"We do as the council bids. Take them all."

The metallic clank of several pairs of what had to be manacles drew closer. The wagon rocked as nervous horses tugged their leads.

The wagon dipped again as a heavy weight stepped up, and Fenity threw herself down, landing on top of another contestant and closing her eyes. Her breaths came shaky despite every effort.

Lantern light pierced the dim space.

"She's in here," the female called out. "The green one is too."

The wagon door rattled, then rattled harder.

A male's curse cut through the night. "They've locked them in. Quickly, find the key."

The weight left the wagon, rocking it again, but Fenity

kept her eyes shut and her ears open. Commotion resumed full force as the goblins searched for the key on the wagons and the bodies of the deceased fae. Yells and curses rose in volume, frustration and desperation clear as more time went on.

A group stopped in front of her wagon, shuffling feet and blazing torches giving their location away.

"It's not here," a different male said in a low voice. "We would have found it by now. It must be with the guards at the journey's end."

"Then use these," the female said. Fenity couldn't tell what she was talking about, but it was soon clear. The loud whack of a weapon chopping at the door almost made her cringe, but there was no way to tell if she was being watched.

What would happen when they broke the lock? She knew all about dampeners. The demon king had trapped her with them. Spelled manacles made by the fae that blocked all access to energy. Once they were on, there would be no hope of escape.

The sharp clang of steel meeting metal combined with the lower-pitched thwack of axes on wood. The horrible noise rang down the road as each wagon was being chopped.

"It's the same as the others. Nothing is getting through." The male's voice sounded worried, and the female growled.

"The wood is chipping away, but too slow. It's not like normal wood."

"They've spelled the wagons. It'll take all night to chop through."

Someone approached from the side of the road. "We don't have all night. Scouts report the fae filth have a patrol coming from the west. We have minutes."

The goblins cursed and growled at that, a chorus loud enough to shake the wagon walls.

"The Waters female said there'd be no patrol," the male said.

Waters? As in Moona Waters? Fenity quickly skimmed the contestants but didn't see her.

"Never trust a fae. We'll take the wagons then," a male growled.

There was a smacking sound, like skin on skin, followed by a curse.

"Idiot. They'll catch up to us with four. We'll take one. This one. Burn the rest."

Fenity gasped. Could she open a portal around an entire wagon? Or or four?

"These wheels can't handle the terrain," a second male said.

"We'll get that door open before we reach the border," the female growled. "Then we ride."

There was a loud hiss as torches caught and roared to life. All those females. She had to do something.

Two pairs of footsteps came pounding up to the group. "They saw us," the goblin said, breathless. "We took some down, but the filth turned on us." The goblin roared, his grief unmistakable.

"Sound the retreat!" the female who must have been in charge said. "Leave the other wagons. Take this one only."

Several goblins—it was impossible to tell by movement alone—climbed onto Fenity's wagon. The reins snapped, and the horses took off.

Fenity cracked open her eyes. Two goblins hung to the sides, their outlines visible through the window bars.

A stampede of horses quickly caught up and surrounded the wagon, but made no move to attack—the goblin hoard catching up. Fenity strained her ears and heard no pursuit.

But hope filled her. At least some guards had escaped.

Renic would know what happened soon, even if she couldn't wait for him. If the goblins crossed back into their lands, it would be a long time before the fae mustered a force big enough to invade, and who knows what might happen to them by then.

The wagon rocked back and forth, throwing them side to side and jostling them with every rut and rock. Trees flew by at their break-neck speed.

"Wake up," she whispered to Sarafine, shaking her. The jewels in her ears, still left from the feast, glinted with moonlight before her hazelnut hair slipped from its pins, covering them. But she didn't stir.

Racing down the road, the chopping continued as two goblins hacked at the door.

Fenity tried waking the other contestants, but it was like they were under a spell rather than a simple draught. Did the spell have a time limit, or was an antidote required to wake them?

Fenity gasped. She knew what to do. It was just the ten of them—the other wagons were left behind. It was a small space. She'd opened portals this size before, and the contestants wouldn't awaken to see what she'd done. The goblins could drive the empty wagon to their homeland completely unaware. Hopefully.

But where could she take them? Thoughts of Marek flashed in her mind, but she pushed them away. He might be able to wake them, but that didn't solve her problem. It only caused more. Going back to the other three wagons made the most sense, but the fae might be there by now.

The wood splintered, but the door stayed shut. "We're getting close!" a male shouted.

That left only one choice—somewhere along the trail where they wouldn't be seen but the goblins couldn't get to them. Fenity summoned her energy from where she'd stuffed it, way, way deep in the place she'd hidden it all her life. It rose, eager and overflowing, like a contented companion ready to appease her. She breathed, fully and freely, without the tightness that accompanied hiding her ability.

The goblins shifted, wood groaning with their movements. "Hey!" A goblin stuck his green, tattooed face to the window.

Fenity released the energy, and a portal grew outward from her.

The goblin's eyes went wide. "Stop the wagon!" he roared.

She quickly expanded to encompass the contestants, but the driver didn't hesitate. He pulled on the reins. The wagon lurched to a stop, and Fenity flew into the wall. The energy slipped, and the portal slammed closed.

"The green female! She's awake!"

Stars. Fenity pushed to her feet, balancing between the contestants' limbs, as more goblins shoved their faces to the windows.

"I told you they'd wake up. Get the dampeners," the female barked. She stuck her face to the window, staring Fenity down. "If I sense any spell from you, fae filth, these warriors will shoot you."

They thrust nocked arrows through the bars, aimed straight at her. Two of them. Fenity froze. Her shaking hands went to her stomach. The goblins scrambled as they gathered the dampeners. She kept her eyes trained on the arrows meant to kill her and her baby.

There was no way out of this. She strained her ears for the fae patrol. Nothing but peaceful insects, and the howls of the night-time predators, oblivious to her plight.

The female goblin returned to the side window. She pushed a pair of manacles through. They landed with a sick thump on Sarafine's face. She didn't stir. Torchlight glinted off their golden surface etched with writing.

"Put those on or die," the female said. Her narrowed eyes watched Fenity closely, lips curled in disgust.

"Shoot her," the male said.

"I'll do what you say. Don't hurt me." Fenity's heart pounded in her ears. She slowly reached for the dampeners.

This is not how it would end. She was stronger than this moment.

"Don't think of trying anything," the female yelled, making her jump. She sniffed the air long and loud, and a small tang of energy coated the air. Her lips split into a fanged smile. "Wouldn't want anything to happen to your youngling."

Fenity's throat closed. Her hand tightened over the manacles. With her other hand up in the air, she slowly stood.

One thing's for certain, the moment the manacle closed around her wrist, her daughter was no longer safe. It would be the demon dungeon all over again.

Never.

Fenity flung the manacles at an arrow. It fired wide.

"Shoot her!"

Fenity opened the fastest portal of her life, shaping it to encompass all the contestants and not the goblins. Almost fast enough.

When the portal closed, the sleeping contestants lay in the middle of the road, halfway between the goblins and the other wagons.

And the arrow was in Fenity.

CHAPTER 46

Under the light of Prisanthony and Pirus, Fenity dropped to her knees in a pile of sleeping contestants. Steam poured from her shaking breaths and from the hot blood dripping down her arm and chest. The arrow had stuck her just under her collarbone on her left side, so deep she wondered if it had gone all the way through, but was too stunned to look.

Fenity squeezed her eyes tight, panting through the pain and straining her ears. They'd arrived exactly where she'd meant to, with no signs of the goblins to recapture them or the fae to witness her portal. The goblins wouldn't dare turn back for the other wagons, not when the fae were already in pursuit. Any moment the guards chasing them would discover the contestants in the road.

She only had to stay awake a little longer, just long enough to be found and ensure it was by the right people.

She shuddered, and not only from the cold. Too many ways she could have died, that her baby would have been harmed. The goblins saw what she could do. They learned she was pregnant—could they tell who the pata was? If the fae caught up to them…

Goosebumps prickled her sweat-and-blood-slicked skin. The moons swirled in her vision. Fenity tugged at her cloak with her good arm, but the sturdy fabric wouldn't rip. She stole the scarf from Sarafine's neck and wrapped it around her wound, tying it with her teeth and good arm. The last tug jolted the arrow, and a sob burst from her. The scarf soaked through, doing little to staunch the blood. There was no way she was pulling it out herself, not without causing more damage and blacking out.

If help didn't come in time, it might not even matter. Could she portal it out of her shoulder? Laughter bubbled out of her, but fear cut it off—she was already growing delirious. She sank to the hard ground and lay on her good side between the other contestants for warmth.

Some rest might be good.

The pounding of hooves startled her to sit up. She screamed from the pain. Black spots mixed with swirling stars. Nausea hit strong and fast. Which direction was the sound coming from? East or west? The goblins or the fae?

The pain was almost too great to care.

Magelights cut through the night, forcing her to blink.

The fae had come.

The horses approached at incredible speed, bearing a dozen guards, with no hint of slowing. Fenity stumbled to her feet, tears springing to her eyes, and waved her good arm.

The guards' eyes went wide, and their horses ground to a halt just in time to avoid trampling the contestants. Fenity scanned their faces, but Renic wasn't among them. How could he be?

The lead guard dismounted, approaching her, while the others surrounded the contestants. She sat hard, the world spinning too fast to keep her balance.

"Lady Fenity... she's awake. She's wounded! Healer!" The guard placed a warm hand on her uninjured shoulder, holding her up as she tried to lie down. "You must sit up, my lady. The arrow pierced through the back."

She nodded, teeth gritted. Tears of pain leaked down her cheeks. She studied her green pants, too afraid to look up and exacerbate the dizziness. "The other contestants, are they safe?"

"Yes. They're already being transported back to Alberry. What happened? How did you escape?"

She opened her mouth to reply, but no answer presented itself. How could she explain this? Tell him the goblins somehow broke through the spelled lock, allowed Fenity to escape with nine unconscious contestants, and then fled unchallenged?

Someone stepped over, whispering hushed words.

Her guard's grip on her stiffened. "We don't have a healer among us. She stayed with the others to tend the warriors' injuries." He hesitated. "We'll have to ride to the nearest town. The pain will be great."

Fenity's hands shook. If she didn't get help fast, she wouldn't live to see Renic another day. "Let's hurry then."

Another guard approached from the side. "We need to control the bleeding. I'm going to remove the arrow and bandage the wound."

Fenity nodded woodenly, then recoiled from his outstretched hand, hissing in pain. "No. The arrow stays in until we reach a healer." She'd hunted and shot too many animals not to know exactly what happened when the arrow was removed.

"She's right," the lead guard said. "Get the contestants on horses, one for each guard. They won't awaken until someone administers the remedy. I'll take Lady Fenity." His kind face and no-nonsense attitude told her she could trust him, which was good because she didn't have a choice. She was fading fast. Every breath was burning torture.

"What about the goblins?" a female guard asked.

The lead guard frowned, staring down the road. "There's not enough of us to pursue them. It's in the king's hands now."

Relief flooded Fenity. If the goblins weren't caught, they couldn't talk. For now.

They hauled the limp, sleeping contestants onto the horses, each with a guard to hold them up. Fenity was last.

The lead guard crouched to help her stand. "I'm Captain Timmay. You can pass out if you need to. I won't let you fall." He pulled her to a stand, and she screamed in agony. Someone wrapped a bandage around her arm and shoulder, stabilizing it and staunching some of the blood.

The horse loomed ahead, impatiently pawing at the dusty ground. Two guards helped her mount, and the pain was so great, she must have blacked out. She woke up with the horse already moving and her head lolled onto Timmay's armored shoulder. Her body was twisted, held up by his strong arm so as not to aggravate the arrow protruding from her back.

She lifted her head, whimpering in pain, praying to the moons she would pass out again as the horse cantered down the road. The others veered off on a different path, a rainbow of females held in the saddles by the guards.

"Where?" she asked.

"They are going to the castle. But you don't have that long. You need a healer." Timmay readjusted his arm around her.

"Try to sleep. It'll help the pain." His presence was reassuring, but she needed Renic.

"How much further?" she gritted out.

"We're close. It's a small village just outside of Alberry. Your wound is still bleeding and we can't risk riding any further."

Fenity closed her eyes and willed herself to fall unconscious. The long, thick arrow jostled with each rise and fall of the horse's gait. The cold air and blood loss leached away all body heat, sending her shivering, which only made the pain worse.

"How did you do it?" Timmay blurted. "How did you escape?"

Clarity cut through the blinding pain and loosened her gritted teeth for a split moment. She hadn't come up with a story.

The horse jumped over a rut in the road, and Fenity couldn't help her scream.

"Easy," Timmay said. "We're almost there. You can tell us when we've seen a healer."

Unbidden tears streamed down her cheeks. Timmay was a good male.

The village sat south of the river that divided them from Alberry and the palace. The world glowed mauve with the hint of a rising sun. Small homes and shops dotted a central square with a well lined with stones. Candlelight flickered within windows and swinging lanterns outside of the common buildings, of which there were few.

The river roared in the background, a constant noise to join the horses' walk and the songbirds readying for dawn's arrival. Otherwise, the streets were empty and silent.

Timmay and two other guards approached one of the

common buildings, while the rest of them carried the contestants on to the castle.

Fenity froze. She couldn't let some random healer tend her wounds. If they had any energy, they would learn her secret. They'd be obligated to tell the king, tell Renic. She'd be eliminated from the Strife so close to its conclusion.

"Timmay, I know I can't travel all the way, but I need someone to bring Fetam. She's a healer at the castle. She's been treating me there." The desperation in her plea leaked through her control. It was too much, trying to pretend and control the pain at the same time.

"We don't have time for that. Besides, she's the king's healer. She can't just leave the castle." Timmay reined the horse at a hitching post and dismounted. He reached to assist her.

Fenity didn't budge. "I'm the king's contestant. I might be your next queen. No healer will touch me except Healer Fetam." Her words slurred.

Timmay frowned in exasperation. "You won't live long enough to win this contest if you're not healed immediately." He tugged at her waist. "Help me," he called to his companions.

They dismounted and flanked the horse.

"You don't understand." She closed her eyes against the renewed dizziness. "I'll lose the contest. You don't want Sarafine as your next queen, trust me. Get Renic." Her eyes popped open. "I mean Fetam. Healer Fetam."

Timmay raised an eyebrow, exchanging a look with his companion. "Let's get you inside before you fall off the horse."

They didn't believe her. It was all about to come apart.

Timmay reached for her again. Fenity grabbed for the reins —the motion stopped short from the blinding pain.

"Don't even think of it." Timmay and his guards didn't give

her a second chance. They grabbed her legs and her waist, pulling her down from the horse. The arrow's shaft caught on the saddle's pommel, and Fenity screamed in agony.

The mauve of the sky split apart into black, then turned mauve again before exploding into black spots that danced like falling leaves.

Hoofbeats pounded against the ground from a distance.

"Fenity!" A voice pierced through her screams. *Renic*. Renic had come.

Her screams of pain formed one word. "Renic!"

"Timmay, her bleeding," a guard said.

They held her upright, all her weight supported by the guards.

"Fetam," she whispered. "Tell him. Only Fetam."

They moved her toward the door, and the pain became too much. The black overtook the lightening pink and stayed that way.

CHAPTER 47

"Fenity!" Her scream was nearly Renic's undoing as he urged his horse across the bridge to the small river village of Autumnrun.

Goblins!

This ill-gotten plan was doomed from the start.

Renic growled and spurred his horse even faster. When the patrol raced into the keep and announced goblins had attacked the contestants, he'd nearly lost his head. The entire castle awoke in panic. Pata wouldn't allow him to go after them, but when word arrived they'd recovered three of the four wagons, contestants unharmed, he'd known without asking who was in the wagon the goblins had taken.

Of course it was her. Of course his pata had taken her dagger and any chance she had of defending herself.

King's orders be damned, he raced for the main gate, Galan with him. Further down the road, they met up with the warriors carrying the other contestants. Fenity wasn't among them.

That was when they told him.

About the arrow.

About her injury.

She'd saved the others, somehow.

Renic charged through them. "Bring Fetam," he commanded Galan.

Galan, a master horseman, rushed back to the castle. He was their best chance of retrieving help for Fenity.

Now Renic raced toward her cries of agony, a sound that shouldn't be allowed to exist in this world. A sound he'd spend the rest of his life making sure never existed again if the gods would just spare her.

Nothing could have prepared him for what he saw. Fenity, his love, his truemate, surrounded by three guards, an arrow through her shoulder, her side turned brown from all the blood staining her green tunic. Her head drooped down where he couldn't see her face. Unconscious?

Renic roared with fury—at the guards, at the goblins, at his pata, at the gods. He jumped from his horse and sprinted the remaining distance.

"Prince Renic!" The guards bowed their heads, halting their progress to the building.

A red haze filled his vision, his limbs visibly shaking as he held himself back from ripping the throats out of these males who held her so callously. *They* hadn't done this to her.

He rushed to scoop her up, to feel her in his arms.

"Careful, Your Highness. The arrow goes through to the other side."

Renic stopped, his stomach recoiling. "Get her inside!"

A guard rushed to the door, holding it open and waving them all in.

The guards lay Fenity on her side on a bare cot inside the wooden building that smelled of alcohol and dried herbs. Her eyes fluttered from the pain, and Renic nearly punched their heads off.

A healer approached the cot, rubbing sleep from his eyes and eyeing the arrow and blood. "This may be beyond my skill."

"Forgive me, Prince Renic, but Lady Fenity requested Healer Fetam." The lead guard looked familiar.

"Timmay," Renic said, finally focusing on him. He'd been a palace guard for years when Renic was a youth. "Fetam is on her way. Send your guards to escort her. Fast as you can."

"Yes, Highness." He bowed, then flicked his arm. The other two guards hurried to carry out the orders.

The healer knelt at Fenity's side, adding another layer of bandage over the wound. "Healer Fetam is coming? Then it's best we wait. I don't have enough energy to staunch the blood flow on my own, and she's lost too much already."

Renic nodded and cupped Fenity's cold hands inside his. "Fetch a blanket!" he snapped. Timmay rushed to comply. The guilt at barking orders wasn't enough to override the fear shaking his entire body.

The fire crackling in the hearth couldn't chase her cold away. He pushed red hair off her blood-flecked face, surprising himself by how much his hand shook.

His heart raced, and it was like breathing through shards of glass. He had to calm down. If everyone in the room hadn't discovered the depth of his attachment to her, it was just a matter of time.

She moaned and jerked in her sleep, causing more blood to seep through the bandage. Renic shuddered and put his forehead to their joined hands. *Please. Let her live.* He'd never felt so hopeless.

The door burst open, and Galan and Fetam hurried in. "Everyone out."

"Do as she says." Renic moved aside to let Fetam by.

Galan put a firm hand on his shoulder. "I'm right outside, my prince."

Renic's deep breath shook, but the inexplicable rage wouldn't bank.

"Even you, Your Highness." Fetam's face and posture were as stern as he'd ever seen growing up with her tending to his childhood injuries.

Renic rose to his full height. "You can burn this village to the ground, march an army of goblins on Asentia, decimate the sun and moons, and still I won't be moved from her side." His hands clenched into fists, ready to do battle.

Fetam blinked her surprise. "Fine. Hold her shoulders. And resist the urge to hurt me when I yank this arrow out."

His jaw clenched. She knew, then, that they were truemates.

Fetam drained a vial of clear liquid into Fenity's mouth, coaxing it down by rubbing her throat. Then she pulled a small saw from her bag. "I've given her a sleeping draught that also helps with pain and infection. She shouldn't wake up, but you must hold her still." She motioned to the village healer who took the arrow in his hands, already knowing what Fetam required.

Renic gripped Fenity's shoulders and held her steady while Fetam sawed through the arrow near Fenity's back. The blood oozed, but Fenity didn't stir. Her face grew even paler.

Renic had seen blood and battle, death and injuries, but this was different. This was his truemate. He closed his eyes, concentrating on breathing and keeping Fenity as still as possible.

With a crack, the saw completed the job, and Renic took a shuddering breath.

"Now I'll pull the arrow out from the front, so the shaft

won't cause further damage." She directed her words to Renic as she unwrapped the bloody bandage from Fenity's shoulder —walking him through it, reassuring him. "Once it's out, we'll have to move quickly. Follow my lead."

Renic's heart pounded.

With the healer gripping Fenity's torso and Renic holding her shoulders, Fetam grabbed the arrow sticking out of Fenity's front and pulled. It came out slowly at first, then fast with a sickening suction.

Immediately, blood began pouring from both wounds. So much blood.

"The arrow was poisoned." Fetam tossed the piece aside and it clanked across the floorboards. "It has thinned her blood." Her brow creased in the only sign of distress Renic had ever seen on the elder healer.

Fetam wasted no time, the village healer moving with her, almost as if he'd trained with her at some point. They stripped her bare from the chest up, one of them holding constant pressure on the wounds.

He'd hunt those goblins to the ends of the earth.

An electric buzz filled the room as Fetam summoned the full force of her energy. "I'll manage the blood. You close the wound, Rupein."

The village healer—Rupein—called his weaker energy forward. "Master Healer, you know the patient is—"

"I know." Fetam cut a glance to Renic. "Begin."

Renic fell to his knees as the two healers bent over Fenity, his body responding to the energy they expended. He needed to *do* something, but all he could do was watch and wait. The blood slowly ceased flowing. The wound gradually closed. But Fenity remained pale and lifeless. Fetam kept one hand on Fenity's forehead, while Rupein kept his hands on her wounds, one in front and one in back. They didn't move, motionless there for eternity. At some point, the sun rose high enough to shine through the window.

The only sounds were Fetam's pants and the slow crackle of the dying fire. Renic rose and added more logs. He could keep Fenity warm. Fetam's movement caught his attention, but it was only to move her hand from Fenity's forehead to her stomach.

The goblins had *poisoned* their arrows.

"She's going to be alright, my prince."

Renic opened his eyes to see Fetam giving him a warm smile. He hadn't realized he'd closed them, hadn't realized there were tears on his cheeks. Rupein sat on the end of the cot, hunched over, head in his hands. Fetam's skin gleamed with a thin coat of sweat.

But Fenity lay on her back, eyes closed, renewed color in her cheeks, and a healed scar on her shoulder.

Renic stumbled to the cot as Fetam pulled a blanket up to her shoulders. "Thank you, Fetam. I don't know what I'd do if..." He couldn't finish the words as he took Fenity's hand, now slightly warmer than before.

"We'll let her rest for the morning, but then we should move her back to the palace where we can keep watch over her. The poison is gone, but she lost a lot of blood. My energy can't replenish lost blood."

Renic nodded, unable to speak.

He left the others outside to wait. Just a few more moments not to hide his love from the world.

CHAPTER 48

Fenity opened her eyes to her mata sleeping beside her, and for a moment she wondered how she'd returned to the hut in the forest. She rolled over, and the softness of the sheets and the weighty bulge of her stomach made her eyes flare wide.

Rich opulence. Carpets and curtains. Beautifully carved furniture. This wasn't her home in the woods. This was the palace.

She held her stomach and smacked her dry mouth. "Mata?" What happened? Her pata had led the defeat of a wyvern incursion and was appointed High Lord. They'd moved to an estate on the southern edge of Asentia, taking her from the only place she'd ever loved. She'd just settled in when the king forced her into the Strife as one of the youngest contestants—certainly the most incompetent and unprepared.

Renic. She'd found her truemate. And the goblins shot her. She reached for her shoulder, shuddering at the phantom pain.

"You're healed, my young one." Mata sat up, eyes shining. "I've never been so worried."

Fenity smacked her mouth again. "How did I get here?" She had no recollection of traveling to the palace. Did she lose her memory?

Mata pulled the servant's cord by her bed and then poured a cup of water.

Fenity drank it eagerly. Flashes of memory burst in her mind—goblins with axes, arrows and portals. Portals—she'd opened a portal to save them.

"Prince Renic went to find the contestants. You were badly injured. They brought you back here." Mata pushed Fenity's hair back. "They are saying you're a hero, that you rescued the contestants, waking up and freeing them from the wagon, though no one can agree on how." She raised an eyebrow in silent question.

Fenity winced and lay down, weary from a simple drink of water. "I had no choice."

Mata hugged her. "I'm sorry for the way things turned out. We should have stayed in the woods, my daughter. Then you'd be safe and you'd be happy. You never would have been forced to take such risks."

"I'm where I'm supposed to be, Mata. I've found my truemate." She smiled. Renic had saved her.

"Your truemate?" Mata sat back in surprise. "Who?"

But then the door opened, and Arinia and her attendants piled into the room, laughing and crying, surrounding her. They plied her with questions and compliments amid joyous relief.

Before Fenity could catch her breath, or barely notice Pata had joined the revelry, Fetam stepped into the room.

"I need to examine my patient," she said, loud and in charge.

Arinia and Mata squeezed her hands, and then the party

left almost as swiftly as it had arrived. Silence descended over the room, and it was just her and Fetam.

"Was it you? The one who healed me?" Under Fetam's coaxing, she eased back down on the pillows. How could she still be so tired after…? "How long have I slept?"

"Three days. And yes, I healed you. You all but demanded it would be me." She placed a cool hand on Fenity's forehead, and another on her stomach.

"Is my baby alright?" Worry stabbed through her weary body.

"She's perfectly fine. And you are too. Your body needs time to recover. And you need to eat when you next awaken."

"Next awaken? Why am I so tired?"

"You were very sick and very injured. I laced your water with a sleeping dram. But after this, you won't need it anymore." She paused, as if readying Fenity for a blow.

"What is it?"

"The king is sending someone to question you this afternoon. Not just anyone. His army general. I pleaded for more time, but they won't wait any longer."

Fenity's lungs seized. Her story. She hadn't had a moment to plan her story—could hardly remember everything that happened. Exhaustion pulled at her thoughts until they slipped from her fingers. All she could think to say was, "Is Renic alright?"

Fetam smiled. "Your truemate is worried for your health, but I've told him all is well. Now sleep."

"Don't tell him about our…" Fenity slept.

She next awoke to the clinking of dishes on a serving tray and Arinia's bright smile.

"You are to eat, bathe, and dress for General Ashryn."

Fenity's mood darkened immediately. Of all the people to

question her. He wouldn't go easy on her just because they were family. He was loyal to his role as the king's general. If anything, he'd use it to his advantage.

She went through the motions of preparation, but the after-effect of the sleeping dram left her head foggy. When the last hair comb was tucked into place, she was ready to go back to sleep.

But Arinia led her to the sitting room—a beautiful room with a private terrace overlooking the gardens, though closed against the cold. A male warrior was already there, ignoring the elaborate tea and treats before him. His stern eyes locked right on her, and then Fenity really did think about going back to bed. Or portaling away forever.

Her sleepiness disguised her nerves, and she all but dropped into the chair across from him at the dainty table he barely fit beneath.

"So you're the lucky one," Fenity said. It'd been a long time since she'd seen General Thallan Ashryn, not since he wed her sister many years ago. "I haven't seen you at all during the Strife." Except when he almost caught her and Marek on his land. "How's my sister and baby Lela?" Lela was her niece, already a year old, and the cutest baby she'd ever seen.

"Lady Fenity." He dipped his head. "They are well." His eyes softened momentarily.

"It's been too long since I've seen them. I'll need to visit soon." Very soon, if she wanted to see her sister before her baby came.

"Do you know why I'm here?" His tone changed back to stern.

"The king wants to know the details of the goblin attack."

He didn't respond. Just sat there expectantly, a male who didn't have to ask twice, and shouldn't have to ask even once.

Fenity respected that. "I can tell you what I remember. It's still slowly coming back to me. It started with the feast. I didn't eat the cake and I never went to sleep. When the guards came for me, I faked it so I wasn't left behind for the next pillar. The goblins took our wagon, and then things get a little fuzzy." She wiped her sweaty hands on her knees. "The others wouldn't wake, no matter what I tried." She swallowed. Truth mixed with lie. "When the door finally opened, they dragged us all out. They had these golden manacles they called—"

"Dampeners. We should have known they'd acquire some."

"I knew we'd never return if they got those on us. So when they tried to put one on me, I pretended to wake up. It became pure chaos. They scattered, fearing I had energy. I pretended to cast a spell, and they fled. That's when I realized I'd been shot. I don't remember much after that."

It was weak. So weak. She'd concocted the story as she spoke, and there were too many holes. But now she was stuck with it. That would be the way of things until her dying breath.

Thallan stared at her. Studying her. Measuring her. "You woke up, and they simply fled?"

"They thought that the others had awakened, too. We were all in a pile, and I nudged the contestants when I stood. The goblins were already on high alert after their plans failed, and our guards were after them. It was like wildfire, spreading until they were all mounting their horses, fleeing."

His brow furrowed, and he leaned closer. "If the goblins were panicking, already on the run from us, why would they take the time to empty the wagon of contestants still so far away from their border, making it more difficult to travel?"

Fenity rubbed her sweaty palms over her skirts. "I don't know. I was just glad to be free of that wooden prison. But I'm sure the horses were tiring from pulling the heavy wagon. I was kidnapped, injured, and fearing for my life. The door kept repairing itself as they chopped. Maybe they didn't want to risk having to leave us behind. It gets rockier the further east you go, right?" She held his gaze despite the deep need to look away.

"Maybe." His deep voice rumbled, and she was surprised the fine tea set didn't rattle.

She let the silence linger, her brother-in-law waiting for her to fidget, or give any indication she wasn't being truthful. He knew the story didn't line up, but he had nothing to go on. She knew better than to use their relationship as leverage. It would only be further proof of her guilt, and further motivation for him to continue with this line of questioning.

But there was one thing she had against him. "How did this happen, General? How did a rogue clan of goblins even know we would be on the move?"

A flash of memory. Something the goblins said.

Thallan's mouth turned down. "I take full responsibility for that, Lady Fenity. The safety of the contestants falls to me, and we were unprepared. In short, I don't know how the goblins found out, but I will soon." He stood, pushing back his chair. He towered over her, heavy gaze still weighing her down. "Thank you for your time. I'm glad you're recovered. Good luck at the pillar announcement this evening, Lady Fenity."

His words faded as the night came to her, full force. Fenity gasped. "I remember." She grabbed his arm as he moved to leave. "The goblins said something. They said there wasn't supposed to be a fae patrol. Someone had told them that." She held her head, headache blooming. "Lady Moona. Or, no. Just Moona. The Waters female. That was it."

His features remained blank. "That is a grave accusation."

"I'm not accusing anyone. I'm telling you what I heard."

"I will relay your account to the king." He headed for the door, and relief loosened her chest. She was safe.

Thallan abruptly turned back. "I almost forgot. Do you know why His Highness, Prince Renic, felt the need to put his life at risk and leave the palace against all rational judgment to come to your aid?" He waited, unblinking.

Fenity stood from the table, gripping it for balance. "We've gotten to know each other during the Strife. He cares for me." What was this new line of questioning about?

"He knows plenty of ladies of the court, but he's never lost his head like that, not in all the years I've watched him grow up."

"Why does it matter? This is the Strife. The entire point is for Renic to find a wife." She couldn't keep the irritation from her voice.

"Our heir is risking his life and safety to chase after the contestants. It very much does matter. And his name is *Prince Renic*." His tone was patient, yet stern, leaving no room for argument. "I've heard the rumors of you and him. What aren't you telling me?"

So this is where he'd catch her lying. She couldn't lie before and be believed if she lied now when he already seemed to know the truth.

She stepped closer and lowered her voice. "*Renic* and I are mates. Truemates."

His eyes flashed wide for only a moment, then something like pity took the place of surprise. "I see."

It felt freeing to share it with someone new, someone she considered family. But he wasn't happy for her. Not everyone found their truemate. It was a thing to celebrate. Instead, he looked almost devastated.

"What do you know?" she demanded.

"Take care of yourself, Fenity." He left, but she wished he

would have stayed. She'd tell him all about her fears and concerns, and he'd tell her that of course she would win the Strife, and of course the king's dislike of her didn't matter.

Instead, she'd survived the questioning, yet the fear he left behind nearly drowned her under its weight.

CHAPTER 49

The time of the Fifth Pillar had finally arrived. Fenity's attendants whispered as they readied her for the ballroom. Apparently, while she was recovering, King Sidian declared the conflict between the goblins had grown too dangerous for the Strife to continue. He canceled the final pillar. According to Fenity's attendant, Alinne, who was married to a guard, the plan had been to leave them in the woods in groups with challenges that tested their honesty and trustworthiness.

It would have been her shining moment.

There was only one thing going for her for the final tally. The Fifth Pillar represented integrity, and who was better suited for that than the person who'd rescued the contestants from the goblins? No one else had the opportunity to stand out in the recent task.

Her hands wouldn't quit shaking as Arinia put the finishing touches on her hair. A green ball gown with sewn-in crystals in whirling patterns, and a matching hair comb tucked into her braided updo. It was beautiful, but still too tight over her belly.

She couldn't even concentrate on the walk to the ballroom where they were to gather before the feast. Somehow, she made it there without even noticing, but some contestants stopped her at the door. The females she'd connected with, Nisha, Mira, Daream, and several more.

"We wanted to thank you," Nisha said, speaking for the group. "We tried to visit, but you were too sick. You saved us." She dipped her head, as if Fenity was royal.

Words caught in Fenity's throat. "I did what I had to."

"We won't soon forget it," Daream said, reaching for her hand, gold dress shimmering.

Fenity soaked up their kindness, clasping their hands in turn until she entered the ballroom. Inside, her friends surrounded her, joined by others in the room. The raised dais sat empty, waiting for the king to make his appearance.

Moona stood to the side, alone and frowning in her pale blue ballgown. Was she a spy? Had General Ashryn told the king? There hadn't been time to tell Renic what the goblin said.

Sarafine also had a crowd of contestants around her, and when they parted and Fenity finally saw her, she gaped. Sarafine was looking at her with gratitude in her eyes. She moved toward Fenity, but the king finally entered, halting the room. Only Renic accompanied him, not his mata. Fenity tugged at the collar of her dress, which was somehow choking her without even touching her neck.

Why was it so hot in this ballroom? Could she run out the back doors into the garden and forget this was happening? She and Sarafine were tied, with two pillars each. This pillar determined it all.

Renic caught her gaze and gave her a small, reassuring smile. Did he know who would win? Was it her? One would think the anxiety of this routine—answer the king's summons, await word on who won, steal whatever glances she could from Renic—would dull over time. It did not.

The herald stepped onto the dais while a horn blared. "Our esteemed King Sidian and heir to the throne, Prince Renic, are pleased with the strength exhibited by the contestants, their ability to recover and report here this evening despite the traumatic ordeal. They would also like to express gratitude to the warriors who saved the contestants, especially those who lost their lives. Please be assured that the goblin threat will not be ignored. His Highness, Prince Renic, rides out tomorrow with a host of our best to join forces at the border. The goblin heathens will learn they cannot harm the people of our court and get away with it."

Renic's lips parted for an instant. Most fae would have dismissed his action—it happened so quickly. But Fenity saw it for what it was. He hadn't known.

What did that mean?

The herald smiled, buttons stretched tight on his vest. "Our king has a special surprise in store for you. Not only are we to find out the winner of the Fifth Pillar, but he's ready to announce the winner of the Strife!"

Amidst the applause, Renic snapped a look over to his pata that would have withered a mighty syraoak tree.

Fenity's heart pounded through her dress. Sounds turned muffled. Renic hadn't known that either. Which meant he hadn't been part of the decision, a decision that should have been his and his alone.

Fenity found Sarafine in the crowd. The female in red was already watching her, waiting for her to figure it out. Her mouth curled into a hesitant smile, though her eyes flicked between Renic and Fenity.

She'd thought she'd won. She thought Renic's reaction meant the king had picked Sarafine.

Fenity prayed to every god she could remember that it wasn't true. The God of woodland creatures, the Goddess of water, the Goddess of spring, the God of decay...

The room applauded as King Sidian stood, the herald bowing and conceding the stage. But Renic's panicked face was all Fenity could see.

"My court!" King Sidian raised his arms to the applause. "The goblins have come and ruined my fun, but that only means we will choose our winner that much sooner."

Renic grabbed the arms of his throne in tight fists, his surprise morphing into hate blazing in his eyes.

"It is my pleasure to announce to the court and kingdom that the winner of the Fifth Pillar of Faedom, and therefore the winner of the Strife—your future queen and betrothed to the crowned prince of Asentia. Lady Sarafine Rivers."

The floor fell out beneath Fenity. The column caught her as she stumbled backward, arm cradling her stomach.

No. It can't be.

The applause disappeared with her pounding heart. Renic's hate remained as his glare bore a hole through his pata's head. He wasn't surprised. He'd figured it out right along with Fenity. Only she'd been too stupid to not keep fighting for hope.

Nausea rose, violent and sudden. She'd been here before, but unlike before, this time it was unsalvageable.

Crowded with congratulating courtiers, Sarafine met Fenity's eyes, but she didn't look exultant. She looked horrified.

King Sidian smiled and held a hand out to Sarafine. She adopted feigned surprise and an innocence that didn't belong to her. He led her onto the dais, then turned and motioned Renic to join them.

To the shock of all, including Fenity, Renic stood and walked straight out of the room. Galan followed close behind.

King Sidian pretended not to notice his son snubbing him in front of the entire court. He turned and smiled, Sarafine at his side. "Congratulations to your future queen. She's displayed admirable qualities and skills in *all* pillars of faedom, and more. Our prince has chosen well."

Sarafine bowed deeply to him, then deeply to the court as the never-ending applause threatened to swallow Fenity whole.

"I congratulate the rest of the contestants and wish them well. I will now announce the bottom ten." The herald unrolled a scroll.

What was she doing here? She'd lost. The strife was over.

Fenity headed to the doors as Moona's name was called first.

The strife was over, and she'd lost.

Renic. Their future. Their baby.

How could she have lost?

Fenity ran out of the ballroom, charging past contestants, shoving them out of the way when necessary. She had to find Renic. He'd make this okay. They could run away together. They could raise their child together.

Renic found her on a blind, tear-filled sprint through the halls. Silent tears streamed down his face too, and he led her inside her rooms, shutting the door with Galan standing guard in the hall.

"I lost, Renic, I lost. I failed."

"No." He squeezed her to him. "My pata chose. I had no say in this. He ignored my wishes. He's angry now, but I will speak with him. We'll tell him we're truemates. I won't let him say no."

Fenity nodded, too upset for words, but traitorous hope

filled her. Yes, of course—now that the Strife was over, once the king knew they were truemates, he couldn't deny her. "When will you speak to him?" Renic was leaving tomorrow. "He planned this. He planned for you to go fight the goblins so you couldn't be here to argue with him."

"Yes. He's very cunning. He never could have predicted just how strong my love is for you, strong enough to disobey the king's command."

Arinia burst into the room, out of breath, with tears streaming. "I've heard. Oh, dear petal, I'm so sorry. We wanted it to be you so badly. It was supposed to be you."

Fenity's own tears responded, welling again, but she couldn't let go of Renic.

"It will be her. I will speak to my pata after the feast. All will be well." But he didn't let go of his grip on Fenity either.

She didn't bother praying to the gods this time. Their declarations would either fall empty or not, but hope was all that remained.

Renic left shortly after that, making Arinia promise to feed her. He would speak to the king at dawn. Their fate rested in his hands.

CHAPTER 50

Renic shut the door upon leaving Fenity's room, and the fury he'd buried deep down, struggling to hide from her, boiled to the surface. He'd never disobeyed his pata before, never once opposed him in public. But this time, Pata was lucky all he'd done was walk away. The hurt and betrayal, the pure agony on his truemate's face, was almost the king's undoing.

Royal choice. His pata has never intended to let him have a say. Royal choice meant the king would have all the control—that the king would have the final say.

He *would* rectify this. Not in the morning. Tonight.

Waiting out the feast was a test of patience he almost couldn't bear, despite a lifetime of training to be patient.

"You should go to bed, Galan. I will see this through." He'd nearly worn out the rug pacing in front of his pata's suite.

"My place is with you, my prince." Galan stood nearby, body language daring Renic to send him away.

They both tensed when a messenger approached Renic, bowing.

"His Majesty demands your presence in the throne room."

Renic glanced at Galan. "Good."

The throne room was empty and quiet this time of night, with the feast still raging, except for his pata sitting tall on the throne, thunder in his face and clenched fists.

Renic left Galan to guard him from the hall. He didn't stop to bow, simply marched right up to the bottom of the dais, his steps echoing across the bare stone with none of the usual courtiers to absorb the sound. "Thank you for seeing me, Pata." As if it hadn't been the king who called this meeting.

The irritation that flashed in his pata's eyes was well worth the insubordination.

The king's voice was low and lethal, but the guards at the doors could still hear, their presence an inevitable part of life. "You humiliated me in front of the court tonight."

"No, you humiliated me." Renic couldn't contain his emotions as well as his pata. Not yet. "You circumvented tradition and stole my voice in this competition. You took away my right to choose my future bride, the female I will spend centuries with."

"And what made you think you ever had a voice?" His pata lifted his chin.

"This is my life. My future. And the future of our kingdom. I know who embodies the Five Pillars of Faedom. I know who passed all your tests. But you're too prejudiced to see it."

"All of my tests?" He stroked his chin. "You think I care where the female comes from?"

"Everyone cares. It's the only thing I've heard since she got here. Anytime I gave her the least bit of attention, there was some courtier there to remind me she's no one with no connections. As good as one of the commoners."

"They're right."

"No, they're not!" His shout echoed around the throne

room, but he didn't apologize. His pata was winning this simply because Renic couldn't contain his emotions. He took a steadying breath. "Whether you intended or not, whether the Strife was designed that way or not, I should have a say, if not *all* the say, in who I marry. And I choose Fenity."

"No. You will marry Sarafine. The agreement has already been signed."

Already signed? "I will not. You can't make me."

Pata raised his eyebrow.

Damn. He sounded like a spoiled child.

Pata stood, his bunched muscles betrayed the anger he hid so well. "A youngling of mere eighteen cannot know what is good for him, good for his future, and good for this kingdom. I'm the reigning king, and I made the decision. I took your opinion into consideration, but your opinion is folly. You will marry Sarafine, and if you test that, if you betray her for a forest child with no court status, there are ways to make her obsolete. I haven't imprisoned her yet for being a spy for the goblins after that flimsy story General Ashryn reported—the investigation is not complete—but I will."

Fiery anger poured down Renic's throat. "You will not harm my truemate!" He bit his tongue to keep from threatening the king. Son or no, the king would not suffer it.

Pata's eyes widened in surprise. His mouth curled in disgust. "Truemates? You're claiming you are truemates now?"

"We are truemates." Renic rose to his full height. "And I will do anything to have her win the Strife and marry her. Anything."

Pata studied him, cold calculation in his eyes. But then they softened infinitesimally.

Renic held his breath.

"Even if I could undo what has been done, I wouldn't."

"What? Why?" Renic demanded.

Pata paused, clearly deciding something. "Leave us," he boomed. Instantly, the room cleared of guards. Pata lowered his voice anyway. "You are aware of the depth of the goblin threat."

"Of course. I've attended the council meetings." He knew the numbers. He'd been to the border, witnessing the preparations for a full-scale invasion, and now the daughters of their court had been threatened. Where was this going?

Pata stood from his throne to the edge of the dais. "We don't have the numbers to protect the entire length of the border. Not without a draft, and I don't want to cause a panic. Only in the case of a portal opening should we call a draft."

"What does this have to do with the Strife?" Renic was burning with impatience. His future hinged on this moment.

Pata ran a hand over his head and down his face. Whatever he was about to say was making him nervous, and Pata rarely showed his emotions. "Lord Rivers has committed five thousand fae from his lands to our cause, in addition to funding half the cost of the campaign to secure the border." Pata sat back hard on his throne.

The world shifted beneath Renic's feet. "What did you do?" he whispered. But he already knew. All those contestants whose punishment for losing was to pay fines to the winner—Sarafine. After Pata had convinced them it was okay to lose a contest or two.

The king had turned the Strife—an age-old tradition formed to steer their people into the next age—into nothing but an auction. Highest bidder wins. And Sarafine's parents had been happy to oblige.

But who was left to pay the ultimate price? Fenity. And himself. And their people.

"What have you done?" His pata was a fair, just king. A good pata, teaching him to be a prince of the realm. Had it all been a lie?

Pata lifted his chin. "I've secured our future, just as our ancestors once did when the humans grew too greedy."

"I won't marry Sarafine. If I can't be with my truemate, I won't survive." Renic felt the truth of that. Even now—especially now—in the face of all he learned, all that was still unraveling in his mind, the need to go to Fenity and protect her was near-crippling.

"Then I'll have to take her life," Pata said. And it was the deep forlornness and sorrow that sent Renic to shaking, looking over his shoulder to see if any guards had returned to await the king's orders and were on their way to murder his truemate.

Renic's words tumbled over each other. "We can find another way. Lord Stormbrook commands warriors, too. Lots of them. Why not even try?"

Pata looked almost pitying. "You're a fool if you truly don't know why. She has no energy. And you have no energy."

There it was.

The great shame his pata would never voice, the secret Renic was sworn to never utter, the words now echoing around the throne room. But his pata wasn't done.

"You cannot be bonded. Your heirs cannot take the throne without energy running through their blood. The Fae Kingdom of Asentia must have strong rulers. And strong rulers must have energy. Without that, we fall to enemies like the goblins and we crumble from within."

Renic nearly stumbled. "I don't... That can't matter in the face of this. She's my *truemate*."

"And if you cannot let her go, I will be forced to make you let her go." Pain lined his voice as if he truly regretted this course of action. "It's the only way." He reached out a hand. Even too far away to touch, Renic recoiled.

The way his pata kept glancing at the exits... something uneasy settled in Renic's gut. His instincts rang like alarm bells. His sincere, caring pata was trying to distract him. To ease him into compliance.

The king had no intention of letting Fenity live.

Renic dropped his eyes while he gathered his thoughts. He had to tread carefully—say nothing that would spur his pata into immediate action. "You're right, Pata. I don't want it to be true, but it is. My heir must have energy." He shook his head. "I know I have to let her go, but this hurts so much." He clutched his heart—no need to fake the pain centered in his chest.

"It will. It does." Pata wasn't buying his performance. Just like Renic wasn't buying his.

"Her family will leave soon, now that the Strife is officially over. Give me until then to figure out how to say goodbye. I know I can do it."

His pata nodded. "Very well, but you must not embarrass our future queen with your actions. Keep this whole affair private—much more so than you have thus far." He narrowed his eyes.

Renic bowed his head, mind churning. His pata wouldn't honor the promised time if he suspected Renic could never stay away from her. If he knew anything about truemates, he'd know the compulsion was too strong. And he knew everything about them, despite not being mated to his own wife.

He'd have to hurry. Fenity didn't have much time.

"Thank you, Pata."

His pata grunted, waving a hand in dismissal. As Renic walked away, he added, "You needn't marry Lady Sarafine right away. Take time to get to know her and grieve the loss of your mistress. Heirs are necessary, but we have time."

Pata thought he was doing a kindness, but really, he was solidifying Renic's theory that he had no intention of letting Fenity survive.

Renic nodded his silent thanks and withdrew from the throne room.

Then he was running.

CHAPTER 51

Arinia dressed Fenity in her softest nightshift while Mata practically force-fed her dinner with warm milk. Fenity didn't even mind she was being treated like a child, incapable and weak. At this moment, she *was* incapable and weak. She'd lost the Strife. She'd lost her truemate. She'd shamed her parents and herself. She needed this kind of care, and there was nothing wrong with leaning on others when life got too heavy to stand. If Arinia's and Mata's comfort could take away even a fraction of this pain, she'd sip the milk and eat the food and let them tuck her into warm blankets.

After they'd gone on to bed, she was left tossing and turning, pacing and worrying. When she couldn't stand it a moment longer, she dressed herself in the first thing she found and headed for the door.

Just as she reached for the knob, someone knocked and let themselves inside in a rush. It was him. "Renic."

His usually sunshiny face was grim enough to make her shiver with fear. Galan entered behind him, plastering himself against the wall like part of the décor.

Renic hurried to her and gripped her arms with shaking hands. "You have to leave. Immediately. It isn't safe for you here."

She shook her head. "What about your pata? Didn't you tell him we're truemates?"

"That's why it's not safe." He hesitated, unable to meet her eyes. "There's something I never told you. You never asked, so I never said. I should have told you. I'm like you. I don't possess any energy."

Fenity bit her lip, frantic to ease the despair pinching his features, her own secrets ready to bubble over. "I love you. Not having energy doesn't change that. I need to tell you something, too."

"It's why Pata didn't choose you. I must marry someone with energy."

Fenity recoiled. "And do you agree with him?"

"No! Of course not. Pata knows the hold truemates have over each other. He doesn't believe I could let you go and marry Sarafine. And he's right. That would never happen."

She gripped his arms. "You think he'd kill me, to free you of our bond. But that's not how it works. I feel it in my blood and soul. I could never love another—the bond cannot be severed."

His mouth thinned. "You don't have to love someone to produce heirs."

Fenity's arms went slack. "He doesn't care about the true-mate bond." Understanding washed over her, like falling through thin ice, plunging into a depthless, freezing death where there was no up or down.

Renic snatched up her hands. "I'm so sorry. If you had never met me, you'd still be safe."

She placed a hand on his cheek. "I don't regret my choices. Everything I've ever done, every mistake I made, everything I wished wouldn't happen that happened anyway, led me to you. So I'll no longer lament my past. I'll no longer anger at the things that happened beyond my control." Her breath hitched. "I was wishing for better when all the while my unanswered wishes were leading me to you. I'll never regret my choices."

His eyes shone, love and pride and sadness.

Fenity covered her mouth. If there was any chance it might make a difference... "Renic, I have to tell you something. I lied too. I do have energy."

"What?" His body went rigid with shock.

Someone banged on the door, and Fenity jumped. Just as Galan reached for the knob, Arinia burst inside, quickly locking the door behind her. Her face was contorted into horror. "They're coming. Guards."

Galan gripped the hilt of his sword. "Orders, my prince?"

"Renic?" She gripped him tighter as his face morphed from shock to anger.

"He didn't waste any time. Hide. We will take care of this. Don't worry, love. Galan, stand watch."

All too fast, Renic led her to the dressing room. He caressed her face, squeezed her hand three times, then shut the door.

Fenity was left in the dim light, surrounded by fancy dresses, her rapid breathing and pounding heart filling the space.

"I'm here, my petal." Arinia's voice sounded from just outside the dressing room, a shield between her and the king. "I won't let them have you. Nor will Prince Renic."

"What about your son?" Fenity clutched her stomach. This couldn't be truly happening.

"Prince Renic will protect my son. The Strife is over. I'm no longer bound by the king's bargain." There was certainty in her tone. Fenity could only hope it was true.

Fists pounded on the door to her rooms. "Open up in the

name of the king." The voice was muffled between the walls, but the urgency was plain.

The door burst open with the splinter of wood, but the rushing footsteps cut short. "Your Highness." A pause. "We did not expect you."

"I know why you're here, and you will not have her. I order you to stand down."

"Apologies, Your Highness, but we are under direct orders from the king."

Fenity's body shook. They would disobey their prince? What would happen when they caught her? How was Renic going to prevent this?

"If you enter this room, your lives are forfeited." Renic had never sounded so deadly.

"Forgive us, my prince. We have no choice." Footsteps rushed into the suite.

There was a scuffle, fists meeting flesh, but there were too many guards for Renic and Galan to take on alone.

Fenity rushed to the dressing room doors, speaking through them. "Arinia, tell Renic I love him. Tell my parents I love them. And please know that I love you."

Arinia sobbed through the door. "Don't speak like that. Prince Renic will stop them."

By the sound of things, she was out of time. "Stand aside. Let them pass. Don't get hurt. I was never really in here."

Arinia cried louder, but the sound traveled as she moved to the side, heeding Fenity's words.

Fenity summoned her energy. Terror gave it strength. "I love you, Renic." Before the guards reached the door, she opened a portal and transported to another place.

CHAPTER 52

Renic launched himself, tackling a guard at the waist as the guard made for Fenity's dressing room. Without a word, Galan joined in the melee, powerful fists slamming into guard after guard.

His pata had lost his mind—sending them to capture Fenity in the middle of the night? He knew his pata hadn't believed the lie about subservience, but to act so quickly...

His fist connected with a jaw as a guard slipped past him. He didn't want to hurt them, only stop them. He and Fenity only needed time to get away.

More guards burst past, piling into the dressing room. None of them hurt their prince or even tried to restrain him. But they held no such reservations with Galan. Renic's friend bled from his nose and a cut above his eye.

Renic rushed to the sounds of Arinia's sobs, arriving just in time to see the guards break through the doors to the dressing room.

"I order you to leave her alone!" Renic yelled after them.

Several guards spread out amongst the dresses and shelves

of jewelry and hair pieces. They rifled through the gowns, ripping them from the hangers, crystals and pearls scattering across the floor.

Fenity was gone.

"Where are you hiding her?" a guard—Yamin—snapped at Arinia. Galan rushed to her side, angling his bleeding body in front of her.

Fenity's guide couldn't be consoled, not even enough to acknowledge her charge had disappeared. Did Arinia hide her somewhere else? Sneak her out a servant's entrance Renic wasn't aware of?

"Prince Renic," Yamin said in a calm tone that did nothing to conceal his rage. "Where is Lady Fenity? Our king does not have the patience for this."

Renic focused on his own expression, ensuring all evidence of surprise was well and truly wiped clean. "You speak for my pata now?" He folded his arms behind him. "I do not know where she is, but I do know I've marked you and all those who dared disobey me this night. Your future king will never forgive your disobedience."

"He tells the truth, Captain Yamin," a female said from behind the bulk of the guards.

A truth-reader. So much energy buzzed in this room, now that he wasn't fighting for Fenity's life. They'd brought a truth-reader in case he tried to hide her away. His body vibrated with anger.

And captain? Yamin must have been promoted for outing Renic for eavesdropping.

"You, maid, where is she?" Yamin stepped closer to Arinia, earning a stare-down from Galan. A young guard on a power trip.

Renic stepped into Yamin's space. "Her name is Arinia Thornreach, head guide and long-time servant of the king and heir. You will address her with the respect she deserves." He couldn't allow Arinia to be questioned. If she lied about where Fenity was—

"I don't know where she is," Arinia said, breaths shaky. "Not one idea."

"It's the truth," the truth-reader said.

Renic growled. "Get out." He'd never felt so powerless. His own guards wouldn't listen. He'd lost his truemate, and his one hope in Arinia had crumbled to dust. Growing up, he'd always hoped his energy would come to him in a great moment of need, that he'd be backed into a corner of helplessness and hopelessness, and this grand power would come to his aid.

Never had there been such despair as he felt now, and still nothing. He was past the age where anything manifests. No great energy was waiting to solve all his problems.

Galan seemed to sense Renic's emotion, as he began shoving guards toward the door.

Yamin bowed his head and waved the others toward the entry hall. "Search the grounds. We'll find her before she escapes the palace."

Guards hauled away the ones Renic and Galan had knocked unconscious. It took everything in his self-control not to slam another fist into Yamin's face.

Renic slammed the door shut behind the last one and rushed back to Arinia. She sat on the edge of a cushioned chair, eyes wide and staring off, tears still stuck to her cheeks. Galan guarded the door.

Renic took her hands. "Where is she?" Maybe Arinia didn't know, but maybe she knew *something* he could use to find Fenity before the guards did.

Her wide eyes met his. "I don't know. She was in the dressing room. She told me goodbye, to tell you she loves you, then she was gone." Her voice lowered to the point of being almost inaudible. "There's no other way out of there. I felt an enormous burst of energy, quick as a flash." She started shaking. "I think... I think..."

Renic blinked, and then his mouth dropped open in realization. "But the alarm." He glanced back at Galan, who'd stiffened.

"I know, my prince. But nothing else makes sense."

She'd tried to tell him. A secret for a secret.

Fenity *did* possess energy. One of the strongest the fae could possess. The kind outlawed under penalty of death because...

"Stars above." Renic dropped to his knees. "She opened a portal. The prophecy."

The doom of the fae. She'd sacrificed the entire kingdom to save herself.

And he was glad. The rest of them could burn so long as she lived.

"I know." Arinia sobbed anew. "I know."

"Never tell a soul." Renic looked at Galan, who gave him a solemn bow. "All we know is that she escaped somehow." He rushed to the window in the bathing room, throwing it open. Way too high to jump. He pulled a sheet from the armoire and Galan helped him tie it around the column flanking the tub, letting the rest hang outside. Let them think she climbed out, then scaled the rest of the way somehow.

Outside, guards carrying torches and magelights spread out amongst the grounds. A manhunt to end Fenity's life.

But where had she gone? And how was he going to find her?

Had the prophecy truly been unleashed?

CHAPTER 53

Fenity collapsed to her hands and knees on the field where she'd once brought Marek. She'd almost gone back to him, the human world, but something had stopped her. So, she'd gone to her sister's house. She shivered under the light of the moons. Winter still clung to the earth. Despite everything telling her to lie down and sleep here, she couldn't.

Trudging through the field and over the hills, she finally came to the small barn at the back of the house. There, shivering under a couple of horse blankets, she spent the night agonizing over how everything had gone so wrong. She'd fought so hard for so long. Worked the hardest she ever had, wanting something more than she'd ever wanted anything in her life. And it had slipped through her fingers, completely out of her control. She hadn't even been able to warn Mata or tell them of their granddaughter.

Now how was she going to get it back?

How soon would the king make her truemate marry Sarafine?

Fenity bit her knuckle to keep from crying again. So many tears. So much self-pity. She was sick of it. She'd never felt so alone and never needed so much help from someone, all at the same time.

At dawn, she brushed off the hay and dust, finger-combed her hair, and knocked on her sister's front door. The house looked just as quaint as she remembered, the extensive herb garden out front, pungent with the promise of early spring growth. A cute cottage in the middle of sprawling fields and scattered trees.

Her sister—half-sister—was decades older than her. They shared the same pata. After her sister's mata passed away, he'd met and married Fenity's mata, all well before Fenity was born. She didn't possess energy but was the best healer around, even without it.

When her sister, Corantha, opened the door, she gasped in surprise. "Fenity. What are you doing here?"

Fenity's face crumpled, and she burst into tears. Even coming here might put her sister at risk.

"Oh, child." Corantha pulled her into a crushing hug, shutting the door against the rising sunlight. She sat her at the wooden kitchen table and busied herself brewing lavender tea while Fenity composed herself. She added a thick dollop of honey to Fenity's cup.

Fenity held the drink in both hands, warming her bones and inhaling the relaxing floral aroma. She took a tentative sip, letting the sweetness wash over her tongue and the heat plunge into her belly.

A fluttering answered, and she gasped, nearly dropping her mug. She pressed a hand to her belly, and the fluttering answered again. A grin lit up her face and her body buzzed with joy.

"I think you better tell me what's going on," Corantha said, sitting across from her and eyeing Fenity's stomach. "Starting with why you've shown up in the middle of the Strife. And speak quietly so Lelana doesn't wake."

Of course, word hadn't reached them yet. "I lost the Strife, Cor." The words burned her mouth. "Lady Sarafine of Alberry won. But Renic—Prince Renic—and I are truemates." Fenity held her belly. "No one knows about our daughter, not even Renic. King Sidian didn't pick me because I don't have energy." Mata never told anyone what she and Fenity could do. She trusted Corantha, but it was safer for her not to know. "The king knew Renic would never give me up, so he sent the guards after me. I escaped, but I don't know what they'll do if they find me. That's why I can't go home." They were likely on their way there now, hoping to capture her. "I can't stay long. I won't put your family in danger."

Fenity took another sip of tea while Corantha blinked in stunned silence.

"You are my family, and you'll stay as long as you need." Corantha patted her hand. "I'm so sorry you've had to go through this, sister. To find your truemate and not be together? Well, there's nothing worse. I can only bear Thallan being away now because he and I had so long to get used to it." Something seemed to click in her. "You'll stay here, at least until the baby comes and we can sort this all out."

"I can't risk you and baby Lela being wrapped up in this. Your truemate, if he's involved in the search for me, he'll eventually come here. I think the king means to end my life, to free Renic of the burden of me."

"Hush." Corantha took her hands. "You're not a burden. You're family. We'll do what we must."

Whimpering came from the next room.

"Right on time." Corantha smiled, and Fenity followed her to a small bedroom off the main living area. A squirming mass sat up, on the cusp of a full-blown cry, when Corantha lifted her from the bed, snuggling her close. The sweet baby, a year old now, grabbed onto her mata, pulling at the top of her shirt.

"Almost, Lelana." Corantha quickly changed Lela's soiled clothes for clean ones. "She's always so hungry in the mornings." She unbuttoned the top of her shirt and nursed Lela, whose eyes drifted closed before opening again. When they found Fenity, the baby unlatched and sat up, making noises and pointing, clearly asking who was this stranger in her house.

"I'm your Aunt Fenity," she said in a high-pitched voice. Stars, Lela was cute, with small, pointed ears covered in fuzz, and short, pale hair. Fenity held a hand out to her niece. The baby stared at it before resuming nursing.

"This'll be you soon enough." Corantha patted Lela's bottom. "How far along are you?"

"I'm not entirely sure. Maybe four or five months?" It was hard to believe she'd hold her daughter like this one day soon. A little piece of her and Renic.

"I'm going to be an aunty." Corantha smiled. "So you'll stay here, right? I need help making tonics and looking after Lelana when I have patients."

"Yes. I'll stay." For now. Just until it was safe to find Renic and tell him everything. Would he even accept her back after knowing what she could do? Should he? "Thank you, Cor."

"You'll be doing me a favor, really." She laughed. "You've been through so much. Use this time to rest, recover, and take care of yourself and your baby." She lifted Lela. "Cousins."

"And they'll grow up to be best friends." Fenity smiled, but inside she was wilting. There was hope again, trying to creep up and fill her head with beautiful ideas.

When had that ever worked out for her?

CHAPTER 54

While the guards searched the palace, Renic spent all night pacing his rooms, worried out of his mind and trying to figure out where Fenity might have gone. Of course, she was nowhere within the castle grounds. But he sent Galan to join in the ruse, and his loyal friend brought back regular reports.

As more guards joined the hunt, then servants, then even some courtiers, the gossip spread—that Fenity was so distraught with the shame of losing, she'd run away. That the bottom ten contestants had banded against her, resenting a forest dweller for taking one of their spots. Even that Sarafine had paid someone to remove Fenity from court so there would be no doubt who the true winner was.

As outlandish as the rumors were, there was no mention of the real reason—nothing about King Sidian trying to have Fenity removed from Renic's life forever.

And then, just before dawn, the king called a session of court to make an official announcement. Since the Strife was over, the high rulers and courtiers gathered in the throne room. These sessions weren't unusual, except they didn't happen at night.

Renic arrived, stopping in the dark hallway inside the door nearest the dais. Bodies filled the space, some still rubbing sleep from their eyes. Rumors and mutterings rang loud, bouncing off the highest corners of the stone room. His pata sat on his throne, regal as ever but with a stern expression on his face.

Renic nearly jumped when a presence came up behind him. "Galan. What is this about?"

Galan gave a quick bow. "I quit the search for Lady Fenity when I heard your pata called for the high rulers. They met in here before inviting the rest of the court."

Renic sidled closer, lowering his voice. "You heard something."

"Not much, I'm afraid. They shielded the room from sound. But it's something to do with the goblins."

Renic's eyes widened. "A secret meeting." That he hadn't been invited to.

A guard found them then. "King Sidian requests your presence." He motioned Renic to his chair beside the king's.

Galan remained in the hallway. Once seated, Renic stayed silent. There was no way to speak to his pata without letting the entire court see his ire. As much anger as he felt toward his pata's choices, they still represented the crown and must appear united.

In the back of the room, Fenity's parents entered and took a place in the throng. Lady Stormbrook's skin was blotched red, and they held each other close. Whether they realized it or not, a detail of guards watched them closely, trailing them.

King Sidian raised his hand, and it was like energy had sucked the noise from the room. All conversations cut off. "As you all know, Fenity Stormbrook has gone missing from the castle. We have received new information regarding her disappearance."

Renic gripped his armrests.

"Someone leaked information to the goblins about the contestants' location on the night they were taken. A spy within our midst. After consulting with General Ashryn and my counselors, we have uncovered the spy—someone recently risen to her rank and desperate to remain in power. Fenity Stormbrook."

CHAPTER 55

A roaring filled Renic's ears. The roar from his raging heart, the roar from the outraged court, the roar of pain from Fenity's parents as the waiting guards seized them, dragging them away.

A goblin spy? So this was how his pata would take Fenity from him forever. Outlawed. Death upon discovery. The entire kingdom on the hunt for a traitor before finally rejoicing in her capture and ultimate end.

"How could you do this to me, to my truemate? You're killing me." Renic's words somehow penetrated the roaring, and the king finally turned to him.

"You will survive and be better for it." He turned away, dismissive.

Renic shoved from his chair and hurried from the throne room through the side door.

Galan followed close behind. "I'm with you, my prince."

"I have to find her. To warn her." But where would she have gone? Her pata was lord over the southernmost realm, but Fenity said she didn't consider that home. Her true home, where she'd grown up, was in the Lirian Forest, somewhere remote and forgotten. That was the most likely place she'd go, but King Sidian would know that too. He'd also have better means of finding its exact location, unlike Renic, who could only guess while disguising any search efforts from the court. The court who would raise a scene if he was found searching for the runner-up to the Strife and a spy.

None of that mattered because he had to find her, and before she came back for him. It wasn't safe here at the palace. Nowhere was safe anymore.

He had almost reached his rooms before he pivoted and headed toward Arinia's. She was the best place to fill in any missing holes about Fenity's life and family. Maybe she had some ideas.

"Galan, go to my rooms and ready our provisions. I will return shortly."

Galan gave a quick bow and hurried away to comply. Gratitude bolstered him as Renic continued toward Arinia—true loyalty and friendship still survived.

"My prince." Sarafine stopped him just inside the main hall from the gardens.

Sarafine. His betrothed, at least once the ceremony took place.

She bowed slowly, still wearing the jewel-encrusted red gown from the night before, dark circles under her eyes. Had she slept?

He'd grown up with her chasing him around, and now he didn't even know how to look at her. He hated her for winning, but it was an irrational hate. Not all this was her fault, though she'd gotten everything she ever wanted.

"There's no time for this." He turned away, giving her his back.

"I'm sorry, Renic," she called after him softly. "I didn't want things to turn out this way. She was a good female."

"Was?" he spat, his muscles clenching as he whirled to face her.

"Is," she said quickly. "Better than me."

"Were you in the throne room? Did you know she would be branded a spy?" He pulled at his collar, nearly ripping it. "And all for part of some farce so that you will be queen, not her. You and I couldn't be more wrong for each other. I'm not even sure you like me, but I know I don't like you."

"I love someone else, too. But that doesn't matter now. We're betrothed. I will be the next queen."

Renic gritted his teeth. "I don't just *love* Fenity. She's my truemate."

Sarafine went rigid. "She told me, but I thought it was a trick."

"She's my truemate, and now—" He ensured the hall was still clear. "And now my pata has deemed her a spy to kill her so I can move on and marry you." His voice cracked, and he swallowed hard. "All because he thinks she doesn't possess energy. But she—" He stopped. "I don't know why I'm explaining any of this to *you*. You and your conniving duplicitousness, your parents' meddling, are the reason everything's gone to hell. You and my pata. He told me what your parents did." He shook his head in disgust. Fear. Rage. Desperation. "I will never marry you. To my dying day, I will remain a wifeless, heirless prince rather than settle for anyone who's not Fenity. I will find her, or I will die alone."

Sarafine winced. "You're right. About all of it. I tried to fix it, but the damage was done and I hate myself for it. I hate my parents for it." Her eyes shone, but no tears fell. "They only birthed me to have a chance at the throne. They told me that.

And that if I failed them, I was no longer their daughter and they would cast me aside. Disown me."

Renic's rage toward Sarafine abated like a fire doused with snow melt. "We were friends. Or, I thought we were. You could have told me." She'd hidden this from him her whole life. Bore this secret while pretending to care for him.

"You changed when you became mated. I thought it was the pressure of the Strife. I should have seen it for what it was." Sarafine schooled the hurt from her face. "I'll help you. I'll make this right."

Renic's shoulders fell under the layers of secrets unraveling upon him. "And are you prepared to step down when Fenity returns?"

"She'll never be able to return after what your pata just did." The words were pitying.

He sank against the wall. How was he going to fix this?

He had to leave the castle and find her. Immediately. "If we were ever really friends, tell no one of this conversation. It's time to start choosing for yourself and living your life for you." She didn't say anything more as he left her behind.

Guards opened the door to his wing. He made for the bedroom, peeling away layers of clothes while gathering some more suitable for travel. He had to find her.

"I wondered if you'd flee like my advisors thought you would." King Sidian's voice rumbled from beside the roaring hearth. Two guards stood on either side of the room, Galan between them, jaw clenched.

Renic tugged his undershirt back on. "Have you come to kill me, too, Pata? Concoct a story branding me a spy in a meeting I'm not privy to?"

Rage simmered in his pata's otherwise blank face. "Where is she?"

"It pleases me to know you have no idea. I was worried you'd captured her and put on this show to save face." Renic picked up a discarded book from the sitting table and thumbed through it, hoping to mask his complete and utter shock. Pata didn't come to him. Ever. "I wouldn't be here if I knew where she was."

"The guards are here to escort you to the goblin border. I trust you did not forget your duty."

Stars. Of course he'd forgotten. He couldn't even say anything about it, though his pata knew that leaving now would nearly break him.

The book fell from his hands, crashing to the floor. "She's not a spy."

"My sources say otherwise. The goblins knew exactly where to find them. How else would she be awake?"

"I warned her not to eat in the dining hall."

Thunder stormed in Pata's countenance, and his energy spiked.

"I can't undo what you've just done, but I will prove her innocence." Renic said his next words slowly, trying to keep the desperation from showing. "If you find her while I'm away, give her a fair trial. And let her parents go. They have no part in this." If the king found her before he did, there would be no trial—fair or otherwise. Everyone in this room knew it.

"Lord and Lady Stormbrook are not my prisoners. He serves me well, despite his traitorous daughter. They are being escorted to their lands in the south for their own protection."

A small shard of the boulder on his shoulders fell away. He sensed his pata spoke the truth. It was as much as he could hope to gain. "Very well. I'll dress and report for the goblin border shortly. I don't need an escort."

"See that you do. The guards will remain here on watch, just in case."

Just in case he got any ideas about escaping. How would he

search for her when he was off at war? Exactly his pata's plan, no doubt. He just hadn't counted on Fenity escaping.

Pata sighed long and loud. "I don't want to be your enemy, son. This was not how the Strife was supposed to go. But I'm king first, and I must do what's best for our kingdom, even if it's not what's best for you."

Renic swallowed. His pata wasn't a bad male, though lately he seemed more interested in protecting his way of life than protecting the people. Or maybe he'd always been that way, and it took meeting someone from outside their circle to see it. Regardless, Pata had threatened Fenity, and there was no repairing the rift his pata knowingly severed with his own sharpened sword.

So Renic didn't say a word. He walked past the king into the bathing chamber and prepared for an immediate departure.

CHAPTER 56

Hours later, bleary and already cold, Renic ignored his gilded carriage and rode beside Galan, along with a company of their finest warriors led by General Ashryn, heading east toward the Goblin Kingdom. Every step took him further away from Fenity, he was sure of it, and every step only darkened his already dark mood. The warriors and servants wisely left him alone.

Did Fenity have anyone looking after her where she was? Guards, servants, and a gilded carriage? Was she even safe? His mind played these games for the next several days it took to reach the border.

He'd been there several times, even recently, boosting the warriors' morale as they defended the fae from the goblins who were ever desiring for more land for their growing population.

Though they'd never been so bold as to invade this deep. Kidnapping members of the royal court was a breach that could not be suffered. And though it wasn't where he wished to be, exacting revenge for the attempt on his truemate's life was a close second.

The base camp looked nothing like it had during his last visit. The number of tents had exploded, looking like a real war camp instead of a simple border defense. No wall separated the territories, only a barely detectable change in vegetation. On the other side of the invisible line, far into the trees, scouts reported that the goblins made their camp—scattered and much less impressive. Instead of fine tents set in uniform rows, they'd cut limbs in random lean-tos, weapons racks holding sharp axes and shortswords. Even without the reports, the goblins' campfires with smoke rising above the distant trees gave away the exact size of their army.

But when Renic inhaled the chilled air, he didn't need to see the smoke or hear the reports to scent their fear. The goblins were divided, the land ruled by several clans under many leaders, making it difficult to amass a force against the fae. They'd made a big mistake provoking their enemies, and they were about to realize it.

Renic and Galan passed their horses to a servant, bypassing the royal quarters and heading straight for General Ashryn at the war tent. Everyone bowed as Renic entered—lords, captains, and high-ranking warriors.

"General Ashryn. What is the plan, and where can I be of use?" He'd studied war, and even seen some battles, but he wouldn't do General Ashryn the disrespect of pretending he possessed even a fraction of his knowledge in defense and strategy. Renic was a glorified figurehead, and if that was how he could help, he'd gladly take it and be proud.

The general crossed to the table in the middle, covered with maps and place markers. "I see no reason to delay, Your Highness. King Sidian wishes us to attack with our full force. The last of the warriors have arrived until His Majesty sends more. But this is well enough. Commander Ravengarde advises the same. He's never seen the goblins so motivated. Best to deter them now before they grow bolder."

Commander Ravengarde nodded. He'd served at the border longer than Renic had been alive.

"What's the risk of the goblins retaliating? Anything they might do that would hurt our people should they decide to enact revenge?"

"You're worried about a full-scale war." General Ashryn nodded. "It is good of you to think of our people. As far as King Sidian is concerned, we are already at war. This show of force will do its job."

"Good. The goblins need to be stopped before it gets worse and more fae get hurt."

"When we move on the goblins," General Ashryn said, "King Sidian has commanded you to stay here at base camp to motivate the troops." There was no hesitation in the words, just a general leading his warriors.

The room tensed, waiting for Renic's reaction. Galan watched from the tent's entrance, ready for whatever Renic decided.

Renic kept his face empty despite the rising anger. He'd been cut off from searching for Fenity, and now he'd be denied revenge for the goblins nearly killing her. "With respect, what fae will listen to me if I don't take part in the fighting?" Several nods accompanied his words.

General Ashryn spread his hands over the map on the table. "We must protect the bloodline. Without a sibling or an heir, our king's hands are bound. Our warriors will listen to you. You are our prince."

"Alright." Renic shoved his pride aside. This conflict was bigger than the rift between him and his pata, and his pata was right. "Let's go over the rest of the plan."

They attacked at dawn. Renic was regulated to the back of their forces, rallying the injured or those who prepared to rotate into the melee, with Galan assisting just as fervently.

Renic hated looking weak and helpless, but he was wise enough to listen to his general. The warriors couldn't do their job while worrying about their prince, capable or not.

In the middle of giving his rallying speech for the tenth time that day, a loud roar pierced the air. Then the screaming started.

Renic cut off mid-sentence, standing taller on the empty crate to see past the warriors amassed before him. All heads turned to the border. Galan moved to his side. Between the tents and the trees, the fighting was nearly invisible, but the roaring and clash of swords grew deafening.

Orders came down the line, and the fresh warriors he'd rallied took off running.

Commander Ravengarde jogged past, and Renic stopped him. "What's happened, Commander?"

His face was drawn, sweat beading his upper lip. "The goblins were ready for us. The campfires were a ruse. Our warriors met a massive, hidden force."

All those fae. "I'll report to the infirmary at once." Had the goblin clans banded together? Renic had underestimated them. They all had. The casualties would be great.

The battle didn't end in a day. What should have been a quick campaign turned into weeks of fighting all along the border. King Sidian would not allow Renic to return until it was over. Renic wrote back numerous times, arguing with the king, but he wouldn't budge, and Renic knew why.

Fenity.

She was his purpose, keeping him going when the warriors he rallied in the morning were gone by the afternoon. They had to win, or he'd never be free to find her.

Renic sent Galan on fruitless searches for information about who the true spy was. He also paid spies and regular citizens to bring word on if she'd been found. It was the same every time. The king was searching, but she remained elusive.

The only good news he ever received was that Fenity's parents were indeed safe. Safe and searching for their daughter. And Arinia—who Renic had worried might suffer from her involvement with Fenity—was appointed Sarafine's lead attendant, a high honor as Sarafine hand-picked her entourage. One of the first things Renic did was promote Arinia's son, Atraius, to captain and assign him to a safer area.

General Ashryn found Renic pacing his tent one morning, clutching the latest finding of no news in his tight fist. "Sorry to disturb you, Prince. The latest numbers have arrived. We are summoned to a council meeting."

Renic threw the letter on his desk. "Do you have a family, General?" He knew nothing about the male except that he was good at what he did, protecting the kingdom against its enemies and serving the king. He'd been doing it a long time. "Or a mate?"

General Ashryn glanced at the crumpled letter. "I do. A truemate and a daughter."

Renic stopped pacing. He hadn't expected that. He cleared his throat, ashamed to bring personal affairs into war, yet he had to know. "How do you stand being away from them?"

There was no judgment from the general, only understanding. "We have been mated a long time. Nothing could have separated us at first, but it grew easier. I take comfort in knowing that by serving my king, I'm also serving my truemate and child." He frowned slightly. "I also take comfort in knowing where they are and that they are safe in their cottage in the fields north of Diatem."

Renic chuffed. "Yes, knowing where they are must be a comfort."

"You'll see her again. In this life or the next."

Renic met the general's gaze. "So you know, then."

General Ashryn examined the tent's flap. "Lady Fenity told me."

Renic tilted his head. Why would she have done that? And when?

"If I may, my prince, you've done admirably given the circumstances. Only a great strength of character could obey his king and remain here, fighting against the instincts I'm sure are demanding you find her and see she's safe." He rested a hand on the hilt of his sword. "You might not be aware, but Lady Fenity is my sister-in-law. I don't wish any harm to come to her either. The good of the kingdom must come first."

"And what do you believe to be for the good of the kingdom?"

General Ashryn ignored the question. "King Sidian has ordered me to report your departure if you should go looking for her."

"I see." The words slipped out through Renic's clenched teeth. Did his pata know no limits? How had he not noticed this duplicity before? Not seeing it was the folly of the youth he'd never be again.

General Ashryn paused, cocking his head like he was listening for something. "Do you trust your guard?"

"Galan? With my life."

The general spoke almost inaudibly. "Your Fenity also told me something else, and I believe her. Something the goblins said about the spy. They said the name Waters, a female, gave them the information."

Renic's mouth dropped open. "And you reported this to the king?" Waters, as in Moona Waters?

"Yes." His stiff posture was the only giveaway for his discomfort—either for betraying his king's confidence, or the injustice done to Fenity.

Renic braced a hand on the table. Pata knew Fenity wasn't the spy and outed her anyway.

The general lifted the flap, flooding the space with daylight. "As I said, it comforts me to know my truemate is safe on our fields north of Diatem. I'll see you in the command tent."

He left Renic standing there with wide eyes.

The general had just told him where to find his truemate, he was sure of it. The fields north of Diatem.

Renic flew into action. He grabbed clothes and food at random, stuffing them into a leather satchel. How long would General Ashryn pretend not to notice his absence before he wrote to the king?

He sheathed a sword and a dagger, and called Galan inside.

Galan entered with a quick bow. "My prince." He eyed Renic's bag overflowing with provisions and raised an eyebrow.

"I need you to hold my place at a meeting in the command tent." Renic shouldered the bag. "And then I need you to clear Fenity's name."

"I go where you go." Galan clenched his jaw.

"Not this time. The goblins said a female named Waters led them to kidnap the contestants. Find Moona and get her to talk."

"Consider it done." Galan bowed. "Have you found Fenity?"

"I think so. But if I want a chance to reach her before my pata knows I left, I need time." He put a hand on Galan's shoulder. "You're loyal to the crown, and my best friend. My brother. There's no one else I trust with this."

Galan crossed an arm over his chest. "I will do all I can, Your Highness."

Renic would find her. They would marry in secret, and the king could do nothing to stop them.

I'm coming, Fenity.

CHAPTER 57

Fenity added more flour to the counter, then dumped the bowl over, letting the heavy dough plop down. Dusting her hands, she plunged her fingers in, kneading the sticky mass until it was smooth and no longer stuck to her skin. She shaped the dough, then covered it with a cloth and left it to rest until ready for her to score a pretty leaf pattern before baking.

Laughter flitted in from the doorway. Her sister stood there, baby Lela on her hip, laughing and pointing.

Fenity looked down. Powdery flour completely covered her protruding stomach. She burst into laughter, and that sent her belly shaking up and down, raining flour down all around her. Corantha laughed until she couldn't breathe, tears rolling down her cheeks.

Fenity barely composed herself long enough to remove her apron and grab baby Lela before Corantha dropped into a chair.

"You're getting so good at that, Fen." Corantha laughed

again. "The bigger the mess, the better the cook." She wiped her eyes.

Fenity took in her hard work, anxious to see how it tasted. She'd cooked with Mata in the forest cottage, but nothing like this. Corantha had an art to her cooking. These past few months should have been the most relaxing of her life—a welcome respite from the Strife. Except it was only a distraction, one task after another until she could be with Renic again. Her heart grappling for new ways to reach him—a message, a portal in the night—before her mind remembered it was too risky. She'd kept her promise not to open any more portals, the demon king's fiery world flashing in her mind each time she felt tempted.

She'd focused on growing her little one while convincing herself this was the right place to be for now. And the laughter wasn't always forced. Like today. Today had been a good day.

Not like the day she'd learned the king had branded her a spy—his justification for the manhunt that would take her life if they found her.

But the good days outweighed the bad thanks to Corantha. Shortly after arriving, her sister sent a coded letter to her parents letting them know Fenity was safe and in hiding, and what Fenity had overheard about the real spy. They'd risked one letter back, and Fenity memorized it before burning it. They'd returned home, unharmed, and were using all their resources to clear Fenity's name.

But the distance and lies separating her from Renic and her parents were a constant thorn in any happiness she had achieved here. The smile slipped from her face, and she handed baby Lela back to her sister.

Corantha sighed a sorrowful sigh Fenity had heard a thousand times. She wanted to make Fenity forget, but they both knew there was no forgetting. The time here was limited, and very much nearing the end. She'd have the baby, recover her strength, then set off for her truemate where he fought the goblins at the border.

Was Renic looking for her even now? News of Sarafine winning the Strife and her engagement to the prince reached them just a day after Fenity arrived. Fenity had finally allowed herself to cry over all she'd lost. But morning came, just as it always did, and she knew she couldn't let go of all hope. They could still find each other. There might still be a way to be together.

That was all she wanted.

Her belly had grown much too big to travel, and no one had found her despite Thallan's letters warning of the king's search.

What if her parents cleared her name? Would the king still kill her if they found her, round with Renic's child?

Most definitely. She'd thought it through several times. If King Sidian was worried about heirs without energy, he wouldn't want this child born into the world. But Fenity would never let that happen.

She placed a hand against her belly as her daughter kicked inside.

Corantha set Lela on the floor, and the baby toddled around on unsteady legs. She'd grown so much already in such a short amount of time. Fenity loved her like her own.

"Fenity?" Corantha looked at her with concern.

She forced a smile. "Thank you for taking me in. Thank you for welcoming me into your home and your family, despite the risk. I'm so grateful for my time here." She could have gone to Marek's from the start, but what did he know of pregnant fae? And what would happen if she gave birth in the human world?

Corantha took her hands. "You have time still. It's been such a blessing having you here. Helping with Lela when I have patients, and spending time together again. Don't speak like it's ending. I hope you'll stay much longer. Let our young ones grow up together."

But it was ending. Fenity felt it in her bones. This near-perfect piece of existence was almost over.

"I'll stay as long as I can."

There was a knock at the door, and they both jumped. Fenity's heart skipped a beat.

"Hide. You know where." Corantha picked up Lela, who fussed from having to stop banging a wooden spoon on overturned bowls.

Fenity grabbed her packed bag from the back door as Corantha peeked through the front window.

"It's Kamina." Their neighbor across the fields. Corantha's breath let out in a whoosh.

Fenity set her pack down, then dropped into a chair, heart slamming against her ribs. Kamina knew Fenity was here, and they trusted her. They were the only fae even remotely close, so keeping hidden would have been next to impossible.

Royal guards had come twice since Fenity had arrived. The first was to question Corantha. The second time, they searched the house. Fenity was out with Kamina, helping in the fields. She'd come back unaware there had been any danger.

Corantha opened the door. "Come in, Kamina, come in."

Kamina wore a finely stitched tunic of the prettiest blues with matching leggings. She and her mate both possessed energy, which they used for successful crops, so they could afford things like tailor-made clothes. Corantha wasn't poor by any means, not with the money she made as the local healer and what Thallan sent back to her from his duties as the king's general, but she didn't spend her coin the way Kamina did.

Kamina stepped across the threshold, one hand holding a basket of fruit, the other clutching a little boy of two years. He pulled from Kamina's grip at the same time Corantha put Lela down. The toddlers immediately squealed and went to a basket of wooden blocks to play.

Oren was his name. Oren and Lela fought as much as they got along, but it was clear they shared a deep bond. Fenity's daughter would be part of that one day, when everything was settled with Renic.

"I don't mean to stay long," Kamina said. She pulled a letter from her pocket. "This arrived at my house a few days ago. Melovin meant to bring it by, but there was a crisis in the fields, and it slipped his mind. I'm so sorry."

Corantha's mouth opened in surprise. "It's from Thallan."

The baby kicked as Fenity rose. The temptation to read over her sister's shoulder was enormous, but a note from Thallan didn't always mean bad news. He'd written to Corantha many times with updates on the goblin battle and Renic's part in it. Fenity had been wrong to assume Thallan wouldn't help her because of his status with the king. He was a good male.

The steady clop of a horse's hooves sounded down the road. Someone in need of healing, or Melovin returning from the fields? Every noise seemed to make Fenity jump these days.

Corantha gasped. "Fenity." She shoved the letter into her hands.

Fenity gripped the paper, crushing it. It wasn't the usual letter. It was written at a wind transfer station.

Corantha,

I send this with haste, hoping it reaches you in time. Prince Renic discovered Lady Fenity's location, and so King Sidian was informed of his departure from the goblin border. His Majesty suspects she resides on our land. If you find her, report her to the authorities at once.

Be ready. King Sidian's forces will arrive soon from an outpost near Diatem. Prince Renic also rides for you. He had a head start but has much further to go traveling from the Westwater Lands.

Do not fear, my love. With the addition of Lord Rivers' warriors, we defeated the goblins in a battle that's turned the conflict. The border is being secured, but organization is still needed. I will return as soon as I'm able.

Take care of little Lela and our family.

Yours forever,
Thallan Ashryn

The letter slipped from Fenity's fingers. Thallan had been wise. Wind transfer stations were open record. He was claiming they had no knowledge of her ever being here.

And Renic was coming for her.

"Fenity." Corantha's panicked voice cut through to her. She stood at the door, opening it wider. The sound of hoofbeats had exploded into multiple horses approaching from the direction of Diatem. "They're coming."

Kamina scooped up little Oren, who latched onto Lela's chubby arm and wouldn't let go. "I never saw you. Good luck." She gently pried Oren loose, then rushed out the door. Lela pushed to her bare feet, trying to follow them.

Fenity watched it all with wide eyes, feet glued to the floor. As before, they envisioned a warrior or two to come asking questions and do some light searching. She would hide in the barn loft until they left, satisfied not to go looking for her.

But this was an entire contingent, armed with the knowledge she was here somewhere.

Corantha closed the door, blocking out the thunderous noise and making Lela whimper with frustration. She shoved the strap of Fenity's satchel over her frozen shoulder. "The warriors arrived before your prince. Leave now, I'll try to stall them. Get as far as you can." She pushed Fenity toward the back door.

Fenity's adrenaline finally broke through her frozen heart. She hugged Corantha hard. "Thank you for all your kindness. I won't tell them you helped me." She memorized her niece's round cheeks and silver hair. Cousins. "Your family will be safe from me. Tell Renic I will find him when I can."

"You are my family. And this isn't goodbye. They won't catch you." Corantha wrenched open the back door and put a hand over Fenity's round belly. "Run, but be careful. You're too close to birth to risk anything dangerous. Come back when they're gone."

Fenity didn't waste a moment. Outside, the spring sun warmed her cold skin, but the chirping birds went silent at the approach of so many horses. The herb garden and patches of trees hid the road from sight, but Fenity didn't look again as she hurried for the hills dividing her from the flower field—the only shelter from their view. One hand supported her belly, while the other kept the satchel from bouncing against it.

The demon king's rumbling laughter echoed in her mind. She wouldn't portal unless there was no choice.

She finally reached the hills, panting and out of breath. She risked a look back, and horses were already spreading out around the front of the cottage, like river water parted by rock. At least twenty warriors. She scrambled up the hill and over, praying they hadn't spotted her. The hills bought her time, but there was nowhere to hide.

The dull pounding of hooves warned of the warriors' approach, and Fenity threw herself behind a crop of trees, crying out in pain as her stomach tightened and cramped. She took deep breaths, struggling to calm her racing heart.

Not yet. She couldn't portal yet.

But they were going to find her. There was nowhere to hide.

CHAPTER 58

Renic pushed his horse faster and further than she had any right to go, but the mare didn't give up, sensing her rider's desperation. He knew what the cloud of dust ahead of him meant. He trailed warriors, trained to fight and sent by his pata for one purpose: to end Renic's reason for existing.

"Yah!" He spurred the poor horse faster, and she complied. He couldn't admire the peaceful fields or the bright greens of spring. There was only one thing that mattered.

He finally caught up to them, heads turning wide eyes as he raced past them. The warriors at the front veered off the road onto fields where a small cottage graced the land as if grown from it. Vines and thatch, flowers and small trees graced the home behind a thriving herb garden. Someone—a captain —waved them past the house. They didn't slow as they split up, dividing so they might find Fenity faster.

Renic reined in his horse beside a row of lavender, launching from the saddle. He unsheathed his sword as he ran to the front. There was no telling what the king told them of the rogue prince, but his pata was all about appearances. He wouldn't declare the heir to the throne a traitor to the crown. Not yet.

"Prince Renic." The captain dismounted and bowed low—no move to detain his prince.

"Call your warriors off. Now," he growled.

The captain took in Renic's raised sword. "I can't, Your Highness. King's orders." He produced a letter from a pocket in his belt and held it out.

Renic stabbed it, slicing it in two. The captain snatched back his hand and lowered his eyes.

Renic marched up the front steps following two males. He grabbed them by the neck of their armor and hauled them backward. They landed with a crash before he stepped into the house and closed the door in the captain's wary face, locking it. "Where is she?"

A female clutched a squirming child in her arms. She backed against the opposite wall but wore a determined expression. "Prince Renic?" He nodded, and she opened a back door. "Hurry. She ran this way, but she won't get far. Hurry!"

Renic sprinted past the female and leaped out the door. Warriors raced on horseback across the field, speeding for the distant hills. That was where she was. He could feel it—he was so close.

"Warrior!" He waved his arms as one came galloping nearby. "Give me your horse," he commanded when the warrior stopped.

The warrior didn't disobey his prince, not this time. Renic sprinted toward the hills as fast as he could, but others were nearly cresting it. Maybe she'd made it to safety. Maybe she'd found a place to hide. He'd know if she'd portaled away. She was still here.

"Fenity!" He urged the horse faster. Almost there.

CHAPTER 59

The warriors crested the hill in pairs, some staying on top and scanning the surroundings, some forging their horses down the other side. Fenity's stomach cramped again, and she panted, still trying to catch her breath. The tree trunks weren't thick, but three of them formed a semicircle, shielding her directly from view. This hiding spot would never hold up. As soon as they passed the trees and looked back, they'd see her. And she couldn't run. Too much distance lay between her and the next crop of trees.

The warriors raced for her spot. More crested the hills.

There was no choice. Portal or die.

Now, before they got closer or they'd sense her energy and know what she'd done. She'd never be able to return.

Not to the demon world. Never there.

She drew the energy up and gathered it. Heads turned her way. Her stomach tightened, the pain loosening her grip on the energy. No time. She was out of time. Panting until her stomach relaxed, she opened a portal.

"Fenity!"

It was Renic's voice. Renic!

Would he die trying to save her from the warriors? Too many.

A guard drew his sword and charged for her trees.

No choice. No time.

She closed the portal in the human world just as a gush of water rushed down her legs.

CHAPTER 60

"Fenity!" Renic called her name again and again, combing the fields, searching the woods, desperate to find her before the warriors did.

But he knew the truth, even as he refused to accept it.

There were no words to describe the panic he balled up inside, shoving it next to his fuming anger over his pata's actions. There was hardly room for it all, but he used it to drive himself on when exhaustion tried to make him quit.

Maybe she'd portaled nearby. Maybe she'd come back and he'd find her if he searched just a little longer. *Anything* to see her safe.

He traveled as far as someone could make it on foot, then weaved back toward the cottage through trees and meadows of beautiful blooms, now trampled by the warriors still looking for her.

The king would not be deterred in his effort to keep Renic from marrying Fenity.

Dusk turned to night. Torches and magelights lit up the land, but there was no sign of her. Of course, there was no sign of her. His truemate was gone, and he knew. She hadn't gone on foot. She'd opened another portal, but the warriors couldn't know that. They had to believe she'd escaped on foot.

Moons, he'd been so close. He'd sensed the enormous weight of her energy. It called to him.

She could have taken him with her. They could have lived with the sprites or the unicorns. Anywhere they were together would be home.

But where had she gone this time? She wouldn't come back here again, and she wouldn't go anywhere the king would know.

Crestfallen and exhausted, he trotted back to the cottage in the moonlight. The troops finally departed, no doubt to report his location to the king.

The female—Fenity's half-sister—opened the back door, motioning him inside. Numb, Renic left his stolen horse to graze and followed her in. If there was any chance she knew where Fenity had gone, he had to know.

The inside was even more quaint at night, dried herbs and fresh-baked bread scenting the air, and candles bathing the small space in warm light. Dirty boot prints covered the wood floor, and every drawer and cabinet hung open, contents spilling.

"Thank you for your aid, Madam Ashryn." Renic's voice scraped like he'd screamed all day. Strange, he thought that had been only in his head. "I'm sorry for frightening you earlier. And sorry for the warriors." Sorry his pata was a terrible king with no concern for anyone not a member of his court.

"Call me Corantha, Your Highness." The general's wife bowed. Her child was nowhere in sight, tucked in for the night, no doubt. "Don't mind the mess. The captain and some warriors spent the better part of the day searching for my sister and questioning me up and down. They didn't find anything. We were careful. We made the barn look slept in. I think they believed I had no knowledge of her being here. For now, anyway."

Renic rubbed his eyes. "Tell me. Please. Where is my truemate?"

Corantha swallowed hard, eyes shining. "I don't know. I thought she'd return after the guards left. I'm so worried about her."

Renic looked up sharply. "Why? Is she hurt?"

"No, no. At least, I hope not. Her condition—" Corantha paused. "I mean, she ran out back on foot." She gestured for him to sit, but he didn't budge. "Do you think the guards found her?"

"No. I would have seen." That much was certain. "Do you have any idea where she'd go?" There was something Corantha was hiding in her careful words. Did she know Fenity could portal? Could Corantha? He didn't press for more. Any knowledge he gained regarding portal opening in their family could only hurt them.

"The only place she ever talked about going was back to you."

A cry of anguish burst from him without his permission. Hot tears rolled down his face. "I can't stand this. I need her. I need to know she's safe."

"I know, my prince. I know." Corantha swiped at her face and took his hand. "Her last words were, 'Tell Renic I will find him when I can.'"

Renic bit his tongue until the anguish cleared enough for words. "Thank you. We owe you and your mate a great deal."

All his life, he'd prepared to be the next king. They told him what to expect at the Strife and how to choose a good queen.

He wanted to be king. He wanted to embrace that duty for his people—just not the way his parents and the court did.

The moment he'd found Fenity, everything that had ever mattered to him became—less than secondary—non-existent. He didn't care about being a prince or being a king. He didn't care about court politics or the plight of his people or the goblins attacking the border. He didn't care if he never went back to Alberry and the pointless drivel that had been his life up to now.

Unless he could do it all with Fenity by his side. Together, they could make the world a better place. And he'd search until forever.

CHAPTER 61

Standing in the middle of Marek's study, head feeling stuffed with cotton, Fenity dabbed at the liquid on her trousers. Not blood. Not urine.

Her water had broken.

Her stomach tightened again, and she gripped an armchair for support, whimpering from the pain. Exhaustion hit her hard and heavy, but panic kept her heart pounding.

Not yet.

The baby wasn't supposed to be here yet.

She was supposed to be in her own world. Tears slipped down her face. She gasped at the sound of footsteps. Marek burst into the room, eyes going wide, then dark, then wide again. His energy flared, then ebbed.

"Fenity. You came back." He just stood there, indecision and determination alternating across his face.

Another contraction ratcheted up, and Fenity clenched her eyes shut, gripping the armchair in both hands this time. When she could breathe again, he still stood at the doorway, gaping. Everything about the room was the same as she remembered. No servants. Clean as if never lived in. But this time there was no fire in the hearth. The snow was gone outside the window. Instead, the manicured trees and lawn cast a green glow over the dining room and into the study.

"The baby is coming, Marek. I don't have anywhere else to go." Fenity dropped to her knees, folding her arms on the chair and resting her head, willing herself not to cry.

She had nowhere else to go. No one else she could safely turn to at a time that should have been celebrated and sacred.

Renic.

She'd recover and find him again. There was no other choice.

Marek blinked, his face blank. "Send for a doctor," he called down the hall. A doctor must have been what they call a midwife here. His brow creased with worry, and he finally entered the room, coming to her side. "There's a bedroom close by. Come." He waited while she breathed through a contraction. She gratefully leaned on him while he led her to a bedroom.

It was vast, and everything was white. White curtains, white fluffy bedding, white cushioned chairs. Corantha had told her all about childbirth, but she was too panicked and too exhausted to warn him about his choice of room. She was safe at least.

He moved to help her on the bed, but she didn't want that. Standing and swaying seemed to help the pain.

Marek stepped back to the door and rubbed his neck. "I have so many questions, but I need to do something before I... before the doctor comes."

"What?" Her head hung low between her arms while she held onto the bed.

"I need to disguise your ears. I can keep my servants quiet, but not a doctor."

She nodded. "Alright. Here comes another." This one *hurt*, and she clenched her teeth against a scream. "What about the baby?" She panted. "This doctor will see her ears, too." There was barely room for thought through the pain of contractions, which were coming faster and faster.

"I've thought of that. If you drink it soon enough, it will alter hers as well." His voice changed, and she looked sharply up at him. He roughly slapped himself on the cheek and then gave her an encouraging nod before rushing from the room.

Several contractions later, Marek came back holding a blue glass vial. He unstoppered it and held it out.

"Is it safe?" The last word came out as a cry as another contraction came. *Renic.*

"It's safe. I perfected it in case you ever came back, testing it on animals with a similar ear shape before changing them back. Your truename unlocks the spell." He stepped closer. "We don't have much time."

Fenity tipped back the bitter liquid. It burned going down. She took his hand. "Thank you for everything. I knew I would be safe here."

Marek licked his lips and clenched his eyes tight—like he was in pain. "It's not safe for you here. You must leave as soon as you're able."

"Why? What do you—" Her whimpers turned to cries with the next contraction. An instinctual urge to push came over her body.

"I have to activate it. I'll do it now." Marek slapped himself again, and the buzz of energy surrounded him. He pulled his hand from her grip and raised them both beside her.

Fear shook her body, but she tamped it down. She trusted Marek, and she'd do anything to keep her daughter safe. His energy traveled sightlessly to her, warming her belly and up to the tips of her ears. The searing pain blended into the pain of another contraction, and she pushed, giving in to the pressure in her bottom.

"She's coming." Fenity planted her feet on the floor and fisted the pretty white blanket. Gritting her teeth, she pushed again, muscles and gravity shifting the baby downward.

Marek's energy cut off, as did the burning in her ears. Had it worked? He stumbled away from her. Somewhere between her panting and the next contraction, the doctor entered—a female who looked confused, but commanded the room. Marek ran away as fast as he could, and after what felt like forever, Fenity gave a final push. The doctor caught the infant who came out crying, filling the room with the beautiful sounds of a healthy baby's voice.

"My daughter." Fenity reached for her, and the doctor lifted her up. Rounded ears. Someone passed her a blanket—a second female she hadn't noticed before—and Fenity held the baby to her chest, still standing beside the bed. "You're okay, little one."

Was this real? Was she really in the human world holding the little baby who'd been busy kicking her all these months? A fae babe with human ears.

The doctor helped her into bed, and she collapsed into the pillows, exhausted.

"We arrived just in time to catch her." The doctor and other female smiled down at the baby while helping with the after-birth and cleanup. Their accents matched Marek's.

Her daughter quieted down and began moving her face back and forth against Fenity's chest as she rocked her.

"You'll need to feed her soon," the doctor said. "What's her name?"

Fenity traced the rounded edges of her daughter's ears, and

her eyes filled with tears. How could a moment so beautiful be wrapped in so much pain? But her daughter was here and safe and loved.

"Oriana," Fenity said, still studying the tiny features of her baby. "Oriana Arrowood."

CHAPTER 62

After Fenity and Oriana were cleaned up and had their first feeding, the doctor and her helper finally left. They'd asked no questions, only remarking how beautiful little Ori was. Fenity, now dressed in a comfortable nightshift, snuggled her sleeping daughter close, weariness taking its toll after such an arduous day.

Renic should have been with her, but she had a piece of him, and for now, that was enough. She hadn't realized just how quickly love could expand. There was never a question of dividing her love, it had simply multiplied with Oriana's birth.

Marek entered just as she was slipping into a much-needed sleep. He carried a silver tray with a glass and a bottle on it.

Fenity blinked at him, willing her eyes open a few moments longer. "Meet Oriana." She stroked a finger over the baby's fuzzy red hair, the same shade as hers, and down her soft cheek.

"She's beautiful. I hope to have a daughter as beautiful as her one day." He smiled wistfully.

"Then you will."

"I brought you something to drink. It will help with your soreness. And some milk for the baby." His voice trembled, and his hands shook as he set down the tray. Having a female give birth in his home must have been quite a shock.

"Thank you. And thank you for taking us in." Fenity motioned to the bottle. "I won't need that. I can feed Oriana myself. What I eat and drink will pass to her." She took the cool glass in her hands and tilted the liquid to her lips, gulping deep. She was so thirsty, and the water was sweet, but with a chalky aftertaste.

She drained the glass and finally looked up at Marek. He watched her, rage in his eyes, worry in the set of his mouth.

Fenity sat up, wincing. "What's wrong?"

"You drank it, didn't you?" he shouted.

"Was it not for me?" The hair rose on the back of her neck. Exhaustion vanished as she angled Oriana away from him.

The room spun.

Marek shook himself. The anger left, and tears filled his eyes. "I'm so sorry. I had to do it. He's in my head." He clutched at his forehead, squeezing.

"Who's in your—" Fenity gasped. The demon king. He'd cast a spell on Marek. Her stomach cramped, sharper than labor. "What did you do?"

Marek pulled his hair, and tears slipped down his face. "He wants your power. He wants to destroy us. He'll be the end of everything. I can't let him have you or your daughter." He picked up the bottle.

The bottle warped into three bottles, waving in the air, approaching Oriana.

Fenity kicked off the covers, scooting away from Marek. "He won't have me." Her words slurred and blackness tunneled her vision. "And neither will you." She pulled at her energy, but Marek leaped across the bed. Fenity twisted to the floor,

Oriana in one arm. Her energy collapsed in a wave of dizziness and nausea. She vomited.

He was going to kill her. He was going to kill her baby. To keep them out of the demon king's clutches.

"You're too weak to escape. The poison has already taken hold of your energy, as I designed it to do." His anguished voice shook. "I'm so, so sorry. You were my friend. I'm in control now, but not for long. This is the only way." He took slow, measured steps around the bed. Waiting for her to die. Waiting to get to Oriana.

Fenity slumped against the wall. Marek thought she couldn't access her energy. But she felt it, ready for when she summoned the strength to use it. Maybe his potion only worked on humans, but she was weak. So weak.

Baby Ori felt so small and yet so heavy in her arms. She had to protect their daughter.

Fenity drew up her energy. Marek gasped and leaped for her. She opened a portal, but something was wrong with it.

"No!" Marek drew a knife.

Fenity closed the portal, and he was gone. Baby Ori slept soundly in her arms. An empty field of green and an endless blue sky spun around her.

Blue.

Her portal hadn't reached home. She was still in the human world.

Pain lanced her stomach. Fenity collapsed where she stood —a dirt road in the middle of sprawling plains with no help around. Baby Ori landed against her chest and began wailing. Fenity was fading fast.

The sound of wagon wheels approached, but she was too weak to move, to hide. Had Marek found her?

A row of bright green wagons, three in all, slowed to a stop. Concerned faces peered down from the drivers' seats and peeked out from windows. Fenity couldn't even lift her head to ask for help. There was nothing these humans could do for her anyway. Her energy was there, morphed and just out of reach—not strong enough for the two of them. She was going to die; she knew that now. And her little baby, newly born, would be all alone. Oriana would never know where she came from. She'd never know her true heritage.

Moons above, please save me. I'm not ready to die. I haven't lived my life.

But if you can't save me, save my daughter. Save Oriana. Keep her from Marek and the demon king.

Fenity's stomach clenched in pain as she realized Prisanthony and Pirus weren't with her now. This wasn't her home.

The driver of the lead wagon, a larger human male in simple brown clothes, jumped down, face contorted with worry as he hurried to her side. "Loddi! Come quick!" He knelt beside her. "What are you doing out here? What happened?"

Others piled from the wagons with equal masks of confusion, worry, and horror.

Fenity could barely comprehend how she must look to them. In a night slip, covered in vomit and blood, with a newborn clutched in her arms. She couldn't even feed Ori one last time or the poison would flow to her.

"Be careful, Mama," a male near the wagons said. Fenity couldn't see that far. The world blurred in and out.

"She's sick. That baby's just born." A female, slender in a plain linen dress, took the larger male's hand, kneeling with him. Her eyes were a mix of devastated kindness and wary caution. She was a mata. She would protect baby Ori. "We have to save her. Boys, help her into the wagon. Devshire is not far."

"No, please," Fenity rasped. If they took her to a human healer, Marek would find them. "Keep her safe." Tears streamed down her cheeks. "Keep her away from mages. Not safe."

Someone handed the female a wooden cup. "Don't talk like that," she said. "Drink this."

Fenity choked on the water the woman held to her mouth, twisting her face away. "Promise me. Please."

The male's eyes filled with tears. He saw what Fenity already knew. "We promise."

Fenity tried to lift baby Ori up to them, but her arms and heart wouldn't allow it. The female gently took the baby from her, cradling her like someone who'd done so many times.

"What's her name?" The female sobbed.

Fenity laid her head back on the grass. "Her name is not safe. Magic is not safe."

"We have to save her." The female whirled to her family, her desperation mirroring everything Fenity felt. "We can't just leave her like this."

"We'll keep your daughter safe," the male promised, putting an arm around the female. "But one day she'll want to know her name."

A gift then. One last gift she could give for her daughter— an anchor to where she'd come from. "Oriana," Fenity whispered for the last time. There was so much more to tell, so much more to say, and no time to tell it all.

Oriana Arrowood, heir to the throne of the Fae Kingdom of Asentia. Daughter of Prince Renic Arrowood and his truemate, Fenity Stormbrook. Inheritor of a great and forbidden energy that would one day haunt her with no one to guide her. Sought after by the demon king himself and trapped in a world that wasn't hers. Robbed of a life that should have been.

Fenity couldn't even weep for the unfairness of it. All the moments of Oriana's life flashed before her eyes—her first steps, first words, first love—and Fenity wouldn't be there for any of it. Her precious daughter would grow up never knowing her. She'd never know how much she loved her.

But she would grow up. And from the way the male and female already gazed with adoring eyes on the little baby, she'd grow up loved. And that would have to be enough.

But not if Marek found them here. There was no way to know how far she'd traveled from his estate. He could find her at any minute.

Her hand twitched. "Go. Not safe here." The words were so mumbled, but they understood. The group tore their eyes from Fenity and Oriana to scan their surroundings for danger.

"We can't leave you like this," the female sobbed. She turned to her husband. "We have to help her. She can come with us."

"No!" Fenity raised her head but dropped it. Bringing her dying body would only draw attention. Oriana needed to disappear quickly. "Please. Not safe."

The male wiped the devastation from his face. "She got here somehow. The person who did this might be close by. We will give her this dying wish."

Fenity closed her eyes. Something warm pushed against her cheek. Her baby.

"We will raise her as our own," the female sobbed uncontrollably, holding Ori down to her. "We'll protect her name. Ricika, we'll call her. Ricci."

Fenity breathed in the clean smell of her daughter and kissed her soft cheek one last time. *Until we meet again, my little one.*

When she opened her eyes, her baby was gone. The family had kept their promise and left before danger could follow.

Oriana was safe.

If only the Gods could do Fenity the kindness of killing her faster as the poison weakened her weak body. Reality was filtering in and out. Blue sky and darkness. A soft breeze with the scent of grass and nothing. She couldn't die here. This wasn't her world.

She reached for her energy, and it trickled to her, unaffected by the poison, yet limited by her own weakness. One last sunset in her favorite place of refuge.

The portal barely opened, just big enough to fit curled up on her side. She never had the strength to bring them both here. When it closed, her body spasmed in pain, limbs contorting out of her control. In the few glimpses of the world around her, she saw what she'd been seeking.

Colorful trees, a sprawling green meadow overlooking a small castle, pink sky, and twin moons slowly rising. This was her parents' land—her favorite spot at the edge of Sprite Forest. She'd been summoned from this spot for the call to the Strife, the best and worst thing to ever happen to her.

Her body finally stilled, breaths growing shallower. The elusive sprites graced her with one last gift as dozens of them fluttered to the edge of the woods and watched her take her last breath.

Oriana was the purpose of her life—even if she couldn't be part of it—so she'd die with a life fulfilled. Her love for Renic and his love for her would live on in their daughter. Ori would bridge the gap between worlds.

EPILOGUE

Wisp Daysong, queen of the sprites, flew for the forest's edge like lightning drove her wings. It was her, Fenity Stormbrook, friend of the sprites. She'd returned, they said, and she was dying.

Her people split apart, making a path for her between the scores of them that lined the trees, watching helplessly as Fenity wheezed in and out, in and out.

Wisp sensed the poison even from here, the wrongness of it radiating from the fae's body, as clear as the scent of death.

But they couldn't let her die. She was their companion, their liaison—a ruler they could trust. The only one who understood them and treated them as equals.

Wisp escaped the safety of the trees, darting to the female's side with her most trusted renders close behind.

Sprites were growers, not healers, but she had served her time in potions and healing, just like they all had. They might not possess the cure, but they could grow it.

"Willow, yarrow root, lavender, savory, boldo," she spouted off.

Each render took an herb, summoning their power to raise them from the ground until a small forest of herbs rooted beside Fenity's limp elbow. Fast as she could, Wisp plucked and ground the required amount using her own energy to make it into a powder.

Axis, her love and her king, arrived just in time with the water pooled in several stacking leaves and carried by multiple sprites. Wisp wasted no time mixing the powder into water, along with some coal dust her people had wisely collected. By the grace of the forest, Fenity clung to life.

"She must drink it. Quickly."

Several of them propped the fae's mouth open, while others poured in the liquid. Fenity swallowed it instinctively. Wisp watched, waiting for a miracle, but no miracle came. Fenity's breaths continued wheezily. Slowly. Her skin stayed pale, limbs twitching every so often.

But Wisp knew a fighter when she saw one. Fenity was holding on to something. Someone in this world did not want her to leave it.

Dusk turned to night. Axis wrapped an arm around her shoulders. Her people formed a circle around the fae, even at the risk of going without the forest's protection in the dead of night. She directed more potion to be made and administered.

Night turned to dawn, and Fenity continued to breathe, continued to live. They gave her more potion mixed with water. Eventually, her limbs stopped twitching. Color returned to her cheeks, and her breathing evened out, yet she didn't wake.

"We can't watch her forever," Axis said, wings flitting with impatience. He worried for them and their meddling in fae affairs.

Wisp stuck up her chin. "Then she will return home with us."

"What? What if someone is looking for her?"

"What if they are? What if that's how she came to be this way? You heard the scout report. The fae king chose the red one as the winner." Wisp's lip curled. "We must take care of her. When she wakes, she'll take care of us."

Axis kissed her hand. "I love your kind, wise heart."

Wisp smiled at him, her fluttering wings giving away her pleasure at his words. "Let's move her then, carefully."

It was a monumental effort to move the fae, compiling a pallet and dragging her through the woods. It took several days, and yet Fenity didn't stir for any of it. She remained in a dreamless sleep.

The elders weren't happy, but eventually saw reason. Wisp had told them of the bond between Fenity and the fae prince, as had many others. It was like a light that shined brighter when they were together. The bond of truemates. And how grateful would the heir to the throne be when they brought his truemate back to life?

The elders even agreed not to tell the fae king, as it wasn't clear who had harmed Fenity, and it was well-known the king did not favor her. The sprites painstakingly built a shelter to house Fenity, and added the responsibility of caring for her to the rotation of their daily lives. Wisp did all she could to awaken her, but the months and then years slipped by while Fenity slept. No one came to claim her. No one came to harm her, and Wisp's judgment was called into question many, many times.

When word of an old fae prophecy being awoken reached Sprite Forest, Wisp almost cracked, fearing the worst for her people if they continued to harbor this secret. Eventually, the fae vanquished the demon king, but the sprites felt it. Wisp felt it. Something was still wrong with the world. Whatever the fae had done wasn't yet undone.

And Wisp knew it, then.

The time had come to venture back to the fae kingdom, even at the risk of the king's wrath. Fenity was important to this fight somehow, and the world was going to need her before the end.

Did you like this book? Please leave a review!

Scan the QR code or visit kristinlhamblin.com to access
Kristin's other books, fun links, and monthly newsletter for
updates and giveaways!

Acknowledgments

There are so many people to thank when it comes to publishing a book, each of them so important.

Thank you to my husband, Jonathan, and our four daughters. I know there were times you had to wait for me to finish just one more sentence. Thank you for your love, support, and patience. I do it all for you.

To my family and friends, thank you for your enthusiasm and for letting me get overly excited about what's in store for readers with this book even though you had no idea what I was talking about. You mean the world to me.

To my incredible alpha readers and beta team, Angie, Ashley, & Jamie. Your early enthusiasm for this book and these characters makes it all worth it. You are the best. Love you guys!

To my ARC readers for showing up and loving this series—you have no idea how important you are to the process.

And, of course, I wouldn't be anywhere without my dear readers. From the ones quietly reading and cheering me on, to the ones who message me, read my monthly newsletter, and join my ARC teams. None of this would be possible without you. Thank you!

About the Author

Kristin L. Hamblin writes young adult romantic fantasy stories full of unforgettable friendships, forbidden love, and strong female characters who kick butt on their way to happily ever after. She lives in Oklahoma with her husband, four daughters, and a menagerie of pets including three wiener dogs, Ruby, Sunny, and Pumpkin. Join her newsletter for exclusive content and connect with her at kristinlhamblin.com